BERNARD LOVINK

No Man's Land

novum pro

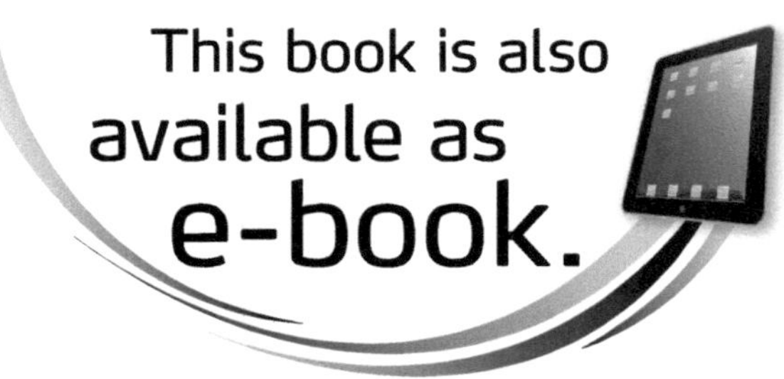

www.novum-publishing.co.uk

© 2021 novum publishing

ISBN 978-3-99107-856-2
Cover photo:
Vdvtut | Dreamstime.com
Cover design, layout & typesetting:
novum publishing

www.novum-publishing.co.uk

*The degree and kind of a man's sexuality
reach up into the ultimate pinnacle of his spirit.*

F. Nietzsche

Contents

Not everyone finds satisfaction in hurtling through time on
the overcrowded train called "society". A single person jumps
off... After the colossus has faded from view,
the cacophony of steel on steel ceases to be deafening,
he becomes aware of the soft sound of the wind through the trees...
He stands up, brushes the dust from his clothes, stretches his limbs,
and hastily clambers off the embankment to avoid seeing
the coming trains, so as not to be overcome by regret and
pity for those who, like him, look like living beings, indeed
like people, and who will quickly become unreal in his
mind's eye...

B.L.

PART I

Reorientation

1.

In hindsight, it would seem as though thirty-four-year-old Christiaan Jacob Janssen fundamentally lacks an instinct for self-preservation. Perhaps Chris — as he is known among friends — is unaware that he has been driving for the last hour and a half toward catastrophe, and certainly he cannot know that he will soon narrowly escape an inferno that will capture the attention of every television-watching or newspaper-reading citizen of the world.

It is a Saturday afternoon, the eleventh of May in a still somewhat nascent third millennium. The air is bright and sunny, a surprisingly warm spring morning. Chris has been invited to give a lecture that afternoon to members of an urban literary society on the "future of fiction". He taps the steering wheel in nervous anticipation as he mulls over his stimulating intro for the dozenth time: *Does compiled writing still stand a chance?*

Chris checks his watch. 2:15 pm. *Still well ahead of schedule* he thinks as he rolls into the city. He will have plenty of time to meet with his old colleague, who has a preference for downtown buildings in the old city. His colleague has recently accepted a post at the Alma Mater in the city and asked Chris to tag along to tour a few real estate listings.

Chris, guided by his Falkland GPS, parks his car in the thin shade of a row of shabby trees in a friendly-looking, but somewhat cluttered 1930s neighborhood. The tranquility all around suggests that many residents of this neighborhood — nestled in a quiet pocket just outside the city center — are today finding recreation outside of the city.

Chris is impressed by the robust supply in the city's real estate market. Notes are made (type, size, location, sun position, visible state of maintenance, facsimile brokerage) on four properties offered for sale. This foursome, plotted out on a field of imaginary lines and diagonals, forms an almost perfect rectangle around a dilapidated plot of land boasting an old, ramshackle warehouse, clearly abandoned. Children have been lighting fires there.

'Sufficient to be going on with,' he murmurs.

While Chris seems to lack the instinct for self-preservation, he does have an eye and an ear for quietly approaching disasters creeping up on him in felt slippers: pale shadows leaping forward, vibrations in the atmosphere, portents like those of an earthquake that cause sensitive creatures instinctively to fly from the trees, crawl in or out of the ground, or softly howl. He will remember slightly later – when the dust settles and the fires dampen – feeling a sensation as if the air pressure around him was increasing slightly, pressing against his eardrums. The heat becomes almost oppressive, with waves of it rustling in the shabby trees and driving the flies to become more insistent, even more aggressive perhaps.

Chris checks his watch again. 2:45 pm. An electronic signboard flashes 28°C at the small corner parking lot. A sound like water gushing into a sewer after a downpour puts Chris on edge. It seems nearby, but as he cranes his neck, Chris can see that the noise is coming from behind a row of houses. With hindsight, and after reading an account in a newspaper, Chris will conclude that it was at a distance of about two hundred meters, at least, and that the sound was not gushing water at all, but a glowing blaze shot high into the air. The ball of fire drops to the ground and shatters as if glass, sending flames in every direction, the effect of which, Chris decides later, was only slightly spoiled by the bright direct sunlight.

Then a sudden, intense heat upends the atmosphere. For a moment, Chris feels as though two glowing hands are tightening their grasp around his neck, then he's thrown to the ground by a hot blast of air. He's on his feet in an instant, looking for somewhere, anywhere, to take cover.

Finding nowhere suitable, Chris turns and runs. The streets are suddenly filling with people investigating the sound, and they stand frozen, awestruck by the grandiose firework display, forcing Chris to weave and jump and shove his way through the crowd as he flees. Moments later (a second, a few seconds?), the blast. Is it one, is it more, is it a series of blasts? Chris doesn't know anymore. For a moment there is only the silence of the grave. *This* is *the grave!* Chris thinks. He will only remember the most heart-rending part of what follows, dazed as he was by that Neolithic explosion: an invisible force like a wave breaking, shattered windows pushed into the houses all around, people screaming, people bleeding, those who are still able to stand rushing for safety. It all seems like a gruesome fairy tale to him, one full of icy reality, written to terrify grown-ups. Roofs are blown off houses, floors collapse. Chris sees a man and woman, both naked, standing in the bedroom of their home whose facade has been blown away, cracked open like a dollhouse. The woman covers her face with her hands and her screams slice through Chris. He sees an outer wall crumble to rubble and a child buried, the sound of bricks collapsing on cobblestones behind him. Window frames burst from falling facades and clatter on the street right in front of him. Roof tiles slide from building tops and shatter on the paving stones all around him, yet by some miracle, he isn't hit, all around him the unspeakable horrors of fiery destruction.

The hot squall is all around him: the blow of the shockwave to his back, birds flying off in every direction, a cat darts in front of him, then a large dog with its tail between its legs, all emerging from and disappearing into the thickening clouds of dust and grit that flow into the narrow street behind him, taking possession, catching and enveloping him. Yet behind this cacophony, Chris hears the soft rustle of last autumn's leaves whipping in the wind of the firestorm, and for an instant, everything is clear: fate has pulled back its dark and heavy cloak and extended a weathered hand to him. Suppressing a whoop of delight, Chris Janssen steps into the fold.

In hindsight, fate should not have staked so much on Chris. A handful of injuries, a couple of victims, one or two missing, a few damaged houses. Why so many dead and missing people for one person's luck? Surely, he isn't worth such a high price, is he?

Consider your next move carefully, Chris thinks to himself. Consider? He runs down another street. The sign above a shop door reads 'party supplies'. He rushes in and, in halting bursts, tries to explain what he's seen — and smelled and heard — to the thin, silver-haired shopkeeper. Shaken, the man rushes outside, and after choosing a wig, a pair of thick framed glasses and a mustache (he picks up a joke nose, then shakes his head and sets it down again), Chris walks out without paying. The shopkeeper is rushing toward the sound of disarray, and Chris hurries in the opposite direction.

Leave nothing to chance. Rounding the corner, Chris ducks between some bushes, to don his new appearance. *There is a plausible chance in our small country,* he thinks, *that someone will remember.* He imagines the reports to come. *Chris Janssen? Yes, I saw him walking just there. No,* after *the explosion, I'm sure of it. Still, I thought…* and on it would go until eventually, yes, they would find him alive and the jig would be up, his moment lost. So, yes. Now. He needs a different appearance, immediately. And also, a different inner self, as he still believes in all his awful ignorance that Chris Janssen can truly disappear. He isn't Chris anymore. He isn't Janssen anymore (a last name he's been unhappy with for at least twenty-five years). He decides he'll come up with a new name eventually, but for now, he's nothing. A Nobody. N. for short.

Chris continues walking hurriedly down the streets in whatever direction feels like the opposite of the explosion. Finally, he comes upon a ladies' bicycle leaning against a house. He, who has never stolen anything in his life, checks whether the bike is locked. It isn't.

He feels like a twelve-year-old miscreant as he jumps on the saddle, pedaling as fast as he can away from the scene of disaster. He waits for the imagined shouts of "stop thief!" to echo through the neighborhood and fade away behind him, but they do not come. It's as though the entire city has been paralyzed by the infernal event. Or perhaps this is the day of judgment freely rendered from Belcampo (N. can already hear Kees Brusse's distressed voiceover). He thinks that perhaps the difference between mine and yours has been blasted away, and the moment has come at last to introduce collective ownership according to Bakunin and the little red books. Some events force different times.

It isn't long before N. leaves the last houses of the stricken city behind. With whizzing, slightly under-inflated tires, he rides to the countryside. Warm wind whips at his face, adding to his feeling of giddy jubilation, like a long-caged bird that's finally been set free. The weight of worry has lifted when suddenly N. realizes that, without purpose or preference, he has set his course for the north. Towards home. Or, at least, towards Chris Janssen's home. Apparently, the tendency to flee back to where one came from, back to home and hearth, is a deep-seeded condition.

But N. cannot go to Chris Janssen's home. As he slows, a thick column of smoke catches him, spreading the scent of burning scrap wood, fired stone, and warm slag from the old coke-fired foundry. He isn't far from where he was born, played, and went to school. At the next intersection he cycles through, deliberately rerouting his path.

Heading southwest and toward the fading sunlight, N. guides the bicycle onto a paved cycle path alongside a wide road. An unbroken procession of ambulances and fire trucks, sirens blaring and lights flashing, stream past him and into the city. It takes some time before N. notices that the traffic is only going one way; the counter-flow of traffic has pulled over along the side, having crept onto the verge, giving the impression of a modesty quite uncommon among Dutch drivers. It is all far too serious. N. is noticeably the only person moving in the opposite direction, the culprit fleeing the inferno behind him; the light, the sun, the summer, the future, to meet his new future.

The road rolls gently through green pastures where cows graze, too stoic to be bothered by this human activity, unaware of the ominous cloud on the eastern horizon, their slow brains interpreting the explosion as a distant storm at most. N. looks around, realizing suddenly that, aside from those tucked behind the glass and metal of their busy vehicles, there are no people anywhere. Not even at the houses he's passing by. Colorful summer chairs have been set out here and there on lawns and patios, but they are unoccupied. There is no one enjoying the cool shade of equally colorful parasols. *What an untapped luxury*, N. thinks as he begins to sweat slightly.

N. muses at the idea of the literary society, and wonders uselessly whether they are all shuffling their feet with impatience, awaiting his arrival, or whether they, like him, have abandoned their literary acuity in favor of the more immediate firestorm nearby. N. cycles steadily on towards the sun. Cars continue to drive towards him, among them still an occasional ambulance, a fire truck answering the call, a police car with a raging engine. There is an insistent drone as a few helicopters hover in the air, pushing toward the disaster that seems to have created its own orbit and was pulling everything in, in the air, on land, perhaps even on water. That filthy plume of smoke still billows up behind him, but as he continues to distance himself the threat seems to fade, as though every mile is making it fade further into history. *Perhaps*, he thinks *I can ride this bike until today is just a footnote.*

But the late afternoon sun has only grown more stifling, and N. is now sweating so profusely under his wig and behind his mustache that they're beginning to slip here and there. His glasses might fog up if the frames had lenses. N. is dressed lightly, in a short-sleeved shirt, cotton jacket with no tie, linen trousers, thin socks, and open shoes, but still the heat is oppressive. By the position and height of the bicycle saddle, N. guesses that the height of the rightful owner is probably not much taller than five foot three. At nearly six foot three, N. is beginning to feel acute pain in his back, not to mention the growing discomfort in his seat. The road widens, and N. dismounts to walk away and rest his aching body. His watch reads 4:00 pm.

The fields and pastures give way to a wooded forest on one side where the bicycle path veers away from the main road and into the deeper shade of the trees. N., grateful for the momentary reprieve from the sun, follows a gravel path to a wooden bench where he sits down in the shade of an oak tree. Behind him a brook babbles, around him birds' bustle and chirp, busy with the task of feeding newly hatched chicks. A spotted woodpecker flies from tree trunk to tree trunk, a jay squawks its shrill call. After some time, two deer amble through to graze along a section of the forest edge. He can hear only occasional murmurs of traffic from the main road now. In the clear blue sky above him, he imagines the invisible exchange of digital waves, carrying increasingly nervous, frenetic sounds and images. He senses the soft sound of wind in the conifers, and then suddenly, N. is aware of a silence that affects him more intensely than all of the past hour's raucous disaster. His ears ring and his head begins a quiet throb. Stretching out on the bench, N. longs for the lure of sleep but is too restless to relax. His hands shake, his heart is in his throat, his neck is aching and stiff.

After fifteen minutes, N. gets up again and walks his bike back to the cycle path, which winds its way through the remaining patch of forest and settles alongside the provincial road again. He passes a cluster of houses – some tiny, forgettable village – with still very few signs of life outside, but here and there he notices the cold glare of television screens flickering inside. The good citizens within are already under the spell of the first images of the disaster he so narrowly escaped.

He pedals on. At an intersection, he changes route, more to the northwest judging from the position of the sun. N. rides into another small village, and then another. For the most part, life seems to have continued, or has returned to, its usual course. That is to say, farmers are getting ready for the evening cow milking, children scutter about side yards in the final hours of daylight. The frenzied one-way stream of traffic has now fully welcomed the return of the oncoming flow again. A clock tower strikes five. Now and then, when not obscured by trees, N. can still see glimpses of the black column of smoke from the city center. The hellish fire must still be raging. It now seems distant to N., less realistic, barely an omen, just a glowing pinhead in the light of the great wide world. Nevertheless, he has the impression of moving against the backdrop of an absurd landscape.

"I'll have to get used to my new life," he mumbles.

It is on the outskirts of the neighboring city that N. concludes that the bicycle's rear tire has a slow leak. The rubber tire slips on bumps, jarring the metal rim against the against the hard concrete and sending jolts up the frame and handlebars. In front of a house where an elderly gentleman muses on a garden chair (N. guesses he is about eighty), he dismounts and politely asks the man for a bicycle pump. As he disappears into the house, N. notices through the windows the flicker of television, the news broadcast glowing across the faces of the inhabitants.

Noticing N.'s attention to the TV, the old Saxon nods toward it and says "That is something, isn't it, sir? Some mess they've got there." He looks rather studiously at N., working quite vigorously at pumping up the tires. N. wonders whether the old man has noticed that the bike is a small ladies' size. He realizes with some embarrassment at how he must look, with a too-small bike and thrown-together disguise. He nevertheless thanks him warmly and continues on his way, in a direction he believes to be westward.

N. throws his leg over the saddle and checks his watch. It is now 5:30 pm. If you kept your back to the billowing plume of black smoke rising from the city, you might think life had completely returned to normal. Some people have begun populating their patio chairs, and the air is filled with the happy sound of children playing on lawns. Down the street, someone is washing their car in the fading evening light. N. can smell someone cooking an early supper and he feels his stomach turn and growl.

By 6:00 pm, N. can no longer ignore the throbbing ache that travels up his tail bone and takes hold in his lower back. When he comes upon Village Q, he turns the bike toward the town center. After stashing the bicycle behind a fence, he sets out on foot to explore the village. The streets are mostly deserted. Here, too, people are transfixed by the television broadcast. *I could shoot a cannon off in the village square*, N. thinks, *and it wouldn't hurt a soul.*

N. finds a corner café still open and orders some fries. He tries to strike up a conversation with the server, whose eyes linger on N. for just a moment before returning a fixing his gaze solidly on a small screen. The fries are lukewarm and greasy, but they satisfy the most aggressive hunger pangs. N. stands, pushing back his chair as he does, counts out the required coins, and leaves them beside his empty plate. Leaving the café, N. remembers the hotel he had seen during his brief exploration on the main road just outside the village. *Hotel Aurora*, lodging and breakfast, 50 euros per night. Decidedly not a big city price. He will spend the weekend there, he decides, and try to put things in order.

At the front counter of the hotel, a pimply young man greets N. and hesitates only a moment before offering him a guest register to sign for a room. He signs in under the name K. van Andel, a name that comes to him on the spot and which, as far as he knows, has no connection with anything. He writes down a fictitious address, pays two nights in advance, and takes a room on the first floor. There is a view of the main road, lined on either side by large oak trees, cutting through a meadow where two ponies are grazing contentedly. His reflection in the shower mirror catches him by surprise; he was in such general disarray from the strange events of the day that he had almost entirely forgotten about the wig, mustache, and glasses. He did not look like a man escaping the calamity of a lifetime; he looked like a part-time clown returning from last night's party in the harsh light of day. He thought he might be good for a big laugh at the Brabant carnival.

N. had felt a bit uncomfortable talking to the young man at the front desk because he felt as though his mustache was out of place. Now seeing himself in the mirror for the first time since donning the ridiculous disguise, he understands the odd look the young man had given him; he remembers now that the grandpa with the bike pump and the café owner and even a few passersby had looked at him so curiously. The mustache itself is bad, rumpled like the one on Nietzsche's death mask. To make matters worse, it's also completely crooked. The left side of this artificial thicket starts an inch above the lip, the right side ends an inch below. One corner of it is curled to reveal the flesh-colored adhesive, a dab of oily mayonnaise trembles on the other end. He's doing a very poor impression of Charlie Chaplin in an awkward pose, a caricature of a caricature. What a ridiculous introduction he's made to this down-to-earth village! N. is astonished that the young man gave him a room without asking for identification. *I think I would've called the madhouse immediately*; he thinks.

He grins at himself, but the grin is so flat and meaningless that he is once again startled to see himself. Upon further investigation, he discovers that there is a scorch mark on the back of his linen jacket, and a small trail of clotted blood has dried along his neck. After taking stock of his body from head to toe, he discovers only one minor irritation from a slight burn. He escaped what will become known as the Gunpowder Disaster nearly unscathed. N. inhales deeply, and after a long and somewhat pregnant exhale, he takes a long shower.

The television seems to be stuck on one of the private channels, but piece by piece, N. is able to build a larger image of the explosion. From the short sound bites and flashes of images and videos between lively, persistent commercial ads, he concludes that there is now a preliminary inventory of victims; many people were injured, dozens are in hospital, and many more are missing. And there are dead to be mourned, some of them badly mutilated. With this information, N.'s confidence in his plan is reinforced slightly. Once the dust has settled and it is accepted that missing people are a sad byproduct of this catastrophe, this blow that has knocked so many people off course will put him on course, he feels certain of that much.

He keeps watching the broadcast for a while, the commentary by breathless and/or allegedly sympathetic reporters, while his thoughts dwell on very different matters. As his mind wanders, his gaze subconsciously fixes on an image of a vehicle. It takes a few moments before he recognizes it as his own badly mutilated, half-burnt car. The wreckage was caught by a telephoto lens, focused, zoomed in. The license plate—relatively undamaged, for the state of the rest of the car—only appears for a few seconds, right before a commercial promoting a new Andrélon line, but it's enough. He knows that it's his Peugeot station wagon on the screen, standing there as evidence to support the high probability that death is the only explanation for his disappearance into oblivion. This image could of course be used and reused later as evidence for investigators, should his loved ones still doubt his total dissolution in a devastating fire. "But Mrs. Janssen, you know about that car. Your husband couldn't have been very far away. We're sorry, you'll have to accept the inevitable."

Poor Paula. After that hellish blast, everything *has* changed! There have been twenty-four hours of silence on his part; there is no credible way back now, if he still wanted to go back. N. would have to call her now, right now (not tomorrow or the day after tomorrow) with some foggy excuse (the explosion – shock – escaped in panic – found myself here – please, Paula, come pick me up). Now or never! Do I want that?

"No, I don't want that, not now, not ever again!" His inner voice is prompt and clear. This is *my* chance! *The supreme moment!* N. has already embraced it; the time that will do the work for him.

He puts his sweaty clothes back on, stinking of smoke and soot, checks his disguise and descends to the restaurant, a spacious sunroom that has been built onto the hotel. He is the only guest there.

2.

N. sits in a chair by the window in his room and begins taking stock of his belongings. Wallet with contents, approximately 500 euros, minus his expenses. He's lucky to have this much cash. When planning his trip at the ATM this morning, he had decided to splurge on a nice hotel and to hire an escort for the evening; to dine somewhere exquisite with her, then do something fun together, and other things, later in the hotel room. This has often been his habit over the past few years.

He continues his inventory: driver's license, his watch, a Lamy pen, a Blueline notebook, underwear, shirt (slightly scorched), trousers (somewhat stained), socks (smelly), jacket (heavily scorched), shoes, the silly disguise and the illegally obtained bicycle. That's it. He'll be able to stay in this hotel for five days, including evening meals. After that, he'll be broke, down to his last penny. Any electronic transactions made after 2:30 pm yesterday afternoon will betray him like tracks in fresh snow. He will have to proceed with caution, deliberation, like a petty criminal, at least at first. He can't forget one thing, make one misstep. His deranged disguise is just the beginning. To get through what is to come, he will have to immerse himself again in that noisy mishmash called society. He must continue to feel its pulse. But from a new perspective, one he will slide back into it with complete silence, smoothly, like a scaly reptile that's just shed its skin. What a wonderful challenge!

N. takes out his wallet. He has 361.45 euros cash (after paying for fries and two days room and board). He has one bank card, one credit card. "Useless," he mumbles "I'd make a fool of myself and my disappearance. Cut them into pieces and flush them down the toilet to be safe." Then driver's license (unnecessary, even dangerous), registration (ditto), an older photo of Paula and of Anke when she was about three years old, a snapshot from a family reunion, photo of his parents, a dated bank statement, the business card from Piet Perfect chimney sweeps, an article clipped from a newspaper (he doesn't remember why), a photo of a charcoal drawing he once made—a nude of an art school friend—a piece of paper with addresses and telephone numbers of people he hasn't seen or spoken to in years, a pin, a mother-of-pearl button, a paper clip.

N.'s heart suddenly begins beating fast and hard. Here indeed is the challenge, at the rock-bottom of his dispossession.

He sits with his back to the television set, which is still switched on, and stares out the window. He lets the sound of the broadcast wash over him—voices of reporters, of first responders, stories of what happened from local residents and witnesses, the shameless politicking by the authorities. Out of the corner of his eye, he sees the dismayed face of a mayor, a fire chief in uniform (why on earth haven't they taken decisive action?) delivering his technical explanation as if from a textbook, conveyed with the necessary gravity. The game of passing the buck begins. He sees traffic passing in front of the hotel: cars, cyclists, a moped, a motorcycle, a jeep with a horse trailer. Across the street, the ponies start to trot, chasing each other.

N. turns to the hazy blue images of the disaster that relentlessly invade living rooms—millions, tens of millions of living rooms around the world—as N. will soon discover. People around the globe all watching the same thing he is now. It's getting dark in his room. He checks his watch. It's past 10:00. The sky in the east turns from mauve to violet. On the other side of the hotel, the sun has already set. The TV images keep catching his eye; people, things and events grab his attention for a second, but cannot hold it. He sees ruined houses, facades torn away, living rooms and bedrooms that have been cracked open and, as if violated in their intimacy, shamelessly flaunt their naked parts. There is a big hole where houses could have stood before (they may well have, but N. can't remember clearly). Damaged and burnt cars glide past on the screen, and only then does he become alert. His Peugeot offers a gruesome and cinematic image, and the camera focuses on it again. "For God's sake," he mumbles, "for God's sake, just leave that car in the picture. Leave it in the picture until everyone knows the license plate and starts talking about it, guessing, gathering information, until it is finally accepted that the care belongs to C.J.J., and that C.J.J. is among the missing." Because that is something people want to know, even if they don't personally know a C.J.J., they still want to know it's him. Then they can all build a story, one they can believe, and one they can create their own ending for..

Reporters now know that dozens have been killed and injured, including two firefighters. A mustached fire investigation expert comes on. His shirt is bright and a bit too frivolous for the story he's telling, of mutilations so serious that identification may no longer be possible (don't mistake the expertise, sir, gathered at the forensic institute). Hope builds in N.'s chest until it aches. He hopes that Paula is also glued to this program and that her days of uncertainty about his tragic end will be short. He hopes that she will quickly reach the conclusion that her husband is one of the missing with a likelihood bordering on certainty of death. He hopes she will not sit and wonder about their future together. The word 'missing' will not officially appear next to his name until the next day.

That will be Sunday. He will have all day and the days that follow to work out his plans, his strategies to counter the usual course of events. N. switches off the television and stretches his limbs. He feels a leaden fatigue, especially in his thighs. He rubs his hands almost contentedly, undresses, laments the fact that he can't brush his teeth or put on pajamas and slides naked into the crisply ironed sheets. In a relatively cool room, he manages to slip away from the historic day.

3.

When he comes downstairs, there are three people in the restaurant. A fairly young couple are sitting together at a table in the far corner—perhaps an already fairly seasoned pair, N. thinks, judging from the impressive silence at that table—and an older man, sitting alone on the opposite side. The breakfast nook is arranged to only take up a small part of the room. Nevertheless, N. manages to stay far enough removed from the other guests to limit greetings to a nod. He has never been much of a morning person and he'd prefer to limit conversations entirely right now.

Surrounded by sunlight and the serenity of tinkling cutlery, lightly interrupted now and then by the waiter zipping past and the older man's restrained cough, N. eats a light breakfast and returns to his room.

Refreshed by three cups of good coffee, he sinks into the creaky wicker armchair by the sliding glass door. It opens onto a modest veranda still shaded by a row of huge oak trees that are just starting to don their springtime buds. The TV continues to stream images of the disaster, still steaming and glowing like a volcanic crater leaking lava. Now, nearly 24 hours later, the commentators and local residents have turned to connecting this horrific accident with the protection of the petty bourgeoisie in this town. Of course, they wouldn't miss such an opportunity to make it clear to the city council and all those other high 'lords' what, exactly, they've done wrong.

Then there are questions about a horse and a locked stable door; the blame game is in full swing now.

A wave of nausea rolls over N., bringing him to his feet. He's a familiar cynic on the carousel of emotions the television-watching nation engages in; he predicts the misery of this disaster will be milked to the last drop. This tragedy is a gold mine for all those broadcasters; devastating news, a pick-me-up, a stroke of luck in the middle of a twelve-month slow cycle. After he hears the umpteenth bureaucrat playing Pontius Pilate, N. can take no more. Completely involuntarily, he deposits the entirety of his recent breakfast into the toilet.

"I'm not myself yet," he mumbles, wiping his sour mouth. Feeling lightheaded, he sits on the porch to get a breath of fresh air and watches the ponies across the road. At first there are only two, then three, and then a fourth pony joins them. Seemingly unmoved by the traffic in front of them, they stare blankly in the same direction. N. hears the growing rumble of an accelerating diesel train (he'd heard it a few times last night) and remembers crossing a track further down the road yesterday.

Regaining his constitution, N. decides to take a bike ride through the countryside to give his spirit a little room to breathe.

After a few hours of pedaling through the varied landscapes (guided by those handy ANWB signs) he makes up for his lost breakfast in a charming restaurant somewhere on the edge of a forest with a tasty double omelet. He has a beer with it. A sweet-looking and apparently unattached young woman tries to strike up a conversation with him, which he reluctantly avoids thinking about his increasingly unpleasant mustache. Nevertheless, he cannot deny that this countryside is full of beauty, even astonishing beauty. The rolling hills are scattered with alternating swathes of forests and farmland, outlined by rows of trees. Some of the larger sections of farmland, with their extensive fields and pastures, are obviously operated by crop consolidation companies. Other plots are small, with rustic farmhouses tucked away, seemingly unaffected by the passage of time. He cycles through fairy-tale cathedrals of trees, decorated with their delicate spring greenery—birch, beech, oak, and alder.

His rear tire has slowly softened over the course of the afternoon. N. rides back to Q casually, stopping along the way to sit on the bank of a brook bordered by cow parsley. Grass carp and a few minnows swim in the brook, and further downstream he sees a kingfisher diving. It does not escape his attention how curative these quiet moments are for him. He had felt it that morning, too, when he awoke in the fresh air of a new environment. On the bank of the stream, N. considers his "plans", both immediate and big picture. His bike ride had somehow transformed his abstract ideas into concrete reality. He will have to be careful, and patient, to wait for just the right moment; after all, time is now the only thing he has in abundance. He can cultivate patience.

N. stands up, mounts the bicycle, and ends his wonderful afternoon back in Q, completely satisfied. He decides his disguise is in urgent need of attention when a young man in a group hanging around the chip shop shouts, "Hey, there's that crooked mustache on his pussy bike again!" He spoke in the local dialect, but N. understood every word. It turns out his disguise was already attracting attention in town. Not ideal. He may have to figure out how to get a new bike, too, if he wants to avoid attention.

N.'s overactive imagination conjures up a little car with police stripes cutting off his path. *Sir, can we see your ID?*

I, and no one else, am the painted bird here. Tomorrow, he will buy sunglasses.

N. had never been to this rural hamlet before, but after the calming effect the day had had on him, and after a hot evening meal and long shower, he decides he will stay in Q. Not in this little hotel itself, he'll have to find something cheaper in the coming days. He'll also need to somehow arrange for a more or less regular, modest income to avoid quickly burning through the capital he might build from the plan he was brewing. If he ran out of money, he'd be in real trouble.

As for the income, N. had already worked through that on his ride. How fruitful these quiet Sunday hours have been! In the village of X, quite a bit larger than Q and some twelve kilometers to the south, which he had visited on his bike tour, his keen eye fell on an advertisement near the entrance to a supermarket: Help wanted, shelf stockers, anyone 16 to 60 years old, part-time or full-time employment, available for other incidental tasks. Hiring immediately. He decides to inquire at the modest establishment as soon as he has everything in order.

N. remembers the moment he first began seriously looking for a suitable moment to make this leap. It was a little more than a year ago, in response to a crucial fragment of an otherwise uninspiring essay, he felt the long-latent need become manifest. One dazzling metaphor that put him on a completely different path—in his fantasies and now, so suddenly, in reality too. Away from unimaginative Calvinism with its utilitarianism, which is ultimately just one of many life philosophies!

N. lies on his back on the hotel bed, thinking. He shivers, suddenly feeling cold as he flips through his mental catalogue of the various options he's considered in recent months: a drowning death without a body, a hike in the mountains gone awry. Paula doesn't like hiking, especially not in the mountains, afraid as she is of the slightest heights. Just two days ago, he had nearly booked a hiking tour through the Italian Alps for this August, but an unscheduled meeting with a colleague and a few students delayed these plans.

But that was the point. For his next of kin, he needs to have died. Without mortal remains, his death must still seem plausible, the only option. For their sake, he needed them to believe that he had not just disappeared into the world from one day to the next for some banal reason: a young floozy, economic hardship, unwanted fatherhood, an unexplainable sudden intolerance for a domestic existence that has become too cozy, too predictable.

His desire is driven by something deeper, more complex. There are three or four elements at play here: a nostalgic longing for a kind of simplicity and perspective he thinks he remembers from before his college days. The need to "slow down"—an expression he actually despises for having been plagiarized and dragged into a cliché by so-called avant-gardism or post-modernism. All this coupled with an undeniable longing for a quiet, ascetic life. He believes he is ready for it. Ready to reject the barren materialism that surrounds him.

Then there is his need for a kind of spiritual detoxification through renunciation or severe restriction; in this case, removal of the television and the written media that are increasingly upsetting to him. And then, finally, there is the distressing fact that if the situation remains unchanged regarding career, income, and social status, he will be forced to continue working into old age, doing something he no longer has any affinity for. The idea of receiving a generous but undeserved salary year after year for academic work that hardly benefits a poorly prepared and increasingly less qualified and less motivated student population, to regularly publish articles that will never be read by anyone, endless participation in symposiums, consultations, restructuring committees who want to reinvent the wheel again and again, and perhaps worst of all, having to keep up the facade that all of this is still interesting, having to keep fooling his colleagues, and his colleagues him, while everyone knows or should know better … it's been enough to drive him to despair.

How long has he been searching, desperately looking for a crack in the lattice of a fast-moving life of which his job is such an inextricable part? Oh, to escape that ever more dizzying speed, to find a momentum more suited to his nature and desire, to escape the merry-go-round of "time" to which he's been tied! Jump off at the perfect spot, hope you don't get hurt too badly, don't crash into anything, knock the dust off your clothes, yes, take a deep breath and point yourself in the right direction. Passenger as he was—no longer aboard a speeding train, but rather on an airliner traveling dizzying distances without any recognition of the landscape below, disregarding its exotic locales, things to reflect on, quiet places to rest, to catch your breath and come to yourself again.

How unhappy he felt then, near despair every time he returned from a weekend away, even during and after every vacation. How can you willingly step back onto that carousel of a "normal" life that is, either unconsciously or knowingly and willingly, sustained by laziness, conservatism, fear of uncertainty, hunger for consumerism or whatever reason?

How much more would my life have soured and decayed, he muses, *had that liberating explosion and acrid smoke not filled my nose, my eyes, my ears!?*

He takes a shower, slides naked into the bed, and falls into a deep, dreamless sleep.

4.

Despite his new existence and his general satisfaction with his beautiful plans, both large and small, N. cannot ignore the fact that his financial situation is becoming dire. The serpent is stretching out in his Arcadia. The refreshing afternoon he'd had yesterday, while modest, had taken a dangerous slice of his meager funds. He has only 265.95 euros remaining.

He books three more days in the hotel, then walks to a corner pharmacy and buys a pair of sunglasses, a toothbrush, toothpaste, and a small patch and repair kit. Total cash remaining: 64.75 euros. As his wallet lightened, his mind grew heavy with worry: it was worrying to watch his reserves diminish so quickly. After having grown used to receiving a generous salary every month, this experience of economic fragility feels foreign. If he wants his first little plan to be a success, he won't be able to eat in the hotel restaurant tonight or he won't have enough to cover his travel expenses. N. contents himself with a bag of fries.

By 8:00 the next morning, he's boarded a train. He buys a ticket from the conductor. He has 14.25 euros left.

The train to Y is slow, and the seats gradually fill around N., the crowd grows larger at every station. After a while, it seems like noisy, provocative teenagers have filled every compartment. N. concludes that, apart from the difference in regional dialect, adolescents in this rural part of the country are no different than those anywhere else. The noisy train was only a fresh reminder of an opinion he had long ago settled on: better to lecture unmotivated university students than try to teach annoying and aggressive fourteen- to eighteen-year-olds. This singular motivation led him years ago to pursue his doctorate. *Why,* N. laments, *don't people go to school to learn something anymore? All they seem to accomplish is making the teachers regret their profession!* By the time N. steps off the train in Y, his palms are sweaty with annoyance. At the station restaurant, N. decides to spend his remaining euros on a cup of coffee and two generously filled sandwiches, which he eats while he waits for the intercity train to take him home.

N.'s irritation lightens a bit as he eats. He observes with great satisfaction that this rural region does offer a particularly beautiful bevy of young women, some of them truly stunning. And not just beautiful, but friendly. One young beauty even sits down next to him, scans him up and down without a hint of reserve, and, rubbing her shapely form against his bony shoulders, tries to chat with him, in excellent Dutch no less. N. stifles the conversation with painful reluctance; his disguise suddenly feels itchy and obvious, like a child playing dress-up. He can't wait to be rid of this ridiculous outlaw facade, his laughable Hercule Poirot mustache. But today, especially today, he cannot possibly abandon it. His mission today requires exacting execution; there is no room for error. N. wraps up his remaining sandwich and leaves the station on foot.

With just a 5 euro note and few small coins left in his pocket (not enough for a bus ticket), at 10:55 am, delayed only 45 minutes, he leaves his hometown railway station. The weather is as beautiful here as it was in Q. Sunbeams break into myriad dapples on the chromed handlebars of countless bicycles lining the station square. In the glassy waters of the canal, a tour boat full of seniors breaks into jubilant partying. None of the locals seem to be exceedingly burdened by the mysterious disappearance of C.J. Janssen. On the contrary, the patios around the city center are decked in cheerful summer furniture. Two young ladies dressed in long, modest burkas fixate on N. as he walks in front of them with his sultanesque appearance (do they think him a countryman? Perhaps a kindred spirit?)

A little before half past twelve, N. turns the corner and is confronted by his own house—well, not his house. Christian Janssen's house. Market value, approximately 400,000 euros. Outstanding mortgage, approximately a hundred thousand, the still legal co-owner at 5.15 euros in the black. Upon the pronouncement of his death or permanent disappearance, a life insurance policy will pay out to Paula that will cover the remainder of the outstanding mortgage. This thought comforts him; she deserves that much at least. The house stands on the corner of a row of semi-detached houses, all built together about twenty years ago, spaciously designed, with enough of a garden for the enthusiast (he never was one for plants; Paula maintained the garden. Chris had proven to be an efficient but entirely unenthusiastic lawn mower).

The Janssen house is on a quiet street, the seemingly idyllic urban home of a picturesque modern Dutch family. Parallel to their street is a pond, lined by bushes and trees hiding another quiet neighborhood from view. In those bushes, at the edge of the parking lot in front of a low-rise apartment building, stands N., fully disguised and desperate to avoid those who, he assumes (one could always be wrong), would most like to see him right now. He checks his watch; it's half past twelve. At 1:00, he's still there, but moves to a bench in the sun. There is a problem. Paula is home, her car is in the driveway in front of the garage. Paula is not the type of woman to leave home without the car. But worse still, she is not alone. Her mother's Mercedes SEL is parked in front of the house. Of course her mother is there! She will be worried about her daughter who, in turn, will be gravely concerned about her husband. That is when mothers should be there.

Would Anke be at home too, he wondered, kept home from school to mourn the tragedy? But N. does not see his stepdaughter's blond head in any of the windows.

At half past one, a Volkswagen Passat pulls up to the house and parks behind the Mercedes. A smartly dressed man in a dark suit with coiffed hair steps out, carrying a shiny briefcase. He walks up the driveway with a springy, purposeful gait. He rings the bell and is let in by N.'s mother-in-law. N. imagines the visitor being offered a chair, balancing the briefcase on his knees as he takes something out. Perhaps he is an insurance agent, sent over to explain what and how much the life insurance policy will cover? But that seems a bit premature. A representative from a crematorium, then, or the funeral insurance company? He imagines the slick argument: "But we don't have anything, ma'am, after all he has already been cremated (ha ha). Well yes, we can pay for an empty coffin as a symbol, perhaps just a small one. As a company, we've been in situations like this before."

After a long half hour, the visitor is let out, again by the mother-in-law. Mrs. De Geus van Wateringen had always been fond of the idea of N. as a son-in-law, a prospective professor within the circle of her illustrious but not very intellectual family. And it was a good thing he'd come along when he did; Paula's distinguished parents were faced with financial ruin after Paula's

childhood sweetheart, turned husband and wealthy bank manager, had brazenly cast Paula and their eighteen-month-old daughter aside for his beautiful young secretary. It had been the talk of
the month in certain social circles; the sweetheart and the secretary, it was later discovered, had been cheating as far back as his
wedding day, and then the sweetheart had gotten accidentally
(or perhaps not) pregnant.

Paula had been deeply traumatized by the event. Even now,
more than six years later, she was still plagued by bouts of mood-
iness and fitful, waking nightmares. It was for this reason that N.
had been so reluctant to start divorce proceedings.

But he knew now, without question, that this attachment
to Paula, and hers to him, was a mistake. It was his mother-in-
law's hasty and premature brokerage that he had failed to coun-
teract in time. Anxious to see her spurned daughter and father-
less granddaughter tucked into a financially (if not emotionally)
stable marriage, Mrs. De Geus van Wateringen encouraged them
toward marriage. He is not the type of person, it would turn out,
who is built to endure a permanent commitment. He is a lover of
casual contact, with a promiscuous nature, relentless in his longing to discover, then conquer, new bodies, preferably the bodies
of young women. And he wanted to let the inevitable parting, the
peeling apart of bodies rather than spirits, go smoothly, without
heartbreak. He wanted to live unhindered by the weight of amo-
rous mortgages, to quickly and easily plunge into new adventures
without the tether of consideration for another person. He sometimes considers himself a Casanova, Don Juan, and Bluebeard, all
rolled into one, refuses to accept a tragic fate of aging and decline
like any of those dubious characters. He'll stave off the wear of
time by settling with a woman at some point, maybe in his fifth
decade, somewhere in the world (but he already knows exactly
where). He'll find a young girl, beautiful and naïve, say about
seventeen, and she'll bear him a few children where he can see
his youth blossom again.

At that time, N. believed that he had taken control of his wan-
derlust, his prowling and seemingly insatiable libido taken in hand.

The sun throws shade on the park bench from behind an oak. N. unwraps his remaining sandwich and eats it, panic growing from his lack of control over the situation. If there is no opportunity to get into the house unseen today, his situation will become truly dire. Where can he go with that paltry five-euro note in this money-driven society; where can he find shelter? Is there some distant acquaintance or colleague he could somehow fool into believing that he is not Chris Janssen, but just his double? He could accost total strangers like a mad man, beg them for an advance, promise to pay them back tomorrow. Perhaps they would trust his beautiful brown eyes? He could take his watch to the pawn shop. It's a Rolex, but it also isn't cheap, and still relatively new. Paula gave it to him last year for his 33rd birthday. It has a gilded case, gold-plated bezel and closure. He imagines he should be able to get two hundred euros for it, at least. There is nothing else, other than the clothes on his back that are starting to stink even from some distance now.

It's a quarter past two. At the language and arts department of (what was once) his university, about 500 meters away as the crow flies, students would be taking their seats in a large lecture hall, waiting for one Dr. Chris Janssen to begin a lecture on general literary history (today's topic is on the influence of Enlightenment and early Romanticism on 19th century literature). He wondered if the lecture had been postponed in deference to his probable death. Probably not, N. muses. Jan Nas will probably step in. His PhD student wouldn't pass up the opportunity to really raise his profile within the faculty. And he's right to do so. Jan could become a worthy successor. Of course, he'll have to cultivate a relationship with Piet de Geer, the dean, and maybe pick up the pace on his dissertation. But it will be worth it; this "tragedy" could really make his career. Again, N. feels some small satisfaction with himself.

N. is up now, anxiously pacing across the parking lot. He feels the pressure of society squeezing around him, like an uncomfortable jacket that's too tight in the shoulders. All around him, people are hurrying for this and for that, everyone's in a

big rush to take home their little piece for the day. He wonders
at how long he can keep up this game if he fails to get into the
house today. When a police car passes slowly in front of him,
the two occupants seeming far too attentive to his presence, N.'s
paranoia gets the best of him. *Sir,* he imagines, *can we please see
some ID?* Or worse, what if he is recognized by some vague acquaintance on their way to console Paula? Or some nosy neighborhood watchman in the apartment block behind him, hungry
to be part of a true crime documentary, decides to alert the police that some man in a bad disguise has been sitting, staring at
a row of bourgeois houses and obviously awaiting his opportunity to break in. He feels his presence become suddenly unten-
able. With feigned nonchalance, N. walks casually around the
block; he'll return once the police are satisfied with their patrol.

Once back at his post, he breathes a sigh of relief. Through the
window, N. can see the busy movements of mother and daughter
preparing to leave. Paula seems a little hunched in her mouse-gray
suit, blonde-haired and pale. It isn't very flattering on her. She
has a closet full of beautiful clothes, and rarely leaves the house
in such drab attire. Is N. only flattering himself when he imagines that his life partner looks downcast, dejected, mournful?
She shuffles down the driveway and eases herself into the passenger seat of her mother's Mercedes; he is comforted slightly by
the knowledge that, at the very least, Paula is not entirely herself.
She is not the type of woman who willingly gives up control of
the steering wheel, either literally or figuratively.

Finally, the big sedan pulls out of the driveway, rays of sunlight glinting off its shining chrome. It seems unlikely to him
that they would leave Anke at home alone at a time like this, so
N. assumes that, given the time of day, the ladies have left to collect the girl from school. That gives him a ten-minute window,
at most. He doesn't have a second to lose!

Although his disguise feels increasingly akin to the emperor's
new clothes, he approaches the house from the rear. He had left
his house key on the ring of keys now smoldering in the Peugeot.
It didn't matter. After the third time they'd hired a locksmith

because someone absentmindedly locked their keys inside, Paula had insisted on hiding a spare key to the back door in a crack under the roof of the shed. N.'s practiced hand, trembling as it might be, finds the key immediately and carefully opens the door. In the utility room, he is suddenly deluged by the familiar smells of home. He moves quietly; he can't be absolutely sure Anke isn't home, otherwise he would storm through the place. Something moves in the next room, and N. freezes in place, until he sees Flap push open the door and welcome him with a tail around his leg, purring imperturbably, expecting a cuddle or something from the refrigerator.

Sorry, Flap, not today, he thinks, pushing past the angora cat. She withdraws haughtily, fixing her unfaithful owner with a distant, yellow green glare.

Is anyone home? N. can smell the nicotine from his mother-in-law's cigarettes. He gathers that she's been here a few days, judging from disheveled state of the guest bed. He is halfway up the stairs to his study when the telephone rings. It is deafening in the silent house, and N. fears for a moment that his heart may stop. He feels suddenly sick with fear, sweat breaking out all over his body. He can't explain away the ominous feeling that has overcome him. *Hurry!* he thinks, and takes the stairs two at a time.

In his desk drawer, stashed in the bottom right corner, are four icons in open wrapping paper. He sets them on the desk, inspects each one briefly, then folds the paper back around them and ties it with some twine from another drawer. Downstairs, the phone rings again, every bit as ominous and persistent as before. He quickly scans the room, picks out a few cassettes of his old recordings, then plucks a recently purchased three-volume Montaigne and *Under the Volcano* from the bookshelf. He stuffs everything into a plastic AH bag and thinks only vaguely of his extremely devalued stock holdings in the parent company of the well-known retailer. Fearing that Paula might notice the removal of anything too personal, N. scans the room again and sneaks hastily down the stairs, a thief in his own house.

Can he already hear the car in the drive, keys jangling at the front door? It's been nearly ten minutes. Of course, he has the story ready, just in case. Close to the disaster, bang, fire, heat, dead, terribly dead people everywhere, numb for a few days, short memory loss, hospitable reception, the slow regaining of self-awareness. He has rehearsed it at least ten times, knowing it isn't credible but hoping that relief at his survival might drown out the timbre of his lie. But the bottom line is still this: he will never, *ever* be offered the chance like this again. Fate surely will not drop another opportunity like this in his lap again, to just slip away, discreetly and permanently. This diabolical chemistry of time, age, reason, spirit, attitude, insight, position of the stars, and, lest he forget, deadly tragedy, came together just this once in harmonic vibration to slice through the fabric of reality so that he might step through and disappear behind the fold. No fabricated story will save him, no devilish trick. How could he return to his previous life, made even more unbearable by the weight of the disgusting lie? Indeed, he'd be pulled back, into the roiling pool of human bodies, elbowing and clawing one another for the space to become respected citizens in this society.

Once in the kitchen, N. has an epiphany that will save his entire plan, or at the very least, keep his watch out of the pawn broker's hand. Tucked in the furthest back corner of the tea cabinet was the Jenssen's "culture fund", a small cocoa tin, the contents of which Paula had assumed all authority over. For years, the couple had made a habit of emptying their small change, two-and-a-half and five guilder pieces, into a small pink piggy bank. When the piggy bank was full, the coins were exchanged for fifties and hundreds. These went into the "culture fund", money reserved for occasional expenditures on art and culture. They'd visit a gallery, purchase a painting, a drawing, a beautiful woodcarving or engraving by an industrious acquaintance, or visit a theater or museum. But as time passed, money went in but rarely came out as the pleasure they had once found in each other's company gradually evaporated. Once, the Janssens even thought of exchanging the contents to euros.

N. reaches for the can, opens it (it is still full, to his great relief), and folds the thick stack of paper into the inside pocket of his jacket. And then, quite suddenly, he hears car doors slamming in the driveway, and this there is no mistake. Hastily he puts the empty can back in its place, darts a quick glance across the living room. Through the window, he sees his mother-in-law flipping through keys as she walks toward the front door, and Anke, balancing on one leg on the sidewalk, hopping, happy to be free from school despite the tragic circumstances.

But where is Paula? N. slips into the utility room and reaches for the handle of the back door when he sees her gray figure walking up the garden path. She often walks around the house when she's bought things for the garden to put in the shed. But what the hell?! She hasn't bought anything at all! As quick as a flash of lightning he shoots into the hall, back up the stairs, and noiselessly pulls his studio door closed behind him. N. hears the back door open and the key turn in the front door. Gasping for air, he slides behind a tall armoire, where, feeling dizzy, his knees buckle, and he collapses on the floor.

N. has no sense of time or direction when he comes to, just a few moments later. As he regains his senses, his watch reads five to four. He is still dazed, but he knows without a doubt that it was exactly half past three when he emptied the culture fund. He hears a hazy rummaging downstairs and a moment later Paula's loud voice in the hall. "You want tea too, don't you?" There is a mumbled confirmation from Johanna Elisabeth de Geus van Wateringen, née de Bruyne. N. regains his strength, doubles down on his optimism, and carefully pulls the door open so that he can listen from the landing. "No, they'll call back, they promised," he hears Paula's voice, again at a volume meant to cover some distance. The TV switches on, probably Anke watching one of her favorite shows. Then there's the tinkling of cutlery and his wife's voice moving into the living room as she emphasizes again that she is expecting to be called back this afternoon. Then the kitchen door closes and N. hears only murmurs. His heart pounds so hard it might leap from his chest as he creeps down the stairs, grateful that they've never been particularly squeaky. As silently as a speck of dust, he moves towards the back door and steps outside. On the garden path, N. had the ridiculous feeling that he was being watched by his family, gawking and pointing at him from behind the curtains. He tucks his chin into his jacket, covering his face with his hat, and disappears behind the shed and fence.

Away from danger, N. exhales and is immediately stabbed with hot, throbbing pain in his head. He walks briskly, putting as much distance as quickly as possible between himself and his previous life. By the time he boards the intercity train, it's a quarter to five. Once on the train and tucked into relative privacy, he peers into his AH bag and discreetly counts the paper-wrapped bundles. He remembers clearly the day he bought them, fourteen years ago during a holiday in Poland, and for a relatively cheap price in a small shop in the center of Krakow. It was at the urgent advice of one of his traveling companions, an art history student who didn't have the money himself but spotted their value right away. That had been just before the Peaceful Revolution. They were confirmed to be originals that for centuries must have decorated the interior of a Polish church, monastery, the drawing room of an upper-class family or, who knows, maybe even the shabby shelter of a farmer or day laborer. They'd been badly weathered by time and climate, but with his tender maintenance and the technical ingenuity of his college friend, they'd been restored back to more or less their original condition. According to him, they would fetch a minimum of ten thousand guilders each, an amount N. could not believe. He didn't need the money at the time and had set his art treasure aside as a nest egg.

Reaching the central station in Y and with finances and spirits somewhat restored, N. decides on a quick meal before catching his connecting train. He happens upon an excellent rice dish at a Chinese restaurant around the corner from the station, which completely relieves his headache. His mood so improved, he drinks two beers before walking back to the station. By half past eight, he is back in his hotel room, inspecting his art treasures again and then, with pleasant anticipation, the contents of his jacket pocket. The two-and-a-half and five guilder coins had grown over the years to an amount of 2,890 euros in denominations of hundreds, fifties and twenties, far more than he had expected. N.'s financial woes of the previous few days were gone, for now anyway. He whistles softly between his teeth, feeling like his new self and congratulating himself on his smooth performance, when he reaches into his pocket and feels the key to the back door. He feels light as he tosses it aside, *I'll never need that again!*

He washes his clothes in the sink with soap from the shower, then hangs them over the curtain rod to dry. Exhausted, he falls into bed, but is dragged through a restless, dream-torn night in which a furious and sometimes howling Paula has caught onto his theft and disappearance. A policeman resembling commissioner Bulle Bas stands in N.'s study, scratching his head thoughtfully, collecting evidence for the missing artifacts in the bottom drawer of the desk.

The next day is Wednesday. N. takes the train to Y again, and does some shopping at C&A and Hema. He buys five pairs of underwear, five pairs of socks, three collared shirts, a pair each of trousers and jeans, a windbreaker, comfortable lounge pants, a stick of deodorant, a pair of slippers, four T-shirts and three sets of pajamas, as well as a suitcase. Then he buys a prepaid mobile phone and leaves the city. Anything else he may need in the near future will certainly be available in Q.

5.

After shopping in the city, N. has just over 2,000 euros left. To keep his money from disappearing like snow in sun, he will have to live simply, which means his first priority is arranging for more affordable accommodations. And besides, he has no other choice. After extending his stay for a week, the desk clerk informed N. that *Aurora* is booked from the beginning of June to the end of

August for the summer holiday, which means there will be no room for him in two weeks.

The next morning is a Thursday. N. rips up the registration for his car. Next he holds the driver's license between his fingers, ready to destroy it, but then changes his mind. He throws the key to the back door into a dumpster; he didn't want to tempt fate by entering his home again. He renounces the borrowed ladies' bicycle. It is obviously too conspicuous here, and beyond that, he cannot shake the symbolic weight that riding the feminine bike might lay on his masculinity. He parks it in the covered bike shed at the railway station, wishes it a caring new owner. He could have traded it in, but decided not to risk that engraved serial number may have been reported stolen.

He walks to a bike shop in Q, greeted by a talkative, ruddy man in his fifties in blue overalls. Among many other things he proudly displays, he has a sturdy, second-hand, three-speed Gazelle men's bicycle with an old-fashioned dynamo. After a pro forma inspection, N. buys the bike for seventy-five euros. For ten euros, the ruddy man says he will throw in a second-hand double pannier bag. Always handy. The man's wife serves them coffee and slices of spice cake with butter, which she had baked and brought to the shop. The three of them chat about the weather, exchange opinions about the recent disaster, news of which still fills screens and newspapers every day. Then Mr. C.J. Janssen, aka K. van Andel, rides his recently acquired, appropriately sized bicycle through Q, the central village of a beautiful municipality where, he increasingly suspects, he will take up a clandestine residence for at least the next few weeks or months. He does a bit more shopping, buys a map of the area, and has lunch in a small park behind the village church; that is to say, he eats a cookie with almond filling and a coconut macaroon on a bench, washed down with the contents of a can of Fanta. It is still sunny, but a bit cooler than the past few days and weeks. N. is grateful for his foresight in buying a windbreaker yesterday.

In the afternoon, he rides to the supermarket in X, still waiting for shelf stockers to apply. He removes the wig and mustache, hiding them in his spacious panniers before entering the store. If he wants to work here on a daily basis, he knows he'll never be able to keep up the disguise. Best if everyone knows his normal appearance from the start. He asks a lanky cashier with a blonde ponytail if he can speak to Mr. de Wilde, the person to whom the flyer directed applicants. The young lady, bored and fussing with her nails, gives him a long stare, probably trying to decide if she'd like to work with him. She points to a room she calls "the office" and tells him to knock. From within comes a loud "come in!", and N. walks into a room with a raised floor, a blank wooden wall with a narrow opening like the gun hole of a bunker through which the activities of staff and shoppers can be observed. All very strategic. Behind this wall a balding, middle-aged man with apple-red cheeks, average height but above average girth, busies himself behind a desk. He introduces himself as Piet de Wilde, branch manager. He's a pleasant pyknic type, evaluating him critically from behind glasses with thick nearsighted lenses.

N. can tell immediately that Mr. de Wilde is put off by his unshaven face. He has a pang of regret about not adding a razor to his shopping list, as he knows first impressions are often all that matter with simple folk. The grocer would not want to frighten his loyal clientele by hiring some unkempt maniac. But Mr. de Wilde humors him, and then there is some back and forth about him, where he comes from, the extent of his education, employment history. N. improvises; he sticks to the general truth when he can, without overcommitting to one story. He finished primary school (true), then started secondary school but made a mess of it and never finished, which he later regretted terribly. He finished tech school and got a job as a metal worker at a construction company, but became legally disabled as a result of psychological stress related to various changes in the company. Upon the declaration of his legal disability, the company doctor had strongly advised him against ever taking a full-time job again (weak, weak, weak).

The grocer sighs deeply.

"Can you read?" he asks, looking suspiciously over his glasses.

N. says he can. His stomach turns as he realizes his application will likely be turned down; he already imagines himself with the first of the Polish art treasures in hand, head bowed, walking into the pawn broker's office. The man sighs again, rubs the smooth skin on his chin with his soft, plump hand, as if subconsciously implying how much more presentable a clean-shaven face is. He sets his pen down on top of a stack of nondescript papers on the desk, removes his glasses, then folds his hands in front of him as he says carefully, clearly trying to discourage N., that he only needs a part-time, temporary.

"That's just what I'm looking for!" N. nearly shouts, he's shown too much enthusiasm. "I'm just looking for a bit of extra cash for a while." This could be the perfect arrangement!

Finally, Mr. de Wilde nods. "Okay, but only Friday and Saturday. Maybe Monday afternoons now and then... and you'll be expected to sweep the store." One last attempt to discourage N.

He eagerly agrees (almost overdoing it again), and decides that he'll push his luck a bit more, asking to be paid under the table and in cash for very innocent reasons that Mr. de Wilde (he hopes) will understand. A little store like this must have a few immigrants working illegally, N. thinks. Mr. de Wilde narrows his eyes and purses his lips for a moment, then sighs again.

"Agreed, seven per hour. No contract; you'll be paid only for the hour you work." He sets his thick glasses on his nose again, as though the conversation has officially ended.

"Eight an hour," N. shoots back, "and twenty-five a week in food." It's been some time since he's had to play the aggressive businessman.

Mr. de Wilde smiles, perhaps a bit condescendingly. "Five and a half an hour plus twenty a week in food," he says firmly.

N. feels the actual pain of Karl Marx's theory of the impoverishment of the working class. That was written a hundred and fifty years ago; would boss mentality ever change?

De Wilde tells him shortly that he can start tomorrow (Friday), but this notice is a bit too short for N. He suggests Friday next week instead, and the man agrees. N. is given some instructions about working hours, dress code, co-worker and customer interactions and so on. Amazingly, he does not ask for an address or phone number. N. is expected to show up at the gate of the shop on Friday at eight o'clock in the morning.

N. leaves the supermarket, a little dazed at how quickly the parts of his plan are beginning to move. N. pulls the disguise from his pannier, glad that he won't need it much longer now. Whistling and humming, he pedals north again, basking in the warm glow of good fortune. He steers his new (legally obtained) bicycle, which he has grown increasingly fond of, off the main road to a path that meandered through a nature reserve between woods, sand drifts, fens, heaths, a pasture of sheep, and a few wandering locals. That brilliant spring green lay upon the landscape all around him, almost as if it has been accentuated a little too heavily by its painter. He stops to eat the remaining coconut macaroon and rest, leaning against a tree trunk. A persistent red forest ant tries to climb his shin, but N. smashes it between two fingers. He pedals on towards Q, arriving at the *Aurora* at exactly 6:00 pm.

After an excellent meal in the restaurant (they've found a truly great chef), Mr. Van Andel contacts an escort agency. With twenty-one hundred euros still in his pocket and the prospect of a steady income, he decides to reward himself with this small luxury, just this once. After all, he's a healthy guy with a healthy dislike for manual labor, and that's just what he'll be doing. She is sweet and her breasts are firm, which gives the impression that she is eager to offer them to him. He tries to hide his loneliness between them, asks if she wants to go out. She doesn't. The evening progresses as one might expect, physically exciting, but lacking entirely in mental stimulation.

6.

That Friday, the hotel slowly fills up. The silence is driven out as holidaymakers fill the rooms and restaurant. The silence of the *Aurora* had been such a pleasant respite after the chaos that had preceded his arrival that fateful Saturday afternoon. The evening before, a small tour bus had pulled into the parking lot next to the hotel and let out eight spry seniors. N. assumes they must be members of an aerobics club from The Hague who have chosen the hotel for a long weekend as a base to explore the surrounding area on foot. They are all morning people, N. discovers, entering the breakfast room around 9:00 (early for him) to find it fully occupied and bursting with energy. The interlopers, without exception, are all over the age of 70, clad in genuine knickerbockers and sturdy walking shoes. Before N. has been served his first cup of coffee, they have all breakfasted and are beginning a hardy stretching routine on the gravel outside the *Aurora* in preparation for the day's big hike.

N., tapping an egg, finds their vim and exuberance dizzying; he really must put some serious effort into finding some living arrangement that, even if not permanent, will at least be private. Two days ago, he had taken a rather disinterested glance through a stack of weekly newspapers lying in the lobby. The Q Post, a free local door-to-door advertising paper, had been shuffled into the mix, and he seems to remember a certain advertisement.

After finishing breakfast, he hurries to the lobby and breathes a sigh of relief when he finds the proletariat bulletin still hidden in the stack. He flips eagerly to page 4. There, in the bottom corner, beneath an almost full-page promotion for the local discount store, a small ad reads: *"For rent: furnished, small suite in a main residence. Vogelpoelweg 14, Q. Rent negotiable. Inquire at tel. no…"* The paper is already a week old. There's no time to lose. He dials the number on his new phone, and a somewhat husky female voice answers. No, she says, it has not been rented out yet. Yes, he can come by this afternoon.

N. found Vogelpoelweg 14 in his map, the Family Guide to Village Q. It's two kilometers to the south, near the expansive nature preserve he had visited on that lovely afternoon when he'd decided to take up residence in Q. The address turns out to be on a B-road, a Saxon farm with a partly thatched, partly tiled roof surrounded by meadows and a row of poplars. It sits back about a hundred meters from the road. He has left his mustache, wig, and glasses in his pannier; if a deal is going to be made, his new cohabitants will have to be comfortable with his regular appearance—if somewhat unkempt, at the moment. He pedals up the gravel road to the yard, where he is met halfway by the ruff-woof-wag-arf bark of a shaggy sheepdog mut.

"Bart… quiet!" The figure of a tall woman steps out from beneath the shade of a canopy. In the full sunlight, N. sees she is dressed in a cream-colored blouse and close-fitting blue skirt, which leaves her rather bony but sturdy knees exposed. "Are you here for the ad?"

"Arf," the sheepdog gives one last woof of greeting, and N. gives him a friendly scratch between the ears. He recognizes the woman's voice. He estimates that she is about forty years old. She reminds him of someone, but he can't remember who.

"I'm Olga," the blond woman says, extending her hand in greeting "Olga Beumer."

N. takes her hand delicately. "Kees," he says, "Kees van Andel," K… Kees. It feels strange to hear this new name as it coalesces in his mind, then takes shape and slips from his mouth. Perhaps it's too similar to Chris? *Ah well, to hell with it*, he thinks, *it could have just as easily been Karel, or Klaus or Kobus, or… whatever. It's done.*

He will be known as Kees here until the last day they see him.

"You didn't have trouble finding the place, did you?" she asks. He feels acutely that her blue-gray eyes are scrutinizing him. The hoarse voice instills in her a sense of confidentiality. She has high cheekbones, pushing her eyes up at the corners, and speaks fluent Dutch with a slight foreign accent. Polish or Russian, N. thinks. As a university student, he had spent some time dabbling in Slavic studies before finally devoting himself completely to general literature. He tells her he did not, the ride had been pleasant.

"Well, would you like some coffee, or would you like to see the space first?"

N. can hear the irony in her voice and opts for the latter. He notices a slight shaking in his prospective landlady, beginning in her shoulders and radiating to her hands and fingers. She is adorned heavily in jewelry—a chain of small rings in her ears, several gold and silver necklaces, piles of bracelets on each wrist, and glittering gold and gemstone rings on almost every finger— which gives the effect of a soft metal tinkling sound as she walks. It's 23° C, but she seems almost chilled in her thick skirt and light silk blouse. *A widow, perhaps?* N. thinks, imagining briefly the course of events that may have led this woman here, uncomfortable in the presence of a strange man. By the deliberate and heavy makeup and shining nail polish, it is clear that she is a woman with the means to leave the rougher work to others. He thinks he detects a few streaks of white swept into her bun, but it was hard to tell against her thick, ashen-blonde.

As he approached earlier, he had wondered where the "small suite as part of the main residence" could possibly be. To the left of the main house, a wooden canopy covers a tall stack of hay and straw bales, a few bicycles, an assortment of gardening tools, and a Honda lawn mower. Opposite that, a shed has been converted into an open garage where a caravan and a Peugeot 204 are parked, with space in front seemingly waiting for another car. To the right, a large stone barn, with a gently sloping tile roof and small, semicircular windows, where he can see curtains have been hung. N. assumes that this shelter was once a horse stable or pigsty. Nevertheless, the lady leads him to this building.

His instinct is to plug his nose as he enters the structure; he doesn't want to smell the last of the fattened pigs. He enters by ducking through a low door, hoping his disgust goes unnoticed. The interior is only barely adequate. A kind of hallway, just large enough for a person to turn around in, opens into a cramped living room, approximately five square meters containing a leather couch, a side table, and an easy chair. The kitchen is a separate room, with modern countertops and a simple table with two chairs. A large window on the far wall has obviously been converted from a barn door opening, giving an expansive view of the meadow to the edge of a forest some five hundred meters away. The section of the meadow nearest the building has been fenced for pasture, where a few sheep, goats and a pony are grazing peacefully. Chickens scratch and peck in the patchy side yard. Bart, the sheepdog and farmyard guard, jumps the fence, scattering a few hens, then lifts his leg on some imaginary tree or pole. When he finishes marking his territory, the sheepdog appears to scan the yard with a glower, as if daring someone to dispute his claim. N. is momentarily captivated by this idyllic scene, and almost doesn't follow when the tinkling of the woman's jewelry leads to a small bedroom with a modest three-quarter bed. Adjacent to the bedroom is a small closet with a shower, bath, and toilet.

The furniture looks a bit jumbled, probably the result of various visits to a thrift store. The floor in the living room and bedroom were a sturdy hardwood, giving the quaint space a certain warmth. It offered the perfect ambience for a man intending to lead a sober, remote, and undisturbed life, with neither economic nor social abundance; transition to his post-modern simplicity will be an easy task here. N. realizes with some irritation at himself that, as was often the case when he encountered new people or things, he had briefly fallen into the trap of his own prejudices. He remembered reading in grad school about one Georg Christoph Lichtenberg, who, more than two centuries ago, had warned about giving over to one's prejudices.

N. keeps his cool, not wanting to betray his eagerness before discussing price, but inwardly his heart rejoices: *This is EXACTLY what I was looking for!* Olga lights her third or fourth cigarette since beginning the tour, then casually inquires whether he is single or if perhaps his wife…

"I'm single… divorced," he says, cutting her off. He's surprised at how easily it comes out; no one would have guessed his lie. She lets out a heavy sigh; N. isn't sure if he's imagining it, but he senses a tinge of disappointment.

"It looks reasonable," he says, trying to sound frugal, "What are you thinking for rent?" He musters his best attempt at a critical look (what does that face even look like?) as he scans the space along the raised ceiling where some cobwebs hang. The whole place looks a bit dusty. His eyes lock on her blue-gray gaze again.

"Two hundred a month," she says, "including gas, water and electricity in normal use." Her resoluteness gives the impression that the "rent to be negotiated" portion of the ad had just been bait. "If you'd like, I'm willing to clean once every two weeks, but then rent will be two hundred and fifty."

"Of course." N. nods understandingly. His relief is palpable; walking through the entire suite again, he knows he's found his home, at least for the coming months.

He'll be able to cook his own food there, the lady assures him. "There are pots and pans in the kitchen cabinets, not new, but well cared for and good quality. Of course, I'll also be willing to cook for you. Then it will be…" Olga rattles off yet another amount, and then some other innocuous service and another fee, and finally some number that N. doesn't register as he has moved into a deeper inspection of the kitchen cabinets. Dishes are stacked in a cupboard with stained-glass doors and a repaired leg. In the drawer, plenty of cutlery and several utensils. A small television has been set on a table in the corner of the living room. His landlady pops out from around the door frame, her face in an open question, staring at him expectantly.

"Uhh, yes, Mrs. Beumer, yes I think I'll take it," then hesitantly, "I'll get back to you about the cooking."

She invites him again for a cup of coffee in the main house, her jewelry jangling as he follows her. Though she appears to be home alone at the moment, Mrs. Olga Beumer informs him that she lives at the farmhouse with a daughter, who is at school right now, and her boyfriend, who just left for work an hour ago. The furniture in the very spacious living room is simple and uncluttered, open and cool without being bare or uninviting. In one corner, a leather sofa faces an old Chesterfield, and between them is a Gueridon table. A writing desk sits facing a window with the same breathtaking view of the meadow, and near it a wooden highboy with four drawers. On the opposite wall, bric-à-brac stone figurines and several intricate pieces of rococo porcelain sit atop a carved sideboard. There is a fireplace set into the wall, and on the mantle sits a Frisian tail clock and several Delft blue ornaments. N. makes a note that there aren't any religious decorations. The interior is tasteful, the designer having successfully navigated the fine line between interesting and lavish. He gives her an approving look. He might even go so far as to say she has good taste (but of course he doesn't tell her that).

She asks Mr. van Andel (as she calls him) whether he has a car. He replies that he does not, offering some excuse about making ends meet on a modest income. With this openness about his finances, Mrs. Beumer seems to soften toward him a bit. She tells him confidentially that until about six months ago, the guesthouse had been occupied by a lady who was married but was living in hiding from her abusive husband. She had been referred to the Beumer family by the women's shelter in Y, and had lived here quite happily until being found by her husband, despite her many precautions. A few unsavory things involving the police had taken place at Vogelpoelweg 14 after that. "I'm sure you can imagine," Mrs. Beumer said. After that, everyone agreed that it would be best if the battered young lady found a new address.

The neat landlady looks distantly out the window, her slight quaking intensifying at the images she's just evoked. She confides in Mr. van Andel that after all that trouble she had strongly considered no longer renting out the guesthouse. "It's just so nice to have the extra income, you know?" Then, almost bashfully, she asks Mr. van Andel if he might consider paying rent in cash, directly to her. She starts to conjure some reason but he waves her off.

"Of course not. Cash is fine."

His luck makes him feel giddy. Not only is he an inconnu who can only do business with cash under the table, he'll also be able to conceal the fact that he lacks a bank account. Such an inconsistency would surely strike this sharp-eyed widow as odd. And so it is that he agrees to willingly contribute to the gigantic black market, where the wasteful arm of the government has no reach into the profits of sinful endeavors. Their situations fit together perfectly, like a rod in a bearing.

A second cup of coffee is followed by a third, and the conversation continues pleasantly. The two discuss everything and nothing, with hardly a mention of the Gunpowder Disaster, which N. takes as a sign of the woman's high level of civility. At some point, the conversation turns back to business.

N. agrees again to the monthly rent of 250 euros, including cleaning (which he really hates doing), but says kindly that he does not set a very high standard with regard to the latter (to which the lady responds with a nice smile). She generously offers to give him the last week of this month rent free—Mr. van Andel should just try it out for a week first. In other words, he can take up residence next Monday, if he so wishes, after she's taken a broom and soap to it over the weekend. "It's been empty for the better half of a year," she says, "and it shows." She taps her cigarette in a glass ashtray full of butts, smiles mysteriously, takes a pull on her cigarette, and exhales, wrapping herself in smoke for a few seconds.

N. looks at the lady's well-groomed hands and suspects that she will secretly outsource the cleaning job; perhaps to her daughter for extra pocket money. They fall into a comfortable silence, listening to the tail clock serenely tick, as though taking bites of the future. N. falls for a moment into the chewing tick-tock rhythm. After such a tumultuous week, the welcoming hominess of the farmhouse is like a balm to his chaotic mind. A fly buzzes against a window, a dog barks in the distance, a goat bleats in the side yard. For a moment, N. is speechless. Apparently, so is his landlady. She looks on at him with curiosity, as though cataloging each impression, compiling a more complete image of who he is. She's still looking at him when she lights yet another cigarette, her wrist bangles tinkling as she strikes the lighter.

"I know I'm still a stranger to you," N. says, trying to put her at ease. "You're probably thinking, who is this weirdo, doesn't even have a car, a wife… but there will be plenty of time for us to get to know each other."

The landlady smiles warmly. She agrees; there will be plenty of time for all that, she'd like for him to get to know her a bit better as well.

The two pass the afternoon sitting opposite each other in comfortable leather armchairs. A cloud of cigarette smoke envelopes her more or less constantly. She crosses one sturdy leg over the other, and N. can't help but notice her rather low neckline. He imagines, considering her thin but tall stature, that Olga is not hiding much behind her light blouse. A pair of noble nipples at most, he thinks. He tries to imagine her naked, but without much success. His eyes stray to a modest bookshelf. He makes out titles by the diligent Merilyn French, Renate Dorrestein, Nelleke Noordervliet, Hella Haasse, Lulu Wang, Adriaan van Dis, Isabel Allende, Henning Mankel and others, so many comforting women's novels by well-meaning writers. On the corner of the bookshelf, to his pleasant surprise, he sees a first edition of Tolstoy's *Vojna i Mir* in Cyrillic. He wonders who speaks Russian in this house? Her perhaps? He decides he'll ask her, some other time.

When he stands to leave, she does as well, jewelry jingling. They exchange a firm handshake and lock eyes before he bids a polite farewell. N. mounts his bike and is dutifully escorted to the B-road by the ruff-woof-arf of Bart. He waves again as he reaches the road and continues out of sight, whistling happily as he cycles towards Q. His plan is falling into place; everything is as smooth as silk. Yesterday work, today shelter. If he can keep his lucky streak going… N. sits up on the saddle, pulling his hands together in happy contemplation for a brief moment, causing him to wobble and nearly crash.

On Saturday morning, giddy with his good fortune, N. makes another trip to Y to shop. He buys hair clippers, a pair of sturdy walking shoes and a transistor radio with a cassette and CD player. At a well-stocked bookstore, he purchases some drawing and painting supplies. Once a passionate but unpretentious amateur artist, N. had noticed right away that his new accommodations offered excellent light and scenery. Indeed, what better time to revisit the old hobby?

Around five o'clock, back in his hotel room, he calls the escort service again. He isn't sure, after all, when he'll be able to spend a pleasant evening with a beautiful girl again after he takes up residence at Vogelpoelweg 14. Sacrifices will have to be made. That afternoon, in the dumpster behind the hotel, he got rid of his disguise. He is now Kees van Andel. The clock strikes midnight, and with it a new era is begun.

7.

If his life were a collection of short stories, Sunday—his final night at *Aurora*—would be the "dark and stormy night" story. The high-pressure system that had been keeping rain at bay for three weeks gave way to a small but nasty depression. In the morning, N. has breakfast with the young girl he'd paid for the night before—a dark little thing—before returning to the room to try for a few more hours of sleep. He was tired. She had cost 350 euros, and he had made sure to get every penny's worth. The girl—she had claimed to be just eighteen, said her name was Monique— had matched his lust and desire with such aptitude and without reluctance that he quickly doubted the age she had given. She was at once accommodating and adventurous, seemed to prefer being on her knees, to be taken *more canino*. It excited him to feel her regulate her own pleasure, pushing first hard then softly against him, spreading her thighs or pressing them tight around him, according to the level of her arousal. She moved her fingers down her body, pleasuring herself, as he caressed her soft and sensitive breasts. And he knew that she had also enjoyed herself, from the wet vibration he had felt when he'd slipped inside her; it hadn't all been fake. Every time Monique had let out a high-pitched, animal-like scream, he had grown to love her more.

Afterwards, she fell into a deep and trusting sleep in N.'s arms, making him feel more like a protective father than a paying customer. The amusing thought went through his head that with her riveted so seamlessly to his chest and stomach, he was almost a hermaphrodite. She really was lovely, and it was a shame, he thought, that she should throw herself away for money. Especially with that energy; surely, she would burn out quickly, and her career would be stunted. But how could he possibly tell her such a thing? He'd just seem dubious, and besides, such questions about personal history and true identities would only result in lies between them. There had been no obvious fabrications (except the Big Lie itself), and N. wanted to enjoy the idea that they had remained two pure souls. But in the morning, she became the first (and the last, for now) sex phantom, added to a series of dimly lit figures, from whom he took leave with some regret in his heart. But she hadn't been just another body; he'd felt a real connection with her. He thinks he would like to know her real first name.

With the scent of the girl's hair still on the pillow, and with the juice of their sex still mixing in the sheets (he can sometimes go to extremes), N. sleeps soundly. Persistent dreams of rosy and purple wonders take him well into the afternoon. He wakes to the noise of other guests slamming doors, children playing tag in the hallway and other noisy games.

It's still raining. The ponies on the other side of the oak trees, having spent the night being whipped by wind and rain, stood imperturbably, ears back, ignoring the gurgle of cars passing on the road. N. eats a sandwich he'd brought up from breakfast that morning and orders a pot of coffee brought to his room. He peruses the NRC newspaper he bought in Y. Even this venerable evening paper is still plastering reports of the disaster as front-page news. There is still the nice round number of five missing persons—can he safely assume that Chris Janssen is one of them? But this paper is already two days old, practically rancid. He throws it in the wastebasket.

He begins *Under the Volcano* while he drinks his coffee, but puts the heart-rending impressionist novel away again after just a few pages. He's not in the mood to empathize with other people's struggles; he has plenty of his own obstacles to overcome. He sits sipping coffee silently for a moment, thinking about the girl who'd been at his side the night before. There had been a bottomless emptiness with her departure, immediate regret over letting her go. Maybe he should have paid for her to stay the whole weekend. He is convinced she would have stayed if only he had asked. When she had said goodbye, there was nothing of the disconcerting contemplation, feigned interest, non-comments or haste to get away, as it always was with the other girls. He sensed her hesitation at leaving, he thought, felt certain that she had liked him. Perhaps they could agree to meet now and then, somewhere, for the next few weeks or months. Two completely unattached beings in a strange environment, silently binding themselves together for a few nights, uniting against an unrelenting loneliness. What a scenario!

His longing to hold a soft and willing body against his own is once again gnawing at him. He wants someone he can hide himself inside of, who can protect him from interminable solitude. Perhaps he can validate his own existence through the pulse of a woman's pleasure.

By 5:00, it has stopped raining and N. decides to stretch his legs. Walking through Q, he takes stock of the proverbial tedium of rural villages on weekends. Indeed it only slightly surpasses the tedium of weekends in cities, just a change of scale and perspective. There is no movement on the street, no one walking in the pedestrian zone, wet sidewalks reflect only the changing streetlamps. Not even a dog walker, out for an evening walk. Through living room windows, N. sees lively televisions broadcasting colorful sporting events and takes it as a sign of living beings inside. Loud singing pours out of a café where a local football club's victory is being celebrated.

It's all so inviting, lively, and cozy, but N. feels a wave of bitter melancholy rise up in the back of his throat. His loneliness is invasive, all-consuming; this, he feels, is a worrying sign.

On his way back to the *Aurora*, depressed and waxing phil-osophical, he sees the moon pop out between hurried clouds. *Without Galileo and Copernicus*, he thinks, *would anyone even know that the moon is round and forms a celestial body with the earth, and to-gether they revolve around the sun?* At 7:00, he has a hot dinner in the restaurant. He'd been holding out hope that his evening meal would improve his spirits, but the busy cacophony of all those unknown faces, the boisterous children, push him eat hastily. At half past seven he is already on his way to his room with a bot-tle of wine, a glass and some snacks under his arm. He makes a half-hearted and unsuccessful attempt to continue his afternoon reading, and upon failing, sits at his bedroom window watching steam rise from the four ponies as the warm evening sun begins to dry their damp coats. He sips the wine, and slowly, happily gives himself over to its dreamy haze.

He wakes, stiff and aching in his chair, at half past twelve. After a hot shower and a thorough toothbrushing, N. slides be-tween the hotel sheets and rests comfortably. Smiling, he notices that his regret and melancholy, that penetrating fear of loneliness, have disappeared. He sleeps peacefully the remainder of the night.

Early the next morning, he's greeted by a friendly sun peek-ing through the oak trees, brightening his gray room.

8.

Monday morning. N. lies in bed, lulled by the sound of traffic passing outside the hotel. All the cogs in the great machine of the economy are preparing for another five- or six-day grind. Even the quiet of the countryside is swallowed up by the bustle of the work week—bicycle, car, bus and train wheels all rushing somewhere. The accelerating diesel engine of the early morn-ing NS train had already woken him twice. Regardless, a deep sleep has left him feeling refreshed, and he throws off the covers, takes an extra-long shower, and dresses for his last breakfast at the *Aurora*. Then, with a carefully packed suitcase balanced on his fender rack, he rides to Vogelpoelweg in a bright mood. He looks back once, with a rhyme, "Thank you, Sunrise, for this early light surprise."

When N. turns up the driveway to Vogelpoelweg 14, he is once again greeted by Bart's loud bark and wagging tail. The mutt seems to no longer consider him a stranger. Two cars are parked beneath the shed this time; N. assumes that the second must belong to the landlady's boyfriend. Bart's greeting has apparently alerted the residents to his arrival. The tall, thin figure of Mrs. Beumer appears at the door, calling to the dog. She is dressed in anthracite gray trousers that fit snugly on her frame, making her appear even slimmer. Her silk blouse is a lovely yellow with a deeply plunging neckline. Sunlight glints off the layers of delicate gold and silver adorning her neck and wrists (is it just him, or is she always glowing?). The cigarette, perched delicately between two well-groomed fingers, curls pale blue smoke into the room. Unlike their previous meeting, today she is wearing strong perfume.

She greets him warmly and asks if N. would like a cup of coffee. He declines gently, saying he'd like to settle into his new place a bit first, unpack his suitcase. When she inquires what time the movers will be here with the "rest of his things", N. smiles sheepishly, replying that there is no "rest". He pats his suitcase with one hand and says "It's all right here." There is a brief moment of silence that is quickly penetrated by the distant barking of a dog. Her mouth opens as if to say something but, changing her mind, she simply shrugs. *Well, it takes all sorts,* he imagines her saying later, when she debriefs her family on the character of her new tenant. Despite this new discovery, Olga precedes to hand him the key to his new residence with some ceremony, allowing him to unlock and open the door in front of her. Inside, the apartment has been scrubbed clean until it shined with a glow that any self-respecting Dutch housewife would be proud of. A very tasteful vase has been placed on a table in the living room, filled with a generous bouquet of fresh cut flowers. The flowers are lovely, and the woman has done a wonderful job of making the small space warm and inviting. When he tells her so, she smiles and her cheeks flush red.

She leaves him to make coffee, and when he joins her again at her house, she calls her boyfriend in from his gardening work. The man introduces himself as Theo: he is middle aged, average height, with dark, receding hair, a dark mustache, and a nasty scar on his left cheek. N. will later learn that the scar is from a broken beer glass, used on him in a fight at the annual fair many years ago. Theo doesn't say much at first, and what he does say is coated in the thick accent of the region, still rather difficult for N. to understand.

The conversation is mostly guided by Olga, with her husky voice and sturdy hand gestures, glittering with gems and tinkling with gold. Inevitably, the topic turns toward the recent disaster. Theo repeats the most recent reports: fourteen people have died, and six are now missing, presumed dead. He reads it off a bit too triumphantly, earning him a reproachful glance from his girlfriend; such a gruesome topic is not appropriate for pleasant conversation, and she would like to assume that her new renter has no interest in such things. Under normal circumstances, she would be right. He was generally disinterested in empathy. But now, with his present stability and future aspirations tied up in the balance between "missing" and "presumed dead", every detail was of interest to him. *If only they knew*, he thinks, grateful they've believed his story so far.

Three more cups of coffee are poured, and the woman smokes yet another cigarette when, somewhere in the labyrinth of the renovated farmhouse, a telephone rings. Somewhere else, the soft sound of classical music flows from some invisible sound system. Theo, visibly uncomfortable that he's been left alone with N.— and in silence, no less—suddenly starts on an enthusiastic monologue about himself. From the broken fragments of language, he can decipher through the man's thick accent, N. can summarize that the man—*please, call me Theo*—served in the military as a young man, and he'd had an *awfully* good time of it with great comrades. Theo's voice rises into a question, and N. realizes a little late that he's asking whether N. had served in the military. He says that he did not, and begins to explain that his older brother had, but was cut off by Theo, launching into his own story again.

"I served with an artillery unit in Nunspeet and 't Harde, with the black berets, or the tank corps. Does that mean anything to you, the tank corps?" It did not. "I became a private first class there, it was *amazing*, but I was glad when I was discharged. You don't earn much doing that."

"Are you a soccer fan, Kees? Can I call you Kees? I'm a big fan of de Graafschap who, by the way, will be relegated again this year. I don't ever miss a game, except when I have to work. I work down at the dairy factory in Z, making butter and cheese. The factory runs day and night, seven days a week, and I'm on a three-shift roster, so I workday and night too. Not today though, I'm free today. And tomorrow I'll be around during the day, but then I go back on the night shift for a week straight tomorrow evening. The pay's pretty good but, man! Do you earn it!"

Theo continues, prattling along in his unintelligible dialect. He tells N. of his many colleagues who have already suffered from heart problems, and he doesn't think he'll keep doing it for long either, that three-shift roster. "I've already discussed it with Mr. de Korte from HR. I don't want to wait until I have a heart attack or something like that, too, because, let me tell you, the policy there is to just ignore a problem until someone gets hurt, but I'm not stupid. I'm not going to be their prey, these bosses, these high lords who take all the money and exploit us workers for as little as they can, then toss us out when they don't need us anymore. I like the work, though. I studied for a year and a half at the dairy school in Bolsward to become a butter and cheese maker. I had a pretty great time there, too, actually. And hey, I bet you've studied a bit too, eh? You look like the type."

N. looks at him, suddenly studious. *Damn it*, he thinks, *this guy thinks so much and knows so little?* Everyone just studies nothing nowadays—only in it for the degree. It used to be that you were only a "student" if you were enrolled at a university or college, but nowadays every silly air head from elementary school graduating into some sad tech school calls themselves a student. His accidental and unexpectedly exuberant conversation partner is still tirelessly describing his grinding down in the Great System (collective bargaining agreements, shift changes, clocks punched). N. hears that Theo has stopped droning, but it is a long moment before he realizes that this proletariat is awaiting some response from him—an encouraging word, perhaps, some expression of solidarity with the plight of the working class. But the former academic does not have a ready answer, no heartening response prepared.

Mrs. Beumer rejoins them then (and not a moment too soon, N. thinks) jingling, slender, and graceful in her perfectly tailored trousers. She looks a bit surprised at her boyfriend, who is suddenly and uncharacteristically so talkative. She fixes her new tenant with a kind of look of understanding, gracefully relieving him from conversation. She tells him that she plans to buy a tablecloth for the table in the kitchen, and that she'll drop it by later.

At half past eleven, N. withdraws to his new home, simply enjoying the quiet privacy for a time. In the afternoon he makes a trip into Q to stock up on groceries. Throughout the afternoon, he is plagued by curiosity about his two new landlord neighbors, Olga Beumer and her boyfriend. The boyfriend is clearly out of his element, shacking up with such a sophisticated woman. They remind him, he decides finally, of two revue artists performing a cabaret show.

<h1 align="center">9.</h1>

'New York, Neewww York!' The new transistor radio hums its first song into the gleaming living room. N. tries to pull the artist up from his memory. Sinatra with Nelson Riddle's orchestra,

maybe? Count Basie perhaps? *Basie… Riddle… what a lot of useless trivia we carry around with us*, he thinks, *and without even thinking about it, we just do it.*

'*If you can make it there, you'll make it anywhere… Start spreading the news…*' the song courses on.

It's been nine days since Christian Jacob Janssen disappeared into smoke and fire, and N. is more or less comfortably settled. He has confirmed that yes, his accommodations were indeed once used as a pigsty. It had been transformed into its current state by framing in a few walls. The late Mr. Beumer had been quite the clever handyman; he had installed every possible comfort in the modest space. N. looks out across the pasture where cows are grazing. The landlady's boyfriend, in one of his dubious monologues, had told N. that deer could often be spotted out along the forest edge early in the morning. ("Do you have binoculars? No problem. You can borrow mine some time.") The room feels more foreign to him than a station restaurant. The furniture is unfamiliar, gathered from God knows where: thrift stores, junk shops, flea markets. He tries to orient himself again after the *Aurora*. On Monday afternoon, after returning from his shopping trip, he just sits in his new room, staring out the window. For hours he can barely move from his chair. All he can do is stare apathetically out the window, watching the animals graze in the pasture outside his window. Driven either by stupidity or curiosity (who can tell?), a pony looks in through the open window, hoping the new resident might kindly toss some delicious scrap over the fence now and then.

N. can feel the waves of melancholy breaking at the edge of his mood again. He braces himself, familiar with this pattern. It's because he's bored, that must be it. Nothing to keep him busy. And the upheaval, like those first days of vacation when it feels impossible to release yourself from stress. It will pass. He'll start his new job on Friday. That's something. First, he'll put his routine in order, then he'll put his mind in order. A daily schedule to map the sea of time before him; this thought is followed by a crashing wave: what about all those days he dreamed of, free from schedules and obligations? But in this respect, he knew he was just an average man, someone who craved a sense of purpose, in spite of his own desires. He has certainly proven that he is no master of the art of *bon vivant*.

He takes a piece of paper from the drawer in the writing desk to quickly write down his thought. He lifts the pen from the page, hesitates, then writes, crosses out, rewrites, sets down the pen and reads the following list, written in a stark but messy scrawl:

"Now finally working out the novel I've had in my head for over two years."

(There had been quite a few pipe-smoking, tweed-wearing would-be novelists among the arts faculty at his university. It always amazed N. how quickly they degenerated into professors to lecture on Nabokov, their initial enthusiasm extinguished quite completely after being rejected by the very first publisher. Unworthy of a writer's future. Incidentally, his efforts are just a leisure activity, so success is irrelevant.)

"Keep working toward the Grand Plan. Figure out how to do it without exposing myself."

(He wants to leave the Netherlands, permanently, within the next year at the latest.)

"Buy a copy of Les Fleurs du Mal *and La Rochefoucauld's* Maxims, *and others."*

(He'd seen both these novels in a used bookshop in Y, but hadn't had enough money to buy them at the time. N. knows that his command of the French language, both written and spoken, have slipped in the past years.)

"Don't neglect my hobby of drawing and painting."

(A relic of his brief life with Minerva.)

"Make a point of exercising regularly."

(Such a wonderful way to take in the beauty of this countryside.)

"Women."

(N. knows his polygamous nature will only cause problems for him without frequent and intimate contact with a few beautiful and strong women.)

He transcribes the list of solemn intentions, which he expects
will occupy the bulk of his anxious energy and free time, onto a
clean sheet with neat handwriting and affixes it to the inside of
the kitchen door. With his course now properly charted, his out-
look is immediately improved. He sits contentedly at the kitchen
table, tapping his fingers on the mahogany tabletop. The late-af-
ternoon sun is shining through the window, and the wood is a
beautiful, rich brown. He prepares a small meal of rice, watches
the eight o'clock news, and spends the rest of the evening reading *Under the Volcano*.

10.

"Do you like it?"

N. can see her watching him through his periphery.

He answers truthfully. "I do … and I think I'm going to like
it more and more."

"You know, if there is anything you need, just let me know."

"A comforting thought, ma'am. But I'd rather be as little of a
burden as possible. It seems like you're pretty busy."

She has come in, now, unpacking the new tablecloth and arranging it on the kitchen table. Her skirt is short and fairly wide,
too short for her age, he thinks prudishly. But it accentuates her
unusually thin waist and sturdy thighs. It's Wednesday, his third
day in the little apartment. Yesterday and this morning he heard
her drive away at half past eight, returning sometime after noon.
Perhaps she has a job? More likely she went off to visit friends,
he thinks. From that blow that constantly complains there isn't
enough time, in order not to lift a finger all day. But what does
he know? There's just something about her—her speech, appearance, her whole presence—that suggests to him that Mrs. Beumer
is exogenous to the countryside and therefore fairly lonely. If she
has any girlfriends, N. thinks, they probably don't live out here.

"You're not a burden to me," she says, "not at all! And I think you'll find that I'm not easily bothered … by the way, what do you think of it, Mr. van Andel?" She points to the tablecloth. "I tried to match the color to the interior a bit."

Her stare penetrates N. so deeply that he almost expects her to call him out: come on now, Chris, the game is up! It would be just his luck that, after all the gifts fate has handed him, that he should end up seeking shelter from a woman endowed with telepathic gifts. N. starts to feel a bit uncomfortable.

N. changes the subject. Her inquisitive gaze is broken when he asks about her work. She does indeed have a job, working two or three mornings a week as an on-call home care attendant for a nearby institution. N. is surprised by this, considering her well-groomed hands and nails, impeccable dress and lavish jewelry. She tends to people in their homes, usually in the municipality of Q but occasionally further afield. Most of her clients are elderly or people living alone, people who have just been released from hospital and can't take care of themselves yet.

"Here in the countryside, you know, there's a lot more loneliness than people think. Young people move to the city or the coast where there are more opportunities, and many of the older people are left alone. The *neighborhood association* is less and less of a given."

Besides, she can't possibly just sit at home all day. So ever since her daughter, Sonja, graduated elementary school, she has had this job. Of course, she would be fine without the money, she tells him, but it's not just that. "I have to be around people now and then. Otherwise I'll go crazy!"

Mrs. Beumer's towering figure, the gentle tinkling of her jewelry when she moves, her husky voice and that strong perfume, barely winning out over the acrid smell of her constant cigarette, fill the small space. Every fiber of this woman's being is feminine; her aura, her gestures, the way she breathes, those strong thighs, even the dewdrops of sweat on her forehead. Her closeness reassures him, but it also makes him restless. She is skinnier than he prefers, but still very pretty. She is well-built, and her face has a pleasing symmetry.

He lets out a long sigh, feeling his longing move a bit inside him. He offers her a chair and a cup of tea; she accepts both.

"After I took this job," she says, rearranging the new table-cloth, "I decided I wasn't going to rent this space to holiday visitors anymore. The money is fine, yes, but I found myself cleaning the place every week or every fortnight. It was too much for me. Of course, I could pay someone to do it, but then there's no money in it. And each time you have to wonder what kind of people are coming to your home."

She looks ahead thoughtfully, taking a drag from her cigarette and savoring it for a moment before exhaling the smoke.

It wasn't usually too bad, but sometimes there would be a whole family and that could get annoying. She told him a story of one family whose children had played soccer in the yard, ran through the garden to get the ball and broke everything. Not only did they not listen when she told them to stop, they had even talked back to her. And then there was the privacy. So she decided to rent it out on a long-term basis and that has been much better. She certainly needs the money, but she has to admit there's also a social aspect for her. She likes knowing someone is always nearby, just in case. It can be very quiet here, especially in winter, and sometimes she finds it a little frightening. She had even had a break-in one night, she tells him, which is when she'd decided to adopt Bart. The burglar, she shudders, was even in her bedroom, although she hadn't noticed anything missing. For this reason, she tells him, she's also glad to be renting to a man now.

N. asks about her boyfriend, but she is quick to inform him that he actually isn't there that often. Unprompted, she lists the days and nights of his absence. And he's not always there on weekends either. No, all things considered, she is pretty lonely out here in the country, so she's happy to have a tenant again.

"I just hope it works out for both of us," she says, glancing up at him and tempering her happiness. Then, smiling affably, she points to the floor in the living area and remarks that she had decided on the parquet floor because it's easy to clean. She had first wanted carpet, but had been warned against it in a holiday rental; people are always doing all sorts of unhygienic things on it, she says, with a conspiratorial smile.

He nods delicately but says nothing.

After a quiet moment, she says, "So, you're divorced?" The question is unexpected, and N. is set momentarily back on his heels. His guard is up now. *Who is this woman, anyway?* he thinks. He thinks carefully about the picture he wants to paint of himself. Of course, he'll have to give her something, some little tidbit about who he is and where he comes from. Besides, he promised her. But which picture, and for what purpose? Should he liven up his temporary existence at Vogelpoelweg 14 with an *affair de coeur*? He feels confident that she would ease his loneliness, and at the very least she doesn't seem averse to flirtation and inuendo. Assuming she isn't some demi-vierge, what kind of person would spark this elegant woman's curiosity, and indeed, her loins? Perhaps she's subconsciously searching for someone with immense personal failings?

N. examines his new, benevolent landlady. She's older than him, that much is obvious. But does that matter? Maybe she'll take a bit more work, but she's definitely worth it. But what will bring her in, a macho man or a pitiful wretch, success or failure, unabashed hedonist or heartbroken fool? Perhaps a mixture? Or maybe she's a romantic? Given her boyfriend's somewhat implausible appearance, wouldn't a hedonistic lifestyle success story ending in disaster be the most effective? The decision must be made now. He can't walk back his story later without causing some uncomfortable confusion between them, or worse, arousing suspicion in her that might unravel his entire plan. Still the failure but, the tragedy? (N.'s artistic preference).

He starts with the broad strokes, picking out highlights from the tableau of his failed life. Then after some time sitting across from each other in the living room, she in the easy chair, he on the leather sofa, he suddenly releases a Niagara of words and thoughts and ideas.

After graduating college, he became a teacher. His first job was at a rural school somewhere in the Betuwe—she wouldn't know the place. But when the government cut their funding, the school was forced to merge with another rural school. Mrs. Beumer commiserates; her daughter's rural school had been forced to do the same at one point. After the merger, he was redundant, but lacking seniority, was ousted by his competitor. On a whim (idealism, he assures her, pure idealism) he decided to apply to an immigrant education program in a disadvantaged neighborhood in The Hague. He gives her a knowing look, asks if she's heard of such programs from the newspaper or TV, and she says she has, that she understands. The fire of his initial enthusiasm, he continued, was quickly extinguished by the day-to-day slog in the classroom; teaching soon became hell. So he bid farewell not only to the school, but deeply disillusioned and mentally damaged, also to teaching in general. He was overworked and in over his head, and the result had been a near total unraveling.

The landlady nods understandingly. He notices her perk up whenever he speaks of hardships. Perhaps her keen eye had already detected some fragility in his spirit?

After this last school, he had been committed (if this story were a painting, he thinks, this detail would be the bright yellow on a palette of grays). The attending psychiatrist, after meeting with him a few times, had recommended that he be legally prohibited from ever setting foot inside a primary school—or any other school, for that matter—ever again. Just like that, his life in education became a thing of the past. So, on the urgent advice of the psychiatrist upon his release, he is now simply seeking peace for a while, at least a year, to recover and start working toward a new profession. Which brings him *à Voici*...

"Oh, and yes, to answer you earlier question, yes, divorced. Twice, actually."

He describes an exemplary, albeit shortened youth, having been brought up by strict parents and the severe Christian Reform church. He lived a rather sheltered life before leaving the nest and had been overwhelmed by the big world and its temptations and enticements, populated with girls and women so much freer in word and deed than the girls he'd grown up with. In short, after a few brief but tumultuous affairs of the heart (surely she understands his meaning), he jumped into a hasty wedding with a much older woman. It was followed not long after by a heart-breaking divorce. But he yearned for *un bon père à venir*, an orderly life. A few years later, he married again.

But what happened? Disaster, of course. His income declined steeply after his burnout and subsequent job loss. His second wife, who was sweet but a little helpless, had never worked herself but nevertheless enjoyed a secure income and the status that accompanies money. She didn't always have it easy with him of course, he understands that, and things got much worse after he started staying home every day; staring off, doubting and pitying himself, he can understand now why she wandered. Anyway, wander she did, into the comfort and company of an older businessman with a successful career and vivacious life. Although he'd been suspicious of it, she did not admit the affair to him for over a year and only then because she was expecting a child.

In short, the second divorce, with all its turmoil and terrible wounds, has been final for a solid month now. Another reason he's glad for his quiet convalescence in Q. Perhaps she can understand that, too?

Yes, of course she can. She shakes her blond head, gives him a sympathetic look. She asks if he has children. He says that he does not. Then, in a low voice, "How long do you intend to stay here?" As he spoke, he noticed that she shifted constantly in her chair, crossing then uncrossing her legs, then crossing them again, invariably showing and hiding a small glimpse of her white panties. She leaned forward to pour tea, lit a cigarette with the smoldering butt from her ashtray, and sucked the smoke eagerly through her slender neck.

"I don't know. Let's just say until you've had enough of me," he suggests with a shy, somewhat crafty smile.

A goat bleats in front of the window, crows settle in the meadow beyond. Mrs. Beumer sighs and raises her shoulders as if to suggest she's caught a chill. Her rings click together as she clasps her hands together, then says gently, clearly weighing every word,

"I don't think I'll be tired of you easily." She looks at her tenant and smiles, allowing him to take from that whatever meaning he wishes.

She inquires whether Mr. van Andel is still in contact with his ex. No, he says. Contact now or in the future is completely implausible. After everything he's been through, he wants nothing more to do with her. When he thinks of Paula, and of Anke, his stomach sours. From May 11th onwards, his life is a lie, his past is a lie. One long lie that will become the truth. N. feels this more acutely at this moment than ever before.

After his tale, he imagines Mrs. Beumer stringing his story together into cautious expectations and conclusions. Perhaps she's creating a story in which this new tenant, not bad-looking but battered by life and fate, could indeed relieve all of her earthly worries, from a steady, under the table income to perhaps her other carnal needs. She nods thoughtfully, her eyes becoming full with what looked to him to be a truly feminine longing. Silence falls over them, becoming even more intimate the longer it lasts. N. is the first to break it, trying weakly to add some details to his tragic story. Then she asks him how old he is.

"Thirty-four," he says truthfully.

She shakes her head. "You're too young to have had all that misery!"

N. agrees, the painful memories—some real, mostly imagined—bring him nearly to tears. He manages to say nothing for a moment.

She looks at her watch, realizes it is half past four, and exclaims that it's time for her daily glass of sherry. Would Mr. van Andel like to join her? He says he would, he has wine but no sherry. It seems only fitting, he tells her, that they toast their new arrangement. He fetches two glasses while she disappears into the larger house for her bottle.

"Sonja won't be home for another hour," she says after returning with the sherry. She has changed into a blue skirt, longer and tighter fitting. They raise glasses to each other. After taking a sip, she sets down her glass and repeats that her boyfriend is rarely there, that officially he lives with his unmarried sister in Z., closer to his work, and that he often goes out with friends on weekends, and although he usually is there on Wednesday nights, tonight he will be working and will not be around.

He can only assume what these announcements are meant to imply, although they really do not concern him. He now more or less has a picture of all the time the two of them might have together, companionable and alone in each other's company. His member swells in his pants, reminding him that it's been over a week since he was last with a woman.

Then the landlady continues with the story of how she met Theo six years ago, two years after unexpectedly becoming a widow. No, Sonja is not Theo's child (as N. assumed). Her late husband had died in a car accident on his way to work in Y. He was a messenger at the district court. It had been a foggy November morning in the countryside. A car had been passing a lory on the provincial road and had been met head on by Mr. Beumer. There were two fatalities, both her husband and the driver of the other car.

She sighs, pulls on her cigarette, and taps the ashen end into the ashtray. Her eyes rest on the pastoral scene outside the living room. One of the sheep in the foreground looks shamelessly into N.'s living room. A goat stares philosophically at the grass in front of it.

"Sounds like you've had a pretty rough time of it, too."

She shrugs. "It was eight years ago, time takes the edge off, but of course you never forget. It was awful. Fortunately, I have my daughter."

N. asks about her daughter, wondering still what country Mrs. Beumer came from originally. She is a foreigner, that much is beyond doubt; her accent becomes thicker when her Dutch becomes more emotional. He remembers the copy of *Vojna i Mir*; perhaps she is Russian or Baltic. He resolves to ask her another time.

Mrs. Beumer fixes her gaze on him again, her fine wrinkles cracking almost imperceptibly beneath her makeup. Sonja is now sixteen, a sweet, affectionate child. Not stupid, but not a great scholar either. But Olga is not the type of mother who pushes a child to study beyond their natural inclination, and N. congratulates her on this. She did do general secondary education for a few years because she wanted to, but it soon turned out to be too ambitious an undertaking for her. Reading and writing had been particularly difficult for her since elementary school, and she quickly decided to follow a vocational education instead. She now goes to school three days a week, and spends one day a week completing her practicum at a hair salon in Y. She wants to become a hairdresser. The rest of the time, Thursdays, Friday afternoons and Saturdays, she is a cashier at a supermarket in X (this catches N.'s interest). When he asks which supermarket, the lady affably says that X only has one decent grocery store, and upon further description, N. concludes that it must be the same grocery store where he will begin stocking shelves the day after tomorrow.

N. tells her as much, adding quickly that it's mostly so he can have some social interaction. He thinks it might be better if she's not made aware of just how dire his finances really are.

"Well, isn't that just a nice coincidence!" She leans in closer to him, taps the ash from her cigarette, crosses her leg so that her foot grazes across his shin. "Hey, you two can ride the bus together." N. smiles, shifts a bit in his seat, and explains that he plans to ride his bike so that he can get as much exercise as possible.

"Maybe you can convince her to join you. Especially in this nice weather. It would be so good for her, she spends so much time just sitting around."

They raise another glass to this coincidence and she pulls yet another cigarette from a seemingly inexhaustible pack. She offers one to N., but he declines. He never smoked much. He'd been shown a graphic video of a smoker's lung as a young boy and it had successfully squelched any inclination he may have had toward the habit. He doesn't tell her this second part; she is too irredeemably devoted to her tobacco.

Sonja's arrival home is announced by Bart's familiar bark. N. has yet to meet the young woman; he's only heard her voice a few times. Mrs. Beumer walks outside to greet her daughter, asking her to come introduce herself to their new tenant.

She enters hesitantly, a somewhat awkward teenager. He recognizes her immediately as the girl at the register when he'd asked for Mr. de Wilde, but she doesn't seem to recognize him. He is stricken by how much the young girl resembles her mother, like identical twins, born thirty years apart. He wonders whether this perfect facsimile had indeed been conceived naturally, or perhaps she is her mother's clone. The younger is about half a head shorter than the senior, but their figures are otherwise the same, with that blond, wispy hair and those blue-gray eyes. The girl's skin, however, is completely uncracked by wrinkles.

Naturally, N. introduces himself, telling her they'll soon be colleagues. Sonja gives N. a searching, incredulous, look. This guy, a shelf stocker? Her mother suggests that Sonja cycle to X with Mr. van Andel on Friday, the prospect of which clearly does not appeal to her at all. She reminds her mother that there is excellent hourly service between Q and X.

"And the bus is hardly ever busy," she adds a resounding argument to her rejection.

The pleasant afternoon intermezzo comes to an end with a last sip of sherry (three glasses in total). Before taking her leave, Mrs. Beumer sets a companionable hand on N.'s shoulder and asks that, going forward, will he please call her Olga, and, if he finds it agreeable, she'd like to call him Kees. He didn't like the name anymore, hearing it spoken aloud. It's too Dutch, the name of a man who wears clogs and lives in a windmill. But it's too late now to find anything better.

"Well, I should start making dinner," says Olga as she and Sonja take leave of him. He can see the path laid out before them now; it likely won't be long before she's cooking his meals, too.

That evening, he adds one more point to his list in the kitchen cabinet:

Keep a diary, beginning with the last 11 days.

(After all, N. thinks, the most impressive years of my life may still be ahead of me.)

The next morning, he makes a schedule for his proposed novel. Working title: *The African Bride.*

11.

He reaches the staff entrance at the grocery store at the stroke of eight Friday morning. After discussing some practical matters, Piet de Wilde introduces him to the other staff. Jan, a fellow shelf stocker, also new. Daan, a fat young man with a wily face and a shaved head is a warehouse clerk and jack of all trades. A middle-aged woman, who introduces herself as Ria, works at the meat counter with another colleague, Nardie who makes a rather nervous impression. Another man named Kees manages the bakery, along with his assistant, a sensible young man who introduces himself as Arthur. Finally, he shakes hands with the four part-time cashiers who are present, of the seventeen who work at the store.

The other Kees, who tells N. that he too was once a shelf stocker, gives him such thorough training that, within just five short weeks, N. is responsible for retail logistics of the entire store. He does stock management, controls supply and removal, calls the distribution centers, negotiates discounts from time to time. In between, he sweeps, cleans, turns items so they're facing forward. He assists the butcher, and the baker, he helps organize produce, and even steps in behind the cash register when someone is out sick (which often happens) or suddenly quits before a replacement can be found.

Mr. de Wilde, who is pleasantly surprised by N.'s unexpected acceleration, offers Mr. van Andel a full-time job, a proposal which N. turns down immediately and with feigned regret, but seeing the disappointment on his manager's face, agrees to work Thursdays.

Thursday, Friday, Saturday. Two hundred euros per week in cash plus thirty-five euros in food. More than eight hundred cash under the table. His monthly expenses are fixed at two hundred and fifty euro. He's glad that he won't be drawing on his reserves anytime soon; there is around 1,800 euros remaining from his "culture fund", and for now at least, his keepsakes are safe. He decides to set aside at least 250 euros every month; a dead man can't apply for health insurance, after all, and with the rising costs of medical care, even an appendectomy could ruin him financially.

Yet another reason to stay healthy. He commits to cycling from Vogelpoelweg to X and back every day, come rain or shine. That should help. After the first week, he discovers a route that follows a gravel path through the woods, which shortens the distance by about two kilometers. He feels victorious in this silent battle he's waged against public transport. Many have been the day when he and Sonja leave the store at the same time after a long day, tired but satisfied, and he arrives home, refreshed from the evening ride, well before her. Of course, she notices, but the fact doesn't seem to bother her enough to accept one of his many invitations to join him. And of course, he cannot take Sonja's proposal that he 'ferry' her on his bicycle rack, seriously.

In the meantime, he keeps his commitment to making a daily record in his diary. He fills his days off with reading, writing, and watercolor painting (albeit still rather uninspired). He commits what he believes is a rather serious amount of time to working on his novel. In between, he goes on long walks, increasingly accompanied by Bart, who has adopted N. as his new best friend. And every day, he puzzles away at the Grand Plan in his mind, although admittedly without much zeal, given the Arcadian living situation he finds himself in. N. realizes he needs to be careful not to indulge too much in a certain *dolce far niente*, a tendency that is not foreign to him given his rather easygoing nature.

By mid-June, the weather was settling into summer, the cooler temperatures and showers growing ever more occasional. He's gained a little muscle from his new lifestyle, and feels quietly proud of his physique.

The vegetable garden outside the house, which is abundant and which Olga has "guaranteed organic", has improved his health greatly. Like Adam in the Garden of Eden, he can make unlimited use of it and the supply seems to have no end. Every day she makes deliveries to his door of homegrown potatoes and walnuts from last autumn, claiming that she and her daughter "simply don't have the appetite for so much food." Of course, N. is left to wonder what they may have the appetite for. In any case, his acceptance of their invitation to dinner has improved their kinship greatly, beginning as a once weekly ritual until soon they were enjoying their evening meals together two or three times a week. There is no lack of appetite at these meals, N. notices. It also does not escape his attention that mealtimes are so often coordinated around Theo's absences.

Olga and her daughter are both great cooks, so their invitations are never a disappointment. Wanting to return the favor, N. was pleased when the ladies not only accepted his invitation, but also found his cooking to be better than acceptable. Sharing food, and especially cooking together, creates a strong bond, and by the beginning of July, it is clearly becoming a struggle to imagine his life without the mother and daughter in it.

Alternatively, his relationship with Theo becomes more complicated. On the few occasions they see each other, N. has tried to show his good will. He'll make an effort to chat with him now and then, out in the yard, or offer to help him weed the vegetable garden. Sometimes Theo is warm and greets him with a hand raised in greeting. But then he'll occasionally scowl at N.'s appearance and go out of his way to avoid him. N. can think of no explanation for this ambivalence, and wanting to maintain smooth waters at home, decides to invite him for a drink.

12.

"I can't help but notice that you don't get very much mail."

The understatement puts N. on edge. He has, in fact, never received mail here, and doesn't plan to, aside from the weekly local papers and other junk mail that apparently even mailboxes in the countryside cannot escape. Tenant and landlady are standing companionably together at the top of the drive above the small farm. Before the most recent cuts to the postal service budget, all addressed mail was faithfully delivered to the house. Since then, more rigid standards have been put in place for countryside mail delivery and only parcels, urgent items and registered letters are delivered to the door. Olga usually picks up the mail and deposits anything addressed to him—that is, a few lifeless brochures and advertising flyers—on a table in the hall. Indeed, nothing of substance ever comes for him.

N. comes up with an easy lie, thanking Olga for her caring attention, but that he had made an arrangement at his previous post office to hold his mail until he was able to provide a forwarding address. He had no way of knowing that he'd land in Q, but now that he was happily settled, he still needed to send his new address to his many contacts and loved ones.

Olga nods. Her bracelets scatter fragments of sunlight (they're outside on deck chairs in her garden, drinking coffee). "The less mail the better, in my opinion," Olga says, "it mostly brings bad news." Then, smiling, she says "And I don't just mean the infamous blue envelope from the tax man."

N. smiles back, mechanically. He knows this could become a problem. Now that he's seemingly dissolved into oblivion, he'll likely never receive mail again. Nothing official, in any case. Every living Dutch citizen gets mail now and then. Even without family, friends, or acquaintances, a person would at least received occasional correspondence from a financial institution, an insurance company, or some government authority. But there will be no such mail for Mr. Kees van Andel. N. leaves Olga, feigning a headache. The conversation has made him uncomfortable; he'll need to come up with a solution to this thorny problem before it festers. She is the type of woman, N. thinks, who is just enterprising and considerate enough to go to the post office in Q herself to record the forwarding address for him, after which she will discover that there is no arrangement with the local post office at all. Indeed, there is no Kees van Andel.

That afternoon, N. rides to the department store in Q (with a surprisingly large array of office supplies), purchases a set of ballpoints in assorted colors (every detail matters), packets of envelopes in different colors and sizes, and a bundle of blank postcards. Then he rides to the post office for stamps. A few days later, at the same post office, he finds a bundle of unused envelopes from a well-known Dutch bank (what luck to find such a thing!). He begins sending himself blank letters with some regularity, making sure to change the color and handwriting of the address each time, as well as the occasional postcard, sometimes with feminine text and signature (secretly hoping to spur a response from his landlady). For business mail, he prints out an address sticker from his laptop, his first big purchase after starting at the supermarket. He makes sure that a monthly bank statement appears on his table. It quickly becomes part of his routine to drop mail for himself at the post office a few times a week.

N. had become accustomed to walking the side of the Beumers' house to the garden on his days off. On one hot Wednesday afternoon, on a mission for a nice crisp head of lettuce, he turns the corner to the garden to find Olga sunbathing, stark naked, her long slender body stretched across a sun chair. Apologizing, he turns his back to her quickly so that she might have a chance to put something on. She makes no such motion.

"Oh, Kees, don't be such a prude! We're adults here, aren't we? I'm sure you've seen a naked woman before, probably much more beautiful than what I have to offer."

She props herself up on her lounger, resting on her elbow. N. is struck by her physique, her skin as pale and as hard as white marble. It is so creamy white that the sun's rays seem to just bounce off of her. She seems impossibly thin, as though there is no room between her ribs and spine for her necessary human organs. Her chest is flat; just two big nipples perched atop her ribcage. Even her pubic hair is pale and blonde, glistening in the sunlight. He notices large scars on her shoulder blade and in her groin, and the vertical stripe of a caesarean section. When she parts her thighs for a moment to change position, the thread of a tampon hangs from her vagina, a sight that makes N. recoil in distaste.

N. keeps his head turned down modestly, trying not to seem affected as he forages among the vegetable beds. But there is an undeniable tingling in his scrotum when he thinks that, perhaps, she had lain there intentionally, knowing that eventually he would come along to see her. With an ache he realizes how long it's been since he's felt the tender caress of a woman, the softness of the female form. For the remainder of the evening, he feels his landlady's friendly stare on his back.

13.

A vagina, a vagina, my kingdom for a vagina!

It's been three weeks since he last lay with a woman. There is always the alternative, what every man turns to for a brief respite from the unbearable weight of solitude. These past few weeks have been too hectic; with his existence in such upheaval, there was little time to contemplate the specificity of his desire. But with life a bit more settled, the landlady's sunbathing awakened his irresistible natural desires.

N. skims the stack of free weekly papers from his stack of mail, the Q Post and the Daily Courier. In the first, a few chaste advertisements for local entertainment, but not even the slightest hint of erotica. In the somewhat more worldly Daily Courier, a few mobile numbers are listed in the dating section for telephone entertainment. Alarmed by the lack of professional escort services offered in Q, N. decides he'll take the train back to Y as soon as possible. There he is sure to find more opportunities; in any case, at least the town has a few nightclubs.

Of course, a provincial little town like Q wouldn't have much to offer in this respect. Surely there must be some enterprising housewife in the village who unofficially serves the voracious male population, but how does one go about finding an informal house of pleasure in this quaint town? After all, N. has no connections here.

But he's heard around town that next week is the annual summer festival, which will surely attract some lovely young girls, looking for a little holiday fun without expectations of lasting connection. N. decides to keep some distance between himself and Olga.

That Tuesday, according to the detailed program printed in the Q Post, the summer festival will open with a cultural evening in the village hall devoted entirely to religious fraternization. The evening begins at half past seven with a performance of *Hallelujah* by the mixed Reformed Choral and Recitation Association. At nine o'clock the Protestant Christian theater association, The Meadow Flower, will follow with a performance of *How Henry Found Himself with Annie*, a piece which, according to the enthusiastic Q Post, has received great reviews in the province. A raffle will be held during the intermission, the proceeds of which will offset the cost of installing a new bar in the clubhouse of the Christian Reformed angling club, The Fat Bass.

Filled with ecumenical feelings, N. rides toward the village on Tuesday evening with low expectations. The mixed choir does its best; they give it an honest effort, but are far from reaching great artistic heights. N. suspects that most, if not all, of the ladies in the choir, sopranos and altos, mostly middle-aged, are all related to the male tenors and basses. The play was performed in the regional dialect, which N. suspects is only part of the reason he found it confusing. In any case, it ended happily enough, with two lovers embracing each other, and left N. floating between dream and reality, with some jealousy at the thought that the female protagonist, so beautiful in her stage makeup, would end up in the bed of her bumbling co-star, whose lines required prompting throughout the performance. With N.'s libido strained as it was, the thought pained him throughout the evening.

In any case, the Fat Bass' treasurer would return home satisfied with decent raffle proceeds. N. won a dry sausage donated by the butcher, Pannekoek, which he congenially offered to a woman at his right dressed in silver-gray and permanently holding a lorgnette, giving the excuse that he is vegetarian. He feels rather detached, alienated from himself, wedged as he is among these simple, tax-paying citizens. These good people who do as they're told, never push the limits, ignorant and uncaring of the mechanisms that propel them and, out of despair or laziness, just trust in the Lord. The grateful audience, in their ceremonious Sunday best, enthusiastically clap when they're expected to, delighted by whatever they're fed from the stage.

In any case, there are no beautiful (or even homely) stray young ladies whose attention he could draw with some strategic eye contact or other cunning maneuvers; the few women who did appear to be unattached had long since passed their expiration date, in N.'s opinion. All of the younger women looked neatly tucked away into marriage or engagement, and those that weren't had the hope of attachment lingering in their eyes.

But N. is not entirely discouraged. If the desire is strong enough, a way will be found. The festival schedule for Thursday evening lists a performance by a regional band in the same village hall. He expects a different audience might attend the event, perhaps less conservative, more worldly, hopefully more young, unattached women with looser morals. And so, on Thursday evening, he finds himself once again among the villagers, this time with Olga and Theo at his side, whose invitation, of course, he could not refuse, although he finds their company somewhat suffocating. He has the vague sense that the landlady and her boyfriend feel the need to chaperone him to keep him from doing something stupid.

The audience is younger. But once again, there are plenty of empty seats, and no one here alone. N. is starting to get the feeling that the general population of Q has, for the most part, whole-heartedly committed to those mutual vows of faithfulness and support in joy and in sadness, for better or for worse at the altar of civic duty. Theo gushes enthusiasm for the singer, who N. believes was let out of rehearsal too early. Nevertheless, the crowd continues to call for encores, even though he is drowned out by the big screaming beast of the carnival (carousel and swing ride, a shooting gallery, high striker, a small Ferris wheel) in the square in front of the village hall. There is little to be done; by the end of the night, N. is in an increasingly foul mood.

Throughout the performance, he casts libidinous glances over the audience, but quickly comes to the conclusion that he, a lonely, yearning man, will yet again return home alone to a cold and empty bed. On the way home, Olga admits that she hadn't been much impressed by the performance either, but Theo, with his simple countryside perspective, simply cannot remember *ever* seeing such an *amazing* performance. N. can feel the energy between them, and his mood is soured even more at the thought that, just some fifteen meters away from his own lonely bed, Olga and Theo will likely be engaging in their own *amazing* performance. *It cannot go on like this any longer,* N. writes in his diary afterwards.

On Saturday, the week of festivities ends with a performance by the country rock band, Frontaal. The village fills to bursting with Teutonic noise that N. can hear from his small apartment on Vogelpoelweg. He laments the corruption of Q's youth's taste in good music, opting to stay home and avoid the spraying beer and godless primal sounds. Afterall, the likelihood of the type of woman he is looking for showing up at a show of such prehistoric violence seems low. N. ponders sullenly at their youthful cries about the supposed costs of the aging population. In a decade or so, they'll be shouting (although likely at more appropriate volumes) about the cost of repairing hearing damage in thirty- to forty-year-olds.

In the end, the festival week cost him close to a hundred euros and gave him *nada* in terms of willing flesh. His need for carnal climax is at a breaking point; he is dangerously close to despair.

14.

In his weekly scouring of the *Daily Courier*, N. finds a notice that a singles' mixer and dance (couples also welcome) is held every two weeks at Wesselmans' conference center in B (a hamlet halfway between Q and Y). There is a mandatory dress code, and musical accompaniment is provided by a live orchestra, The Romanticos. The next one will be held this Saturday, and the final event for the season in two weeks' time. The next season is to begin again in October.

His first order of business must be to satisfy the dress code. Taking the train to Y, N. buys two brand-name shirts, a trendy blazer, jacket and pants and a pair of Bally shoes. It cost him 610 euros, an amount he could never begin to save from his modest income. His reserves are beginning to run low after last week's 500 euros purchase of a second-hand laptop and a printer.

That Saturday evening is a bit chilly, but after a rainy week N. is grateful that at least the weather is dry. The bus stops right at the entrance to the conference center, and N. can hear the sweet sounds of old-fashioned accordion and saxophone music even before his feet touch the pavement. It's nine o'clock. The mixer has been going for an hour now. N. buys a ticket for 15 euros and enters a smoke-filled room. From the foyer, which is raised slightly above the rest of the hall, N. has a full view of the dance hall. To his left is a bar (buffalo skull, White Feather painted on a galloping horse with a lance. On the terrace, there's a balustrade and the wooden swinging doors of a saloon, behind which about fifteen men, mostly dressed in jeans, stand slouching, drinking their beer. At the back of the room, on a small stage, several well-dressed figures stand amid a sea of noisy instruments. A large sign in colorful letters leaves no doubt that these are The Romanticos (in N.'s experience their English isn't quite correct, but lacks the knowledge to correct it). Next to the stage, a large group of men and women mingle together. N. assumes these are the couples. Finally, to his right, in the middle of a jumble of tables and chairs, he identifies the group he's primarily targeting: a fair amount of solitary ladies—N. estimates there are about thirty-five of them—roughly in the all-or-nothing age range of twenty-five to forty (but N. will reserve judgment; he's no longer going to be picky). A shiny oval-shaped empty dance floor stands between them, a vast barrier between them and the men at the bar.

N. waits for a break between the musical numbers before entering, and manages to attract some attention. This is no surprise, as N. will soon find out that nearly all the ladies and gentlemen here have known each other since elementary school, catechism, girls' club, boys' club, work or other social events. In this couples' circuit full of eternal roamers, procrastinators, serial daters and late bloomers, N. is the odd one out. "Who's this guy?" The new visitor sees this question pass across the faces of the male echelon like a wave of light in a neon tube: „What is the best strategy for this type of party," N. wonders. He is, by nature, quick to master strategies that will make the most of situations like this, but at the moment he isn't sure how to act. Sitting down among the ladies to his right seems a bit premature. He needs a little more time to get a feel for the situation. To his left, the men jovially squeeze between each other to the forefront, obviously observing him critically, their heads bowed together in discussion. The new arrival instinctively feels that he'll need to gain favor with these gentlemen before showering any of the ladies with his charms. Clearly, he reasons that he'll first need to establish some rapport with the men before making a pass at any of the women.

He descends to the dance floor quite confidently in his new Ballys, with a purposeful stride—head raised, shoulders back, hands loose at the hip, entering—Bill Buck's saloon. He orders a beer. which is served to him by an impassive bartender with a melancholy expression, reinforced by a high pile mustache that in less refined circles is called a "snot mop". Among the talking and drinking group of cowboys leaning against the bar he spies a bass-tenor from the Christian Reform choral group *Hallelujah*. There is no doubt; N. remembers his trembling throat as he belted out a Bach cantata delivered with dedication. Maybe this is his opening. So, he approaches the singer, tells him he saw his performance and that he'd been impressed by Hallelujah's *amazing* performance.

"Practice man, practice. Two or three times a week in the week before a recital." The man smiles proudly and boasts that he's been a member for thirty years, allowing N. to quickly calculate that he must be close to 50 years old. He would have guessed younger. They began chatting about this and that like old acquaintances and N. buys the amateur singer a beer. They've both loosened up. N. begins to wonder if the man has a slight tic or suffers from shyness because he keeps turning his head to the left almost every other word during their conversation.. Fortunately, this is not the case. Everything becomes clear, the moment that The Romanticos start a new song, when the man's apparent discomfort completely evaporates. Stopping in the middle of a rant about the quality of regional singing, the singer shoots forward like an arrow from a bow, jumps over the balustrade with surprising agility you that wouldn't expect at his age, and runs across the dance floor to where the single ladies are gathered. Even before the other men have emerged from the jostling saloon swinging doors, he's succeeded in asking a lady with dark hair for a dance. In N.'s opinion, she is certainly not the unsightliest of the bunch. She refuses.

So, all of a sudden, Mr. van Andel finds himself alone at the bar with a beer in his hand, under the impassive gaze of the bartender and his mustache. The other men, who have now thrown themselves upon the ladies like motorcycle racers on their machines at the start of an endurance race, are busy showing off their skills on the dance floor. This stampede of, which will become more apparent as the night goes on, is being boycotted by the same dozen or so ladies throughout the evening. (It's always the same, with the odd exception —beauty standards, it seems, are hard and fast in all cultures), The stampede will be repeated many times as the evening progresses. After each dance, the sexes separate as if there is a contagious disease on the dance floor. The Romanticos' repertoire, it turns out, is limited to purely Dutch hits, with songs by Frans Bauer, Jantje Smit, Marco Borsato and Henk Wijngaard. The classic, *Zangeres Zonder Naam* [Singer Without a Name] is also included, and even Johnny Hoes is every now and then resurrected from his artistic grave. Each and every one of these sing-alongs, knee-slappers, torch songs and other tear-jerkers are performed with conviction, The lead singer is feeling the emotions, tears streaming down his eyes.

As the band prepares for a new set of songs (three songs each time), N. pushes forward, also jumping over the balustrade, ruthlessly storming forward, elbowing out a sea of competitors to ask a lady to dance. She is close to what he considers his ideal type of beauty. He casts his bait, in hopes that she bites. With a shy smile, she does indeed take the bait. The song by Mary Servaes is one of mourning.; N. tries to lead her to an old mourning song in three-four time by Mary Servaes. This requires some fancy footwork since she is constantly hopping – she clearly has no sense of rhythm. He assumes that she is tipsy, and thinks forgivingly, *just leave it at "dear, oh dear… just don't drink anymore."*

During the dance—which is really more like a wrestling match—he tries to make some light conversation. His dance partner nods, responds with a few sentences in the regional dialect which N. barely understands, only to again give full concentration to her dance steps. Her brow furrowed from the effort, and she can't manage a real conversation. When the song is over, he safely returns her back to her chair and courteously thanks her for the dance. On his way back to Buck's bar, the Hallelujah man offers him a beer and introduces himself as Karel. A few other men have returned to the bar, one of them with such a profuse amount of chest hair that N. imagines how it could be styled into braids. Impulsively rolling a cigarette, impulsively, he tries to make conversation and asks N. who he is and where he's come from. These questions trouble N. and so he gives vague and evasive answers.

The men drink their beers, keenly awaiting the band's signal to invade the dance floor once again. This time, N. has his eye on the brunette who had earlier rejected Karel's invitation.

But as the band begins their set and the men begin charging forward, a dancer stumbles over a chair and badly hurts himself on the armrest. His glasses are broken beyond repair and drips of dark, red blood from a bleeding cut over his eyebrow, attesting to the man's decisive force.. Yelps ripple through the row of ladies and the bandleader decides to hold an extra break.. The injured man is taken behind the bar to be treated.

Taking advantage of this unexpected lull in the music, N. tactfully acquaints himself with the brunette. He is the only rooster in this particular chicken coop. The other roosters have abandoned the hen house, but he doesn't care. It still seems ridiculous to him, this strictly maintained watershed of the sexes. Why loiter at the bar when just twenty paces away are the sweet pigeons that, just maybe, might be able to quench his enormous thirst tonight? He sits down next to her, introduces himself, and starts a conversation about ordinary things, and then offers her something to drink. She shifts in her chair; N. can't decide if it's the stiffness of her seat or his obvious advances, but she seems to be uncomfortable in her chair. The rural belle would like a tonic water, which N. retrieves at the bar. She has a pleasant voice, speaks standard Dutch, with a bit of an accent.

A bit later, the wounded man, re-enters the battlefield, his head wrapped in a white turban of bandages to cheers. The Romanticos prepare for a new set of dramatic Dutch ballads, the woman is so captivated by his conversation that she categorically rejects Karel's request for the third time. At this, Karel's face turns red, his eyes casting a malevolence glance at N, which he can't fail to notice. Karel can't possibly think that he came to B. just to annoy him; of course not! It's just because he thinks she's the most attractive lady there. After all, it's only human nature; reproduction with a beautiful, strong woman brings a beautiful, strong offspring. A few moments later, he notices the Hallelujah singer sulking at the bar, commiserating with the abundant chest hair guy, who might have also been rejected. N. can't help but gets the impression that their dark looks may reveal some sinister plan. He doesn't want to pay attention to it, so he pushes the thought from his mind.

At some point, the brunette wants to know what kind of person Mr. Van Andel is. She's never seen him here before, she says, and judging by his accent, he must be from somewhere else… Of course, N. can't let such a perfect opportunity go to waste without putting his imagination to use. He has come to enjoy these impromptu challenges to his imagination. He considers the details, gathers his thoughts. What new story will he tell today? She seems like a good type, so he tells her, with a slightly raised voice in order to be heard over the music, that he is originally from Randstad, that he's been a civil servant at the sub-district court in Y for some time now (thank you Olga, for your candor). that he hasn't found his own home yet. He tells her that he's enjoying living with a family in Q while he looks around for his own place.

"You aren't married then?" she glances fleetingly at his still-beautiful hands of the professional class, and casts her eyes mistrustfully over new *Men-Shop* clothes. N., already wrapped up in his new existence, tightens up under her inspection. With a low, sad voice he explains that he was previously very absorbed in his judiciary work, to the extent that his wife and child became estranged from him. Since then, he's realized there's more to life than just building a career, but unfortunately, it's too late. A year ago, mother and daughter decided to move on, sharing their lives with a new, more loving man..

N. sighs and tries to stare sadly in front of him. He reveals that he wants to build a new life here in the country with a woman that he unfortunately hasn't found yet and yes, if you're completely unknown in the area, of course you'll find yourself at such a singles' night out. Surely the lady can understand that.

The lady (he puts her in her early thirties) understands completely and again breathes deeply, which N. cannot fail to notice. She tells him that he can call her Tineke. The band finishes their set and flips on some recorded music while they take their break at the bar.

Breaks between the sets of torch songs are sometimes filled with recorded music, when the romantic musicians take a longer break to indulge at the bar. In this way, a liberating quickstep suddenly bubbled through the room, providing N. with the ideal moment to invite his conversation partner into the ring for a quicker step. Tineke looks at him in alarm, protests that that is not at all the custom; nobody here does that and what will the others…

But N. is already pulling her by the hand to the floor. They do a fast foxtrot, attracting the gaze of about seventy pairs of astonished eyes. A fiercely blushing Tineke is well-guided, with rapidly diminishing resistance, and N. can feel her body starting to relay. This is followed by *Samba Pa Ti* by Santana, one of N.'s favorite beats. His partner is not as well-practiced, and he graciously releases her when her steps are too slow, finishing the quick Latin dance as a solo performance. For the next rumba, Tineke, naïve to the steps but with an all-or-nothing effort, tries to reunite with her dance partner only to surrender to the mind-and-body transporting secret of this lingering cadence. She allows him to lead her, trustingly and willingly. Something in N.'s depraved brain whispers that all her defenses are melting away, as she slowly gives herself over to his lead, while N. imagines her melting into his touch. He instinctively pulls her body close to his, grasps her firmly staying close for at least five minutes. When the song is over, they remain standing on the dancefloor, still embraced, staring deeply into each other's eyes.

The Romanticos resume their set, dragging on through the evening with no mentionable highlights to speak of, except perhaps that they stop pretending to find an uninterrupted musical highlight. N. sits down next to Tineke, knee to knee. He realizes that he has a bit of a bite on the line; and that, who knows, this evening might end with a bang after all. He orders another tonic water and a half wine for himself. Clearly, this is not a common order,, because, as it so happens it takes the bartender a while to come up with the requested carafe – along with a dark look over his quivering moustache with the bottle of red after an uncomfortably long wait. N. senses some grounds for his suspicion, and that the bartender's facial expression reflects the thoughts of many of the men: get out of here, faster than greased lightning;

we don't want you here! The mood seems to have turned from benevolent curiosity to veiled animosity. His suspicions are corroborated when he notices their cold, unfriendly glances, eyes narrowed and pushing against him slightly, trying to blocking his passage as he returns to Tineke with the refreshments. He resolves to pass it off too lightly.

"Aren't you also unmarried?" he enquires, not looking to either side in order to avoid the gazes of the others as he sits next to her again. He is primary concern is how he can get her out of there as quickly as possible, if necessary. She lays her hand emphatically on his thigh and says a bit sadly that she does date occasionally. She had been in a relationship for a number of years and even had plans to get engaged, but in the end, she had to give up the engagement because her parents were against it. As she was their only child, it meant the world to her parents that she chooses a good match. He counters by asking what exactly does she means by "a *good match*?"

She hesitates and blushes to a raspberry color and begins to look more and more personal and endearing. "Well… someone who is good, and independent," she says, then glancing at him "who takes good care of himself, is well dressed… that's what I mean."

Someone who speaks good Dutch, that is also important to them.

"And isn't there anyone you like?" N. wants to play it safe; the mood in the room is starting to feel acutely belligerent. He nods to the array of gunslingers in Buck's saloon whose eyes are intently fixed upon them.

Tineke disfigures her pretty face with a slight grimace. "Well, they're always the same. You keep hoping that someone new will show up. I've been coming here almost all season. But to take one of them as a boyfriend…" No, she doesn't see that happening. All they do is drink beer, which gives them bad breath, don't brush their teeth regularly, and she expresses serious doubts about whether some of them even take a shower or put on clean underwear before they come here. Sometimes, they smell so bad. And there are a couple of real creeps you always have to keep your eye on.

"See the one with the chain around his neck?" Pointing at the guy with the curly monkey hair out sprouting from his open shirt.. Well, apparently, he feels up women while they're dancing.

"What about the other one, Karel? I think he has a crush on you."

She is surprised: "Do you know him?"

N. tells her about Hallelujah's performance last week. She says she likes him, that he's more presentable than most of the others. He also has a decent job as an accountant at the Rabobank in Q. But she thinks he's too old. He's already fifty-two, and terribly boring. All he talks about is work, playing soccer, and his singing club.

N., becoming more and more engrossed by her body, asks if she works and if so, what she does for a living. She has a good figure, in fact, a very good figure. She is very beautiful with her full face, beautiful teeth, and a pair of firm breasts which she dares to flaunt with confidence. Her legs are nice too, and he imagines that the place where they come together will also be quite nice. He notices that the combination of beer and wine is nicely starting to get a hold of him, and he feels a warm glow rising up inside him.

Tineke reveals what he'd very cautiously suspected, that she's employed as a telephone operator and receptionist. She works at the town hall of Z, which is where she also lives. She has a…

Just then the musicians start the next set, and N.'s increasingly candid table companion is rudely snatched from him by Karel. He forcefully snatches Tineke under her arms, caveman style, drags her to the dance floor, like a cannonball with a determined look. Her protests, weak as they are, are drowned out by the noise of the instruments, singing, and unskilled clomping on the dance floor. N. is rather bewildered, but decides to make the man pay. At the next song,, which is this time dedicated to André Hazes, the bank clerk launches again. However, N. had asked her for this dance and cuts in. Karel protests weakly, but the glorified teller from the farmers' lending bank is politely but resolutely rejected by Tinneke.

At this, the atmosphere begins to resemble a scene from the wild west. You can already hear Morricone's fateful music. After the dance, N. returns to the bar to get Tineke another drink. While waiting for his order at the bar, he's pushed and tapped from behind. When he turns around, he is struck in the neck. Fifteen hateful stares are directed at him, some jaws move as if they want to eat his raw flesh wild animals in a feeding frenzy, testosterone lurching through reproductive organs. N. realizes that he has, without a doubt, become *persona non grata* at the Bucks bar, if he utters a single wrong word the pistols will be drawn. But he is not the fearful type, blessed with a sturdy build, not to mention his pride and honor. The neck of the guy who sucker-punched him – one who'd leered in his direction from the beginning while the hairy stranger unsuccessfully tried to start a conversation with him – is now being grabbed by the throat and warned not to try that stunt again.

But then they are all around him. What was he thinking?! Here in this room, he is the asshole, mister high-and-mighty newcomer, and these men know how to deal with such a shitbag who's after their wives, knock them up, and then never be heard from again... *Oh yeah, they know your type around here all right, and you better just fuck off very quickly if you don't want to eat porridge in the hospital tonight,* he reasons.

The men's faces don't leave much room for interpretation, and now it dawns on N. that he's been invading their territory all evening, and the time has come for him to pay for this transgression. Restraining himself with all his might from swinging hard at one of these guys' heads, he decides that under the circumstances, a much better idea is to drink up and promise to do better. Tineke is not that important to him. You can find a nice pair of tits and a sweet face anywhere; you certainly don't need to risk your life for that..

He suggests a round of beer. But his offer is rejected derisively; and they forcefully direct him to the exit. We don't want a guy like that here, so full of himself, such a stuck-up prick, such a la di da, such a windbag from the West who'd better *go on* into politics, but not here (chuckle). He distils all this and other intelligible things from their growling dialect. Karel gives him a nasty poke in the side and N. is on the point of retaliating; at the very least to competently floor that bookkeeper. The problem is he is overwhelmingly outnumbered by these hapless and desperate seekers of pleasure and happiness, and his slightly misty brain warns him to not knock on that door, for God's sake, do not provoke them and do not allow himself to be seduced, because a completely different danger suddenly looms in his mind: the district sheriff and his deputy. No, sir! That guy started it, he started the scrap, we can all testify to that. Well then sir; let's see your name and address, as well as your papers.

N. realizes the type of life-threatening situation he's in danger of maneuvering himself into. While being banished into the darkness with cries of hatred, repelled and chased away, he feels something warm glide along his hand, so he opens his palm and presses something into it. He hears the glass door of Wesselmans' conference center for singles (and couples) slam shut behind him. Feeling lucky to have not been beaten down in the middle of the sidewalk, he opens his hand under a streetlamp. With difficulty he unravels a piece of paper folded into a tight cube, with a telephone number and a note beneath it, saying: *So sorry, please call me. Tineke.* The *please* is underlined no less than three times.

N. whistles softly to himself, smiling. Shoving the paper into the inside pocket of his *Mens-Shop* jacket, he looks up to see the last bus to Q pass right in front of his nose to briefly stop, then close its doors and continue into the dark. This is not enough to lessen his smile, freed at last from the mock-melodramatic lyrics of the sentimental Dutch songs, which he felt more and more ingrained in his soul, and he feared they would be stuck in his head for some time to come.

The ousted man will need to rely on his legs. No problem, he thought, he was a well-practiced walker by now; those four kilometers to Q won't do him any harm. Indeed, there is a nice bike path next to the main road. Aside from his ignominious exit, his Ballys are a bother to him. Wearing these brand-new shoes gave

N. a couple of serious blisters along the way. But even this pain is sweetened by the note that was so hastily pushed into his hand and which seems to hold such promise. Who knows, perhaps it is the beginning of a beautiful, summer-long country idyll. It is enough to get N. humming.

At midnight, he arrives in Q, completely exhausted., His toes are crooked and there's blood in his shoes. Perhaps a half size bigger would have been better. Behind the church he finds his bicycle untouched– an undeniable advantage of rural life. At 12:15 a.m., he is back at Vogelpoelweg 14, where he is silently greeted by the sensitive Bart and where everything seems to be in deep slumber. His faithful four-legged friend happily accepts two slices of liverwurst, wagging his tail and softly whining, laying down on the couch to rest. By 1:00 a.m. N. has also drifted into a happy sleep.

15.

"I heard that you can dance *amazingly* well."

Theo is in the yard when N. returns from his afternoon bike ride. It is Monday, half past four, and the weather is nice. The chuckle in the man's voice betrays that he's heard some other things about N.'s memorable evening. He asks who he heard it from, without a trace of curiosity and not at all reassured.

"A colleague. He was there too; he told us how you looked. You couldn't miss it. And Olga heard you when you came home on Saturday night."

N. couldn't help but wish these people heard less and slept deeper. He parks his bike under the shed, grumpy from memories freshly provoked poked back into glowing embers. Theo follows him, trying to smooth things over with alternating reassurances of *don't worry about it,* and *you really ought to go for Tineke Bosman.* She only lives a few streets away, Theo tells him, and by the way, she's an *amazingly* pretty girl who has quite a few eyes on her. "But anyway," he says, shrugging, "she's very picky and from a rather distinguished family. Her father's a notary, so there you go. But yeah, if you don't have a pre-college diploma or higher, well…" Theo licks his lips at what has always been unreachable for him.

Bosman, Tineke Bosman, resident of Z, name and address. Theo knows more about her than N, he realized. All at once, it becomes clear to him just how small of a world he lives in, how easily you stand out at even the slightest hint of unfamiliarity; while he had considered himself so well hidden here.

He invites Theo into his home. They have a drink and make small talk until N. excuses himself at half past six with the announcement that it is time to cook dinner. The name "Tineke" wasn't mentioned again, and neither was the dance. Apparently, it isn't something that would take a prominent place in the man's hierarchy of daily facts and figures.

Nevertheless, N. has been restless all weekend and now the feeling has returned again. He feels unmasked and therefore hunted, and begins to wonder if it was a wise decision to stay in Q. Apparently, he still isn't far enough from the allegorical railroad embankment and trains are slowly passing by, with highly attentive passengers behind the compartment windows. His dark hair and his beautiful dark beard have grown long by now (Alan Bates in his younger years, according to the landlady), providing him an illusion of protection. Perhaps he should have cashed in his icons right away to finance the immediate purchase of new documents and then packed his bags for Brazil for good? What if the postponement drives him to disaster in the near future, permanently forestalling the Great Plan? How can a person make the right decision in a dramatically wrong situation like his?

He puts off cooking dinner. Lounging apathetically in his chair, he looks outside and observes a butterfly fluttering past the window outside, which is to say that he does not really see it, so completely absorbed in his thoughts. He doesn't hear Dikkertje, the potbellied pig, staring in and snorting, coming for her scraps of potatoes, rice or pasta to eat, as if she had never been accustomed to anything less. He doesn't see the sheep and the goats that raise their heads toward the door every other moment because they know N is home and it's around this time that he dumps his fruit and vegetable waste over the fence. By now it is half past seven. Bart walks in and out as often as suits him because the door handle holds no secrets for him. N. doesn't lock the outside door during the day out of respect for his landlady. Bart yawns heartily, moving to the other chair with a sigh. He scratches himself behind an ear and looks at N. wisely, as if he guesses and shares the other man's worries. That evening, N. keeps it simple, making an omelet which he eats from his lap.

Before long, it is ten o'clock. A pair of seagulls flap past a silky evening sky as darkness begins to fall on earth. Like every evening at this time, the roe deer stalk along the edge of the forest to graze. No, there is nothing wrong, certainly not; judging from the animals' intuitive rhythm, there's no need for worry.

16.

The next day is sunny and warm again; what a relief after a cold and rainy June. As N. returns from the village, his eyes already catch a glimpse of Olga from the Vogelpoelweg, sees the flash of her bright blonde hair from the top of the drive. As he approaches, she is lying on her back on an air mattress, sunbathing *au naturel* once again. He has unlimited access to her vegetable garden ("to his heart's content", she said) and he intends to pick some early tomatoes from her greenhouse. He could make paella later. Why shouldn't he? Of course, he could have ventured into her garden quite a bit later that afternoon. After all, there is no hurry. But the tenant has had a sexual frame of mind regarding his landlady's overt sexual overtures for the past few weeks and he doesn't want to leave any signal, however weak, unexamined. He wants to know, preferably as soon as possible, how the lady's flag is hanging in a certain respect and what signal these sunbathing sessions might be intended to send (it couldn't be a red flag now, he has established, but perhaps a rather beige one, pale beige to white). So, he asks from around the corner of the house before reaching the garden, in an attempt to be polite, giving her the opportunity to preferably not cover her nakedness but to not to be put on the record as a voyeur, so calls to ask if he can walk past.

"Go ahead, and for God's sake, Kees, don't be so spastic again."

That sounds hopeful. With his head averted pro forma, he steps across the patio and walks along the lawn (which is the only way to pick the desired fruits without having to cross the barbed-wire fence of the adjoining meadow). She laughs at his feigned modesty and asks if it needs to be done right now or he'd like to have a drink first.

A beer would be nice. When she's back with bottles and glasses and her loosely wrapped robe slides off her shoulders again, she points him to a lawn chair. From that position in the garden, he can look down in peace and covertly have the pleasure of observing the landlady's firm but breastless nipples, waist and tuft. He sees her navel cavity collecting a shimmering pool of sweat.

"It might be good for you to get some sun too," she suggests. She pinches a blade of grass from her belly.

N. probes with a remark, and attempts innocence, claiming that he doesn't have any suitable clothing.

"No swimming trunks, you mean?"

He nods eagerly.

"What do you care? I'm not wearing anything anyway." She rubs through her vaginal slit unabashedly, an act that gives N. a popping erection.

"Can I sit here with you like this? Suppose Theo was to…" He was obliged to raise the point or something like it. Because a haze had fallen over his eyes, light blue and green in color. Would he have really used one of those phrases from the book of amateur theater, the one that always asks for the familiar path?

"Theo won't be back until Thursday."

"Or Sonja," N. continues, to probe, still struggling with his erectile haze and stumbling speech while meanwhile, busy taking off his clothes.

"Her…? Well, so what?" She lights a cigarette with trembling fingers, inhales abrasively without taking her eyes off him. N. puts his clothes in a neat, gentlemanly pile, sits down again and takes another look at her thin body, the soft white scar at her groin, the vertical stripe above her mound of Venus. She sits facing him, her legs spread unconcernedly, fidgets once more at her pudenda.

Still testing, he says, "Aren't you afraid she might know something?"

"Sonja? Whatever…" Sonja could think whatever she wanted of her mother and at the very most, only get jealous.

The erection remains. N. doesn't know what to do with this lively body language and is unsure what to do next with his body. Her nudity makes her a stranger to him again for a while. She takes a sip of wine; he drinks his beer almost reflexively, smoothly changes the subject by assuming, referring to her accent, that she was not born in Holland.

She answers quickly, as if she was expecting that question, and wants to answer it once and for all, she says "Russia. I was born in Russia, in a village near St. Petersburg." She tells him that she was a member of a Russian girls' gymnastics team. She was an excellent gymnast. When the team took part in an international tournament in Hamburg, she made her escape. She was eighteen. She applied for and got political asylum. She'd had more than enough of the USSR and was sick of the regime and the lack of freedom. She never regretted it. The most difficult moment for her was the death of her mother, seventeen years ago now, because she wasn't allowed to return for the funeral.

"That was hard Kees, really hard."

Olga, suddenly caught up by her memories, looks into the distance. She says she never knew her father and she has no brothers or sisters. After escaping the USSR, she joined a gymnastics team in Hamburg for another year, then travelled through Europe. When she was about twenty, she met a much older man from Belgium. She followed him to Antwerp lived with him for several years. At long last she couldn't endure it any longer. He drank heavily, became morbidly jealous and aggressive, and quickly lost his appeal to her as he was too old; by then, he was in his sixties. When she could take it no longer, she left him. Sometime later, during a trip to Rotterdam, she met Harry Beumer. Harry lived in Rotterdam and had a job in the port. They shacked up and only got married after she got pregnant with Sonja. Harry was from Q; this little farm was his parents' home. He inherited it when his mother died; they renovated the house together and were able to move in because he found work at the subdistrict court in Y. So, Sonja was born in the city on the Meuse.

N. nods, a little bemused by this change of topic. which he sincerely hopes will not sour his mood and cause his vague libidinous vistas to darken and fade away before bearing fruit. Bart comes to sit next to him. He empties his beer glass and asks if she's managed alright here in the countryside.

"I don't need to be in the city, if that's what you mean. The wonderful thing about this little Holland is that it's so small, you're close to everything. If I particularly want to be in Amsterdam for a day or so…" She'd been accustomed to vast distances in remote and rural Russia.

N. nods again, reaching down to stroke Bart's coat, then he tries to casually recline his chair before realizing—and feeling somewhat foolish—that it is in a fixed position.

"Come lie next to me." Olga runs her gaze fleetingly over his chest hair, patting the air mattress invitingly. But it is so narrow that body to body contact cannot be avoided. He allows himself to rest against her skin, registering her satisfied sigh, smelling her sunscreen and, for lack of any better conversation, warns that she should be careful with her white skin.

"I haven't been out here that long," she says, "and besides, one who wants to be beautiful for the male has to suffer pain." Her laugh sounds hoarse and lewd, a bit too lewd, when. as a casual expression of innocent camaraderie, she takes his still-hard member in her hand and massages the tip.

On his back with his arms under his head and (in a foolish, incomprehensible attempt) to forcibly distract his attention and appear unphased by this forward display of intimacy, he asks how she got that wound on her groin.

"Appendix. I still lived in Hamburg. They messed up in the hospital there. The wound got inflamed and I had to have another operation. Because of that, I couldn't do the splits properly anymore." In the same breath, as if wanting to get ahead of the next question, she explains that Sonja was delivered surgically. Although she'd been doing gymnastics for years, her pelvis and birth canal turned out to be too narrow. "Hey, Kees," she changes the subject so suddenly that N. is completely caught off guard. Although he had been expecting it, sure enough, she asked the inevitable "Did you have a pretty good time last Saturday?"

The man groans; there is certainly no need to go, once again, down this well-worn path.

Why is he looking so far away, while what he is probably looking for might be found closer than he thinks, yes, there might be a woman very close who can give him what he might be lacking in life right now—pure, unattached, carnal pleasure.

He groans again and asks such a redundant question when he mumbles it, that it makes him think of a dialogue straight from a performance by The Meadow Flower once again.

"I'd better keep my eyes peeled."

The man nods again. End of discussion. They lie silently next to each other for a moment and N., in his extremely paradisiacal state of the moment, is only slightly hindered by the consideration that it might be better to not be in this state for Sonja's arrival. She is at school, one of the last days of the school year. Still a child, she is certainly old enough to be able to draw certain conclusions from their state of *purabilis naturabilis*; he isn't at all sure that he wants that. In any case, that does not prevent him, now that he has the warm body of a woman so close to him, but it doesn't stop him from wondering how the landlady will react if he turns to her, kisses her nipples, strokes her scarred belly, brushing her golden tuft and pretends to want to take full possession of her. Will she get up, reject him, leave him spurned and insulted? Not likely. Will she lie down, look at him with a smile and spread her legs with something animalistic in her eyes, anticipating his entrance, letting each have their way by joining together in the sacred act for which males and females were created separately?

For a brief moment, he rests his hand on Olga's crotch, feels abundant vaginal fluid. She is ready to receive. She is ready for him! Mr. van Andel, who has now been more than five weeks without a woman, literally and figuratively rubs up against the moment when he can no longer control himself; and will stake everything, even if it was a ridiculous million, for those few sweltering minutes around which the sun and zenith revolve. He is ready to stake anything for those few minutes of coital bliss. He would… but then… then there are the minutes, hours and days after that. He realizes that one wrong move could spoil everything: either (again unlikely) the instantaneous destruction of his present privileged existence, or ending up in a confusing (what is the boyfriend Theo's role and place?) and banal relationship with this woman – which in fact, boils down to the very same thing. But at the same time, every fiber in his being shouts out to him that if he wants to, he can go ahead with this skinny, almost translucent, but also strong and sinewy body. For a healthy, hyper-hetero five weeks is long; a terribly long time. So, drowning out any other thoughts, he climbs on top of her, and she has already spreads her thighs, reaches down to guide his member and take him inside, and looks directly in the eyes, her lips, her thoughts, her body fixed on his penis, his movements, his hot sperm, receiving, cherishing. Bart (outstretched ears, tail between the legs) witnesses how he enters his mistress, slicing like a knife through butter. Then there is only the breathing of two people in ecstasy, and the sound of wet flesh and… then he sees Sonja entering the yard through the opening between a shrub and a bed of hollyhocks. That is, he hardly sees her because she's still hidden behind the bushes along the roadside, but he knows it's her. Bart knows it too, because he raises his head, sharpens his ears, stands up wagging, and moves away. And that is why, mere seconds before the Terrible Shot, he stops his act of pro-creation, very much against the will of the landlady, who makes that perfectly clear. When he stops, mere seconds before the fi-nal thrust, the landlady moans her discontent.

"Oh Kees, go on, don't stop!"

"Sonja's coming."

"Who cares, what do *I* care!? Damn it, take me, fuck me!"

But Chris, alias Kees, dismounts her and already sees Olga's daughter cycling past the house, noisily accompanied by Bart who also thought it was enough. He gets up, his rock-hard erection shining in the sunlight from the mucus of her sex like an unhol-stered revolver directed at this lonely, aching creature, just like him, and gets back into his clothes. Tomorrow he'll call Tineke Bosman. That seems like a much better idea to him.

N. takes another look at the alabaster anatomy, feels a pang of regret, mixed with relief and reprieve. That evening, he in-vites the landlady and her daughter to come and eat paella with fish and minced meat with him.

17.

She's sorry, very sorry about what happened. Tineke has spo-ken with the owner about the fact that something like this, what happened to him really shouldn't happen in his business; that he should have intervened, that she's a little ashamed of this region where she was born, what N. must think of it, and what he might think of her, going to such evenings after all.

"Oh Kees, I thought it was so embarrassing!"

The desire is high, so high after the interrupted, psycho-neu-rotic fusion with the landlady, that the very next morning, N.

calls the number that was slipped to him. He gets a man's voice on the line that briefly informs him that Ms. Bosman is only there on Wednesday afternoons; he should call her back then.

So, on Wednesday he calls, and they make a date for that evening. If N. is coming by bus, he should get off in the center of Z. She'll wait for him there, and perhaps he'd like to go with her to the cinema near the bus stop where Bridges of Madison County will be shown again, a movie she's been to twice before and would love to see again.

N. gets off in the center of Z at a quarter past seven. When he sees Tineke again, he's a bit disappointed. With her rather deep neckline, her short skirt and firm legs, she definitely had something seductive going on last Saturday. Nothing is left of that now. She wears dark blue jeans, which makes her look as ordinary as all the women in this voluntary uniform with an utter lack of imagination. Over the eternal jeans, a black turtleneck makes her complexion look pale. N. doesn't immediate recognize the woman who walks up to him. He really thinks Tineke would look more stylish in a dress or skirt than in these jeans that obviously don't suit her. They are baggy around her hips, almost frumpy. Hasn't anyone ever told her that?

They shake hands, and her first words are to ask him if he has a car.

At the local cinema (open on Wednesday, Saturday and Sunday evenings plus a Sunday matinee), the everlasting Clint Eastwood talks and frolics with the immortal Meryl Streep. After the intermission with coffee and cake, N. and Tineke become emboldened enough to hold hands; three-quarters of the way into the show they begin playing footsies. *He, musing in the meanwhile, thinks that for God's sake* he *shouldn't focus so much on her appearance!* Regular sexual intercourse, that's what this is about. Preferably with a woman with a well-developed awareness of the relativity of human contact, without too much pressure on a relationship, someone who values discretion and hygiene; in other words who takes healthy pleasure in copulation. How beneficial it would be for his peace of mind and his inner care in general. What a boon to his general sense of well-being! Why shouldn't this solid Tineke, who is now in the process of winding her fingers through his, why shouldn't she bring this blessing to fruition? Nice face, beautiful white teeth, good figure, firm bosom, a tad on the chubby side perhaps, petty bourgeois by day, world traveler by night, with an active eye for the erotic challenge. Because otherwise why wouldn't someone like her have been taken long ago, if that's not who she is, if she truly longs to be respectably married, mother of a couple of rosy-cheeked kids? Perhaps she also fears commitment, or hasn't quite left the experimental stage of life. Recently liberated from a previous, overly restrictive relationship, maybe she is now passionately longing for something new, something exciting with an outsider. That story of her strict parents is surely just a cover to avoid laying it on too thick. What girl is so crazy these days?

N., intoxicated and enraptured by the fantasy and the closeness of the feminine, suddenly no longer sees the boring countryside around Des Moines, but a romantic Alpine Austrian countryside. Here, he sees a naked, dancing, singing, dashing Tineke that he is allowed to catch and spread out on a mountain pasture, to weave some Edelweiss through her abundant pubic hair before pleasing her with his alphorn. What images! This alchemy of ancient Lawrence and sixties *Eastman color* gives rise to a very pleasant feeling emerging from his loins. It makes him hot and he begins to sweat.

After the eternally youthful Streep has reunited with her family and good old Eastwood has disappeared into the pouring rain with his pickup, the lovers, satisfied with this happy ending together with the other eight members of the audience, disperse from the cinema. It is eleven o'clock and the wind has begun to blow. Tineke proposes a drink in a restaurant nearby. N. orders two glasses of wine. At her request, he tells the story again, adding a few more details about his fizzled-out marriage and his desperate attempts to get it back afloat. Tineke will probably realize, he thinks, as he concludes his bitter tale, how ready he is now in "certain aspects". This muted cry of distress leads to her first kiss. She, in turn, assumes that of course Kees understands that at the age of thirty-five she has already had several affairs with men. Unfortunately, Mister Right was not among them. She thinks it would probably have been better to take her chances in another part of the country. A few years ago, she made serious plans to move to Utrecht where she had a nice job lined up, but her father put a stop to it. Not only does she still live with her parents, she's also in charge of caring for her mother who had a stroke four years ago and has been confined to a wheelchair ever since.

"Daddy doesn't want me to leave under these circumstances."

N. also learns that any possible marriage comes with the condition that the couple lives there. The house, a mansion with a deep garden somewhere in the center, is big enough. The young couple will not only have the second floor but also part of the ground floor at their disposal.

"But" she sighs, "where do you find a man who wants to live with his in-laws these days?" She looks at N. a bit sadly. What's more, if the son-in-law-to-be is going to make the cut with her parents, he should preferably not speak in the local dialect, look neat and tidy, have a solid education and a good job, preferably in the government or a related sector or else in the legal profession. She asks about Kees' education, to which he, no longer entirely at ease, mumbles something about an academic level. She had already thought so, she exclaims enthusiastically, because of his choice of words and how he expresses himself in general.

N., slightly gratified, asks to ask something: if she thinks her father would like him.

Tineke looks at him suddenly, with a very serious look. The caress of her hand over his hand, wrist and forearm becomes more emphatic. "I think, Kees, that Daddy will really like you… By the way, now that you've found a job all the way in Y, do you plan to keep living in this area?"

N. reassures her, saying that he will, that he'll be looking for a place of his own in Q or the surrounding area soon.

"Are you Catholic?"

N., taken aback a bit by this totally unexpected question from another century and believes he can reassure her with the definite statement that he is *not* Catholic. He aims at the highly probable circumstance that this stolid region is mainly populated by the gritty descendants of the Calvin and Lutheran backbone of Dutch society, with a hint of desperate Camusian atheists or the occasional Muslim shuffling along the shady sides of the street, interspersed among the population.

Ms. Bosman sighs again, and N. orders one more glass of wine because his companion would rather have a tonic now. They chat a bit more. At a quarter to twelve, they are asked in a businesslike tone to settle the bill and to leave because it is now closing time. The last bus to Q has left, but Tineke takes it as a matter of course that she will bring him home. As they drive off in her brand-new Fiat Stilo, she asks if he thinks they should see each other again, and, if so, she wants to discuss a few things with him tonight "so we don't misunderstand each other."

N. thinks they should "definitely" see each other again. He keeps it to himself that his need is intense, really intense, and he'd actually like to see *all of her* on *this* late evening. The information that she lives with her parents has made him realize that the regular warm contact he had hoped for with this lady could run into logistical problems, which is why he is already considering (it costs a lot, but you have some money) renting a *petite maison de passe* now and then.

He says he would not only like to see her again, but also to enjoy her presence a little while longer tonight, because yes, it's been so long since he had a good conversation with a woman. N. could barely get enough and the evening passed so terribly quickly.

In response to his words, she almost immediately turns left into a parking lot on the edge of a vast forested area between Z and B. Surrounded by soft instrumental music from a German radio station and a strong breeze that rustles the trees, she kills the engine and they talk a little more. N. gradually puts one hand on Tineke's shoulder and the other on her firm back. She puts her arms around his neck. Then she gives him a kiss, and then, another one, longer, stronger, pulling him into a powerful embrace. She allows N. to slide his hand under her turtleneck, to whip her breasts out of the cups. When he works her nipples with his tongue for heavenly stimulation, she bends over to him and hooks one leg around his hip. For a short, golden moment he thinks that tonight he will finally reach his climax. She fiddles with the closure of her pants – who knows, she might be throwing herself onto his white sabre with complete dedication, and N. is already hastily fiddling with his. But then, his ears hear the following...

She sits astride his crotch, with her breasts swinging freely on this midsummer night, which means that it is not completely dark at one o'clock. She says, somewhat reproachfully that the fact that he's not Catholic is annoying her, that this could be a major objection from her father, since her family is almost the only Catholic family in Z. This is something that follows ––N. summarizes to himself – the principle of "the smaller the minority, the stricter the doctrine". Her father more or less insists that his future son-in-law recognizes the Pope of Rome as the highest spiritual authority on earth. But she believes that once Daddy has met him, spoken with him, and knows about his education and so on, he will agree, although of course she would still prefer that Kees convert to Catholicism, – "yes darling, I think that it's all for the best". – Of course, she realizes she can't force him to, although as far as she's concerned it is definitely love at first sight, doesn't Kees feel it too? She really wants to be with him, sexually and otherwise, and no matter how great her desire is now and how much she herself wants it, she only wants it after they, he and she, are officially engaged. That as far as she is concerned, they can get engaged soon, because then they can be married a month or so after that, and he won't have to go looking for his own home, and then they'll be able to have hot sex every night and soon have children, and oh, how she looks forward to that, together with him in one bed, husband and wife and a child of his, and what does he think of that...

And oh yes, before she forgets, she would also prefer him to shave off his beard and moustache. It's true that she fell in love with him from the very first moment, but she has been warned several times that men with beards have something to hide.

His libido draining away and almost with tears of rage, regret and disappointment in his eyes, N. says this is all very sudden, that he will call her tomorrow or the day after tomorrow to make a date for the weekend. He goes on to say that he understands that he shouldn't take up too much of her time now, because of course she has to be fresh for work again tomorrow, while he has the luxury of sleeping in for another hour if necessary. He asks her to drive him to Q now where she drops him off in the city center ten minutes later. She bids him goodbye with a kiss and her cheery declaration that she is "completely, really completely" into him.

Retrieving his bike from behind the church, N. pedals home to Vogelpoelweg in the light of the stars that peek between racing clouds. He pedals through the night against the strong wind – disenchanted but holding his head high, as a man who can bear his disappointment (but his diary chafes afterwards with a piece of text that is better to leave out here).

Only half a kilometer from his rented accommodations, he rides into a downpour that ruins his beautiful new Men-Shop clothes.

★★★

PART II

Arcadia Devastated

18.

The moon, only a fragment blown off in the night by a cosmic storm. To N., this is perhaps one of the most beautiful metaphors in world literature, the moon in the morning sky. What sky would it have been? The one seen from Mexico? Or British Columbia, perhaps? Before or after the conflagration? In a daze after a bout of drinking, during a moment of realization, perhaps after an argument with Margerie Bonner? N.'s imagination glides on to Albert Finney and his portrayal of the consul. This was undoubtedly, subjectively and objectively, supported by the ukase of Minerva and her half-brothers and stepsisters, the best role in film history. Would that still have been the case, he ponders, if Richard Burton had ended up getting the role?

He puts Rowley's intoxicating nebulous visions aside, looking up at the gray lowland sky with its drizzling rain. Today, forty-five days after that momentous eleventh, the honeymoon period of his new existence has come to an end. A random moment. Because what, then? What changed yesterday, and what will change tomorrow? It will only get easier for him. On this drizzly Tuesday morning from the comfort of his chair in front of his living room window, he relives the birth of his new existence; it's less shocking now, already polished by time and stripped of the sharp edges. All that remains is a little shudder wrapped up in the warm realization, once again, that fortune could not have done any better for him. Then, with the compulsion to imagine it, he feels the air pressure on his back again—an unyielding hand—the hot breath on his neck. Then he sees himself as if blown away into his new cosmos, transparent and unharmed for now. As if it was fate itself that had given him, amongst all the noise, dust and grit a way out: here's your chance, man, don't fuck it up, get out, that way, and quit your whining! A hard slap on the back to say goodbye. A close shave, a matter of seconds and being in a lucky position; it was either a new existence or ashes.

Low and slow, a grey heron flies over the meadow, his beak heavy with the young minnows from the brook further on. A short way into the forest, the heron lands in a small pond where the creature begins to eat frogs, which N. sometimes hears creaking when the wind is blowing in the right wind direction, to add variety to its menu. A few weeks ago, the heron hatched two chicks in its nest in the crown of an old Scots pine (N. knows where). He breathes deeply, and again, sits down in his chair, still not completely relaxed. As far as his present existence is concerned, for some time now he has had the nagging fear that he'll like it here in the countryside too much, that a narcotic *dolce far niente* will cause him to further delay his Great Plans. He is paralyzed by the near certainty that the landlady wants something much more from him than just rent. This lady is not exactly attractive to him, but he finds her undisguised ambiguity and her recent warm initiative increasingly intriguing. He's been stopped in his tracks before by a woman's sex, which happens to so many men. This could well prove to be a fatal delay in the execution of his plans. If only she were old, or at least very ugly! If only she was a normal "landlady", businesslike and in it only for the rent money, then, he might be able to resist her. And as for that new transparent cosmos: it has all been clouded by lies and eroticism, brought down to earth, vulgar, human. "And where the girls are, there is the vale…" As long as it lasts, nothing is lost. He senses some adventure in this valley of Jericho (that's how it is, isn't it?), where he is offered shelter and which he will traverse after some time. Sooner or later, he'll definitely do that, he is sure of himself in that respect. Never mind, new horizons are shimmering in the distance. If it comes to an actual relationship borne by custom and habituation, it will become too banal for him, that's for certain. The desire to stay here at Vogelpoelweg

14, its allure, will evaporate as soon as the flesh of this skinny, bushy woman holds no more secrets for him, or as soon as, who knows, that body will one day be pregnant by him. There are certainly greener, more tempting pastures to be found elsewhere.

"If only I could get by without a woman around," he mumbles hypocritically, because his heart rejoices at the situation. She, Olga, pleases him, and she has him under her spell with her provocative attitude, her forwardness, her openness, whether or not affected; her candid gaze, her paleness, her thinness, her way of doing things, her smile, her hoarse, raspy voice. Yes, even the fact that she is a chain-smoker holds something seductive for him. She is also hiding something that he wants to know. She has something worldly about her, not of the countryside, rather a certain style of argumentation that also points to a certain *je ne sais quoi* gained from a life of experience. She has a way of putting things in perspective. Her restlessness, her quick gestures and mannerisms make him believe that somewhere in her Mother Russia, or after that, in the Europe of her younger years, there is a secret connected to her existence. As they become more and more intimate, one day, it will come out of her. Maybe, he guesses, maybe only after I've really slept with her a few times, after long, exhausting lovemaking, during an evaluation in a moment of reflection, a candid *après*. She is eight years older than him; he, who has never been intimate with anyone older than himself. Still, who knows? It is a new experience. She is a woman, through and through, and perhaps only during and after such intimate moments will she be willing to reveal her truth.

N. feels a shudder through his penis because, as if the air has completely cleared, he suddenly sees little elf E. dancing through the sunlight with her shimmering glass wings. He is very keen to let the beautiful spring of this relationship continue, to increase its tension, to let the bow be pulled to the fullest. It must remain a beautiful game, a breathtaking fairytale. Until the arrow soon flies toward its target (but not too soon); the heart of the rose that she offers him will become more and more fully open. Isn't he himself an archer? Ha. Oh, and to placate his conscience over this delay, he has at least made some phone calls, half-hearted preparations (but preparations, nonetheless) for implementation of the Great Plan. Phone calls that did not yield much more than what he has long known: that the right time to pull the trigger is really in the first half of next year—February maybe… probably March. Another six months of this quiet sabbatical.

N. sits at the corner window seat, offering a strategic view of the vegetable garden so that he can see when his landlady appears in his field of vision. She is dressed in an old raincoat with a cape that gives her the appearance of an old woman. This image is reinforced by her bent posture as she cuts vegetables – the first action in preparing the hot meal for later. He looks at the hollows of her knees, which N. thinks is certainly the least attractive place on a woman's body. Would someone like that be able to…? She stands there like an old enchantress, doesn't she? Unattractive, no mystery at all, middle-aged with gray streaks in her blonde hair. No doubt, she will be completely grey in about five years' time, if she survives her nicotine addiction. She is ordinary, so ordinary and predictable. In forty years, she'll look like this for real. But what is forty years? He's already thirty-four.

But even all this holds some temptation for him today.

When she turns and sees N. sitting, she raises her hand to wave. A mechanical display of camaraderie, a small act of solidarity with this strange man, sometimes silent-seriousness, sometimes talkative-extrovert whom she has managed to snare in her cottage. N. realizes, foolishly, that true to her feminine nature, she'll keep plowing and rooting, advancing with ambiguities; he'll become putty in her hands. Until she knows everything about him, or at least has the impression that she knows everything about him, his dark secrets will be hers too. Hardly a day goes by during the week without sharing a cup of coffee in the morning or a drink at the end of the afternoon, or, for some time now, both. She cooks for him more and more often. He has become her confidant and her advisor in all kinds of things as well. Sonja, too, has started to show an interest in this strange, lonely guy who is now also her colleague. The three of them sit together and chat about all sorts of things. The landlady weaves her exploratory questions in between the bits of news, tactfully gaining bits of information about him, cross-checking stories for consistency, and then stringing them all together to slowly knit the image of him—in her head, failed schoolmaster and renegade.

"What a find," he murmurs. Would she have believed my fabrications without question? N. has his doubts, from time to time. She is certainly enough of a psychologist to sense the shabby cliché baked into his story, which will drive her to keep investigating until she is satisfied. This also poses a danger to his identity because he'll have to keep coming up with more intricate lies about himself, lies for the sake of corroborating other lies and fabrications. This intricate web of lies is becoming dangerous; one day he will almost certainly gets trapped in all of them. And then what? Just leave with the northern sun, from one day to the next? And where will he go? Will another Arcadia that he has enjoyed for the past five, six weeks open up for him somewhere else in this totally demythologized and standardized little country?

N. still feels his erection like a forgotten echo of his earlier thoughts and fantasies. After the Bosman fiasco (how can such a stale soul live in such a sumptuous body?) his need for a woman is greater than ever. "If only I could do without," he says, hypocritically again. There is a nightclub in Q, but he really doesn't want to risk ridicule among Q's youth. Near Z, there is a sex club *surrounded by rustic woods* according to an indefatigable advertisement in the regional daily newspaper that the Beumers get. But it is a swingers' club, and N. has visions of solidly consenting couples, who, without exception, openly cheat on each other with both parties knowing. What can he, as a single man expect to find there, except perhaps another exit through the side door, or even worse? In Y, actually only half an hour away by train, there is a red-light district. However, N.'s sense of aesthetics always wins out over the power of his libido, even in his current sexually distressed situation, which is something he always congratulates himself on afterwards. He can rationally parry the occasional impulse to invite an escort girl into his humble abode, which also doesn't seem sensible to him in view of the landlady's sharp gaze, because a surrogate might stifle future warm developments here at Vogelpoelweg. N. is certain that when it gets sunny and warm again, a lawn scene is sure to present itself. Sometimes he clings to this dream just like a parched traveler in the Sahara clings to the inevitable mirage.

N. gets up, opens his laptop, lets the printer do its work, sighs as he bends over the first printed pages of the novel manuscript, and then makes some corrections.

… Aisha has fallen asleep and I walk outside. Every now and then I am pierced by the sound of unintelligible voices from the street below. I hear a scream, and then laughter. Just now, a car passed under my study window; judging by the sound of the engine, it's an old Jeep, one of many that drive around here. Still, after more than three hours, the fretful, compelling call of the marabout echoes, alerting the faithful to gather for their evening prayers in the mosque located on the other side of the street. The severe, punishing hand of Allah upon his faithful and servile populace that, thanks to all the international gods, does not have at least the only say-so here.

Suddenly a gust of fresh wind comes in through the window, as if it could rain at any moment. I shudder with longing, but perhaps also because of the gradual, chronic lack of sleep. When I walk onto the rooftop and look out over the city, it is as if the bright stars of the Central African night are reflected below, so dimly lit are the sporadic streetlights.

We live in a new housing development on the outskirts of the city. In places like this, it is normal to find the inevitable combination of official habitation, along with its utility connections and clandestine shanties with their illegal splices. They are periodically cleared out by the authorities but with time, they invariably return. These shanties are just the outward symptoms of an incurable disease. You can smell the close proximity of these poverty-stricken folk, preparing their cheap meals in the early evening, — generally too ill-equipped to be terribly stringent about hygiene. Later in the evening, when the dew settles down, you can catch a whiff of the aroma of silica swelling from the semi-arid desert, ceremoniously riding in on a warm breeze, and, when blessed by the right wind direction, it mingles with the scent of the kapok trees from the plantation

Olga enters, accompanied by Bart snorting with joy, the guardian of paradise who will eventually (and anonymously) be put under but for now, he knows nothing of that. There was a soft tap on the kitchen door that she opened immediately, as he had instructed her to do, because, under the impetus of erotic desire packaged in hospitality, he once swore that she should always feel welcome and at home with him. But N. had not expected her to come now, more or less directly from her visit to the garden. Mindful of her prying eyes, he quickly closes his notebook and lays the printed pages face down on the table. Better to avoid misunderstandings before they happen.

"I saw you just sitting there, doing nothing. I thought you must already have the coffee ready."

In the vegetable garden she wore low wooden clogs with leather insoles. She took them off at the outside door, as well as her raincoat, and entered in socks. Her intro, already redundant, makes him smile.

"No, I still have to put it on. I wanted to know that you were coming first. You might have had better things to do." He gives Bart his rightful piece of sausage, only to let the animal out again.

"Everything inside of me gives way to your coffee, including my last bit of decency and resistance." Olga's glances inspects the room, lingering a little too long and a bit sadly on the upside-down papers.

He makes coffee and they sit across from each other, and chat a bit, watching the two goats that instantly appear now and measure each other's strength with their heads before grazing. Farther away, two magpies alight, and a hare is startled by Bart's patrol on the neighbor's field, who considers that plot of pasture to be his, even though it belongs to the farmer at the end of the Vogelpoelweg pavement. Again, N. feels himself enchanted by the completely relaxed atmosphere of the pastoral scene. He closes his eyes for a moment. Suddenly, the novel's protagonist Aisha M'Kromo, naked and willing, with a conspiratorial smile, is no longer facing him; but in her place there is Olga Beumer, who puts her hand on his shoulder and says she has to go infirm an old lady this afternoon to fill in for a sick colleague. There is the question of whether N. can tell Sonja, who comes home at three o'clock, where her mother is and that she'll be back around five-thirty.

They drink another cup of coffee; N. counts the landlady's third cigarette. Then she informs him that he'll have the place to himself next weekend because Theo, Sonja and she are going to Den Bosch to visit her sister-in-law. They will leave on Saturday and come back in the evening on Sunday. Perhaps N. could water her houseplants once, close the chicken coop in the evening and open it in the morning (another fox has been spotted in the area), pick up the eggs and please make sure Bart gets his food and water.

The last question is strictly superfluous, and she knows it. Bart, and indeed, no animal will ever lack for anything with him around. Sometimes it's better to be a dog, but not always; it depends on the people you depend on. To take advantage of this exquisite weekend, presented so suddenly, he calls an escort service as soon as Olga leaves him to dress for work, mildly excited at the prospect of warm pleasure.

That Saturday evening, he does something not entirely without risk. It involves Olga's otherwise agile Peugeot, which has been left lonely and deserted under the awning, the family having taken Theo's car to Den Bosch. To save her (and her possible protector) from what might turn out be an endless quest through the countryside, N. directed his escort to meet in the square next to the church in Q at an agreed-upon time. She arrives, all alone — no protector, no companion, in a big SUV, no combed-smooth, good-humored pimp with a mustache, sideburns, sunglasses and a pistol in the inside pocket, humming and perhaps keen on, who knows, a nice little extortion racket. After the greeting and brief identification process, she drives behind him to the Vogelpoelweg. The whole way, he is constantly tormented by the knowledge that any accident of any magnitude with the landlady's car would expose him mercilessly and put an end to his status as a "nobody".

After all, the first thing he'll be asked is to show his driver's license, the only document from his previous existence that he hasn't destroyed yet. His true identity will be entered into the state computer system, which will then connect to the next one, for example a population register, and this will lead to inferences and furrowed brows, and municipal officials and cops will take off their glasses in amazement. Oh, N. can see it all, clearly and lucidly, this inescapable course of bureaucratic events. He is so concerned about this obscure possibility that he ends up driving extremely cautiously. Later, his follower asks if he's only just recently learned how to drive.

She is young, about twenty years old, neither pretty nor unattractive, quite tall, almost ethereal, and fragile, too fragile for this profession actually, especially her long slender legs. Like many of the companions he's had before, her name is Nelleke and like many of her colleagues in fornication, she is a "student" who is forced into the profession to earn some extra money. But after he questions her further, it turns out she really is in third-year French student at the Radboud Institute of Language and Literature. What's more, Nelleke, she claims, is her real name. Born and raised in Arnhem, which N. is inclined to believe because there is something *"Ernems"* in her accent (he has family there). She tells him that she is working on a dissertation on Marcel Proust to finish her bachelor's degree. She loves his long sentences, the verbosity of his text, his universe, how he slows things down. She thinks he is a master at this last point, and the way he unravels thoughts and motives is truly inspiring.

N.'s enthusiasm is piqued. As he prepares a tasty pasta, they drink a bottle of Chianti and have an animated, sometimes even rather heated discussion about literature, art and culture. They talk about Camus, about Sartre (who, according to Nelleke, was a failed bandwagon jumper in both literature and philosophy, his existentialism overrated—N.'s ears perk up at this tidbit). They discuss the *enfant terrible* Michel Houellebecq, and modern French literature in general. A second bottle is long overdue, and it is well after one o'clock when he inseminates her with all the power of his month and a half of accumulated loneliness. A wakeful night follows; they sleep until noon that Sunday on his three–quarter bed, wrapped closely together. They drink coffee, have a late breakfast and, when asked, she says she'd like to offer her services to him again, so he should call and ask for her specifically. When they say goodbye, she gives him a bonus kiss and then an embrace, so tender and impetuous that it feels unnaturally emotional for intercourse between provider and customer, which he has always found to be fictitious by definition. He and Bart watch her as she disappears down the Vogelpoelweg, Bart wagging his tail, N. definitely feeling a slight twinge of regret in his heart.

He makes sure that the accomplice Peugeot is parked in exactly the same place as it was before, and that afternoon, accompanied by his faithful four-legged friend, he goes for a long walk.

19.

For the time being, the elements refuse to cooperate for a *gazon-passe* with the sunbathing landlady. It is a changeable July: oppressive periods of rain interspersed with bright summer days prevent what seemed to be a matter of course a month earlier. The weather gods must be getting back at him, N. thinks, for his heretofore *bonheur*, letting the sunshine exuberantly either on those days when he has obligations to Pete de Wilde's shop or on the weekends and beginning of the new week when he has Theo to contend with.

It is at one such satanic moment that he returns from a lively walk in the forest. Lovely warm weather, this morning he has specially taken off work, you would think all the ingredients are there for a *voulez-vous*, naturally pale and stark naked on her sunbed, waiting (after all, she saw him leave an hour and a half earlier), with her strong legs provocatively lifted and apart, *mons pubis* pale blonde shining in the sunlight. He is expectant and aroused, all that remains is to get out of his clothes make the leap he's dreamed of for days and nights… if she wasn't (what cheekiness!) so solidly chaperoned by Theo, as pale pink as a piglet. who was nowhere to be found in the fields or on the roads an hour and a half ago. But now, he sits there like an attentive lifeguard instructed by his boss to prevent the municipal swimming pool sunbathing area from getting completely out of hand. The landlady's boyfriend, dressed in only dirty gray shorts that are a few sizes too big for him despite his beer belly, is perusing the newspaper.

"Hi Kees, back already?" Her husky voice is accompanied by the rustling of the regional newspaper that keeps her protector distracted. Olga shoots into her bathrobe, modestly averted from both men *comme il faut*. N. puts on the coffee.

Fate has only modest compensation in store, a handful of surrogate pleasures, for all those delightful moments that have heated his imagination for so long and remain so fresh in his memory. He is encouraged with the prospect of numerous beautiful days and a favorable weather forecast laying out a longer stretch of sunny days. Sonja shows a willingness to go to work by bike as well, so they travel through the lanes together in the morning and afternoon, chatting companionably about everything and nothing, but mostly about singers and rappers, guitarists and bands and concerts. Then there's the recently started soap opera *Love Is For All Times* that features appearances by the famous celebrities who often appear in TV quizzes, saying that Kees surely watches it, too — and his denial is met with great amazement, not to say indignation.

He does manage to figure out that it's not so much laziness that makes her prefer public transport. It is rather the unattractive prospect of a girl, cycling alone through the desolate woods that stretch out relentlessly between Q and X. There, on one of their journeys, she shudders and shares with him that a year or so ago a girl was assaulted and seriously injured (eternal innocence destroyed by the guilty man's ruthless hands). Her imagination ran wild after that, and now she simply doesn't ride there, not during the day and certainly not in winter when it gets dark early. And her mother agrees; in fact, she would prefer to pick Sonja up from the bus station in the evening, although she admits it might be a bit exaggerated.

There is a shortcut to X, but N. has come to find that it seems to be a particular hotspot for hungry, lonely men. It's a dirt road that runs right through the nature reserve, and outside tourist season, it is as lonesome by day as it is by night lying under the forest canopy. The bicycle path is paved with shell grit and loam, lending itself to quick routine acts by a pedophile or some other slavering degenerate waiting behind a bush or tree, where desperately, but fruitlessly struggling plunder could be caught. No one would ever know. N. later found out that it used to be the main road between Q and X, but fell into disuse at the beginning of the last century when a new asphalt road was built as part of a massive make-work project, mostly around the forest area which N. suspects was probably chosen for land expropriation reasons. The pre-modern stagecoach and diligence route is, however, two kilometers shorter.

Under a warm, cloudless Friday afternoon sky in early August, Sonja and N. cycle home together. She's a nice kid with a healthy interest in earthly matters. She shows some wit when N. asks, for the sake of asking, about how she's doing at school. She replies that he'd do better to ask the school about how she, Sonja Beumer, is doing at school.

"Difficult student?"

"Mmm, let's say a difficult school. Both."

"How much longer do you have?"

"One year. And from September onwards, luckily, only a day and a half every week."

"You really hate studying?"

"Mmm."

"And the hairdresser training?"

"Two days. And I get paid. Thirteen euro fifty cents a day. How do you like that?" She giggles.

"Well, at least then you can give up your job as a cashier, I guess." A buzzard circles above them, together with a fly in N.'s eye, such a small annoying insect that reinforces its death struggle with a caustic secretion onto the eyeball. For a moment he loses sight of the bicycle path and almost falls.

She, almost shocked and is already working on removing the discomfort from his eye with a tissue: "You can't be serious," she says, amused. "I'll have to stick with it for now. I don't want to keep relying on my mother." She looks at him sideways. "Or is this your way of telling me you've had enough of me riding with you? I'll take the bus again, no problem."

Please don't, dear child; his heart aches at the prospect. He is a lonely old bird, and her youthful voice, her warmth, her naïve spirit adds color to his dark days. He relishes watching her skinny, angular shape as it becomes more and more feminine, her beautiful calves whose musculature becomes more pronounced every day that she rides with him. Do you have a boyfriend already? I hope not, I don't think so, I've never seen a boy near you. She's probably still a virgin, he muses, with her untouched, unsullied abdomen.

It is the first time she's stood next to him like that, touching him in different way than just a casual handshake, and he tastes her breath at every word, so close that she seems to speak right into his ear. Flies, bees, wasps, hornets pull the silence beneath the blue into pieces. High, higher than the circling bird of prey (the optical illusions are strong in the thermally vibrating air) with the faint rumble of a four-engine airliner, whose milky white streaks flow through the alchemy of hot gases, cold and physics. There is a pine grove to the left, on the right a heather field with birch and a jay cursing the bird of prey. It is in this warm, and verdant atmosphere where sounds muffle, voices stifle and everything becomes personal, and the daughter's image begins to supplant that of the mother's for the first time (N. realizes this later).

His vision restored, the two mount their bikes and continue down the path. "No, no, please keep riding with me. I enjoy your company too much." Then, smiling in expectation of her response, "besides, I'm also a bit scared of riding alone through this forest. Have women ever assaulted grown men here?"

Bingo! She lurches, swerving toward him so that for a moment their bike handlebars nearly touch and N.'s front wheel averts into the loose sand next to the shell path. He brakes, falling behind to regain his steering. The path is too narrow to ride side by side,. N. enjoys his minor success, as he is generally not very direct. More dead boring.

"Good one," she says when he catches up to her (where the path widens), "I'll tell Mommy about that. The best I've heard today."

"You do that," says N, still basking in the afterglow a hundred meters later. They come to an intersection with an unclear ANWB signpost that just seems to indicate the four directions of the wind. "But seriously," he presses her again, more serious. "What do you have trouble with at school?" Of course, he already knows that she is failing school, although she is certainly not stupid. Older sisters and mothers are always looking out for the younger sisters and daughters, in Russia or the Russian Netherlands, or in the rest of Europe or anywhere else in the world. That doesn't matter, even if they sometimes give a different impression. Somewhere in the distance, a plaintive rooster crows, the misguided creature at this wrong time of day. Sonja explains that she's always had bad grades and struggled with reading and writing. She doesn't know why, either. Math and all that, in fact, anything to do with numbers, well, that was just fine. But writing, and especially reading, has always given her trouble. Even now, for example, with the newspaper. She even has to read things that interest her two or three times before she can begin to understand what it says.

Dyslexia or alexia? Or both? Muzzle, moustache, mosquito, mission; bin, tin, sin, win. Perhaps a classic case. Stubborn problems with word identification and written imagery.

"Have you ever been tested for that, have you told them that you have trouble with that?"

"I've told my teachers, but no, they've never tested me." They always said it would improve on its own, get easier as she gets older. Some children are simply bad at certain things, and good at others. With arithmetic, multiplication, fractions and so on, and then later on with accounting, she was always ahead. She got it right away. She could even calculate huge multiplication problems in her head, given enough time. Nobody else could do that. That's why Mr. de Wilde lets her work the cash register, even though she was technically too young for the position.

Does she ever read books? Stupid question of course. No kid in vocational school reads text that isn't wrapped in a brightly photographed soft cover from the supermarket shelves between cleaning products and toilet paper, loved by cashiers, saleswomen and shopping mothers, which is why they are so aptly called "pulp". But she shrugs her shoulders, says that she sometimes does try to starts books that that her mother borrows from the library, for example, but she never finishes them. She can usually read no more than five or ten pages before she gets frustrated and abandons the effort. "I have," she says, hesitantly (the scamp), "secretly tried to read your books too, when you weren't there... But it's all too difficult for me; I don't understand any of it." (Lowry, Musil, Borges, Jeroen Brouwers, Grünberg; he has nothing else to offer at the moment, at least not in Dutch. Do you think their writings are weird, girl?)

She giggles, looking at the other guiltily. She is quite a beautiful child, actually. Common, yet beautiful. "Suppose" he suddenly bets on a vague prospect, "suppose you'd like to read a whole book. Would you feel OK with asking me to help you?"

What tender situations could come from such an arrangement, him, the lone wolf, the two of them, alone in his rooms, or perhaps here in the woods, on a bench, in the sun, heads together over a book under the believable guise of remedial teaching, for example. Olga at a distance of course, discreet and expectant, because then they can't be disturbed and Olga will have to be patient, and it could take up to a year's time... His imagination begins filling in the details, and a panoramic view expands in his mind (which is so imaginative in this particular area), an undulating landscape populated with slender blond girls, eighteen-year-old escorts for instance, hand-in-hand with (what's the difference really?) teenage sisters of sixteen. There are some radiant sub-panoramas too, sudden, almost hallucinatory, and it gives libidinous N. rise to such fierce goose bumps, leading him to believing for a moment that he really is cold.

He had to speak the last words of his completely disinterested proposal with a raised voice because he got stuck in the loose sand again, pedaling with a foot off, and fell off his seat from behind. She gets off her bicycle again to wait for him, looking at him in a surprised and suspicious way – yes, suspicious, that's how he'd describe her facial expression.

"How do you mean?" She brushes her hair back, those strands of hair at her temples that don't reach the band around her ponytail falling forward. For just a moment, he can see in her eyes the whole sun, or perhaps maybe the whole solar system like within an aleph. She squeezes them into slits, because she has to look within herself. They stand facing each other, man and girl, both panting a bit, albeit for different reasons (he assumes), and to an outsider they must look like two ruffians, the bicycles like parapets between them, and the sunlight seems to hold an impetuous and heartwarming promise. That damn cock crows again. But much farther away now, and less doleful than before.

"Exactly what I said. I will read to you, have you read, make corrections, improvements... But not as a teacher of course." He adds because he thinks he reads something resembling disgust on her face, he assumes, resurrecting the memory of her frustrating elementary school days. My god, dear child, spoiled – unspoiled creature, don't pretend you don't understand this calculating man. Pretty young girls must have an instinctive feel for older men.

That's life, the dangerous adult life with calculating highwaymen and their supposedly unsuspecting Little Red Riding Hood prey, for which he didn't cast off his old stuffed shirt in the middle of May last damn year for nothing!

"Do you have time for that?" She still looks surprised, not to say inquisitive, but her distaste seems to have turned into curiosity.

"For you I do. And if I don't have time, I'll make time. It's as simple as that." He tries to look neutral, decisive and casual, maintaining an attitude of apparent obviousness.

"But..." There is a request for an explanation, but the protestation, or whatever it would have become, is broken off (and never finished) due to a young egotistical motorist crossing the sand road, showering them with a curtain of fine dust and sand, changing their conversation to disparaging "boys like that" and both are forced to take a shower as soon as they get home.

A few kilometers and minutes further on, she says she'd most like to have a part-time job, and she doesn't care what. It wouldn't necessarily have to be in the hairdressing profession.

"What's stopping you? What would you want to do with your free time?"

"Reading," she says, "a lot of reading. There are so many books just in that stupid library bus, about everything. I don't want to go through life like a dummy." Her face darkens as if a shadow of shame has suddenly fallen upon her.

"Who says you're dumb?"

"Nobody... no one will tell you that to your face. But you can tell from anyone who... Well, if you get involved in something, they think you're stupid if you haven't gotten farther than elementary school and a few years of primary vocational education..." And if she'd been better at school, she certainly would have gotten further than being a hairdresser, which is actually in her estimation a stupid profession. For girls like her, she thinks, life is already fixed. A stupid job for a while, a stupid guy who never makes it farther than being a mechanic or something, or works in some stupid factory and who can only talk about work, cars and soccer. Then have some kids because that's the way it's supposed to be; always worries, you're always short of money, and that's your life.

Her look darkens more and more, and N. would like to make an objection, an answer to cheer her up, yet he knows she's right. Here speaks the instinct of a working-class child who, even without a substantial education, study or experience, already feels exactly how things stand in life, how the places, the opportunities are distributed, pointing unerringly on this sore spot of the human condition. She has the awareness, he thinks, but not the capacity to change it. He believes he feels sorry for her.

Promise me, Sonja, that we haven't spoken the last word about this. If you think I can help you with something, please assume that I want to help you. Will you accept that from me? The world with its possibilities is there for everyone, including you, certainly for you... He should have told her this, or something like it; words to that effect would have fallen onto very fertile ground. But he doesn't say them out loud because they already sound a bit inflated in his head. In his heart, he hates what he considers to be pathos, and also because all his life he's had difficulty being personal, empathetic (this unfortunate word), and how unadorned these words might have sat with this child with her natural inclination toward soaps and glitz and glamour. How he might have been able to achieve immediate success with her by stepping off his bicycle, wrapping his arms around her—an action which, in the given situation, is completely natural—then pressing her against him, rocking her, comforting her and kissing her (also completely logical) and perhaps even more things in the time to come, maybe soon. Away with this image too, of Adam and Eve in the garden of Eden, fig leaf and less, tree and fruit and compassionate snake and innocent-looking nature. It was just another opportunity lost; too bad.

But even this unspoken fact cannot prevent her face from clearing again and she laughs at him, teasingly punching him on the shoulder (working-class girls are hard, including on themselves, that's the only way for them to survive). Then she holds his hand on the bicycle handlebars for a moment, looking at him intently.

Some kind of confirmation? Of what? Camaraderie? Unity? A sorrow shared is a sorrow halved?

They come out at the main road between X and Q, cross it and soon arrive at the unpaved part of Vogelpoelweg, near the De Geus family farm. From there you can already see the Beumers' modest domain. Who'll be living there in fifty years? N. has thought about it before, during a walk or something. And will the De Geus farm still be a farm, or will it long have been bought up by some big shot who's had it rebuilt into his country house, a riding school or a stud farm? If, as he sincerely believes, if someone today leaves his native village at the age of eighteen to return there at the age of eighty-five, he can form a picture of how much human existence is one continuous war, even in a rich and free society.

"Waf-woof" woof-waf – Bart greets them, having already seen them coming from far away but who has been trained never to go any farther than the end of the exit on his own. N. gives Sonja a playful punch in a late answer to hers, which earns him a stern dressing down from Bart who is then wagging his tail and jumping with pleasure now that everyone is back around him. He turns then and runs out in front of them to announce their arrival to his mistress and her boyfriend, who are getting ready for the free weekend.

Olga and Theo put the summer chairs in a circle, something alcoholic is concocted in the garden, and they toast the upcoming free days (Sonja and N. have also taken Saturday off). It is during this pleasant get-together that the tenant, who is in a very good mood, promises to teach the Theo the basics of checkers.

That evening and night he works on his novel like a man possessed.

20.

That Monday morning, having finished his breakfast, he sits at the kitchen table and looks outside. It is cooler than the past Friday and Saturday, but the sky is clear blue, with an occasional whisp of white clouds on the western horizon yesterday: a diffident spy coming in from a rainy front near Ireland. The wind comes from the northeast, where a powerful high-pressure area has nestled as firmly as a castle, at least, for the time being.

When Olga comes in, she uncharacteristically closes the kitchen door behind her, indicating that she had come for something more than just coffee and a chat. She asks N. if she can talk to him about something, and he pulls up a chair for her, sitting down expectantly.

She tells him that she knows Sonja has talked extensively with him about her difficulties in school, and would Kees perhaps take a look at her daughter's reading and writing? After all, he was a teacher himself, so…

Kees nods, not exactly flattered by that additional comment. "I told her she can call on me any time. She can also treat this space like hers and come in as often as she wants." Seriously, as far as he's concerned, she can trample the door down. The more often the better, the alluring proximity of this specimen of forbidden fruit, given the manner of allure prevailing in his previous life and profession. N. shudders, as he'd been shuddering all weekend whenever he saw the child in her bikini, her completely superfluous top. The landlady's face is drawn into a shy smile.

"She said you gave her hope again. She said she wanted to try again because you wanted to listen to her."

"I've told her I want to help where I can."

"Her difficulty reading… could she have gotten that from me, by the way? I have a problem with that too."

When he learns that she had no difficulty with her mother tongue, he shakes his head professorially. No, he doesn't think so. He listens to her exogenous accent from somewhere in that endless Russian countryside with its varied phonetics, accents of innumerable dialects, each with a larger geographical spread than Dutch and Flemish put together. He asks, although it makes little difference, if she had taken an integration course in the Dutch language.

She tells him that she had taught herself to speak Dutch, by trial and error, by listening, from the subtitles on TV programs, and so on. When she had met Jan Beumer, he had helped her further so she could read the newspaper as well. But her language skills were insufficient to assist Sonja. "You know, Kees, sometimes I felt so helpless when I saw how much trouble she had with the language and I couldn't help her. That has eaten at me from time to time."

Chris nods. "Didn't they do anything for her at school?"

She shrugs her shoulders, fumbles for a cigarette. "At the elementary school here, they said that I had to resign myself to it, that Sonja just wasn't very gifted when it came to language, but that sort of thing didn't have to stand in the way of a nice job. Not every child is a top student. That kind of defeatism... I've been quite angry about that. But what can you do?"

N. emphasizes again that he'll see what he can do and that she can send her to him any time. Tucked away in some pocket of his brain where he stores images of photo and film room within his cerebral cortex, he entertains images of taiga and steppe landscapes from *Zhivago*, *Vojna I Mir* and *Pokhozhdeniya Chichikova* et cetera,. Off in the distance, a fragile blond girl, wearing a spotless white dress and with hat and ribbon from Chekhov waves at him, dancing and floating as if in slow motion. When the landlady unexpectedly bends over the table to clinch his offer and seals it with a kiss, he closes his eyes, realizing that these two people, Olga and her daughter, whose existence he'd been completely ignorant of just three months earlier, are now the only ones in his life. *I don't have anyone anymore,* he confides dry-eyed to his diary later that day, *my base has become very thin.*

They drink a cup of coffee, and Olga leaves for work.

A week passes before Sonja joins him at his table. A simple test with a few newspaper articles is enough for N. to determine that the child suffers from word blindness. Bearing in mind that dyslexia is often compounded by frustration and a lack of confidence, he downplays the problem in advance. He types a piece of text on his laptop and prints it out, then prints another sheet of paper with the words spaced out more widely than usual works wonders. He quickly diagnoses Sonja's problem as a *cas limite* (about thirty-five words per minute). Strangely enough, she seems to have difficulty with vowel connections. She doesn't know how to blend *au, ou, oe, ei, ie* and the like into a single sound when reading aloud. Onomatopoeias also causes her problems because she doesn't know how to connect sound imitations to the objects that cause the sound. "Sincerer," she stumbles with this word, sometimes with this form of adjectives, and afterwards doesn't recognize the same word in similar forms because she is constantly seeing nouns in it. In the spoken word, he occasionally hears a contamination (he had noticed it before). However, in a piece of text written by her the common inversion of the *b* and the *d* is not present, as is common, nor does she write the *s* in mirror image. There *are* a number of linguistic errors, but he thinks that she likely has a very light case, barely any dyslexia at all, he initially estimates; but most likely a simple reading disorder; an inevitable grammatical disadvantage that could easily have been remedied with a little extra attention, but had now been compounded by years of discouragement.

As his suspicion grows, he inwardly, curses those people who apparently came to the conclusion so easily that there was nothing to be done about the Beumer girl's weak reading and language skills. She is a victim—one of many, N. thinks—of what is by now the biggest national scandal: known as public education. Bureaucracy, departmental meddling down to the last decimal point, incompetent ministers interested only in fame, status and career advancement. who lack force or vision, considering money spent on special education, remedial teaching, management and coordination functions a waste. Given the chance, these people couldn't get rid of the actual teaching quickly enough. This whole scandal crystallizes in the case of Sonja Beumer, who deserves better.

I would have too, he guiltily thinks afterwards, *I, too, would have shirked that responsibility.*

He draws up a comprehensive treatment plan and she turns out to be a loyal and motivated student. Before the end of the summer holidays, he even dares to promise her that in a year's time, if she sticks with it, she will read and write as well as the average Dutch person. He watches over time as girl who used to make a rather quiet and humble impression on him brightens up, just like dew melting off a flower under the first rays of sunshine. More and more, he becomes her confidant. N. realizes that his help and dedication have bound him more and more to the small family, and he is aware of the danger this liaison entails. His "disinterested" commitment will make the two ladies conspire in tireless attempts to drag out the past of their still somewhat incomprehensible tenant and benefactor. He foresees graceful little fingers scratching at the canopy of his self-chosen exile and considers that if you are not served by such interest, you'd do better to be swallowed up in the impersonality of a big city. Perhaps it would be safer, he thinks, than to remain in a transparent countryside where every movement, every positive or negative side-step is noticed, analyzed and discussed among the tightly-knit population. He will need to remain alert.

On the other hand, the ladies' strategy of the advance party amuses him greatly; to be able to keep watching from the background, to catch and analyze probe vibrations and to decode all the reports from this post and to weave them into their pattern of suspicions and expectations. This advance party is, in any case, a happy development, because he too is gradually becoming curious and because N. always has his favorite brand of beer and liquor in stock.

21.

… Under the light of my desk lamp, a cockroach crawls cautiously onward, with its feelers scanning every unknown object it encounters. It's finished its investigation of a couple of pencils and has now moved on to my penholder. A few weeks ago, just after the first keystrokes, all at once, three suddenly came crawling out of my typewriter. Frightened and indignant, they rustled over my fingers, and for a brief moment, the hair on my arms stand on end. Since then, I have never failed to put the cover on the machine after I've finished working. Where do they come from?! It is a periodic plague. I recently saw an army of these insects crawling around on one of the tree trunks of the toddy palms along the street. They often lie trampled to death by pedestrians along the sidewalk; or crushed by car tires on the asphalt. Maryse was desperate. Cleanliness is important to her, and she doesn't understand how these creatures find their way inside. With my advice, she affixed strips on outside doors sills and along the edges of the mosquito nets, yet these pests just keep on invading.

N. sits before his laptop, pausing and re-reading. Feelers or not? Does an insect like that even have any damn feelers? And is that what you call those things? I'll have to check… And toddy palms? Is that how you spell it? Tomorrow I'll check Olga's encyclopedia or the internet.

N. corrects a few more typos, puts a few question marks in the margin, deletes a superfluous sentence, and resolves an inconsistency. He has no ambition to be a great writer; he lacks the talent or the genius for that. And perhaps also patience and the ability to sit still for any length of time. On the other hand, he has no desire to compete with all those egoistic Dutch celebrities who flood the market with unnecessary documents, written by hired ghostwriters. His main interest is in the creative process. He will be able to finish *The African Bride*, which he has now definitively started. But—and of this point he is sure—it will be, at best, at the level of secondary literature which might, like all secondary and trivial art anywhere, make the top ten best-sellers list before bubbling and fizzling out at a dizzying and dismal turnover rate.

A modest immortality is what he has in mind with *The Bride*, aside from expressing on paper his unmistakable preference for the *fruit vert* (skin color unimportant) and to some extent, who knows, also an artistic reflection of his everyday life, now and over time. He might also pursue the first of these in another medium. A reasonably successful drawing, a watercolor or oil painting for example, that adorns a private wall somewhere for a few generations as a forgotten or traditionally tolerated attribute. But he chooses the written word, his artistic preference. Once this manuscript is finished (he expects by the end of the year) he wants to have it printed independently, about a hundred copies (he already knows how and where). He'll provide an appropriate cover illustration himself. Then smuggle this non-ISBN-registered book into about twenty of the larger urban bookshops and discreetly leave them there in not-too-inconspicuous places in piles of five, without any prices, hoping they will find fans. (How would that go at the checkout…? Hmm, how much is this book… Just a moment, let me ask a colleague. N. chuckles at the thought a little bit) If one or two browned copies were found somewhere on a dusty bookshelf a hundred years from now, sold cheap at a book market, thumbing through a few grainy pages, his name being uttered one more time, he thinks he will have achieved his purpose. That's all he wants; a modest immortality, something very personal, something that survives his ever-so-fleeting mortal flesh for a few years.

N. is overcome by a riotous feeling of happiness, which suddenly drives him to work on the manuscript throughout that evening and into the night as if he were possessed.

<h1 style="text-align:center">22.</h1>

Theo—short for Theodorus Sluiter—is five foot seven, paunchy, and balding. He is dressed in shirt sleeves today because it is warm, oppressively warm, even in the evening. The three roe deer has grown into a herd of five some time ago Theo says it's because the "youngsters" of spring have grown up and joined the others. The landlady's boyfriend sits at N.'s kitchen table, prostatically uncomfortable, – he begins shifting in his chair, especially after a while. The advance party is a faithful, albeit not very quick, pupil. His stiff workman's fingers with rough nails grip the checker pieces as if they were tools. His eyes, as well as the frantic movements of his eyebrows and arms, reveal that this is completely strange and perhaps even dangerous territory for him. Even after some time, he struggles to set up good lines of attack and defense, to create combinations. It takes a while before he sees openings, even if they are as big as a barn, and when he does get there, his face brightens and a smile curls around his lips, but, sure enough, he still makes the wrong move. He always stays focused on the center play, so much so that he systematically neglects his wings. When he makes an attack, he invariably forgets his defense. N. has to play crazy moves just to reach a draw once in a while, let alone let him win. Occasionally, as they play, he stares at the other person so intently that N. can almost read his mind as they materialize into questions: who is this guy who's been living here for more than two months now? Who is this guy who is walks out into the woods with his landlady and her daughter just like that. This oddball doesn't seem to need anything more in life than a computer, a second-hand bicycle, a rickety TV and some furniture that doesn't even belong to him.

In turn, N. increasingly wonders how exactly to place the relationship between Olga and her boyfriend. Sometimes he is there almost every evening and night, even on the weekends, playing the role of an exemplary husband, partner or boyfriend. Then he disappears again for long stretches of time. N. also gets the impression that there are occasional fierce quarrels which drive the man and woman apart for longer times. N. reckons he's overheard such tiffs three or four times by now. Two days ago, for instance, he noticed the bickering of female and male voices in the house next to his door, growing louder, then followed by sounds of items being thrown, valuables smashed, and slamming doors, vehement enough to penetrate into his hut. Inevitably he heard Theo start his car and drive off. Maybe you could conclude it was a Russian temperament clashing with a Saxon willfulness, who knows.

To avoid discouraging his opponent too much, N. pushes for a tight draw. They conclude with a short evaluation.

"It seemed like the two of you perhaps had a difference of opinion the night before last?" N., as the host pours another beer, sits down opposite his guest at the window. The roe deer graze in the distance.

"The day before yesterday...? Oh, that," Theo shrugs his shoulders. "Ah, women, you know."

"Ehh..."

"Ah, them... them..." He nods towards the main dwelling, "Mother and daughter, they're two peas in a pod. You know how it is."

"What was it about?"

"Ah... nothing. Issues, just issues because vacation is coming." Theo looks troubled, takes a sip of beer. "They want," he continues after a brief silence, "*she* wants me to check the whole caravan again. I did that last year. There's nothing wrong with it, that caravan. Absolutely nothing. We can take it straight onto the road, but she says 'yes, but this' and 'yes, but that'. Those two, they see problems everywhere."

Then he reveals that he and Olga are going to France for four weeks in September, as they have been doing for years. They've never had any problems with the caravan, although it is already twenty years old. But he checks it every other year, but that "madam" thinks that, given its age, it should be done every year now. Again, Theo thinks this is completely unnecessary.

N. nods confidentially and throws a little oil on the fire, just a little bit. "You know, Theo, women always want to be a hundred percent sure of every angle before they start anything."

Well, exactly. Kees has been married too, so he must have had that experience too. Once they've set their mind on something, it's *impossible* to get them off it again, no matter how much nonsense it is to tear that old wreck apart again, to take the wheels off and check the bearings, the axles, the suspension. Of course, there was another stupid article published about it from the ANWB, something like a carefree vacation starts with a good inspection of your caravan. So then of course there's no stopping her demands then, and that Sonja—that dummy who is of course completely on her mother's side, even though she isn't even coming. – also thinks you can't take it on the road without it.

"Sonja? Dumb? What do you mean?"

Well, she can't even read a newspaper. If they watch a movie someone else has to read the subtitles for her. "If that's not stupid, I don't know what is. I really think she's retarded. She's not even dating anybody."

N. carefully enquires directly what the latter has to do with the former, because he doesn't see the connection right away. But his checkers partner opens his eyes with a highly enlightening move. He jumps his piece over two of N.'s, moving within a single field of becoming king, He bends over to the other confidentially, and says, "She doesn't want the pill... Well, then you'll get it of course." He winks, and nods, donning a conspiratorial smile between men.

"Why not?" Highly curious, N. very much wants to know, while he makes the question sound as casual as possible by starting to tidy up the checkers game.

"Olga scared her. She's been taking it since she was thirteen or so and thinks that that's where it comes from... that, with her throat." Theo points at the dark hairs under his Adam's apple.

"Her throat?"

"Her throat... her vocal cords, I don't know. That rasp. She's already been treated once. She thinks it's from the pill, and the little one is scared to death."

N. recalls the landlady's nicotine addiction, her greedy inhalation. A totally different cause seems obvious to him. Looking off for a moment into the distance, he is lost in thought; Farmer De Geus's tractor drives methodically into the meadow and across his field of vision, prompting the pair of roe deer to jump gracefully over the fence and disappear behind the forest's edge. The host empties his glass, says he wants to do some more work. The other takes the hint.

The Bride has really begun to take shape. N. fancies himself an occasional novelist, who is now finishing chapter five, and he did all that within two weeks, so he now dares to draw this cautious conclusion.

... The evening is slightly cooler for the first time in months. A gentle breeze has come up from the west, from the Volta Basin, a possible herald of rain. I hope so, I hope so with all my heart because I long for the promise of at least two or three days of clean streets, so we can sit on the rooftop terrace in the evening without constantly having to rub sand out of our eyes, to be able to breathe without dust in our throats. And if it pours, like last time, there will be at least a momentary pause to the water rationing. But then we'll have to worry about the fickle power supply due to short circuits in the overhead wires. There is always something wrong with the utilities here, and in order to survive in this jungle, we have learned to resign ourselves to this kind of inconvenience...

I am indeed expecting rain; my ankle has been nagging me for a day or so. The healed breaks and fractures make their presence known just to remind me that I should have used my crutches for a few more weeks.

He makes some corrections, reconsiders Theo's words, then settles in to read Montaigne for an hour.

23.

"Hello sir, this is OOZB life insurance… Can I ask you a question?"

Silence.

"You might have experienced an interruption in your pension at some point in your life. We at OOZB…"

"Ma'am, can I ask you something? Could you free up this line again immediately? Five minutes ago, the police called to say that my daughter has been seriously injured in a traffic accident. I expect a call from the hospital any moment. Can you imagine how *terribly* un…"

"Oooh, that's awful. Excuse me…"

(Half moaning, half screaming, half crying, pretending utter desperation): "For God's sake, madam, if you want to make some extra money, fine. But can you please find a more decent profession!"

"Oooh sir, please take…"

Damn, this device he muttered to himself. He was intensely irritated when his concentration was broken by spam calls while he was busy writing something in his home office. He always had to pick up because it could have been the faculty. A year or so ago, a broadcaster in its program guide, made useful suggestions about how to deal with this annoyance. But N. noticed that on the other side of the line, he had to deal with insensitive intruders, who sometimes laughed and had ready answers to questions like "how did you get my information?" and "can I ask how much you earn from these calls?" He saw this callousness as yet another proof of the degradation of manners, the total lack of respect for others, the penetration of abhorrent consumerism into the farthest corners of the personal sphere. All the more reason to jump from the moving train. *What a world*, he muttered to himself.

He hopes with all his heart that his response has given this OOZB hawker a ding in her conscience, but he doubts it. As far as he can tell, the average consumer is too stupid or lives too unconsciously to see what they're actually doing and what kind of world they live in.

His landlady handles her cellphone gracefully. He has a telephone available to him in his little dwelling that he doesn't, use, because he prefers his cellphone for the rare occasion that he makes a call. A while ago she asked if she could forward the phone to him when she wasn't at home because she preferred to keep her mobile number a secret, and you never know if there might be something urgent and someone may need to get ahold of her.

In this way, N. was able to form a general picture of the Beumers' social life. Of the phone calls received since then, two were for Sonja from a young lady who introduced herself as her friend and called herself Gea (N. has not yet seen the child visit Vogelpoelweg, though her voice is pleasant and civilized). Some phone calls are from the family care, usually with work messages that N. writes down and puts on Olga's kitchen table. Theo has been on the line a couple of times. There is also a lady who introduces herself as Tilly, who turns out to be a friend of Olga's. (N. caught a glimpse of her once.) A dark-haired Valkyrie (big and solid, about fifty years old) from Osnabrück with a green Land Rover and some horrible, yappy nervous non-Germanic dog that N. sincerely hoped would settle down once he saw Bart might (but Bart is much too good-natured, as the little thing even phlegmatically smelled under his tail). Sonja called once from Q asking if N. would pick her up from the bus stop because she had gotten a flat tire on her bike (N. picked her up and patched the tire). Then there were some silent calls where the connection was broken immediately after he made himself known.

And it is also in those weeks that he once spotted a car, a no-longer-new BMW, at the entrance to the main house which was empty at the time. A tall guy got out, walked down the driveway to take a look at the property with binoculars. When N. came out, he hustled back to his vehicle, backtracking down the Vogelpoelweg. To avoid causing commotion, he did not report this incident to the ladies, but it added to his vague sense of unease that had arisen after the first "silent" telephone calls.

This afternoon, another oppressively hot afternoon mid-August by now, he is on the lookout for Olga. He is sitting in front of the living room window, having just cleaned his brushes, letting the last strokes of oil paint dry (a landscape of a none-too-successful but nevertheless, recognizable De Geus farm in the background). He went outside for a while at lunchtime on his own, but the heat quickly became too stifling for him. When he saw the sunlight reflecting the blue of the Peugeot behind the bushes along the B-road, he quickly walked inside, and then studied Olga's movements in and around the house. Almost immediately after returning home, she began her predictable sunbathing routine. N. thought the habit to be somewhat in vain as he could detect only the slightest change in her skin tone, at most some red spots here and there. She does need to take precautions in order not to burn.

The previous day she had allowed herself to be tortured by the sun from as early as one o'clock, couldn't come up with an acceptable excuse for an apparently disinterested entrance. By the time it was four o'clock, and he'd gawked long enough at her white body and the reveled in how easily she prostituted herself to the sun, and with testosterone coursing through him, he walked out to greet her. Damn, hit had already been four weeks since his last carnal contact and he felt like he could pump at least half a cup of sperm into the landlady, and then again, and again. Observing her through the veil of his libido she was divinely beautiful with a long, slender and almost transparent body, and in his imagination, N. had already walked to the yard, onto the lawn, kneeling there, in trunks or without, and Olga welcomed him with an understanding smile, full of cooperation… And then he was jolted back to reality by farmer De Geus, that nasty devil, who seemed to think it was necessary to drive his tractor onto the pasture adjoining the landlady's property to start spreading fertilizer. Coincidence or criminal calculation, N. wonders. In any case, it was most clear not the most suitable time for coitus. N. sneered at the thought of spreading fertilizer in this sunshine, with no prospect of rain in the coming days; even a city slicker would know it wasn't the right time for such a thing. The man seemed to be insane. Surely the farmer did it on purpose, having seen the neighbor lady lying there from his farmyard. What do you want, his own wife isn't much, at least as far as her figure is concerned.

But today, there was no sign of tractor or car, even in the remote distance. And as for making an entrance: it's been agreed that he'll make fresh vegetable soup tonight for the three of them: Olga and Sonja and himself. High time then for the soup vegetables from the landlady's garden paradise, and maybe for more… And here is Sonja already.

Sonja pulls up on her bicycle, cool and collected and whistling cheerfully. She must have taken the afternoon off, the impossible child, to enjoy the beautiful weather. She calls to her mother. What's going on anyway?

He remains at his observation post for a while longer, suppressing his disappointment. She doesn't stir much as she lies there with her head in his direction holding her a hand above her eyes (where were you Kees, you idiot, what were you waiting for?).

But everything is movement and change, and if one doesn't come to the other, the other will come on its own. That is how creatures were created. She stands up, puts on her thin cotton robe or kimono and walks along the house to his front door. She knocks, then opens it immediately, and calls into the hall if she can speak to N. for a moment. Inside, she casts a glance over his painting in the works. She has already framed one of his watercolors (N. found an excellent framer in Y), and hung it in a very visible place in her living room. He promises her that if she likes this one as well, she can have it when it's finished.

"I'd love that. I already like it very much." She wishes she could paint too. But then he'd have to advise her on the choice of subjects. She sits down, lights her cigarette and her hoarse voice catches in a deep inhalation of smoke.

"But uh… what I'm here for, Kees… I think you know by now that Theo and I will be in France next month."

N. nods. "He did tell me, yes." The thought of that lucky dog being allowed to root around between her strong thighs uninterrupted for a month suddenly stirs him strongly, making him rather curt. He swallows something, a lump of jealousy.

"It's about Sonja," she continues. In the past she's always come along, but for the last couple of years, she hasn't wanted to anymore. Last year she was content to stay with her sister-in-law in Den Bosch, but now she didn't want to do that either. But the child is only sixteen and her mother doesn't feel comfortable letting her stay here alone for a month.

N. nods and she continues: "Would you… would you be willing to take care of her a bit?"

"How do you mean, Olga?" He feigns ignorance, wanting to stretch out this conversation, stretch it out endlessly. Because what sits opposite him in the chair, is the magnificently tight body of a self-confident, self-caring woman in her early forties who, the norm once developed demands it, it is covered, even at 30 degrees Celsius. Due to the extreme temperature, the cover only consists of a thin layer of fabric, so nonchalantly draped over her shoulders, which somehow makes her appear to be more naked than without it. He thinks back on their short penetration, an unsatisfactory, interrupted coitus, which she has made no allusion to afterwards. It's been six weeks already—my god, where does the time go! This has to be different, definitely different. N. sweats with lust and desire; it is as if something is snapping in his loins and at this very glowing moment he decides that he will contact the escort agency again tomorrow, the day after tomorrow at the latest. If necessary, he'll book a little hotel in Y.

Well – she says, in a flat tone, as if to deliberately ignore N.'s scandalous Eros, maybe to make him insane with desire – my daughter says she doesn't want to be put up anywhere, but she is also afraid to be alone. For example, perhaps he and Sonja could eat together in the evenings. She doesn't have to bother him beyond that, and they could also eat at her home, for example, if it made things easier. Sonja said she'd even be willing to do the cooking. "The important thing is that she knows you're around. Then she'll feel OK about being here alone at night."

The lady looks at her tenant; seasoned as a nurse to her patient intuitively knowing how to temper his hot state of mind. She lights another cigarette, she would have jangled and sparkled with all her jewelry if she had been wearing it and N. notices she lacks her usual adornment. "You know, Kees, she'll be fine as long as she can be sure that she can knock on your door if she thinks there's any danger. And Bart will still be here, of course. We keep him in the hall at night."

"Doesn't she have a boyfriend?" (Still stretching the time, as well as an attempt to invalidate Theo's hypothesis.) So far, he's never seen Sonja in the company of her peers outside of work.

"Well, not that I know of. She was flirting with someone a bit for a while last winter. But that's over, at least I haven't noticed anything. I don't think it did much for her, either."

N. agrees spontaneously; he can imagine less pleasant company. His fevered desire has simmered down a bit, but he continues to taste bitterness at the prospect of the landlady's imminent absence. They chat a little about the vacation destination. It emerges that for years the family has been going to Franche-Comté for a month each fall, to a village not far from Besancon. For Olga, it is the countryside that attracts her. She describes a type of paradise on earth that the locals, usually see so very differently day in and day out as they work for a living.

"I'll show you pictures tomorrow, then you'll see what I mean," she says, then adds after an inhale of her cigarette, "I'd prefer to sell this place and start a new life there."

"What's stopping you?"

Her gaze penetrates him as she studies him carefully.

"Well, then, what would happen to you?"

That smile, all smiles, but nevertheless, without any trace of joy: "Maybe you can count me among your things and sell me too, like your other possessions. Maybe to another nice landlady like you." He laughs out loud; at his own stupid, yearningly desperate words.

She sighs and licks her lips. "I think I would get very jealous. I'd much rather keep you for myself." Now she laughs too, loudly, at her own stupid and yearning remark, who can say?. She bends forward a little so the cover around her upper body falls open, exposing one of her areolas and smiles at him. Then she crosses one leg over the other, which exposes her thigh so far that in the hot warm space in between her golden blond edged pubic crevice winks at him for a second and, to avoid letting his erection make a fool of him, he is forced to make the same movement. Then he is struck by the powerful realization again that things can fall into place in a completely natural way. His existence here, with a matter of patience and initiative, could soon be punctuated with a bit of excitement. Of course, it is a shame, a great shame about that month-long vacation; a useless lost month of extra delay. N. knows that he can only blame himself.

The conversation stalls, the veil of their desires had been exposed a bit too far. Two people, still searching, groping for words now that emotions have been revealed. A step back is appropriate, a false retreat, a moment to catch your breath to be able to re-assess your position once more. Then, there is N.'s question whether Theo has already checked the caravan.

The landlady scoffs, giving him a disturbed look that says very clearly: clearly She would like to talk about anything other than Theo.

"Leave that to me," is her grumpy reaction. She feels her firm nipples, scratching thoughtfully over her masculine chest. A flesh-red stripe along the underside of her breast betrays that an implant has probably been put in. He pours a soft drink with mixed fruit juice. They talk a little longer about her vacation, and he tells her of his own vacations in past years, where he went, where he didn't go but wished he had, what he saw. Then suddenly she interrupts him.

"Kees, listen. I don't know if you're aware, but Sonja is, uh… well, she's become quite fond of you. Ever since you've been helping her read and write and you've been riding together. She's constantly talking about you. It's Kees this, Kees that. I can't rule out the possibility that in the time to come, if you two… let's say that you are left to rely on each other, she may decide to show it. I have that feeling… Can I assume, Kees," She looks at him probingly, "can I assume that you will handle that, uh… in a sensible, let's say mature way?"

What does she mean by sensible, what does she mean by mature?

"I mean," she says slowly and emphatically, staring pointedly at him now, "I mean, I don't want to have to deal with a teenage pregnancy and then the trouble with an abortion. Not here, in this neighborhood. Do you understand?"

He groans noiselessly and must have almost literally opened his ears at these words. He wants to say something, words of reassurance, or even indignation (come on Olga, what do you take me for?!). He owes it to his honor, to defend his values. There is a fire glowing inside him again, alongside a feeling of frustration because of the fact that he, precisely with his watchful eye and an ear for certain dispositions, has apparently overlooked her growing affection. At that very moment, the teenage child enters, having showered and all, even though she's only walked the short way from the center of Q. It doesn't seem to matter how beautiful the weather is, how clear the monthly forecast may be, she only wants to cycle to work when N. is with her. He pours Sonja a mixed juice too, trembling almost spasmodically, and then he and Olga agree that it's just about time to switch to something alcoholic. The three of them chat about vacations and other light topics of conversation. N. casts a completely different gaze at Sonja, with furtive eyes over this young girl who might make herself available to him. At the end of this conversation—all of which he wouldn't be able to reproduce a single word, passes through his mind without any permanence—he reminds the mother and daughter that he plans to prepare dinner for them tonight. Then, with an internal cheer and feeling completely sloshed from two glasses of white wine, he hastens to the vegetable garden. With a head rolling and spinning from the tantalizing scenes, both real and imagined, he cuts parsley and celery.

An (in)explicable cheerfulness has come over him, one that he manages to enjoy for the rest of the afternoon and evening. The ladies lavish him with praise over the vegetable soup; the evening is pleasant and it all merges into warm thoughts and a golden out-look. He lets go of his prior intention to call the escort service.

Later that evening, rather than letting himself be lulled by Montaigne's righteous babbling, he gives in to the comfort of very different imagined pleasures. The next day, he promises Olga, playing docile schoolboy to compassionate teacher – to be good for four weeks, and very sensible too.

24.

No Rochefoucauld anywhere in Y. The town has three decent bookstores and a well-stocked antiquarian bookshop, but it is apparently ignorant to the oeuvre of this French moralist. Finally in the friendly town of Osnabrück, in a book stall along a crooked warehouse lane, N. finds an untranslated pre-war edition of *Maximes* as well as a collection of aphorisms by Chamfort and a stray copy of Bernhard's *Beton* (he likes to read his German). The books are rust-brown from age, stacked beneath a mountain of other second- and third-hand books. He'd made the trip with Olga who was visiting her German girlfriend, Tilly. She had dropped him off in the city center with plans to meet each other there again in two hours, a couple of hours without each other should be manageable, and then go have coffee and lunch; it seemed better to her that Tilly didn't see them together as long as Theo was still in her life. As far as he could tell, the entire conversation was coded in innuendo.

The current arrangement makes N. feel untethered and more than a little put out. In recent weeks, he'd put a lot of time and energy into tutoring Sonja, strengthening her perception and text interpretation, and his temporary hiatus caused him a slight depression. Sonja was on vacation: ten days on Terschelling together with her friend, Gea. Meanwhile, on the home front, Theo had become inseparable from Olga so any erotic *passe-temps* had become out of the question. All the days off looked dead and useless. N.'s reluctance and existential despair crept up on him strongly.

But yesterday morning the sun shone with all its warmth, and it seemed to radiate through to his mood. In the post box at the road, he had found an envelope, its golden contents addressed to him, with a shiny blue and pale yellow postcard from the Wadden coast on one side and on the other Sonja's hasty handwriting. She wrote of the lovely temperatures of the North Sea, that she can barely wait to cycle to X together with him again soon. She closed with, *Lots of love and willingly, your Sonja (please don't tell Mommy!)* It was undoubtedly because of this slightly personal tone that she decided to place her postcard in the envelope. The thought gave N. a tingling sensation in his scrotum which injected a bright energy into his afternoon; bold, tantalizing thoughts swirled in his head unceasingly. Was Olga right, after all? Would the kid truly make herself available to him? (He hadn't allowed himself to believe it until then.) The depressive slump passed on the spot.

Olga and Theo are in full swing with preparations for their vacation. They will leave in a week. Theo's caravan has been scrubbed down thoroughly, inside and out, as if it was a labor of love. Patches of paint have been applied here and there. With inevitable grumbling, Theo had given in, crawled under the vehicle, unbolted the wheels, and greased the wheel bearings. He replaced a broken brake light. At one point, N. noticed the jack sagging and, seeing that the poor soul was about to have the whole caravan come down on top of him, stepped in to offer a helping hand. On August 24th, the three of them celebrated Theo's fifty-first birthday. They toasted Theo's many attributes—both real and imagined—in N.'s suite before the three of them stumbled off to a small but cozy restaurant hidden in the woods somewhere, halfway between Q and X. One advantage of the countryside, N. noted, are the labyrinth of roads between B and C, to avoid police surveillance.

Nevertheless, even this momentary diversion offered by N. (and appreciated by the landlady and her boyfriend in every way) was not enough to erase the lethargy still dragging away at him. He thought he had detected the cause: all those hot promises and warm prospects, of which nothing had yet been redeemed, made him feel abandoned, empty even. He began to feel withered. Later in his diary, which he has begun to refer to as 'cynical' he writes: *Maybe I unconsciously caught a glimpse into the essence of things, and in so doing, I looked at that truth which kills action. I have lost the illusion that action might change something about the eternal nature of things.* He too believed himself far away from any metaphysical comfort and saw himself confronted with Maya's unraveling veil. This misinterpretation and misjudgment of his mood and general state of mind (he would soon realize) led to an artificial and somewhat shameful "cry of distress". *Maybe I am suffering from loneliness after all. Three months ago I would never have believed it could get hold of me. One must be careful not to overestimate his own humanity. When it comes to essential existential matters, we are all just trivial cogs in an immense universe.*

A consolation, and anything but metaphysical: four days after the postcard and two days before the landlady and her boyfriend are set to leave, Sonja returns from Terschelling. Windblown, relaxed and, despite her fragile skin, a little tanned, her return puts an end to his moping and moaning. *Although this will not change anything about the eternal being of things*, he still dares to write in his diary, *this simple soul that is now back at my side lights up my temporality here on earth, and with her, returns meaning to my life.*

Two days later, he and Sonja wave goodbye to Olga and Theo, first on the bumpy driveway and then until they disappeared out of sight in a bend of the Vogelpoelweg. Bart, as if to dissuade them from leaving, had continued to bark at the car and caravan all the way to the pavement before he finally gave up and rejoined N. and Sonja at the house.

25.

N.'s initial optimism regarding the degree of Sonja's dyslexia fades as their work together continues. But, having long been made aware of this deficiency, she clings to his modest therapy with persistence and is indisputably making progress.

She still has a week remaining of vacation time from work and N. has just started two weeks of leave, one week paid (thanks to Piet de Wilde's infinite goodness), and one week unpaid. The younger Beumer and he have agreed to have hot meals together and to take turns cooking. To celebrate both their vacations, they take the slow train to Y a few evenings to visit a pizzeria. Sonja asks with surprise why he doesn't take her mother's car, and he responds with the convenient excuse that he wants to drink a few glasses of wine and doesn't want to drive home impaired.

One afternoon as N. works on a watercolor she enters his suite and, deliberately making noise being still a bit shy about entering uninvited, sticks her head around the door. At his invitation she shuffles inside, looks around humming, studying the few paintings he has set around the room. There are pen and charcoal drawings, a few of which he has had framed and hung on the wall.

"Hey, do you draw nude too?"

"A nude or nudes," he corrects her, and they both fall into an uncontrollable laugh that is extinguished suddenly in the awkwardness that reigns in every area they have not yet explored together. Sixteen years ago, during his short spell at the art academy, N. met another student who he lived with for a while and who posed for him. He carries the photo of one of these nudes, the best one he did, in his wallet. And he used this photo last month to bring the beloved memory of his former roommate back to life artistically. A fusain, somewhat stylized.

"A friend of mine. She went to art school with me."

"You went there?"

He nods. "Six months, and then I'd had enough already. I knew I would never become a great artist." He means to tell her that when he had expressed the desire to learn to draw and paint

146

to a few gathered teachers, they answered with Homeric laughter, followed by a question, asked in slightly too high a tone, what he thought he wanted to draw and paint. What he failed to understand, young and naïve as he was, that museum basements were full of figurative art. "There are piles, young man, towering piles, just lying there moldy and rotting." It was quickly made clear to him that continuing down that road would mean the end of art. Indeed the future lay now in the cinematic arts. N. realized quickly that he was facing an institution which, although they were right of course, embodied the end of art. He wished afterward that he had said it their faces. But his insights were not mature and not well-formed enough, and he was not confident enough to know that his distaste for the whole thing had been instinctive.

A week later, he dropped out, and even today he is a little bit proud of this decision to want to take himself seriously in the face of the chaotic, dreary mix of art directions, art explosions and the infamous "isms" of the twentieth-century avant-garde. This was the inevitable result, he firmly believes, of the absurd attempt to democratize art and make it accessible to a wider public. Art that is not at least somewhat elitist, that doesn't shun artistic illiteracy, art without a canon is, in N.'s opinion, stronger today than ever. It has doomed art as a whole to death because it is corrupt.

He had drawn these conclusions when he was nineteen, and he is pleased at how well they have stood the test of time. More or less like the mathematician who waits eighty years for the world to catch up and see the blatancy of his truth, N. believes that a human life is probably too short to wait for the age of new, truly groundbreaking work in figurative painting, or art in general actually. He does not yet see the long-expected paradigm shift he yearns for, peeking above the horizon, which is all the more reason to take himself seriously and keep his back straight.

Oh, how he wishes for a moment that Sonja was someone he could have such a robust discussion about all this with today!

She has looked around with a studious face, and then says, "I think what you make is quite beautiful."

"Beautiful perhaps, but, in any case, amateurish. An art critic would be annoyed, or die laughing." (Probably not even. On the contrary, they might even give it serious consideration.) For her, the words "Art academy", "art critic", "amateurism"; the entire conversation, really, for falls in the category of just "difficult words". Most definitely.

"I don't care. I like it." She's looking at the oil painting he finished at the end of last week. "Is this Jan de Geus' farm?"

N. nods. There is too much black mixed with the green where he's shaded the forest behind it, suggesting the threat of a thunderstorm rather than the edge of a forest. De Geus, a tough blond man in his fifties, will occasionally chat with N. when he comes back from a walk. Mrs. de Geus, a skittish little woman, always hurries away behind a wall or outbuilding when she sees him coming, although she did once raise her hand to him from a distance.

"Do you have to take all your clothes off when you make that?" She giggles, pointing again at the charcoal drawing.

"Not necessarily, the model can keep her panties on."

"Did she keep them on then?" Suddenly she stares fixedly at him with a punitive gaze. What an affected and therefore beautiful person, a child who can lay no claim to you, to see you pretend so clumsily.

"I don't remember." He lies; these sessions almost invariably ended with lovemaking. He remembers them clearly, including the smell of her sweat, her vaginal fluid and his cum. Mabel always fluttered around naked through his bedroom-cum-studio. She had a beautiful figure, nothing that even remotely suggested that adorable body would soon be swallowed by fat in such a relatively short amount of time. Yet it was her, the blimped-out woman he had unexpectedly bumped into in the city center one morning two years ago, her hair pulled back into a spindly knot, holding the hand of a child, a daughter, with one hand and pushing a stroller with the other. It was a shock to him, the first time he experienced the transience of physicality. And she must have read that dismay on his face, seeing herself suddenly through his eyes. After a brief exchange in recognized glances, she turned away with a grim look, feigning interest in some innocuous item in a shop window. They did not exchange a word and afterward N. had had a bad day.

"Would you like to draw me naked as well?" She giggles again, a bit forced now. this girl who N. thinks that in all likelihood will still have the same fragile figure in ten- or twenty-years' time, at least if she takes after her mother in that respect, and why wouldn't she?

"If you'd like," he says, vaguely. His immense desire is nicely wrapped, the way back is already closed. He doesn't want to lose face— no guy wants that. Still, the affections poured upon him by the mother and daughter have given him occasion to live through this fantasy, recolored and replayed by his imagination. He has anticipated the questions, answers, sentences, entanglements, and already he's developed something of a strategy. These fantasies are a delicious, intoxicating drink, a heady elixir that raises questions like, *is this not the aim of all masculine endeavors? Even in the time of hunters and gatherers, in those first agricultural settlements of human existence, and in all the later centuries of Greco-Roman enlightenment, Christian-Muslim darkness and profane rationalism*, N. thinks, *doesn't it all come down to men's desire for female flesh?* Caliph and seraglio, emperor and prostitute, king and maintenee, cardinal and concubine, Picasso and his Dora, Rodin and his Camille, he and his Beatrice, J.J. and his visions; throughout history, the acts are always in service of the sacred task of planting the seed in beneficiary females. *What is man's purpose but to care for the reproduction of the species and then to die? Be fruitful, and multiply!* (Genesis 1:28). After all, isn't the rest of life just a prelude and an afterthought?

All these thoughts parade through his mind, but his only response is, "If you'd like." Indeed, why do girls so easily sell their souls and salvation to the devil and his damnation for the thrill of posing naked? N. asks himself this with the sly smile of a clever older fox. Is there still a sacred need to sacrifice the body? He is sure that Olga will catch wind of this sooner or later. Between her cunning instinct and the camaraderie she shares with her daughter, the events will come to light. And then what? Will he be forced to hastily pack up and leave? That would be a pity, a great pity.

"Will I take everything off then?"

"Go ahead." N. suddenly feels a tremor roll from his head to his toes and back up. The tangibility of his fantasies laid out before him with her eager "When are we going to do that, then?"

She looks at him, mischievous and lewd and suddenly conspiratorial.

"The day after tomorrow? Then I'll be done with this one." He shrugs toward his easel.

"What time?"

"In the afternoon. Then I can keep working for a while in the morning."

"Do I have to pose the whole time?"

"Only when I need you, on call. You can do other things in between. I don't have to watch you the whole time."

They drink coffee and then she proposes—practically buzzing with the anticipation of this exciting prospect—cooking at his place tonight, saying that she finds it much cozier at his than in the big house.

That morning at about eight o'clock he sees her riding away on her bike. She returns at noon with a shopping bag on her carrier. That afternoon she enters his house, her ponytail pulled into a bun. She's put a hint of rouge on her lips, making her look older and a lot more feminine and lending a vague sense of depravity, considering her age. She wears a loose blouse, probably from Olga's wardrobe, with the neckline cut so low that the slightest movement of her upper body reveals the hint of her nipples. Around her belly and thighs, her cotton pants are so tight that the sacred cavity between her pudenda is clearly visible. Red pumps give her tall frame a certain awkward regality. All this, N. expects, has been done to give the impression of an experienced woman's maturity, but to N. it seems just a bit ridiculous. Her performance is the fruit of her imagination, how she believes a model moves in a painter's studio. And she looks at him, so obviously seeking a compliment, so he lies and says that she has good taste, asking if the blouse is one of her mother's.

"Darn it, nothing gets by you. Don't tell Mommy. Does it really suit me?"

N., who will do anything, anything at all, to maintain the anticipatory atmosphere of the afternoon, repeats his compliment. They eat a sandwich, drink coffee. Then he pulls up his easel, silently, and gives her a look of *well, shall we…* She disappears to his bedroom, giggling in the hallway, and returns a few moments later, naked except for translucent panties.

"Is this okay? What do you think? I went to Y for them this morning." She points to her delicate lingerie. She stands there, looking at him and around like a white chicken in a completely unknown environment, alone in the wild. The fabric is so scant that an edge of her white-blond pubic hair remains uncovered. There is a slit at the vulva making him fall instantly in love. Christine le Duc in the countryside. Once again, the profound amateurism of her attempt to look sexy endears her to him.

N. clears the table and asks her to pose in front of it. Buttocks against the edge, hands flat on the top, chest forward, head up, one foot on the ground, one calf crossed over the other. In all her unabashed nakedness, without realizing it, the position is not at all erotic. He has promised that he will capture her life-sized in pastel, as she thinks charcoal is a bit boring. It will be a slightly sexy image, also at her request, to which he will add stylized touches here and there. Because her chest is so completely flat, he proposed giving her breasts, and she readily agreed.

As he begins his work, he inquires if she has a boyfriend.

The slim blond muse releases her stretched posture for a moment. "Not a chance, man."

He gives her an inquisitive glance.

"You see this?" She lifts up her chest, looks down. Two peas on a shelf. "Guys want girls with big tits. I've been with boys a couple of times. But, when I let them under my blouse, they suddenly have all kinds of excuses for why they stop coming around."

"They could still come, you're still young."

"Not likely. Mommy never got them either, not even when she was pregnant with me."

"Big boobs aren't important to all boys." He has to swallow saliva. He suspects his face bears the empty, sperm-white expression of the anonymous child molester, standing at the edge of the near-empty schoolyard, trying out a repertoire of naïve suggestive remarks on that one timid, hesitant schoolgirl who stayed behind.

"Yeah but," she continues, "there's a big difference between big boobs and nothing at all." She looks a bit sadly at her flat front. "If I didn't… if I didn't have that there (she points between her legs), I could pass for a boy."

"I think when it comes down to it, 'that there' is much more important to boys than boobs," the failed teacher retraces his own glowing past. A yearning shiver runs up his spine again, cuts between his buttock, exits through his toes.

Then Bart goes crazy with his savage warning of strangers approaching. N. looks out the window. and sees a car approaching down the drive. Sonja swiftly disappears to his bedroom as he walks outside. They are people who (it has happened before) missed the "no through traffic" sign. He manages to explain to the occupants—the driver a young Turkish man, next to him a blond wife or mistress, and in the back seat two creole-looking children—that they are on private property. They apologize profusely in a thick accent and reverse the car joltingly back up the driveway.

In any case, after about an hour and a half the session is over. The main outlines have been set; he will add the details later. Sonja dresses again and he puts on coffee. She offers to cook again tonight, and he eagerly accepts. That evening they watch TV on his couch, a completely trivial music video program with three-quarter naked singers backing up a young, hot-blooded but third-rate front man. The girls in the crowd faint with hysteria. Sonja sits with her arm around his shoulder, the picture of an innocent child next to her kind-hearted, patient dad. He can smell her skin, her body; it's the very specific scent of a young girl, with something perhaps a little spicy. He wishes he could discover what lies in her head and soul and desire, turning over cell after cell to find out what place he occupies in her experience.

At half past one, a little drowsy from two glasses of red wine, she returns to the big house to sleep. He gives her a modest and innocent kiss at the door. She had allowed him to occasionally to run his fingers over her flat bosom, feeling her nipples grow hard under his fingers. Then she would look up at him dreamy and smiling, over and over again, displaying herself to facilitate his trembling groping. Now and then he could smell her vagina, like a bitch in heat. When she laid her head against his belly, he pulled the pin out of her tucked up hair, releasing her ponytail from its band, and stroked the edge of the hairline at her neck. She purred like a cat and became putty in his hands. She started humming again, her long blond hair loose and seductive. He made out the undeniable outline of a condom in the pocket of her pants, tightly stretched over her thigh. Just in case? What outcome of this memorable day might she have had in mind? It was also close as far as she was concerned, and they had sighed. Olga's admonition and her fixing gaze became suddenly clear in his mind, and he stopped, just in the nick of time.

She put both arms around his neck a few times, kissing him wetly and deeply. She returned her attention to the TV, dreamily, and at one point fell asleep with her head in his lap.

A few days later he finishes the pastel drawing of her, pleased with the likeness. He has it framed and gives it to Sonja, whose pleasure and appreciation is uncontainable.

26.

September came in with beautiful weather and a quiet peace, signaling the end of summer holidays. Sonja and N. cycle to and from work together daily without any need of raingear. An easterly wind brought dry, clear skies and an innocent high pressure system nestled over the Baltic states. But the forecast is calling for a change in the weather, which is accompanied by an increasing, sweltering heat.

It is on one such sweltering Sunday in mid-September, following breakfast together, that N. and Sonja sit at his table working at some text exercises. They study style forms, and, to improve her visual-spatial capacities he has her write longer sentences. He coaches her through sentences with subordinate clauses and parentheses, adding more and more adjectives until she completely loses control over the text.

What would we be without language? he lightly muses as he waits for her to puzzle through a challenging clause. Language makes us what we are, or so the philosophers of language would have us believe. But isn't it also true that language helped us create our own sense of being? Language is also a pre-eminent cultural resource, a trick we use to smooth out and cover up the bumps and knocks of the process of life, making it seem more fluid and unbroken. It is a vehicle on rails so we don't feel the unevenness of the ground beneath us. *We read*, he thinks, *and write and speak without any notion of this artifice. Unless we're especially dyslexic.* one can only can only consider language as a construct, in constant confrontation with the crumbling nature of this process that flows so smoothly to the eye and the ear. They are the ones who keep stumbling over the fact that each individual word is a unit, unmasking the artificiality and preventing them from whirling across our senses like skaters on ice. *Who knows*, he thinks, *perhaps that's the reason for their instinctive aversion to text.*

Later on, in the afternoon, they sit outside on a bench in the shade of a pear tree. The sound of a propeller plane plowing its way through the air rumbles somewhere above them. Sonja looks at yesterday's newspaper that had been dutifully placed in the old front door mailbox by the delivery woman, a beautiful Sri Lankan adopted child with big innocent eyes, all black and white and pink and smile.

"What is esth... ethereal?"

N. looks. "Ethereal." He explains it to her.

"And child… squaw?"

He also tries to explain, but without much success. because he doesn't know how to interpret the metaphor that contains the word.

"Why do they always use such difficult words? Who understands this?"

He doesn't think there are many difficult words in this newspaper.

"Mmm, I think there are." She coos, folds the newspaper and puts an arm around him. He wraps an arm around her, lightly grazes her nipple, then asks why she brought a condom with her the previous week. She blushes; her face would have turned crimson if her pale skin would let her take on such a color. She looks at him, and when she realizes it is pointless to deny it, she says it all so quickly and in a single breath, which he is not used to since she usually expresses herself in short sentences – that he should know that she only wants to have sex with a condom because she hates the pill because she doesn't know what it might do to her body. She looked at him then, pleadingly, and when he did not respond, she continued with a second breath. Well, what did he think of all the boys she's had so far—and there really haven't been many—they all snapped at her when she brought out one of those things, and once they know that about you, rumors spread like wildfire and then everyone knows you're not cool anymore. But boys have plenty of choices; almost all the girls she knows choose not to use one, even take the morning after pill if necessary. And if things get completely out of hand. there is the clinic. She tells him that one of her classmates, a girl even younger than her, has already had to travel down that route twice.

She chuckles, giving the impression again of a much more experienced woman. "Mommy said once…" she says shyly, then gives N. an appraising look, "she said… well she said that all guys want from you is to fuck you, get on, get off, without any nagging, then leave you with the worries. They don't care that, that… Oooh, why am I saying all this to you?" She puts her hand over her mouth as if suddenly realizing that she's talking with a near-stranger. "Are you someone like that, Kees?"

A hush falls around them like a heavy atmosphere, every word seems to assume a tone of intimacy, now. Excitement tingles in his scrotum as N. realizes that *the* moment is close, in other words, tangible. He is silent. Shivers and trembles move through him and he puts his arm around Sonja's shoulder, pulls her to him, feels the warmth of her body combining with his own. She wraps both arms around him then, kisses him, saying she is lonely and cold, even though the temperature is nearly 100° F. His head spinning, already intoxicated with desire. It's now just a matter of tactics and strategy. He must proceed with caution to avoid crossing the line; she is still just a girl, new to emancipation, provocation, with still a hint of childhood, adolescence, just on the edge of adulthood (depending on her mood and temperament). But still, somehow, she has gained empathy, perhaps an (over)sensitivity and obvious considerations for the opposite sex, brought up in an era of pervasive persuasion by mass media with its excessive array of mixed messages and complications between both sexes, love-laden (maybe even puppy love to spice it up) ... With caution he perseveres, onward toward the holy grail: her sacred body.

Something like that.

They take another look at the postcard that had been sent from eastern France five days earlier. On the front is a photo of an autumnal Franche-Comté, full of seductive brown and green, grand desolation and sublime nothingness. On the back, Olga's graceful handwriting tells of fine weather, with the exception of a few hefty thunderstorms which actually provided a welcome break from the heat. In blocky handwriting, Theo adds a few comments about the food and drink on their holiday. Above them, two buzzards float high in the air over De Geus's meadows, beset by sanctimonious crows. Flies and bees buzz, and butterflies, damselflies and other net-winged insects flutter and dart about. Bart, ever-present when food is set on the table, occasionally snaps at wasps that swarm to the sweetness of the fruit of the plum tree, grinding them between his teeth apparently without being stung. Then he sighs, looks at the man and girl, and rests his head on his front paws. There are a few thin clouds overhead, but no wind, and the temperatures spike to 30°C in the shade. Another propeller plane rumbles overhead, out of sight. One of the sheep, panting in the heat, finally turns to chase away a goat that was annoyingly bumping her behind; the pony incessantly swishes her tail at flies. A motorcycle, a two-cylinder four-stroke, burbles over the Vogelpoelweg. Maybe a Harley, N. thinks.

He closes his eyes and senses the return of silence around him. An image suddenly occurs to him; he imagines taking Sonja to Manaus, next spring, to join him there as his life companion. In that verdant jungle he could take her as his girlfriend, partner and wife if necessary. She will barely age outwardly for the next twenty years. For a moment he imagines himself in the cliché of the "paradisical" situation; an old man with his child bride in some foreign but pleasant climate. *I have to be careful*; he thinks, *I can't get too cozy here*. Behind his eyelids he sees a railway embankment and a rushing train, at once so clearly, so vividly, that it becomes real to him. But now, suddenly, he sees himself *inside* the train.

The thunderstorm finally came near dusk and, after a short break, continued through the night. It had been rumbling at the edge of their horizon to the southwest all afternoon, the atmosphere becoming increasingly muggy and the blue of the morning sky imperceptibly turned into a hazy and then milky white. At just after six o'clock, however, the calamity is still at a distance. N. is busy in the kitchen; it is his turn to prepare a nice evening meal for the two of them. Sonja has wandered to the other house to watch a video, something she said she could not play on his old TV set. A prismatic effect of sunlight creates a purple and greenish sky that washes over quickly and implacably as the first signs of thunder and lightning—still a few kilometers to the north— roll toward Vogelpoelweg with wind and rain. Then a hard light wraps the surroundings in silver foil for a moment, and almost simultaneously a sharp, hard crack. There is a "ting" in the telephone and the fluorescent tube over the sink goes out. Rain and wind lash his place in an instant downpour and then he hears the front door open and then slam close. A soaking wet and dripping Sonja enters the kitchen, with Bart following closely at her heels.

"Oh Kees, I'm so scared! The lights have gone out!"

She wraps her arms around him, her wet hair clinging to his cheek, her fright conveyed directly to his chest which hammers with joy as he holds her and kisses her.

Another flash follows, with a bang shortly behind it, and then another. The small, dark apartment lights up as if a glowing mass is smashed into pieces in the yard, the wind rattles the roof panels, the trusses groan and sway. This short salvo is only a prelude to a thunderstorm more raucous and wilder than any N. can remember in his lifetime. Then as suddenly as it came, the wind abates and a threatening, anticipatory silence falls over the small apartment. Outside, all that remains is a gray sheet of rain that lays upon everything in a deluge before giving way to hailstones the size of ping-pong balls, bouncing off the roof pelting the pasture outside. For a moment, N. feels as though he is in the middle of an artillery offensive. The sound is so deafening that he has to yell to be heard by Sonja. Then there is another flash-bang, this time right in front of the side window, so close that it looks as though it has actually struck down in the pasture outside. The goats and sheep begin bleating wildly, yammering in their pens with a harrowing lament. Bart whines softly, his ears stretched out and his head and tail hanging down. He slinks through the kitchen, resting his head on N.'s knee with a look of "is really this necessary?" In another flash of light, N. can see De Geus's cows standing huddled in the distance, backs turned, facing in one direction.

It takes about three hours before the hail and rain starts to recede. By half past nine there is the beginning of a leak in the kitchen and a small stream of water has wound a path across the doorstep. N. is sweating from every pore and Sonja sits next to him on a kitchen chair. She has held his hand through the entire storm, shrinking from terror into his body with every bolt of lightning. He feels sorry for her.

By half past ten, the storm front has rolled to the eastern horizon, clearing the sky for a few twinkling stars. N. finds some candles in the kitchen cupboard, and after mopping up the kitchen floor, he and Sonja share a refreshing drink over small talk about the storm. Finally calm, Sonja returns to the other house at around midnight, accompanied by Bart whose tail is still tucked between his legs.

But Thor, in his godly might, sends his rumbling to the Vogelpoelweg once more, this time from the east. The encore settles, seemingly, directly over N.'s house with a similar ferocity as before, causing Sonja to run back to N.'s rooms again. He improvises a sleeping place for her with a sheet and a blanket on the couch in the living room, but as the thunderstorm loses its power during the course of the night and turns into a regular rainstorm, he hears her enter his bedroom. Shivering she crawls under the covers beside him, clinging to him, naked. They make love, at first teasingly, gently, then fully.

She's sixteen. A child on the precipice of adulthood. But what does that matter now. *For once let me reject my existential values in service of my personal life and as an expression of my personal strength,* he thinks, *let me for once be the creator of my own morality!*

"Fuck me," the child moans, pulling him from this thought. She tells him she's a virgin, but now she lays before him as a little slut, just as all women are, once they're overcome by certain desires. "Fuck me now... hard... all the way! Damn it, Kees, I'm almost seventeen, I can take a dick for once... All the girls in my class fuck like crazy whenever they want. Why not me, why...?"

She makes love like a third-rate porn star, with exaggerated movements and sterile pathos that leave no question as to what the viewer is supposed to achieve. It is, he believes, the resolute imitation or mimicry of images from a video or show she must have seen. His assumption is confirmed some days later, it turns out, when she confides in him that it was precisely such a video that she had purchased in Y a week earlier and had watched just that afternoon.

After he finishes and pulls away, there is blood on the condom. In response to his look of concern, she whispers that it had hurt, initially, but that it will probably hurt less the next time. She flushes when she tells him that she hopes she hasn't put him off, knowing now that it was indeed her first time. After all, there must always be a first time.

The sun rises the next morning with a bright energy, its rays busily assessing what's been left behind by the downpour. A small pond has formed in the vegetable garden, as well as in an adjacent piece of meadow. Vegetables have been smashed by the hail stones, and the goats and sheep huddle together in a high corner of the meadow, sunk to their knees in water and mud. The electricity is still out, making telephone calls, even by mobile, impossible. Power would not be returned until sometime later in the afternoon when the utility company repairman is finally sent to repair a switchbox some way down the Vogelpoelweg. A couple of roof panels were torn off the corner of the main house and carried away. The plum tree, already top-heavy with fruit, had been snapped at the trunk. A pear tree was blown down, yanked by its roots from the earth. A large poplar along the edge of the pasture about thirty meters from the house was split in two and stripped of its bark. And then, in the middle of all this wreckage, three dairy cows that didn't survive the lightning and are lying in the meadow on their backs; their straight, stiff legs pointing upwards, as if thrown disdainfully and carelessly from the table by Zeus and Odin, sacrifices of their angry celebration. By morning's end, De Geus has dragged them out of the field with his tractor and they are loaded into the back of a large truck with a crane. N. spends the day busying himself with whatever task he can find. With a shovel he scoops away large quantities of sand and mud from the yard, mops the now stagnant stream of water from his hallway, and, finding a few new roofing tiles under the shed, makes his best attempt at repairing the damaged roof. Even with the bright sun overhead, the temperatures have become significantly cooler than in previous days, and the pleasant weather makes his work easy.

Sonja returns home from work several hours earlier than usual, and for the next week and a half, until the homecoming of the two holidaymakers, they will create a symbiotic union. For ten days and nights they do not stray from each other's sides, exchanging fluids three to four times a day, drunk on the aphrodisiac of their togetherness. When the phone lines return, they call Piet de Wilde to tell him they are both ill and won't be able to come to work. They abandon their reading and writing exercises. One afternoon a coworker of Olga's from Family Care Services arrives without notice, opening his outer door after hearing voices behind it and nearly seeing Sonja naked as she emerges from N.'s bedroom. She was under the impression that Olga was back from vacation, but after a few tense moments with N. politely ushering her from the house, she returned to her car and the two were left undisturbed for the remainder of their time. After a ten-day ramble between Charybdis and Gomorrah, fellatio and cunnilingus, the child has become an adult woman in his arms, completely mature in a certain sense. On the receiving end, Sonja is as fresh as a daisy in spring while N. is broken, wonderfully devastated by these most beautiful moments of his life. He cannot be sure that he has left her unimpregnated. The awkward fumbling of condoms had quickly given way to suddenly emerging passions from both sides, and too often there was the giggling warning: "I'd be careful now if I were you, mister," or: "Don't you think we're being a bit reckless?" or: "You shot it into me!" Olga's admonitions rang in his memory a few times, but were quickly drowned out by the passionate moans of his young lover.

27.

It is on the last Tuesday of N.'s historic September that Olga and her boyfriend return from vacation, two days earlier than announced and at a most inconvenient moment. On his bed, soaked with the stains of their sin, he and Sonja are naked and preparing for another exchange of love juices when the cream-colored side of the old caravan reflects off the half-open bedroom window. Moments earlier, overwhelmed with passion in the hallway of the big house, he carried her giggling and naked across the yard in his strong arms. Before Olga and Theo could get out of the car, before he could enter her, Sonja had pulled on N.'s robe and fled out the back of his house and through the rear door of the main house. Quickly pulling on the T-shirt and jeans that had slipped off her in the hall near the front door, she went out the front door and greeted her mother casually.

Olga's intensely white skin has gained a light brown glow, aside from some slight burns. Theo looks like a caricature of a Roma. When Sonja tells them of the thunderstorm, they explain that they also had had terrible thunderstorms, several times in fact. They've seen a lot and other things as well, and had quite enjoyed themselves, but had begun to feel homesick and decided to end their trip a bit early.

That evening in the garden, while the temperature is still pleasant, they light storm candles and drink to the couple's safe homecoming. Every time N. looks at Sonja sitting opposite him, she lowers her eyes with a demure smile; they now share a great secret, which will be cherished and replayed, and they pass it between each other wordlessly so as not to alert the instincts of the girl's intuitive mother. A tremor of pleasure passes through him every time the girl gets up and, exactly as they agreed, rubs her still-toned abdomen to give him the intimate reminder of how much she enjoyed the past week and a half with him.

Olga sits next to him, almost shoulder to shoulder, still smelling of the French countryside. She recounts their vacation in a lively, irrepressible tone, touching N. on the arm or shoulder when she wants to strengthen an opinion or convey the conviction of her memory. She talks constantly and they drink heavily. It is after twelve o'clock when they break, all four of them a little bit tipsy. Theo and Olga stumble together into the big house, giving Sonja and N. an opportunity to press against each other around the corner and kiss each other deeply. She pulls him close and whispers that she is happy with him and that she hopes very much that he will soon be able to make mommy a little bit happy too. (During one of their last open-hearted conversations she had given him unsolicited confirmation about what he had, for a long time, strongly suspected.) Sonja's eyes swell with tears, causing N.'s heart to flutter again. The image he conjures in his mind's eye is wonderful, and he is almost giddy about the prospect of the next four to five months. It even brings him to swear to her that he loves her, and he lies when he tells her that he wants to commit to her and her mother for the rest of his life. He presses her delicate body against his own, heavy with sin and deception, soaked in sensuality and alcohol.

They make plans to ride to X together again and, perhaps, along the way they can engage in other activities in the forest. He hardens as he imagines taking her body on the spongy underbrush, the smell of their sex mixed with the rich earthy scent of the forest floor. Breathless as he is from the heady imagery, he yearns for tomorrow and the day after tomorrow and all the days to come. But for now he seeks peace and quiet, a moment to recapitulate everything, to count and to consider his blessings in the seclusion of his own rooms.

In his coming days off, he works on finishing the portrait of the Beumer girl, which is now only head, neck and shoulders, her chest and midriff this time neatly hidden behind a nice blouse, imagining the uninhibited teenager she is, or should be, because of her age. In between, he continues to work on *The Bride*.

N. returns from a walk the following afternoon at four o'clock to find Olga lightly dressed in a blouse and short cotton summer dress. She enters his apartment humming; she has something *so* exciting to share with him from her vacation. N. pours them both a drink and they sit, she with her adornment of jewelry shining and tinkling, lighting one cigarette after another as she recounts the entire vacation story again, but this time concluding matter-of-factly that she would like very much to make a life in Franche-Comté. She had seen some cute little farms for sale there and had already spoken to a local real estate agent. She was disappointed, however, that aside from Sonja, there was no one who wanted to share this French adventure with her.

He begins to ask about Theo, but stops himself, remembering the altercation that morning conducted at such a volume that it vibrated from the main house to his. He had the impression that the landlady's relationship with her boyfriend had become a bit strained during their vacation, and the amount of fun they had together in France may had been a bit exaggerated. Considering this, N. decides it might not be wise to bring up Theo's name, and continues instead with "Well, Sonja and you, can't you…"

"That's just it," she interrupts, and her eyes light up. Sonja doesn't like the idea of the two women alone together. And neither did she, by the way. She purses her lips, allowing round circles of smoke to rise from her mouth, her eyes in a trance of contemplation. He realizes suddenly that she is about to ask whether he would be interested in joining them. When the question comes up, he deliberately stays silent, which creates an awkward pause between them. Silence ticks away emphatically for two minutes before he says:

"You know, Olga, I'm not handy. I really have two left hands. Surely an old farmhouse will need all kinds of fixing up." He's had this excuse ready for some time now, initially afraid that she might compensate for his ridiculously low rent by asking him to do occasional home repairs, something he absolutely hates.

But her eyes brighten again, and she responds with, "So what… you don't have to worry about that. There are skilled people there too."

She laughs hoarsely, without any nervousness this time; she must have drawn courage from his words. She crosses her legs seductively, her dress falling quite some way past her knee. They drink a little more and N. changes the subject; Olga, correctly assumes that her sideways suggestion has caught him off guard and he therefore needs some time to reflect on it, and doesn't push the matter further.

At exactly six-thirty, Sonja appears on her bicycle at the top of the drive. Olga takes her last sip of sherry, then as if to suggest that she considers the matter more or less settled, kisses him deeply for the first time since they have been in each other's lives, she gives N. a real kiss, a warm, moist in the middle of her mouth, one that suggests that, for her, the matter is more or less settled. An hour later, he still feels as though his face has been pushed into an ashtray full of cigarette butts.

28.

<... *Die Zeitungen und ihren lokalpolitischen Dreck lesen zu müssen tagtäglich, ihren stumpfsinnigen Politik- und Wirtschafts- und Feuilletonistenschmutz. Mich diesen Zeitungen und ihren ekelerregenden Erzeugnissen nicht entziehen zu können, weil ich andererseits diesen Zeitungsschmutz so begierig in mich hineinfressen muß tagtäglich, wie wenn ich geradezu an einer perversen Zeitungsgefräßigkeit leiden würde...>*

N. reads a passage by Thomas Bernhard, the Austrian famous for his cynicism, and smiles remembering his college days when he offered a couple of publishers to translate a few of TB's latest novels into Dutch. There was little enthusiasm for it then, and he wonders if and when his *Zeitungsgefräßigkeit* will ever become popular. How long has it been since he took a serious look at a real newspaper? It must be at least two months by now. The Beumers' regional newspapers hold little interest for him anymore, and they don't subscribe to a national newspaper. He also ignores TV news and the inevitable current affairs programs that accompany them. Cut off from all events outside his immediate environment, his interest in "the world" has been reduced to an absolute minimum, and a warm silence of nothingness has completely engulfed him.

The media silence makes him feel more and more like he is living in a dream world, and he is only occasionally jolted by the monotony of reality. It seems as if indeed nothing exists beyond the small family at Vogelpoelweg, especially on the weekends and his days off. Ever since he decided to stop playing the game of everyday life four months ago, his financial contribution to society has shrunk to a negligible amount. Direct taxes cannot be paid by the deceased, of course. He assumed that neither the wages paid in kind or under the table, nor the rent paid to the landlady should be included in that calculation. Kees determined in a wasted afternoon hour, including the current sales tax rates, that his indirect contribution to the treasury in an average week amounts to about 2.14 euros; roughly the financial equivalent, he notes with satisfaction, of a box of paper clips. And due to his ascetic way of life, his contribution to the daily mountain of garbage has also been reduced to a minimum. These realizations suddenly give him so much joy that he is rubs his hands with a satisfied smile before he even realizes it. No doubt, today is one of his good days.

It is pure coincidence that N. sees his brother Hans on television. He and Sonja are naked together, in *coitus a tergo* with her on his lap, preparing to enter her as a cowgirl or more *canino* (depending on her preference), with plans to watch episode 112,334, or thereabouts, of Good Things & Bad Things. Olga is visiting acquaintances in the village and will be home late, and they don't hesitate to take advantage of the opportunity. The eight o'clock news has run long due to some small catastrophe, and there on the screen is his next of kin. N. is startled, not from seeing his brother (his appearance on TV isn't uncommon as he's gained a reputation as some sort of macro-economic oracle and forecaster) but by the sudden sensation that he has stepped back into his old world.

Hans face is composed, almost blank as he answers questions automatically. He's gotten fatter, N. thinks, especially in the face; he should definitely eat less and stay away from the alcohol. He might benefit from more exercise as well. He has started to look more and more like their father, who eventually succumbed to the inevitable heart attack due to physical inertia. Then the segment ends, and the face disappears, but N. sinks into thought, hardly reacting to Sonja's passionate moans which are elicited from time to time by the mechanical caressing of his fingers or the exciting plots conceived for this episode of the soap opera. But the naked body in his lap pulls back his attention, and with ten minutes he makes her sigh and moan and wriggle under the movements as he fills her sacred cavity with his hot fluid. A warm, rosy bubble of air is rises to the top of his mind, almost as if in slow motion.

29.

At work, N. continues to prove his value to such an extent that his boss strongly encourages him to take an online a course in lower management. He sees potential for N. to someday become an assistant branch manager, and although it's unfortunate he didn't finish his three years of lower vocational education; he believes that N. probably has enough intellectual capacity to successfully complete such a course. For the most part, he is well-liked by his colleagues, who call on him for all sorts of tasks and find that he is always willing to help. He happily fills in when someone is sick or has to leave early, and never hesitates to confront "the boss" with any of their complaints. They use him to do their dirty work, Sonja tells him disapprovingly. He can of course see this for himself, but he doesn't care. His relationship with Sonja lacks all inhibition at work (she is the youngest of them all), and he is not sure if anyone notices, nor does he care. If they did, it would only gratify his ego.

When he is accidentally side swipes the company's grocery delivery van, he has a few tense moments in which he is almost certain he will be found out. It was stupid, he realizes; he should never have taken the delivery driver task. Even though there was only minor material damage, the other driver insisted on calling the police. The officer asks for N.'s driver's license, and has no choice but to show him identification for C. Jansen, N. begins sweating bullets. But he does not enter any information into the computer, only admonishes him for having an outdated photo now that N. has grown a beard and demands that the oversight be rectified as soon as possible. He says that he will, wondering how on earth a man in such a ridiculous uniform can make him feel like little more than a naughty child. Immediately upon returning home, he cuts the driver's license into pieces, and swears to never again get behind the wheel.

There is one colleague he hasn't hit it off with quite so well. Daan van Dorp, a young man in his early twenties, is a warehouse clerk who works closely with N., sharing responsibility for stock management. A vague animosity started to fester from the moment the young man fixed on the idea that N. was trying to interfere with his rising career in retail. No matter how much N. promised him that he wasn't after anything more than a temporary position, their relationship became increasingly icy. With his relentless pranks, digs and irritating banter, Daan could sometimes make his workday completely miserable. When the young man knocks over a three-meter-high pile of crates full of empty bottles loaded on a hand truck—supposedly by accident—just as N. walks by, smashing him and cutting him open with broken glass, he grabs Daan by the short hairs. Daan has a stocky build, but N.'s height and weight give him the upper hand. With a bit of luck, he knocks Daan to the floor. When the other gets up, dumbfounded by this lucky move, he takes a swing at N. with a piece of pallet wood. N. grabs him by the throat with both hands, very nearly strangling him, and loudly warns the gasping and retching boy that if he tries something like that again, he'll break his neck. Then he pushes the rest of the pile of crates over him and orders him to clean up the mess.

There were no more problems with Daan after that. When he recounted the incident to Sonja, however, she chuckled and asked how quickly Daan had piled up the crates again. N. furrowed his brows, not understanding the question.

"You don't know? *Really?*"

N. shrugs his shoulders and shakes his head.

"Well, here's the deal: Daan once saw Nardie setting some meat aside to smuggle home at the end of her workday. Well, he's held it over her ever since. He threatened to tell everyone if she didn't do what he wanted, and I'm sure you can guess what he wanted. He's been doing it with her for over a year now, on lunch breaks or in the after closing. There's an old mattress hidden in the warehouse behind the crates."

The story shocks N., and his naivety makes Sonja giggle.

"There's more. Do you know about Jan-Peter and Ria?"

"No," he says, shaking his head again, "which Jan-Peter?"

"Mr. de Wilde's son." He's a lanky schoolboy with a sparse goatee, grown in an attempt to look mature, or to cover a face riddled with acne. N. occasionally sees him pass through the store like a shadow. Apparently, he saw Ria pilfering some grocery items and threatened to report her to his dad if she didn't submit to his sexual advances. So Ria, a middle-aged woman, widow, and mother of three school-aged children and scared to death of losing her job, disappears behind the pile of crates once or twice a week to let a sixteen-year-old boy find sexual satisfaction. If he believes Sonja—and N. has no reason to doubt her—then the entire meats department must disappear during their lunch breaks or after closing into the warehouse to provide a free supply of other meat products there.

These revelations leave N. breathless. At first he wants to believe that his young girlfriend and maintenee's imagination has just run away with her, but he verified these stories that afternoon with another cashier he trusts. She confirms Sonja's story emphatically, even adds that one of the men had tried to blackmail her as well but she threatened to expose all of them and their despicable warehouse activity, claiming that she had secretly taken photos.

N.'s head spins. He'd always thought of himself as a worldly man, and the idea that such activities had escaped his notice annoys him. He immediately begins plotting a way to put a quick and final end to these blackmail schemes.

In the third week of October, an extended period of rain comes, driving Sonja back to public transportation, and puts N.'s raingear to the test on every trip to and from Piet de Wilde's burgeoning brothel.

30.

<A company on its way back, getting old, ancient soon, perhaps indeed still occasionally wildly lashing out around it and proclaiming stupidities. Their existence is anchored in their families, their offspring, pensions, policies, their homes, their cars, vacations and other luxuries. Their drunken, dull faces reveal the many signs of their prosperity and success. In a year's time, they'll be sitting here again, chattering about the good weather, nothing will have changed for them, nothing will ever change again, blind and deaf as they have become to the fact that, under their feet, everything is changing, changing quickly and profoundly. The cries of fear, horror or indignation they will utter when time no longer tolerates their existence and pushes it over the edge of oblivion; it will be the last bad act in their artificial lives.>

He notes these lines of skepticism in his diary late one Tuesday evening in early November during a drive hunt in the fields to the southeast of the Beumers. N. doesn't know anything about the hunt, but the timing seems unfavorable to him. It's been raining for days on end and whole stretches of the empty fields and meadows are flooded. Mud and water are everywhere. A few days earlier, some brave or desperate fieldworkers were out harvesting parcels of corn, and more than once the corn harvester got stuck in the mud, requiring a tractor with a long chain to get the operation running again. A caterpillar had even crawled across the fields like a giant amphibian from another age. According to farmer De Geus, who N. had stopped one evening to inquire about all the activity, any crop still standing on the fields after such heavy rains would have to be considered a loss (he will be proven right).

But the date for the hunt had already been set months prior and given the number of notable figures who had made room in their overcrowded calendars to attend, postponement was unthinkable; at least, according to Theo. Around this time every year, it turns out that N. occasional checkers buddy is charged with organizing a hunting party for hare and pheasant. Aside from him, six other hunters will be present, and Theo proudly lists the names of his high-ranking guests: It seems that those who will visibly be honored in this company are the mayor of a neighboring hamlet, one Mr. Van Panhuysen-Slot (half-noble); the district commander of a regional police force; the local notary, Mrs. M.J. (Mina) Drooglever-Kneppelhout MA, chartered accountant; one Pannekoek, owner of a chain of butchers in and around Q; and a real purebred nobleman, a Count bearing the solid name of Pieter ("call me Piet") van Hummel tot Keppel Esquire (landed nobility). The prestigious group will be assisted by seven beaters for the occasion, mostly farmers and other commoners from the area. Theo had asked Kees with a pleasant but somewhat urgent tone to join the guild of beaters, fearing that it was still too small. He kindly but resolutely refused. It is difficult for him to have sympathy for this sport, or for horseback riding, which seems similar to him. He prefers live animals of all sizes and species, in their wild habitat, to dead or stressed ones.

Olga invites him to join her to prepare the communal meal instead, a traditional dish of a hearty pea soup, catered by Pannekoek's restaurant. But judging from Theo's winking giddiness, there's more to the meal than just the main course. And indeed, Olga tells him, the pea soup is just a base for a hearty intake of beer, gin, cognac and other spirits afterward. They have an *amazingly* good time every year, Theo tells him, and it soon becomes clear that this day is the absolute highlight of the man's existence. Regardless, N. tells them both he'll need time to think about it.

An hour later, N. is in his rooms working on some writing when Olga comes in, asking as a personal favor if he will please join her for the meal. "I would really appreciate it," she says, "and Sonja too. I don't like having all those strangers in the house, and I've become very fond of you. Surely this isn't a surprise to you by now."

Then his landlady puts her hand on his shoulder and starts caressing his neck; the tenant quickly yields his reluctance and is rewarded with a generous hug and kiss.

On the day of the hunt, N. feels as though he's awakened in a war zone. Shotguns blasted at random, the hunting dogs barks and howls, the belligerent beaters prowl the forests shouting and yelling; everywhere is noise and chaos, and with every bang N. can imagine a hare or a pheasant tumbling to its demise. At five-thirty that afternoon, already dusky due to a steady drizzle, farmer De Geus's tractor arrives at the Beumer's yard with a flatbed trailer. On it is laid the pride of the disguised bourgeoisie, a *tableau mort* of about twenty hares (N. would have never suspected *so* many animals in such a relatively small area). There are also twenty-three pheasants, two wood pigeons whose small bodies were blown almost to smithereens and four partridges, which he seriously wonders whether it is actually allowed to be hunting them. The bottle goes round and wide-angle photographs are taken of the harvest from every angle, the beaters kneeling in front of the take, the hunters next to it, standing proudly with their rifles upright.

In Olga's spacious living room (movable panels have been slid aside to open up the kitchen and living room for this occasion), furniture has been cleared and replaced by rough planks balanced on wooden trestles. Garden chairs have been brought in to make up for any shortage in seating. This improvisation creates an atmosphere of cozy disorder with plenty of space for the whole company, a total of 17 people, including Olga, Sonja, and himself. *Unfortunately*, he records in his diary later, *the house did not have a half-dark room adjacent to the living room with a wing chair where I could retreat before and after the pea soup for an ocular psychoanalysis of these people and to quietly cultivate and nurture my own reflections*. No, as an honorary member of the family, N. is required to participate in full light.

Farmer De Geus sits to N.'s right at the table. He has a good sense for sportsman's yarns, and he starts the dinner conversation with stories from previous driving hunts, aided heavily by the gin bottle. Across from him is the country squire who, now that he's taken off his hat and havelock, N. realizes is almost bald and a pale pink in his hunting attire. He is well into his seventies but quick and alert with lively eyes and, N. guesses from his generous girth, probably a little hypertension. He talks and gesticulates without pause and clearly plays the part of animated centerpiece and treasured jewel of this company. N. muses at how rare it is to see such an archaic display together in so few square feet. It's as though he's stepped into the first French empire and then transferred to Q, an impression which is at least partially reinforced by the antiquated style of Olga's interior decorating. Atavisms, people and furniture, reminiscent of a nineteenth-century hunting party captured by an expressionist or naturalist, with a provincial nobleman who spent a day with the bourgeoisie and *Tiers État*. His casts a lascivious gaze on the hostess when she sets in front of him a bowl of hot pea soup and when Sonja brings extra cutlery to him at his request, his hand rubs suggestively just above her knee. *A glimpse of the circumstances in which bastards were conceived,* an inspired N. writes afterwards, *faded glory of the Ancien Régime, having escaped the frenzy of the guillotine, which could polish itself to a shine on such an evening here in all its Old Testament antiquity.*

One of the beaters, office. recognizes him as the postmaster, is pretty well plastered early on in the evening. N. learns later that he, a round little man with a snub nose and red cheeks, can't handle strong liquor at all but in an effort to belong in this group, he often drinks himself into oblivion. Anyone still coherent is content to wait for the moment when this honorable official, father many times over and elder of the reformed church in daily life, will completely abandon his honor and decency. He is already beginning to utter obscenities.

But the conversation has moved on. Mr. Van Panhuysen-Slot, seated just a few chairs away from N., gives a detailed analysis of the current state of politics in general, and more particularly and with much more fervor, that of his beloved Christian Democrats. A country, he summarizes, where the political power is in the hands of parties that do not in any way put the guiding, corrective role of the "C" into their principles, such a country – "…including our beloved Netherlands, because for some time now, we can't just point our instructive Calvinist finger at Southern Europe!" – A country like that inexorably becomes ruled, yes, he would like to say, by natural law – "…yes *natural law*, that's the word! On the dead-end road to shameless selfishness, nepotism, hedonism and other pernicious 'isms'." He is, he wants to say in conclusion, how happy he is that the Christian Democrats have once again become the ruling party.

"And above all amateurism, amateurism and political hooliganism," Mrs. Drooglever adds in, shuffling in her chair as she sees her opportunity to jump into the conversation. "Those idiotic carnival goers, stupid soccer fans, sports fanatics, in other words people with zero intellect shouldn't be allowed to vote. They let the wool be pulled over their eyes by the first big mouthed political cowboy that comes along!"

"Exactly," says the mayor. "And then, as we all know at this table, governance gets into the hands of people who only care about personal power, money and other gain… in other words, it degenerates into political adventurism."

He assumes that the good company around him does not need examples from the recent past, and the man gets shouts and words of approval.

"Without the Christian stamp on daily politics, nihilism will surely take over," Mrs. Drooglever sneakily and quickly cuts off the notary, an apple-cheeked man, red from cognac and a long day in the open air. He sees great danger in the unmistakable moral decay in an increasingly decadent society, a development that previous (thank God) coalition cabinets in particular have had so astonishingly little attention for.

"And contributed to, don't forget!" corrects Mrs. Drooglever for the eleventh time.

"Yes of course," says the other, with slight irritation in his voice, "and yet I still see troubling signs of the times around me today."

The Master of Law looks around as though seeking supporters, but his ominous words only draw modest approval.

Then the Master of Arts (three hares and a pheasant) Drooglever-Kneppelhout—a woman in her early sixties, long gray hair pulled into a bun, pearly forehead, sleeves rolled up with her hunting jacket hung on the back of her chair—begins to speak irrepressibly. She fervently agrees with her comrades, but would go even further. She makes the assertion that for the sake of moral rearmament (she doesn't care if this term is no longer politically correct), s there is the need for a new purity to be brought into politics. After all, politicians have to set an example. But still she presses *even* further. "Dear friends," she says with a trembling voice, casting a probing glance at everyone present, one by one: "It may seem unthinkable, even today. Nevertheless, it is my firm conviction that this purity can only be achieved when the political party CDA is… *disbanded*…! Yes, you heard right! Disband that project, as soon as possible! What I mean to say is this…"

The lady pours herself another glass, rubs her flushed face and continues: "If we want pure, genuine decision-making once again, the immaterial must have the primacy instead of the material weighing up of interests that keeps everyone in The Hague and elsewhere nowadays… also, yes even the confessional parties, certainly them," she wards off some oppositional mumbling with a mighty wave of her arm, "in an iron grip… Now, it is my firm position that the original confessional parties need to be revived. Folks, we need to go back to the old days!" She herself has always remained Christian Historical in her heart and soul, she admits. Even as a young girl, she walked away with Lady Wittewaal-van Stoetwegen, a beautiful lady and *living proof* that in those years, women were once given plenty of opportunity in the Christian Historical Union. Her voice at the CDA is, she wants to say here, her voice at the CDA has always spoken from the heart and soul of the CHU. She has faced all those years since '73, with sorrow, watching the increasing political marginalization of the Christian historical principles and goals, which nevertheless remain high-minded principled ideals. The philosophies of Piet Steenkamp and company regarding the CDA is nothing but a foolish hodgepodge, she proclaims indignantly.

"Yes, I say a hodgepodge, a construct…! Permeated by the papacy!" She shouts scornfully when someone raises a feeble protest. "People who continue to kneel in front of their idol… that Polish fathead in the Vatican with his morally bankrupt brigade in their silly robes… ! Yes, it's idolatry… Worthless! Degrading devotion! Yes, really! Someone has to say it!"

Mrs. Drooglever's apodictic outrage is accompanied by her right fist pounding on the rough planks. She throws a shot of gin against her palate before lighting a fresh cigar.

"And," she continues after a short, stunned silence, her face ablaze with the world's highest righteousness, "it is precisely this foolishness that is just *asking* for political degradation…" And, well, she personally never expected any salvation from this "construct", she says, motioning air quotes around the word. The concept of Christian politics in those turbulent 1970s, she believes, was far from sufficiently crystallized, blinded as they were by the idea of performing a historical act.

She looks around, searching the faces of her peers for support. She finds none, however, and the room fills with a low, mumbling disapproval. Two hunters exchange dark looks across the table, a beater clears his throat loudly. But an increasingly merry Count bubbles up with a jolly "Mina, you're a girl after my own heart."

N. realizes he is making a face of utter astonishment only when Olga breaks it by presenting him with a second bowl of pea soup. The soup is delicious, so thick that the spoon stands straight up in it, and the second round is devoured heartily by everyone at the table. Theo manages to thaw the icy mood with some much needed comic relief. He and the postmaster draw upon an almost bottomless reservoir of jokes and antics, each trying to outdo the other's quips, and drawing roars of laughter, especially from the beaters' side of the room. The mood rises warmly with the appearance of dessert, a decadent compote of plums, peaches, strawberries and blackberries (Olga's personal contribution) and coffee with fresh cigars and chocolates that are devoured without interruption and these, too, melt and smooth out the last snowflakes and wrinkles. Olga and Sonja, bustling about as if they were being paid, visibly enjoy the many compliments they receive.

N. wonders exactly what these people have been told about him. His checkers partner must have long been gossiping about the oddball who's been living in his girlfriend's cottage for the past six months, and who, sure enough, has been teaching him how to play checkers. N. deduces this from the occasional knowing glances cast in his direction. The gaze of the district commander, who has had very little to say throughout the evening, makes him slightly uneasy. He regularly leans in to listen conversationally to Theo's non-stop talking, often looking suspiciously over at N. from time to time. He is a robust man with a moustache, graced with a powerful jaw and a double chin. N. puts him at about fifty years old. He does not allow himself to be distracted by the din around him, and drinks very little, basking in his ataraxia. In a month's time, when he finds himself forced to leave the countryside of Q, at a moment's notice about a month later, he cannot shake the suspicion that, perhaps under the encouragement of Theo, this gentleman may have had a hand in his expulsion. The image of the driver staring intently at the Beumers' yard returns to him. As the evening progresses, N. feels increasingly less at ease. Suddenly it's as if, little by little, an explosive charge is being packed under his rural, so far, almost idyllic existence.

"And you, mate, what's your story, if you don't mind me asking?"

It is Esquire Piet, who is personally addressing N. for the first time, when the room has grown suddenly quiet. The nobleman looks at him with glinting eyes, and *then* all of a sudden N. finally realizes why this man is so familiar. All at once, he places him, the image of a certain old and disenchanting minister of police and internal affairs, deprived of uniform and decorations. Without the hat, thin hair, gray face, short chin, flabby mouth, small nose, the moustache, the glasses—it's him, exactly. Police chief or chicken farmer, what does it matter? An incarnation, he ponders, of this Mr. Van Hummel tot Keppel, becoming the flesh of the capricious and unfathomable decision-maker that led to Europe's dismal and incredibly bloody past.

N. recounts his fictitious and tragic history in vague, general depictions, in an intentionally low voice so much of what he says is swallowed by the surrounding din. N. can tell by the squire's face that he is having trouble hearing him. Moreover, the man's interest was feigned from the beginning, so his interest quickly wanes. When a thunderous laugh erupts a few chairs away (hilarity related to the blind-drunk postmaster) the man's attention is drawn away so quickly that he leaves N. talking to the air. The postmaster has in fact fallen asleep, his head slumped in his dessert plate, snoring as if possessed.

N. spends a bit more time chatting with farmer De Geus, until about ten o'clock, when he considers his obligation fulfilled and excuses himself, feeling heavy from two bowls of soup, a big scoop of compote and a few glasses of red wine. He thanks the hostesses for their good care, and Olga makes an excuse to walk him to the cottage.

"Thanks for coming, Kees. I never like it much myself with all those men. It's Theo's company you know, he invites them." She tells him that she would have liked to have a glass of wine with him alone now and perhaps listen to a nice piece of music. "But I can't get away you see, I shouldn't leave Sonja alone with all of them."

She gives him a deep, ashtray-flavored kiss before returning to the party, leaving N. slightly tipsy from both the wine and the lustful kiss. He rubs Bart's head; the animal stands next to him with his tail tucked between his legs, not really understanding what is going on and none too pleased with all the hunting dogs shut up in the cars in the parking lot. In the light of the outdoor lamp, N. sees a dull gleam on the eye of one of the hares lying on the flatbed, and reflets for a moment on how unfair it was that they weren't allowed to stay alive, cozy as they were together in the fields and meadows, not harming anyone.

By eleven thirty he is in the shower, still hearing the sound of the party singing together, shrieking with laughter, and the sustained screaming of Mrs. Drooglever-Kneppelhout, sounding as if she is being groped, and then celebratory shotgun fire on the other side of the house. There is some drunken palaver, words spoken with ambiguous meaning, and then the Beumer ladies are thanked and kissed farewell. Slowly they disburse, then someone goes back into the house to fetch something forgotten. In the yard two slurring beaters are swearing eternal friendship, the hounds howl and bark, happy to rejoin their owners. Doors are slammed shut, Land Cruisers, Patrols, Jeeps and Range Rovers are started, whining as they reverse up the drive. Someone has taken it upon themselves to drive the postmaster home, despite his spluttering protest. The dead game will be picked up from De Geus the next morning by a poulterer and the proceeds will be divided among the beaters and the Beumer ladies.

N. still can't shake the police commissioner's relentless, fixing gaze. He tends to his diary, checks something, and by twelve thirty has retired to his bedroom. He is ready to close the curtains when he sees Olga's face, standing in her bedroom window directly across from his, about ten meters away. Last summer, when it was warm and all the doors and windows were wide open, he could hear her bed creaking when she turned in her sleep. With his light still on, she can see him plainly. She waves at him, peers out of the window for a moment, then closes the curtains; to open them just a crack a few moments later. She does this so precisely that N. feels suddenly overwhelmed by unease. Once more he sees her face peer from behind the curtains, at first disregarding her, then realizing with surprise that her light is still on ten minutes later. His cocked male instinct has already seen through the nature and purpose of all this.

With a pounding heart, he goes through the hall to the outside door, opens it carefully and walks towards Olga's bedroom window as silently as if on felt slippers. What he sees behind it baffles him; it is so obviously staged that there is something obscene about it. Like a scene pulled from a poorly lit porno film, the landlady kneels on her bed, and once he is finally able to discern the tangled mess of naked flesh, he can see that she is being mounted by her boyfriend, who is making fierce efforts to pleasure her before taking his own satisfaction. N. looks down on Olga's legs, spread wide to accommodate his heavy, laboring body. She stares unblinkingly at the window. It is slightly open, and he can hear her primal sounds of surrender, sounding forced to him, like the imitation of an ascent. The sounds seem as though they are meant for him, so that he can then fit them into his own imagination and fantasies. Indeed, isn't this display meant for him? As if to say *that could have been you, sucker, if only you'd shown a little more initiative.*

He skulks back to his hut, damp from the drizzle and in a pained disposition, a burning desire in his chest and a massive boner in his pants. Around one o'clock there is a noise, giggling and laughter. He jumps out of bed to see Olga's head in front of the window again, and her naked torso. She's opened the curtains again and is staring into the darkness, her face just in front of the window glass, a hand above her eyes, and always in the direction of his window. Then the curtains are closed again, roughly and with finality, and the night falls, heavy and humid after a noisy, dull and useless day. N. realizes it is time to start taking some initiative. If Olga knows about Sonja and him, she is hiding that knowledge masterfully. If she really does know, a suspicion that has become stronger every day, he can no longer leave the mother to hang and grope for his affection. He doesn't want to disrupt a subtle balance to create an atmosphere that will harden with envy and indifference and make his temporary stay here unpleasant. He decides to go back to his stock of roguish tricks that Asmodeus once gave to him with a grin.

It takes a long time before N. falls into a restless sleep.

31.

Three days later, they are technically a couple. It's a Friday afternoon. since N., after taking an extra shift the previous week, has been given the day off. He phones her and asks in a somewhat muffled voice if she would like to join him for "a very nice time together" for an hour or so. Of course N., being as hesitant and cautious as he is, can take this invitation in any direction if there turns out to be some diabolical misunderstanding. Without a word she disconnects and five minutes later, she stands in front of him, without knocking or greeting and without jewelry and rings, noise or sparkle. She is wearing a raincoat, despite the dry and sunny weather these past few days.. Underneath she is completely naked. With an impertinent smile she throws off the garment and orders him to do the same.

They take each other where they are in the kitchen, standing at first, the woman's legs powerfully wrapped around the man's hips, her arms around his neck, he puts his hands under her buttocks and uses her own weight to lower her onto his rod; when he can no longer maintain, he takes her sitting on the couch in his living room and then lying on his bed. The small cave opens beneath him with all its secrets of conception and birth; of life and its sources. He releases all that is animal, perishable, bloody, stinking and oozing with mortality. She's soaking wet from her longing for him, which had been awakened months ago for his clumsy member in the short term, and for his love and affection in the somewhat longer term.

It is dead quiet in the house except for the sound of their jolting breathing and the sloppy sliding and passing of moist genitals that found and taste and approve of each other. Never before had he been with a woman who took so much pleasure in copulating, with a body that offered so many erotic variations (but they have a source that will soon be revealed to him). He thinks there must have been an arrangement made between mother and daughter, maybe even a bet. When Sonja arrives home at half past six, the girl does not, as she invariably has of late, enter his home for a quick cuddle and to unburden herself of the difficulties of the day before the three of them enjoy a hot meal together. That night there is no hot meal. After a few stiff drinks, the man and woman tumble back into bed—ecstatic shadows in the three-quarter darkness of the bedroom—to mix seed and vaginal fluid.

"Aren't you afraid of having a baby?" he asks, not sure whether and what kind of prevention they ought to be using. In between comas, some sense of responsibility always dawns on him.

"You're a bit late with that question, sweetheart. But I don't care, I'm not afraid of anything. I'd have ten more children with you."

"Getting that cut in your belly re-opened and closed again ten times, would you…?" Every time he enters her, he's amazed at her tightness; he imagines her like a virgin girl of twelve to fourteen. This is no body for children, and certainly not for ten of them.

"I'd be willing. Sonja was an exceptionally heavy baby. But for you, darling, I'd be willing to do it. For you I could do anything. As long as you stay with me, stay with us, as long as we can always be together. Oh sweetheart, if you only knew how much I love you, how much I've loved you from the very beginning…"

Later that evening, still on his bed, she retells with more detail her sobering, romantically drawn, life story. She is indeed Russian, born in Kaliningrad in 1960. Her mother had been deported from Belarus to the town on the Baltic Sea after the Second World War as part of Stalin's policy of Russification. She never knew her father; according to her mother a subaltern with the Baltic fleet who left her after he got her pregnant. It was common there, she told him. After finishing school in Kaliningrad, Olga found a job as a waitress in an officer's canteen of the Russian Navy. When she was seventeen she met a merchant fleet captain who proposed to take her to Western Europe and promised her the moon. He smuggled her out of the country on his ship, where he raped her whenever he liked during the sea voyage. She was put ashore again in a port that turned out to be Antwerp and put into contact with a man who would help her get work. She surrendered her passport under the pretext that if she was checked by the Belgian police, there would be no proof of her nationality and she could not be sent back. After some time, she had been able to get new papers, but not until after she'd been forced into the obvious occupation at a nightclub, forced and scared into impossible situations. Although she did try, she couldn't go anywhere without papers, and she and two other Russian girls who worked in the same nightclub under the same threats remained doomed to "the life".

"I won't tell you any more, Kees, about the time I was there. It was a horror." But she does say that she tried to escape twice and was taken back and used and abused twice by the nightclub owner's henchmen. She spent a few days in hospital after a drunk client slashed her with a knife: the wound in her lower abdomen and the scar on her shoulder are silent witnesses of that. For six years she was held in that line of work, transferred a few times to other clubs in Flanders and Wallonia, all run by the same owner. She worked in Bruges, Brussels, Charleroi, Knokke and other places, where she learned how to speak French and Flemish. After a feud and a reckoning in the Charleroi underworld in which two nightclubs went up in flames, a number of girls fled, including her. They crossed the Dutch border in a delivery van. She had some money she had managed to hide away and used it to rent an apartment in Rotterdam. She worked as a waitress in a bar on the south side where she met Jan Beumer, a security guard in the port. They became friends and eventually started dating, and then Sonja was born. As the mother of a child with a Dutch father she was eventually able to gain Dutch citizenship. They were married and after four years, when her mother-in-law died, they moved to Q to live in Jan's parental home. He managed to get a job as a messenger at the district court in Y.

"You know what the worst part was, Kees?"

Chris nods, he already knows.

"That I couldn't go back to her when she got sick." She didn't dare go back to Russia, afraid that even after all that time there would still be a score to settle. They had managed to stay in touch all those years, but when she fell ill and had to be hospitalized, there was nothing that Olga could do. When her mother died in 1986, she didn't dare to go to her cremation —she couldn't even send for her ashes; it is the worst thing, she thinks, that could happen to anyone.

She cries, and Kees alias Chris or Christiaan makes no attempt to comfort her. Why is that? He wonders at himself. Every word of consolation, he thinks, would feel hypocritical in about four months' time when he plans to forget this family and the Vogelpoelweg altogether. He does put his arm around her in a half-hearted attempt to get her back in the mood for some more sex. He can't get enough of her body. They lie silently next to each other for a while and the name Kaliningrad looms in N.'s mind. Kaliningrad, he muses, the city of Immanuel. Until 1945 it was Königsberg, a German enclave. Taken by the Red Army in '45 after several grisly battles. It was a symbol that Stalin, absurd as he was, wanted to destroy at all costs, where sometime in the eighteenth century Frederick I had himself crowned the first king of Prussia. But that history was precisely why Hitler, in his own absurdity, had wanted to keep the city at all costs. An absurd private war unleashed by two madmen who somehow became the world's most powerful men, resulting in the greatest bloodbath in human history.

Wasn't it always that way?

But Olga, despite all her hardships, is not someone who is easily discouraged. She has quite a cheerful disposition. They rise in the middle of the night to eat, then crawl close together again. N. stimulates her big nipples and she giggles; with her bit of a vulgar tone, a remnant, perhaps, of all those years in Belgium.

"I guess you couldn't imagine me in the sex biz with a chest like this, could you?"

He nods cautiously; he could imagine anything, and wants to say something, but she interrupts him by stroking her areolas.

"I had a boob job once. They were small and hard and felt very unnatural. Guys loved them… You know, Kees, a little bit of silicone does wonders." Soon after her escape from the club, she quickly had them removed. One of the bags had started leaking.

In the end, all that crap would end up in her body. N. catches himself anticipating her next question which seems inescapable, and he dreads it, tired of the twisting and lying.

"Tell me honestly, Kees, now that you know all this about me, could you still love me a little?"

She looks at him, with sudden intensity, bent toward him, and he lies. Indeed, in the same three-quarter darkness of his bedroom and right under her gaze, he lies through his teeth. What else could he do?

"Shall we do more of this…? I mean making love and talking and all that, late into the night if we have to?"

He asks how she wants to handle Theo.

"Leave that to me," she answers grimly.

He is happy to set aside the issue of "Sonja", but his ears prick when she asks: "Would you like to live with *us*?" It is the emphasis she places on the plural that intrigues him, and the words that follow intrigue him even more. His temporary Arcadia looks more like a fairytale everyday—daring, challenging, enchanting. "I want," she says then, picking up her earlier train of thought, "I don't want a tempestuous love affair. That time of life is passed for me. But I want someone who will care about us a little, Sonja and me, give us a little attention, lovemaking and other things, to show us that we don't mean nothing at all to you."

N. nods. She demands so little of him, but would Sonja be so undemanding? He nods ambiguously, but Olga, positive as she is, and perhaps also a bit naive, interprets it as consent.

That weekend he will paint her.

32.

By the third Wednesday of November a light rain has been falling steadily for a week. N.'s usual inconsequential but nevertheless joyful bustle has all but halted since gaining carnal knowledge of Olga. He listens to music, reads a bit, walks occasionally with Bart, but nothing more. Oh yes, Olga did call in sick for a week, and they spent the time wrapped up in each other, alternately making love and talking constantly through the day and deep into the night. Sonja seemed content, grinning vaguely as she cooked food and otherwise kept to the background. She is "in his blood" as they say. Olga and her daughter are like a strong virus, pulsing in his veins, and at times he is almost overcome by the permanent state of euphoria; it paralyzes him, leaves him without a will of his own.

He doesn't exactly understand it. Perhaps he's just exhausted from the frequent erotic activities. A sort of fog has settled over his eyes, thickening significantly by a visit from Theo for a friendly game of checkers.

The conversation immediately turned to Theo's incomprehension at the inexplicable recent change in mood at the Beumer household.

"How do you mean?" asked N., while coaxing a couple of pieces off the left side of the board (he was playing white).

Well, he explains, Olga had been scolding and grumbling at him for days, for no apparent reason. It seemed like he couldn't do anything right anymore, and it was getting *amazingly* annoying.

Indeed, their arguments have been growing in volume and intensity, often penetrating the walls of N.'s humble abode. Very early on, when he first heard conflict rise from the house, he imagined some kind of rift growing between mother and daughter because of him. He created a type of fantasy with him in the center as a catalyst and, in time, becoming a bridge between them, a great conciliator; he already envisioned these glorious roles for himself. Eventually he realized that the arguments only occurred when Theo's Opel Astra was parked in the yard, and it dawned on him that there was a male voice in the bickering chorus. He has begun to suspect that the ladies had concocted some sort of strategy to drive Theo away. Mr. Sluiter's presence has clearly become less desirable to the Beumers in the new situation, maybe even an albatross around their slender, lovely necks?

They must be making his life miserable, N. thinks, in an attempt to end things the hard way.

"Is there something in particular you're fighting about?"

"Ach!" Theo makes a dismissive gesture, clipping the checkerboard, and shifting the pieces to such an extent that the game might be considered spoiled. He assumed that the two were planning to move to France, with or without him, and if he didn't get on board soon, then he may as well just scram.

"Don't you think there could be something for you there? You could close up shop here, start farming somewhere in France or something? It's a beautiful climate, after all. A change of scenery." N. mechanically made another move, a little to the left of the center.

"No chance in hell; if that's what they want to do, they'll have to go alone," he said.

"Suppose they actually do. Would that mean you and Olga would break up?" N. assumed the answer but wanted certainty.

"Of course! I'm not signing up for something like that." Then chortling, eyes closed, he says "I guess that means you'll have to look for something else then too, huh, if they get rid of this place."

He looked triumphantly around N.'s paltry little domain. N. tried to look put out; he felt himself growing into a role again.

"I advised her against it. Those hospitals in France, they seem like an *amazing* mess."

"What do you mean?" His interest was suddenly piqued.

"Well, that thing with her throat… I think she's still a long way from being done with that. She smokes way too much too. But I can't say anything about it, or it turns into a fight. It's for her own good, but she's *incredibly* stubborn when it comes down to it."

Theo tells N. about how the landlady underwent radiation therapy on her vocal cords. They had assured her it was benign. But in his heart, he knew that Theo was right.

The conversation moved to somewhat lighter topics, then. They talked a bit longer, finishing a beer together, and before long, Theo left around eleven o'clock. N. didn't know it at the time, but it would be the last time they ever spoke to each other.

N. can't shake his restlessness. The rural silence of farm and pasture is unnerving. At dawn, he counted five roe deer that had returned, despite being driven from their territory during the recent hunt. Maybe they know that hunting season is over. One of Olga's goats peeks inside curiously, jaws working away at their usual circular grinding. They seem to watch over the house like sentinels, and they are always exactly aware who's in the house and when they can expect to be thrown a snack. It's the same for all the farm animals. The goats are perhaps the most persistent, but they only venture out when the weather is dry. The rain does not dissuade the chickens, the sheep, or the pony Dikkerdje, who is now being herded about by a mother goose's aggressive pecking. She grunts indignantly and then goes about her business, unperturbed.

At this scene, N. smiles involuntarily; watching animals on a farm brings peace to even the most confused of minds, and it soothes his own mental turmoil a bit. After his early morning walk, he again finds himself sitting apathetically in his armchair for hours. He has the place all to himself. Olga is tending to a patient and Sonja, with whom he spent the previous night, is sitting behind the cash register in X. His mood sinks even deeper with the absence of both ladies. Bart keeps him company for a while but eventually leaves him, bored by N.'s malaise, opting instead to wait for the return of his mistress at the end of the driveway.

The phone rings suddenly, breaking the intense silence with raw urgency. N. picks up, offers a greeting, but is met only by the sound of audible breathing on the other line. It's the fourth time this week, the umpteenth time in recent weeks. These empty disturbances of the atmosphere, which he calls (with some emotion) "telephone terrorism", have put him in an increasingly higher state of agitation. It used to happen to him before, in his other life. There was a period when he got an average of ten or twelve calls a week, both at home and at the institute, without anyone announcing themselves. And then there was the disturbing call—equally anonymous, but with a woman's voice—in which she told him there was a student in one of his lecture classes who was in love with him.

The pronouncement had titillated N.'s polygamist leanings and it had made his day. There had been no wanting for such attention in those days, passions that were sometimes fruitless, but more often times not. Statistically, there was almost a guarantee that a number of his colleagues would give over to their admirers, secretly or not. Similarly, and partly because of this, it closely matched the statistics of divorces and alimony issues. His routine performance in front of a room filled with students, which seemed so boring from his side of the podium, had an apparently strongly erotic effect on some of the young ladies.

N. wonders now if those young women saw a lecturer or scholar as a powerful official instead of what he really is: a handsomely paid and, on average, deadly boring civil servant.

The student in love with him, the anonymous voice revealed, was named Chantal. He knew it, Chantal Bleeker with the long brown hair. He was sure of that, that Chantal had long brown hair; he'd known that for the past year and a half. She was that gorgeous sophomore who used to sit right at the front of his lectures; of course, that fact alone was not proof that she was in love with him. But the woman on the phone had a completely different voice than Chantal, so it couldn't be her who had called him then. Her face or her attitude did not give any hint of special affection for him. However, after another call, he spoke into the receiver, "Chantal, please admit it's you, I know it is, we can talk about it!" The connection was broken before he'd finished speaking and the anonymous phone calls as well as her presence in his lectures became a thing of the past.

Upon inquiry, he learned that Chantal Bleeker, a fine student by all accounts, had left the university for unknown reasons. N. had deep regrets about not having approached all this a bit more inventively, and above all, with a bit more patience. He hoped she would contact him again, and when she didn't, he hoped at least that she ended up well and that, above all, she hadn't done anything hasty and irreversible.

Although he intuitively feels it is one of the Beumer ladies that keeps dialing his number, his experience with Chantal prevents him from confronting the caller by name. Because, he feels, something else is going on. The presence of these calls fit seamlessly into his idyll on the Vogelpoelweg; he simply accepted them as part of his experience. What reveals more about women's true feelings than precisely such interruptions? N. is almost certain it's Sonja who is calling, calling from work, perhaps still under the spell of their night's work together and needs to vent her feelings about it. But his heart is weary because, although they are the fruit of her romantic spirit and adolescent inexperience, she does not realize the effect such things have on the minds of healthy adult men.

But even these pleasant musings don't help relieve his disquiet; on the contrary, his anxiety is heightened by the uncertainty they bring about. And because he realizes that, as soon as the silent caller becomes known or gets tired of the thrill they induce, this piece of idyll will dissolve as well. Everything, N. thinks, eventually dissolves into drabness, habit, formality, banality, convention, old age and death.

"I guess today just isn't my day," he mumbles.

And he can't be altogether certain that those phone calls don't have another source, something hidden from him in the angry world outside. N. still remembers the strange incident a month and a half ago, on a beautiful autumn afternoon. He had and Sonja had just finished a rural lovemaking session in a young pine plantation somewhere between X and Q. He was lying heavily on his young girlfriend, recovering. Sonja had just asked whether he liked making love with two women, and as he was about to answer when he saw in front of him, half-hidden behind a pine, the white skin of a shin, that part that shows between a pant leg and a sock, and a men's brown slip-on, size forty-four or forty-five perhaps.

For a second, an image from a crime documentary flashed before his eyes. But then it seemed as if the owner of the leg and shoe knew they'd been spotted because they retreated nervously. The silhouette of a round man, dressed in light brown pants and a dark brown shirt, quickly disappeared behind pine branches.

Even if N. had wanted to run after the man, he felt compelled to stay and protect his young lover. They were both completely naked. She hadn't seen or heard anything, and he opted not to tell her. But N. hadn't felt completely at ease since that sunny afternoon in early October.

That event, the memory of it, makes him begin to think that maybe he's been struck by unnecessary paranoia.

He also deduces the fact that he may lack mental stability. Despite all the momentary fairy tales of his new life, at times like this morning when he is left alone with his thoughts, he has to fight the urge to abscond with his bicycle and his few belongings. There is a sense, he thinks, that something is hanging in the air that will lead to the discovery of his true identity; and he feels that his unmasking, is not far off.

It is for this reason that he still makes the occasional phone call in an effort to bring The Great Plan into reality.

All these considerations, endless lists of pros and cons, make him more and more insecure, his existence more undefined. His mood becomes mercurial, leading to even more inactivity. His mind is so flooded with hypotheticals that he can hardly achieve anything intellectual. Work on his novel has been neglected for over a week. He just doesn't see the point of it anymore. Sonja's tutoring has also stopped, and the diary remains untouched. He is simply overwhelmed by apathy.

But then, Olga's blue Peugeot drives past the window and moments later his room is full of life.

"Who do you think are the best writers?" She puts the question to him after—at her request—he let her read a piece from his manuscript.

In the past, when inexperienced freshmen would ask him which writers he thought were the best, he patiently explained that there's no such thing as "the best writers". Even similar questions about which books are the best, he taught, were useless; the answer must always involve a sum of subjective and objective sentiments. He paired these and similar questions with the invariable counter-question of which books made the greatest impact. This was a criterion for him, although also controversial. Does he have to explain all this to Olga? Does he have to explain why, for such different reasons, Sterne, Stendhal, Hermann Broch, Musil, Kafka's Metamorphosis, Célines two great pre-war novels, some short stories by Camus and Borges as well, have made such great impressions on him and sometimes still do?

In answer to her question, he explains once more why no writer is the "best writer" as far as he's concerned, and then he tastes the somewhat familiar tang of cynicism on his tongue, He had begun to notice this more acutely as he stood delivering this argument to a lecture hall full of students. He had taken this as a sign that his interest in his profession—and for literature in general—was on a terminal decline.

He decides to end his lecture prematurely, and they have a drink before making love elaborately and intensely. Unlike Sonja, the mother's lovemaking is unguarded, and N. equally invariably wonders how long it will be until she makes her solemn announcement. She is ready for another child., N. can sense this by that wordless language spoken between lovers.

33.

Something else is making him restless, heightening his confusion about his growing paranoia. In an effort to keep his mind and body fit, he recommits himself to his daily walking or cycling tours, winter weather permitting. He actually spends more time walking than on his bike, except on the days he rides to work, despite losing Sonja as his riding partner. Despite the rainy weather in the past few weeks and the fact that Sonja no longer joins him, he still rides over to Piet de Wilde's store with his steel steed. Either out of habit or mental laziness, he notices that he has started taking the same walking route every time. Ten kilometers, alternating between clockwise and counterclockwise, along forest paths and heathland, past manicured meadows and pastures.

It is this silent season of waiting, of late autumn gossamer and falling leaves. Overhead somewhere there is a quiet rumble of a propeller plane plowing itself through the air, but otherwise he meets no one, until he's passed by a man, walking in the opposite direction. He must be a local to the area, N. thinks, as his face is familiar to him and seems to be popping up again and again for the past month now. He is middle-aged with a normal build. Today, N. notices that he has a balding head; he seems to remember the man's head is usually covered with a green trilby. He is carrying an umbrella on his back today, and is wrapped in his usual long loden cape. Every time they pass, they exchange a type of greeting; nothing exceptionally overt, just a smile in response to a short nod of the other's head; a simple gesture of friendly acknowledgement. Normally, N. would not give him a second thought, but it is becoming more and more difficult to shake the feeling that he knows the man from somewhere, from some distant period in his past. But no matter how deep he digs, he never manages to drag up the exact memory.

But that is not the reason why N. has been strongly considering the idea of striking up a conversation with the man. It was risky, he knew that. Pulling ghosts from the past into his new life would inevitably place his entire anonymous existence in jeopardy. But what is of particular interest to N. is the fact that, regardless of the day, the time, or the weather conditions when he takes his walk, he invariably encounters him. And what irritates him even further is that no matter which direction he starts his exercise, clockwise or counterclockwise, the other always passes him face to face, walking in the opposite direction. N.'s paranoia heightens his restlessness, and he has begun to suspect that the man is watching his cottage from a distance to see which direction he chooses, then sets off in the opposite direction to meet him halfway.

N. makes a sincere attempt to ease his own mind; he decides that the man must not have full surveillance of his recreational activities because when he chooses a different path or deviates from the usual route along the way, they do not pass each other. But even when the man is not visible, N. still feels his watchful presence, and his paranoia gradually turns to fear and panic. Finally, about a week ago, he decided he was going to find an excuse to address the man, hoping that an innocent chat would offer some clarity regarding his identity and intentions.

So, on this particular morning, when N. sees the man approaching, he begins walking towards him. They are on a dirt road, a bit muddy from the recent rain, at a point where the path cuts through a Scotch pine forest. N. approaches him with the intended objective. As the two draw nearer together, it's suddenly as if the man guesses N.'s intention (maybe from N. posture, or body language – he keeps all the possibilities open) and at about fifty meters apart, the man suddenly jumps over a ditch with one strong, athletic leap, his coat tails fluttering, arms outstretched like a ballet dancer. Then he bounds over a small heath onto a forest path and disappears into the pines. The man's unexpected agility—he had the nimble quickness of a young boy—leaves N. standing in a daze.

That night, N. relives this absurd spectacle as he tries to drift into a sound sleep. He can't stop himself from obsessively fixating on the man's appearance. Throwing caution to the wind, N. decides that the next time he sees the man, he will accost him, grill him for information. But it's almost as if his thoughts are being broadcast before him, because the next afternoon (another Wednesday, cool but sunny), at a distance of about a hundred and fifty meters away, the man already turns around, retracing his steps and walking quickly ahead of N. He breaks into a jog, but the man looks back quickly, then begins jogging as well. N. picks up the pace; so does the man. The chase has clearly begun, but N. cannot gain on him. He starts shouting. The man then breaks into a sprint, and once he's about two hundred meters ahead of N., jumps as high as a deer over a hedgerow, once again effortlessly smooth and unrestrained, and disappears into the bushes further on.

N. turns around, retracing his steps to the Vogelpoelweg, . his movements hasty and frantic. Olga who had seen him leave, was surprised when he returned from the same direction (nothing escapes a woman in love, nothing at all, N. thinks). She invited him for a cup of tea and a sandwich, which he gladly accepted. They made small talk, then stripped naked and fell into her bed together. Even the protection of her warm body, already so familiar and comforting, and the soothing balm of ejaculation were not enough to calm his poor heart. She was kind to him, despite his restlessness; N. wondered if she knew that he would soon be leaving her.

The events of the last two days have sent in him a rollicking panic. He can no longer find innocent excuses for this strange behavior, and after deliberating through most of a sleepless night, he decides that he must pack his bags immediately and begin implementing his plan to leave the region, the country, and preferably Europe as quickly as possible. He can feel some dark part of his past tugging at his mask; staying in this place means imminent exposure.

The next evening, N. tries to make contact with Manaus. The connection was terrible. A woman's voice came on the line, and through crackling and static, she conveys to him in almost unintelligible Brazilian that *senhor* Versteegh is not available and tells him to call back another time. He tries again two days later. This time, Manaus himself answers, and the connection is clear. Plans are set.

There's something else that has heightened N.'s paranoia. He will eventually discover that it is diabolically linked with something else. Since about mid-September, during his walks, he occasionally sees a girl. He guesses she's about eighteen years old, with long dark brown hair. She is not unattractive: slender, almost fragile, and quite a tall thing. She is invariably standing with her bicycle at a six-way intersection of sand roads and B-roads in the middle of the forest. There's a bench there where she sometimes sits, a cigarette balanced between her fingers, staring off aimlessly into space. When he arrives, their greeting is friendly, they've even exchanged a few words. At one point, N. thought she might be interested in him—she seemed rather flirtatious—and the thought was accompanied with a certain leap of his heart.

In early October, N. discovers what brings her to this spot, alone, over and over again. N.'s happy assumption that she was interested in him when he learns she is there for a rendezvous. The warm summer days had returned one last time before departing for the rest of autumn, and he rode up on her with a boy. He was about her age, probably of Mediterranean descent, and also had a bicycle parked near the bench. He discovered the two of them by chance. He approached the intersection with the intention of taking a short comfort stop behind some bushes. The two were undressed, bodies so intensely intertwined in the act of lovemaking that God, who oversees everything from His strategic height, could barely have concealed a smile. N. withdrew diffidently and with a touch of disappointment.

A few weeks after this *entre nous*, he witnesses the same girl being harassed at the same intersection by a dark boy. He cursed at her, calling her a Muslim whore, then slapping her across the face with the back of his hand. N. rides toward them quickly, wanting to intervene, but the boy quickly pulled her into his car, covering N. in dust as he peels away from the intersection. The young ladies' bicycle was left behind the bench; when N. returns the following day, the bike is gone. N. didn't see her again for most of November, until last week when he saw her again with her dark boyfriend. There were traces of injuries on her head; while N. looked on shyly.

When he saw her yesterday, alone, he decided to sit next to her on the bench and chat a while. The air wasn't cold, about fifteen degrees, and cloudy but dry. They talked for half an hour and when no one showed up, he asked half-jokingly whether there might have been a misunderstanding. Her answer warmed N.'s heart and mind and made his rural idyll—, somewhat dulled due to the monotony of frequent intercourse with the landlady and her daughter—suddenly began to shine again like new. The dear girl, cheeky and flirtatious, said:

"Well, I've noticed you're always alone here, too."

He nodded, rather surprised by her sudden familiarity

"Well, why shouldn't I be here on my own? Two lonely souls, side by side on a bench."

She laughed and put her hand on his knee. Her voice was pleasant, without a trace of an accent, and she was beautiful when she laughed.

"Did you come here to find me?" He was surprised that the question came out clearly, that his voice didn't break, despite the pounding in his chest.

"Hmm, maybe? Who knows." She looked him straight in the eyes, her pupils dark. He wanted to know the myriad of thoughts passing behind those eyes. With suddenly, his throat felt gripped by an odd feeling, he took refuge in generalities. Another half hour passed before they got up, and N. said, his voice hoarse like that of an older man, "Well, there's no time like the present to ask you your name."

She laughed again, standing about ten meters away from him with her bike, one foot on the pedal, ready to mount and ride away.

"I'm Suzanne," she said, smiling. "And you?"

"Chris," he said, and he was shocked. He hadn't uttered that name since leaving the explosion more than half a year earlier.

"Well Chris, see you next time then. I'm looking forward to it."

She smiled at him suggestively, then waved, and rode away. After about a hundred meters she turned her head and raised her hand again. Neither of the boys he'd seen her with previously had ever shown up.

That night he shared his bed with Sonja. He was very sweet to her. And she was to him, giving herself over to him completely, as she always did. The entire time he enjoyed her body, he thought only of Suzanne.

34.

Over time, the healthful abundance he'd cultivated with his prophylactic lifestyle began to be eroded by ghosts, delusions, fears and other irritations. Olga and Sonja had invaded his veins like a virus, and now Suzanne added to the inoculation. Heavy rain showers forced N. to take public transport to and from X on occasion. One morning, a lady next to him on the bus sneezed without having the decency to cover her face, and N. found himself sick with a terrible flu. In his feverish dreams, N. sees different faces pass in front of him. The police commissioner appears, pointing his shotgun at H. and wanting to charge him for tearing up his driver's license. Then the squire from Theo's hunting party, arguing suddenly like Voltaire in his best moments, coaxing N. back to health with pieces of raw hare leg. The faces of Sonja and Olga appear before him too, and even Paula, who reprimands him strongly for his strange behavior. Paula's mother, to his great surprise, takes his side and forgives him for her daughter's mésalliance. Farmer De Geus passes by with his tractor, spying on him as he makes love with Olga (or is it Sonja?) in the vegetable garden, amongst the kale, in the rain. Bart is there too, on several occasions, wagging his tail until Sonja (or is it Olga?) ushers him out of the room.

In between visits, both real and imagined, he floats through a wispy and colorful haze, darkened now and then by the shadow cast by an unknown man with glasses, moustache and goatee, who gropes at him from all sides and tries to engage him with insane, childish remarks (to which N. rigidly grits his teeth). He is laid on his belly like a baby being put into a clean diaper, they press on his shoulder blades; he is ordered to breathe in deeply, to breathe out, to breathe in again and to breathe out again. Blood is drawn, his precious blood, and sometimes he finds evidence to convince himself that the enemy has him behind bars and he is being interrogated and tortured under bright lights.

His fever reached temperatures of forty-two degrees, then even a little higher. At a certain point, N. struggled to breathe, and the situation became so critical that they were on the verge of calling an ambulance. The crisis lasts for four days. On the fifth day, the fever breaks, and after some inspecting by the doctor, N. is allowed to convalesce at home under the express custody of both Beumer women. He is informed that what started as a severe cold turned into a nasty respiratory infection. It would be another week before he could gather enough strength to enjoy a short walk or bike ride.

When the doctor's bill arrives, the office insists that he must pay an amount of 414.95 euros with a giro account using the attached payment form. He pleads with the receptionist, finally convincing her with an easy lie about plans to leave the country for good. He tells her that he's already cancelled his giro and bank account here, and she finally concedes to letting him pay in cash, wishing him all the best for his new life abroad.

N. worries for a time that in his delirium, he may have exposed his true identity, but after several days with neither Sonja nor Olga showing any signs of this knowledge, he relaxes his fears a bit. Sometime later, he thinks of Suzanne and worries that his absence from the bench in the woods would lead her to conclude that he's played her for the fool. He resolves to attempt the trip by bike later that week.

It is the first of December and Olga celebrates her forty-third birthday with a small party. Tilly has driven there from Osnabrück and plans to stay the whole weekend. Also in attendance are an acquaintance from Y and two female colleagues from the family care foundation that Olga works for. Theo is conspicuously absent from the birthday gathering that evening. When N. inquires about his whereabouts, Olga tells him with a conspiratorial smile that Theo had been shown the door for reasons that Kees is sure to understand. N. was surprised to realize some small regret at the loss of his late-night checkers partner. During N.'s crisis, Olga tells him, he had picked up his caravan, loaded with his things. A little later in the evening, farmer De Geus and his wife stop by, filling the house with the unmistakable smell of silage.

The mood is joyful and boisterous. There's a lot of talk and anecdotes that are too far removed from N.'s experience for him to contribute anything meaningful. After a few drinks, Jan de Geus talks loudly about his youth. Born and raised at the Vogelpoelweg, and eventually to be buried at the cemetery in Q, he knows everything about the surroundings and the people. He holds the audience for a time, but his soon overtaken by the ladies' enthusiastic chatter and gossip. Being the only other man in the group, de Geus turns his conversation toward N., yammering about the agricultural policies of The Hague and Brussels, about the consequences for the farmers' stock when agricultural subsidies are cut, and the fear of cutthroat competition when Poland and other former Eastern Bloc countries join the EU. Jan is a soft man, and his many worries seem to weigh heavily on him.

This evening babbles on in unencumbered conviviality and for a few hours N. is freed from his fears, worries and confusion . For one evening, it is the old Arcadia again. Although it is not discussed explicitly, he soon realizes his presence at the party is a formal introduction to these people, Olga's most trusted companions, as her new companion. At least, she makes no attempt to dispel these suspicions clearly being raised by her friends with their inquisitive and deductive glances in his direction. When he catches one of the ladies studying him—the curious stranger with his proper way of speaking—he smiles. By the end of the evening, there is a wordless understanding that their "relationship" has been formalized; N. feels a pang of regret knowing that he will soon be leaving this domestic paradise.

It is past midnight before Olga has said goodbye to the last of her guests. Sonja has gone to her bedroom and Tilly has retreated to the guestroom. In the spacious living room, messy from the gathering, Olga finally asks the question that has hung like a shadow over them for so long: Would he be willing to move with her and Sonja to Franche-Comté if she sold her property here next spring? She has enough money to buy the farmhouse on the edge of a hamlet, twenty kilometers to the southeast of Besançon that she has her eye on. She knows the local real estate agent and the *maire*; a man who she is sure N. will like very much. He won't have to worry about anything, she assures him. She's already hired a local contractor to do all the necessary renovation work. He's already sent drawings and specifications for her approval. Kees can continue to write and paint every day, take his walks and bike rides. She's taking Bart to France too, of course, and considering bringing along the pony, Dikkerdje, and any of the other small livestock they'll allow her to transport across the border. She plans to work just part time, probably in Besançon, and Sonja will certainly manage to find a part-time job there as well. She'll have enough left over from the sale of her house here to provide her with a hefty safety blanket, and it would be so wonderful if the three of them could stay together. She, Olga, would love it if one day he would become the father of Sonja's children. Oh, and she would actually like to have another child with him too. Surely that is still possible, she must still be fertile enough, because she's almost three weeks late, as of today. She begs him to stay with them for the rest of their lives.

He suddenly finds the phrase—and its implied expectation of him—irritating. For the rest of our lives? For God's sake, thinks N., why? Why not temporarily, maybe five years for instance. This idea that love is meant to last an eternity is so stupid, naïve, or conservative. And how could she, with her sordid past, not instinctively sense how it is between people in the world, with agreements, commitments, tenderness and promises? How could she possibly expect such a guarantee?

He immediately feels a bit grumpy.

But he doesn't want to disappoint her, leaving her with a sinking feeling to end her festive birthday. He simply tells her the proposal is quite straightforward, a bit overwhelming at the moment, but of course he will continue to think about it. They make love intensely that night. He hasn't forgotten her earlier words, and by the feel of her body, he is absolutely certain that she is pregnant. He is also absolutely certain that his future lies elsewhere. He wants to become who he *is*, and he cannot achieve that if he ties himself down to these women for the rest or even part of his short human existence.

He finds that he is pleased with Olga's pregnancy, however. His list of values taped to the inside of his closet door lists it as the 6th point as the natural desire to plant his seed in multiple strong females to be assured of immortality with strong and healthy offspring. And isn't that all the hunting male really wants? No fixed address, no fixed wife, no commitment. Transient, from bed to bed, tirelessly searching for the egg desiring his seed. That is the least he wants for himself in the years to come. A life without offspring seems biologically useless to him; and what, he thinks, is life other than biology? In the creature called "human", a rudimentary layer of spirit is wrapped up in the colored paper of culture. He knows that his yearning for more exotic habitats and living areas is sprung from this same desire; he imagines tribal cultures, where the rules and obligations attached to fatherhood are less rigid and easier to violate than in the so-called humane West, which is confined by an abundance of legal, moral and religious codes. After Olga's informal proclamation, he makes a quick calculation. Suppose a child has indeed been on the way for about a month. If he plays the happy father-to-be here at the Vogelpoelweg until no later than mid-March, she will be five months pregnant; morally and medically too late for an abortion. Certainly be it will take some time before it is clear to the ladies that he has definitively decided to skedaddle.

Anyway, even these considerations cannot dispel his annoyance in the moment. It is a long time before he is able to fall asleep next to her.

They are awakened the next morning around ten o'clock by the sound of a tremendous rainstorm clattering on the roof. N. is still off work, because he is officially still recovering from his illness. Through the clatter of the rain, he hears Olga and Tilly driving to Y; they had plans to spend the day shopping. He stares at the giant fruit basket from Piet de Wilde & his co-workers, plucks a handful of grapes and pops them into his mouth, one at a time. Then he gets up and eats some breakfast before he begins editing a portion of the novel he'd written just before his collapse.

…In the adjoining room, I hear Ayisha breathing, my dark warm-blooded angel. After we gave ourselves to each other and she, at her age not yet accustomed to the power of male passion, fell asleep exhausted in my arms, I very carefully extricated myself from her entanglement to get up and do some more work. I don't think she noticed anything; her sleep is deep, unlike mine. It is the heat of the day that I still haven't gotten used to, that bothers me and that lingers in the rooms at night despite the whine of the air conditioning.

Maryse, my "bara muso" is away for day or so at her mother's in Sanaba. We've already offered a couple of times that Fatima come live with us — she is almost blind. But she still can't decide. She doesn't want to leave the people she knows there; she says. After all, she still has family there…

N. notices that his story has increasingly begun to parallel his actual existence at this moment, and perhaps for this reason he finds the foreshadowing of coming developments a bit barefaced. He shakes his head; it all seems cheap to him, suddenly, and artificial: in short, the writing is bad, worthless. "Writing?" he mumbles, "this is just annoying vanity, useless exhibitionism. It's almost as useless as an office job or a management position in education. Anyone who claims to write for pleasure, claims to just write for the sake of writing, is lying through their teeth. The reality is that everyone is after money and fame and hoping for a wide and enthusiastic audience. I'm just as bad as any hypocrite, a self-denialist, no better or worse than the rest. Maybe that Van Langstraten was right with his half-drunken ideas."

His memory takes him to a Friday afternoon from his former life during one of the monthly faculty cocktail hours. Alcohol would loosen the tongues and ripen the minds of his colleagues, opening the door for some of their more daring albeit less scientific theories. On that afternoon, Van Langstraten, a sixty-year-old German literature professor, referred to his colleagues as „All those Betje Wolffs and Piet Paaltjens' of late twentieth-century Dutch literature." N. heard him say it again, after what must have been the man's fifth whisky. According to Professor Van Langstraten, it was high time for a new Olympia Press and a man like Girodias to finally give fringe writing another chance. History was repeating itself, he claimed, and book censorship was happening again, but this time it wasn't just governments, but the commercial publishing circuit which, despite its protests to the contrary, actually only cared about the sacred sales figures. Culture had long since been replaced by commerce. The stench of the newly created industrial middle class wafted from the doors of all Dutch bookstores today. When he walked by a bookstore, he told the faculty, he always quickened his step and held a handkerchief in front of his face; not only to be spared the sight of those pathetic stacks of *libris* blocks "with their boastful back flaps," but also out of fear that the scent of death of these ephemera would lead him to collapse, unconscious at the entrance of the book seller's door.

The professor continued his loosely eloquent rambling for a few more rounds, causing the crowd to giggle or cheer appropriately.

"Books, thick as fists and heavy as bricks," he said, "sit in crates, boxes and trucks, abandoned. I always tell my students that before they choose a thankless career in authorship, they ought to take a long look at the central book warehouse in Culemborg and ask themselves sincerely who would really want to read what they write. "By his ninth or tenth whisky, however, his high-brow philosophizing had disintegrated into little more than drunken rambling, and the crowd's interest has been lost altogether.

N. later discovered that Van Langstraten had once produced a forty-page novella of his own, grandly presenting it to all the literary publishers in Holland, and after being unanimously rejected, translated the story into English and German hoping for better luck with foreign publishers. . Alas, the effort was made in vain. Incidentally, it was discovered that he had done the writing and translation work during his working hours and sent the manuscript in university envelopes and by university post.

The memory makes N. think about the time he has spent writing and then editing the *African Bride*. His heart and soul haven't been in it for a long time, now. He has been far too restless. But there's something else now, too. He realizes with this memory that there is a deeper fear, an anxiety over time spent on imminent failure. He only has to look at the growing stack of manuscript paper to trigger the thought of Rimbaud. That bard was barely twenty-two when he gave up poetry for good, abandoning a fruitless career in favor of a real, more rewarding life. N. is now thirteen or fourteen years older than Arthur Rimbaud was at that time, and is just now diving into a story which he strongly expects will never surpass the passing whimsy of the cultural middle class. He doubts his story will be impactful enough to offer any real added value. The paper is dead, the ink is wasted. He thinks with unveiled disgust of the people, hundreds of thousands of them in this country alone, some of them well into their eighties, sensible people, intellectuals even, who toil away on meaningless poems and short stories or essays, only to have their work rejected again and again by editorial boards of publishers, eventually driving them to despair. Even so-called "established" writers can never hope to rise higher than the impermanence of the fickle middle-class, and only then by denigrating themselves by seeking favor on some daytime talk show. They become exhibitionists, answering meaningless questions from program hosts who are ultimately only interested in ratings and are not really interested in their guests' works. The whole business is disgraceful! *For God's sake*, N. thinks, *don't people have anything better to do? Don't I have anything better to do?* And then he tosses the manuscript under a chair, vowing to never again, commit pen to paper for the sake of "writing". No, never again! And just like that, his commitment to modest immortality is abandoned for other, more important priorities.

Suddenly there is an overpowering feeling of liberation...

And then the phone rings. He picks up, listens again to the familiar quiet breathing on the other end. Inspired by his newfound self-determination, N finally vocalizes his suspicions into the receiver: "Sonja, I know it's you. Why are you doing this?"

Then suddenly there is an explosion of laughter on the other line. A man's laughter, of that much he is certain. The laughter will echo in his mind, taunting him long after the receiver is set down. N. recoils, looks at the phone in horror. For a moment he worries he'll black out. But he regains his strength, comes back to himself, and hangs up abruptly. A grim foreboding slides and locks into place where it will remain his sardonic companion by day and by night.

35.

On an afternoon in mid-December, watching the last flights of geese passing overhead, N. struggles to comprehend the events unfolding around him. He has no control over them; he has become their plaything. The weather is calm, with a pleasant temperature for this time of year, forming a humid mist of twelve degrees.. He is on one of his beloved walks, contemplating how he can say goodbye to the Beumer ladies, preferably in some decent way (although realizing that they've passed the threshold where his leaving cannot be considered "decent" by any means, anymore). He has abandoned the original plan to stay until March, that diabolical phone call had spoiled any hopes of that. He hasn't seen Suzanne again, who he now realizes, with stinging regret, was little more than a stranger to him. But his priorities have changed; he is now concerned with somewhat loftier concerns than the indeterminate flirtations of a girl who, if their ages were any further apart, might even end in scandal.

He hasn't seen the man on the walking path, either, since his attempt to make contact. N. assumes he must have given up, frightened off by N.'s impetuous initiative. With the man's absence, N. feels once again that the extensive forests and heaths are reserved solely for his enjoyment.

He is about halfway through his walk (he's started with the clockwise pattern today) when a few hundred meters in front of him, on the left side of the dirt road, a police car approaches the intersection at full speed, throwing up mud and leaves, followed immediately by an ambulance. They don't have their sirens on, , but they are moving with no less urgency. At the intersection, far ahead of N., they turn left onto the sandy path toward the six-way crossroads, about a kilometer and a half further on; it is the same direction N. had planned on going.

N., whose sensitivity to the authorities unleashes yet another feeling of disquiet, decides not to take his usual route past the former meeting point today. Instead, he turns right and follows another path into the woods. It isn't long, however, before his curiosity—ignited by the hasty approach of the two vehicles— drives him to veer into the woods in an attempt to approach the bench with a flanking movement. He thinks for a moment that he is like a moth, drawn to the lamp that will cause its inevitable doom, but he cannot resist. From the cover of the undergrowth, he can see the first police car and ambulance parked along the roadway. Next to them is another police car and a few private cars. There are about eight serious-looking people, including a male and female paramedic lifting a lifeless figure on a stretcher and carefully but mechanically sliding it into the back of the ambulance. Leaning against the back of the bench is Suzanne's bike.

N. registers a shock tingling through his body. Something instinctively tells him that he should not be seen. With a pounding heart he retreats, stepping cautiously backward, careful not to make any noise. He quickly makes his way to the B-road— the fastest route to Vogelpoelweg—where he runs frantically toward the farmhouse.

He reaches the De Geus farm in about fifteen minutes and catches his first view of the Beumer house. He stops suddenly where he is met with another unpleasant surprise: the fact that Olga's yard, between the main house and his cottage, is jammed with a number of unknown cars, including two or three bearing the colors and seals of regional law enforcement. The mist has thickened to a heavy fog, but N. can still make out a healthy swarm of uniforms, some blue, some green and possibly camouflage. Bart is frantically running back and forth, barking furiously at a pack of hunting dogs. To his horror, N. sees a large, brutish man going in and out of his rented accommodations. The barefaced and unapologetic trampling of his rights enrage N., but under such threatening circumstances, he knew he couldn't do anything about it.

Trusting a deep inner voice, N. retreats quickly to the thickness of the forest; he had no doubt that the swarm of agents at the Beumer home had been led there by his existence. He also felt sure, but without evidence, that the scene he had witnessed at the bench was directly connected to the scene playing out before him. His heart begins pounding high in his throat.. There is a loud whistle immediately followed by an enthusiastic chorus of whining and howling from the hunting dogs. Then doors are slammed and a company of about ten or eleven men and dogs begin moving slowly *en carré* from the yard towards the B-road, spreading into an unmistakable search party, heading generally in his direction.

The hunt has begun, and he is the prey. What other reason do these men have for desecrating his home? He has to assume that they are all good, hard-working, tax-payers professionals, civil servants doing their honest duty to serve the greater good. N. shoves his hand into his jacket pocket; to his unspeakable joy he feels the outline of his wallet. The evidence of his true identity is safe, for now anyway. Then he quickly starts a retreat, hoping to outflank the search party.

After only one kilometer, this foolish hope is dashed. Another police car is parked on the next street that N. encounters, and past that another suspicious vehicle. His detection and arrest are imminent; he's sure that he's already trapped.

In one final attempt to escape, he leaves the beaten track. He is familiar with the area by now, having walked so much of it that even individual trees and shrubs are familiar to him. He runs through the woods in a crisscross pattern. But as plentiful as the hiding places seem in this forest, there is no hiding from the snout of a hunting dog. They will find him, pounce on him, or at the very least form a howling cordon around him until their owners can overtake him. And the trees and shrubs and burrows and all the good animals there will watch motionlessly as he is hauled away.

In an impressive display of panic and with still only a slight suspicion of why this is all happening, N. scrambles through the cover of bushes and trees, at one point crossing the road between Q and X, disappearing into the woods on the other side. He makes it to the part of the forest where the arbitrary municipal line between Q and P, the neighboring rural township. The image comes to mind of a scene from an American movie he'd seen once, a fugitive runs to safety across a bridge, the river being used as a great political border, probably the Missouri or Mississippi. But this is not a film or fantasy, and blood-set hounds do not recognize jurisdictional boundaries.

N. throws caution to the wind and sets into a dead sprint. If they decide to release the dogs, the chase would be hopeless at this distance. Then, quite suddenly, a police officer steps out from behind a tree unholstering his side arm in a single fluid motion. "Freeze! Put your hands in the air!" N. stops, immediately complying. The officer circles in on him, weapon still drawn, then says in a somewhat more subdued shout, "Are you Van Andel, Mr. Van Andel?" His voice attempts to hide a quiver, betraying the officer's youth. On closer inspection, N. thinks he looks way too young to be allowed to carry a service weapon at all. A representative of Justitia, that damned institution with its time-wasting formality, still managing to block his path to true existence. Why is it so impossible for a man to arrange his existence as he sees fit? With something as pathetic as the amateur efforts of this young automaton, K. van Andel will once again become Chris Janssen. No more nonsense, no more foolishness; a great mystery will soon be solved, and the whole world here will know it, shrug its shoulders and then simply return to the order of the day.

A terrible rage takes possession of N. How had he come to such a grievous end? As the young officer approaches, N. suddenly steps forward, grabbing the man first by the forearm and then by the neck, throws him to the ground. He strikes him with the side of his hand between the throat and neck, just under his ear.

This is the single move he learned during a few self-defense lessons, and he is surprised to feel it come back instinctively. The blow lands, and the officer is knocked unconscious.

With the cop lying there looking foolish but comfortable, one ear resting in the soft pine needles, N. grabs the pistol from his hand, looks at it for a moment, then throws it into the bushes. He darts into the thick undergrowth again, just as another man approaches. He kneels over the pitiable policeman, checks his pulse, then looks around, stands up, and unholsters a pistol from under his coat. He runs with the gun drawn, disappearing into the bushes, in the exact opposite direction of N.

N. is thankful for the physical fitness he's acquired over in the past year and a half as he runs confidently from woodland to heathland and back to woodland without the slightest shortness of breath. Running through a particularly thick section of heathland, N. comes upon a dirt road, looking around carefully before crossing. He's been running like this for at least a half hour, and the fog has thickened and grown dark. N. looks at his watch. Half past three. Perhaps he can lose his pursuers under the protection of the approaching dusk. If he keeps going in his current direction, he knows that in about two miles he will have crossed the entire forest between Q, P and X and will reach a vast expanse of farmland, scattered farms —laying fallow for the winter months; in other words, he'll be visible for miles in all directions.

N. decides to keep moving. It's been some time since he's heard any sign of the dogs that he knew were dangerously close behind him for a while. His pace slows, feeling a slight ease in pressure. He is on the edge of an extended heathland, perhaps five hundred meters across, with scattered pine trees and some juniper-like shrubs. He is about to cross over when he suddenly hears a loud, enthusiastic shout. "There... there he is! Look! Over there!" Immediately a whistle sounds, and again there is the barking of dogs. N. can see his that the situation is closing in on all sides; he is trapped. He shoots back into the cover of the woods, certain that his efforts are useless, but in the thick fog, he can't see even a meter in front of his face.

He comes to what he believes is the edge of another, smaller field but hesitates to cross it, sensing that he is surrounded on both his left and right sides. Mathematically, his path forward is eliminated.

Realizing this, N. suddenly becomes calm, his head clear and calculating. In front of him in the heathland, about fifty meters away, two or three large spruces stand tall, above the fog and twilight like heavy giants or God's fingers pointing upward. In twenty or thirty long steps he reaches the first spruce. He grabs the lowest branch that is thick enough to hold his weight, as far from the trunk as possible, and works his way up the tree. As skillfully as a spider monkey, he climbs higher and higher, feeling a calm wash over him with every meter he puts between himself and the ground. As he passes the top half of the tree, he moves toward the trunk for more balance, then climbs even higher. He stops near the top of the tree, balancing on a branch. From here the base of the trunk is no longer visible and he still has some view over the surrounding field. He thinks he is comfortable enough that he can rest here for a while. Once again, he hopes that the fog and falling darkness will soon become impenetrable.

Sweating and vibrating from the effort, he waits for events to unfold below him. He hears men and dogs approaching from the left. They walk under his tree. Between the branches, N. can see one of the beasts, nose to the ground pulling at his leash. Suddenly his head jolts up and the dog sniffs at the air exactly where N. had jumped onto the branch. But in the next moment, the hound returns its nose to the ground and continues searching. Eventually it becomes clear that the dogs have lost the scent.

"He *has* to be here, somewhere. I saw him running in this direction," he hears someone say in a thick Belgian accent. He hears several voices fade in and out, and then another group of pursuers approach from the left. Both groups of hunters greet each other companionably. There's even laughter, at which N. feels a certain indignation; it is, after all, a man hunt. N. now hears the men's voices more clearly now, but they are still too far away to distil any factual information. He has the impression they are marking time, perhaps discussing the next phase of their search. Then one voice cuts above the rest: "It's getting *amazingly* dark," he hears a familiar voice saying. "Maybe we'd be better off to start again tomorrow…" The rest of the sentence breaks down into a short cough.

N. is suddenly feels a heavy blow at his heart at this betrayal; on some level, he had begun to enjoy his time with Theo, and had considered him a friend. Although he can't see him, N. can tell Theo has come closer to the truck of his tree because he can hear him clearly as he explains to his cohorts that he "always knew there was something suspicious about that guy, he'd suspected from the beginning." He described his initial suspicion that Kees van Andel was far too interested in young girls, and in hindsight he isn't at all surprised about what they discovered today. "My only regret," the stocky man says boisterously, "is that I didn't turn him into the authorities sooner."

"Well yeah, but as long as you don't have proof…"

N. can hear the two men clearly and assumes that they must be at the foot of his spruce tree. He imagines one man rolling a cigarette, passing it to the other fraternally. Through the branches, N. can barely make out the shape of a brown spotted hound, sitting on his tail a little further away, sniffing the air and looking dumbly in the opposite direction.

"What do you base your assumptions on?" It's Theo's partner posing the question. He seems a bit more intelligent than both the dog and Theo. Then he hears Theo present a razor-sharp analysis of his character and personality. He describes a man who (in summary) is always holding something back, never looks you in the eye when you're talking to him. Theo describes how the man tries—in vain, mind you—to get between himself and Olga Beumer, and when that didn't work, he went after the woman's daughter.

"Well, you know how it is. People like that keep searching until they get what they want." In short, no woman from sixteen to eighty-six was safe from his depravity.

N. notices that the detail Theo conveniently leaves out of his story is that Olga and Sonja had kicked him out some weeks earlier. He wonders whether the man actually has any proof of N.'s wrong-doings, or if he is basing his accusations on suspicion alone. Olga had played it all very cleverly, after all. Perhaps too cleverly for a brute like Theo, to be sure.

After finishing their cigarettes, N. hears the two men stand up and brush off their clothes. He hears fragmented bits of the end of their conversation. Words like "nasty wound", "messed up" and "worrying how she…" reach the higher regions of the spruce tree. N. strains his ears as they move away, but soon he can no longer make out exactly what they say. He was hoping to glean some knowledge of why they were pursuing him and what kind of evidence they had. Not that it actually matters, N. knows that. What he *has* seen and heard from the day leave him certain it is serious enough. After some time, N. feels certain that the search has been called off for the day. In the distance, he thinks he can hear a roll call sounding off. There are a few distant whistles, a dog barks loudly and then the sound fades. A dead, damp silence falls over dense undergrowth.

Between the moonless sky and the heavy, wet fog, the ground is invisible. When he holds his hands in front of his eyes, they disappear; there is such an inky darkness that N. cannot read the dials on his wristwatch, no matter how close he brings it to his face. In the neighboring spruce, the squirrel stands on the end of a branch and indicates his displeasure with short, staccato sounds that he should get out of here. He guesses he has been standing in the tree for about an hour and a half. His hands are cold, a cramp is growing in the arch of his left foot. He very slowly makes his way down the tree, landing softly on the branches. His hands are sticky with sap and pieces of tree bark stick to his palms. His pants and jacket are soaked with sweat and humidity.

When he reaches the lowest branch, he pauses for a moment, listening. With a gentle thud he drops to the ground. He takes a couple of steps before he nearly buckles at the knees; someone is tapping gently on his shoulder, demanding attention. When he turns around, only a silhouette is visible. The figure is smaller than his own, but that is about the only detail he can discern.

He is about to attack the man, when he says quickly, "Chris, I would get out of here right now if I were you. If you're still here at first light tomorrow, they'll get you. You've caused too much commotion for them to abandon the hunt now."

"Who are you?" N.'s voice sounds strange, choked with shock but nevertheless loud and coherent. But the silhouette , that of a man, is already disappearing. Twigs break under his footfalls, then the sound of heather whipping against boots. Then once again an intense silence descends and the mist becomes impenetrable.

He struggles through the darkness, gaining a stronger presence of mind with each couple of meters. Wherever possible, he avoids open areas and paths, stops now and then to orient himself by the sound of traffic passing on the main road between Q and X. At a certain point, the sound barely manages to penetrate the thick fog, but he comes to it eventually and crosses it, waiting until there are no passing cars in ear shot. A few times he stumbled over a tree root, stepped into a full ditch. He tripped over a log in the dark, fell forward and twisted his left wrist. In the periphery of a beam of light, he was just able to make out on his watch that the time is now nearly six o'clock.

He estimates that he'll be back at the edge of the woods near De Geus's farm by about half past six. Because of the fog, he cannot see even the faintest sign of light coming from the Beumer farm. N. is aware of the risks, but he has no choice; there are some things in that cottage he simply cannot survive without. He'll need the relics, of course, and the pile of cash he's been stashing behind a stack of plates in the kitchen counter cabinet. Without those two things, he'll be forced into theft, burglary, or begging by tomorrow.

36.

Who was that man? Where did he come from? How does he know my name? N.'s mind is racing with questions; his brain is an explosion of tiny sparks. But he must address the most immediate concerns first. Fate weighs on him heavily now. The last five months of *dolce vita* have lulled him into a dangerous sleep and the time has come to regain control. Someone knows that Chris Janssen is alive! This small fact alone is enough for N. to abandon his construct of reality. If one person knows, isn't it reasonable to assume that others do as well? His entire existence is now suspect.

N. waits for a few moments at the edge of the De Geus farm, disillusioned and uncertain, feeling every bit like a fugitive. A cow coughs wetly in the barn, but no other sound permeates through the heavy blanket of fog. What can he do? His cottage is too dangerous for him. Surely someone has been posted there, awaiting his return, with orders to politely escort or—failing that—outright drag him to the police station. After a brief moment of consideration, he decides to approach the Beumers' house from the side, right through the neighbor's pasture. If anything is amiss, he can retreat back into the protective fog and wait for a more favorable opportunity. N. makes his way along the edge of the woods by following the pasture fence to the low path where the roe deer like to graze. From here, he knows it's about three hundred meters straight to Olga's vegetable garden. He has a sudden pang as he thinks of the Beumer ladies; it saddens him that he will never see them again.

He climbs over the barbed-wire fence, and is shocked twice by the electric fence. *Damn it!*, he thinks, *why hasn't De Geus turned that damn thing off yet?* The cows have been in the barn for two months now, and he's suddenly struck by a memory of De Geus complaining to him about their astronomical power bill.

Then he remembers that after deciding that the winter would continue with somewhat more mild weather, the farmer has been letting some young cattle graze the pasture during the day.

When N. leaves the fence line, he loses all sense of orientation. In the middle of the field, he feels his way hesitantly in what he thinks is the right direction. After several uncertain minutes, with arms outstretched before him, he feels rather than sees another fence, and is immediately delivered another jolt of electricity. N.'s irritation at the shock is tempered by the knowledge that this fence divides the pasture between the Beumer and De Geus farms; he is nearly there. With some difficulty N. crawls under the fence this time, managing to avoid receiving another shock. A little further on there should be a gate that is open. He walks to the right and after about twenty paces finds the opening he had hoped for. He lets out a soft whistle of relief. After a few more minutes, N. can see a light in the yard ahead and then the familiar contours of the buildings very gradually emerge from the fog. Dikkerdje is probably in his stall and hopefully the noisy goats as well, but the sheep cautiously approach N., recognizing his scent as they snuffle him. He is relieved when the two geese do not perform their usual guard duties and hopes that Bart is inside for the evening. If the dog were to bark with the joy of recognition, N.'s plot could be revealed and the whole game could be over.

Very carefully, he climbs over the fence and finds himself standing in the patch of curly kale; his heart nearly jumps out of his chest. The kale makes him think of the delicious meal Olga had made for him the previous day, the dark green leaves were doused in vinegar and cooked with pickles and chunks of bacon and smoked sausage. His stomach growls angrily. He circles the house widely and comes out behind the parking area at the shed annex. Olga's Peugeot is the only car parked there; the exterior light struggles to penetrate the fog but offers enough light that N. is sure no one else is parked there. The lights are on in the house and N. can hear Sonja's voice coming faintly from inside. He approaches his front door cautiously, feeling not for the first time today as though he may have a heart attack or stroke. Then suddenly, out of nowhere, something jumps against his back. Bart, his faithful four-legged friend, must realize the gravity of the situation and decides not to display his enthusiasm with his usual joyful barking. When N. turns to greet him silently, he lets out a gentle whimper. He is on my side, thinks N., certainly he must know those men are wrong; his companion is not capable of rape and murder.

The next step of his plan is crystal clear: go inside, grab a few things by feel, put them in the pannier bags, grab the bike and get the hell out of here. The front door to the rental property has been sealed; no surprise there. He can't imagine any harm in them discovering tomorrow that he's returned to the house, but he is still worried that someone might be watching him from the yard. If he were to be ambushed while inside the cottage, his only escape route would be through the living room window on the other side. The best he could hope for is a retreat back to De Geus's meadow, relying on cover of darkness and fog. But he must take the risk; without his cash and relics, he may as well just give himself over to the authorities. The thought fills him with a hot rage.

N. opens the door carefully. Bart shoots inside in front of him. Silently, he removes his shoes in the entryway; judging by the smell, he thinks he must have stepped in a fresh cowpat in the meadow, and doesn't want to track it through the rest of the house. He moves to the sink, keeping the room dark, and tries to wash the pitchy residue from his hands. In the bedroom, he steps into his Ballys. He hasn't worn them in a week, since the dinner with he'd had with Olga and Sonja, when they toasted his recovery and discuss their departure to Franche-Comté. So much has changed; from where he stands now, the dinner feels like a lifetime ago.

He is wearing his winter coat and his favorite pair of hiking pants. He finds the box with his small savings, takes out the money and puts it in his wallet. Then he moves to the bathroom, still in darkness, and finds his razor, toothpaste and toothbrush. He pulls the packet containing the four icons from its hiding place, puts everything into a heavy plastic bag from De Wilde's store, and looks unsuccessfully for his diary but can't find it (later he will realize it was next to his bed). Hastily he makes his way to the entryway again, stopping in the kitchen to pull a large piece of sausage from the fridge, throwing half of it to Bart and eating the rest.

He opens the front door and looks cautiously around. From what he can see, it looks like the coast is clear. N. hurries to his bike, which he left parked under the shed, and quickly distributes his things among the two pannier bags. As he mounts his bike and begins up the drive toward Vogelpoelweg, he realizes that he is leaving with as few belongings in his possession as when he arrived here six months ago. It seems appropriate. Anything he acquired while living here—clothes, laptop, printer—will be easy enough to replace.

He doesn't even think about his books, paintings or painting supplies.

When he walks past the front door of the big house with his bicycle, he overhears Olga and Sonja in what sounds like an argument—a rather rare occurrence between the two of them. Sonja's shrill voice comes to him more clearly, so he assumes that her mother must be standing further from the door. Suddenly light falls into the hall through the opened living room door, and N. presses himself against the facade and pulls his bike close. He hears Sonja's voice again, now much more clearly. "Don't believe any of it mama! It's all very mean… they're just trying to fool you." Then the living room door closes again with a bang, and after some muffled commotion, it is once again quiet.

N. mounts his bike and prepares to ride. "So long, kind people," he murmurs, but when Bart licks his hand, a lump forms in his throat. "Goodbye to you, too, faithful beast," he whispers, scratching his head thoroughly. The dog whines softly and licks N.'s hand once more, and then he sets off, disappearing down the driveway.

He's been riding down the Vogelpoelweg for less than a hundred meters when he hears a car approaching from the opposite direction. He barely manages to hide his bike in the bushes as headlights cut through the fog and the car drives past him. It's a police car; N. can see the silhouette of lights and a siren in the faint light as it passes. The vehicle turns into the Beumers' drive-way and N. suddenly realizes that his immediate plan is likely too risky to continue. He was riding toward Q where he had planned to take a slow train to Y. Of course, with that being the closest train terminal, it could be swarming with officers anticipating his attempted escape. Maybe they've even closed everything off. He turns the bike and pedals toward De Geus's instead, then past the farm, and back into the woods. Here he realizes that he's forgotten his phone, and he has a brief moment of panic.

Cautiously, and still without light, he points his bike onto a dirt path through the pitch-dark forest. He doesn't dare use his bike light, afraid that if the light itself doesn't give him away, the sound of the dynamo might. He recognizes a large beech tree and finds a comfortable place to collect himself in some familiar terrain. Rummaging around in his pannier bag, N. pulls out the razor, relieved to find the batteries still charged. As carefully as he can without light or a mirror, he shaves off his beard and moustache. He cuts himself on the upper lip and tastes blood.

Back on his bike and with a naked face, he suddenly realizes how cold the air is. Still, he pedals fast, and reaches the road between Q and X fifteen minutes later. He has decided that he'll go to Y, twenty kilometers away, and take the train west from there. When he comes to the provincial road that runs from Q to Y, he steers his bike to the wide path that runs between the railway and the road. He is protected from the road there by thick woods.

It is still foggy, and there is little traffic. Regardless, N. decides to keep riding without his bike light.

This decision, it turns out, saves him from what would surely be a catastrophic confrontation with law and order. In the silence, and without a light forecasting his approach, he is able to hear voices ahead of him in the distance. N. stops immediately, dismounts and quickly pulls his bike off the path. At first, he thinks he is being approached by oncoming cyclists. But then about ten meters in front of him, he sees the contours of a van parked in the strip of grass between the bike path and the road. A few seconds later in the light of a single passing car, he sees on its side the seal of the regional police. Then there are voices behind him and the faint glow of a flashlight cutting through the fog. Feeling trapped, he reacts quickly; his head is surprisingly cool, and he moves with such silent grace that he feels almost as though his body belongs to someone else. Leaving his bike in a ditch next to the bike path, he squats down. When the light of the flashlight approaches, he groans and shouts, "Hey, man, I'm trying to go to the bathroom over here!" There's a brief apologetic mumbling and flashlights move away. Then N. grabs his bags, crosses the road, and jumps to the path on the other side of the road.

"Henk, are you there?" The voice sounds like that of a rather worried lady with a slight Saxon accent. A bit further on, a man's voice—Henk, assumingly—answers back that he needs a minute. Feeling sure that he's still undetected, he tries for the shelter of the forest. Moments later he comes to a wide ditch, full to the brim with swift-moving water. He hurries along the ditch in a crouch away from the voices. He has ridden along this route so often in his spare time that he knows there is a dirt road leading into the woods about half a kilometer further along. This road crosses the railway after a few hundred meters. N. climbs the railway embankment. He has a new plan. The area is practically crawling with law enforcement, but he knows a train will be passing soon. He takes a deep breath and tries to build his confidence—he is going to jump *onto* the moving train.

The fog absorbs the sound of the approaching slow train, moving towards Q, but its engine lights cut through the fog and glide over N.'s bent figure. He lets it pass. Fifteen minutes later another train approaches from the other direction. N. wishes he could stop the train, flagging it down and climbing aboard without detection. Unfortunately, he is forced at the last minute to flee below the embankment as this train passes as well. He is afraid the driver will notice him and phone the police to report suspicious activity on the track.

Halfway between Q and Y is the village V, which N. only knows from the little station where the trains stop. It is about eight o'clock when he approaches the hamlet along the railroad embankment. To avoid looking suspicious, N. leaves the embankment and approaches the railway station from the street. He sees no one. Along the street, a row of houses stand with their backs facing the street; they remind him of the grotesque selfishness of society towards the individual, and the streetlights spread an equally bleak and selfish light. N. shudders; behind the curtains in their windows, he imagines countless sheep, trembling at the story being blasted at them from the eight o'clock news report on the television. Surely the story is of a monster, Kees van Alden, who did terrible things just past their doorstep, and worst of all, the perpetrator still at large and could be standing in their own front or back yard right now.

"Oh Jan, Marieke still isn't home! What should we do?"

Quelle horreur réaliste!

He walks down another equally dreary, seemingly abandoned street that leads to a wider street further on, which in turn leads to the train station. He remembers a cafeteria near the station, and is suddenly hit by the smell of fresh French fries. Caution quickly gives way to hunger. He thinks for a moment, and realizes it's been seven hours since he last ate, not counting the piece of sausage he shared with Bart.

At the snack bar, he orders a bag of French fries with mayonnaise, a hot dog, and a bottle of tonic. He takes the food and finds a spot out of sight of people. Although he's never been to V, he recognizes his surroundings from the times he's passed through on the train. He looks at his watch; it's half past eight. If his calculations are correct, the next train to Y should arrive in about ten minutes. He eats his hot fries in a hurry, empties the bottle of tonic, and carefully walks up the stairs to a sparsely lit platform. Nothing and nobody moves until the yellow lights of the local train appear. The brakes squeal, and the train sounds almost as though it is celebrating its survival of its journey through the fog.

After reaching Y, N. boards the local train to Apeldoorn. Here the fog has lifted, and N. boards a late intercity train to Amersfoort. He arrives at around eleven o'clock. He finds a hotel room close to the station, registering under the name J.H. Raben. When he finally flops onto the bed, he is exhausted and numb but forces himself once more to rise and take a shower. His reflection in the mirror is a true shock. He now fully understands why the few people he's come into contact with—the man at the snack bar, a train conductor, some fellow travelers, and the girl at the hotel reception desk—stared at him with such gawking curiosity and perhaps a slight aversion. Chafe marks, blood, and tufts of missed beard hair speckle his face. He looks like a man who has just narrowly survived a struggle with a lion or tiger. And it's not only his face; his coat and pants are torn and covered with green and grey smudges. He realizes at that moment how lucky he is that none of these people informed the police. He's shocked that the hotel clerk had even been willing to rent him a room.

N. decides it will be best if he is not seen in public for at least two days and commits to using only room service. He takes a long, hot shower and brushes his teeth. Then he lies on the bed, in his underwear and still smelling strongly of sweat, and falls asleep.

The next morning over a late breakfast, he reads an article in the Netherlands' largest tabloid that the previous day a twenty-year-old named Suzanne Heusinkveld was strangled in a forest near the village Q. Contrary to earlier reports, no evidence was found that would indicate that the girl had been raped. The suspected perpetrator is at large and may be armed with a police firearm. What N. finds most disconcerting, aside from the horrific death of the pretty young girl, is that at the bottom of the article, a composite photo of the suspect, one K. van Andel, has been printed in black-and-white. N. sees the photo and realizes that the beard and mustache, which he decided to shave more or less on a whim, make his face look so different that the decision may very well have saved his life.

It is afternoon before he remembers it's his birthday. Thirty-five years old. He treats himself to a piccolo of sekt and some cocktail nuts.

★★★

PART III

The great plan

37.

Countless questions crash over him like a set of waves in a storm. N. has no answers, but they draw him into an ocean of apathy. He barely has the strength to keep swimming. He fills his days mostly with sleep, fully aware that every empty day drains more of his energy. He lacks motivation to work toward the Great Plan; the task before him seems so enormous that even committing it to paper, to weigh the risks and the chances of success, feels impossible. But the necessity of doing so has becoming urgent.

Sometimes, in his more pessimistic moments, he feels that he lacks the courage to even approach such a plan. He is seized by panic at the thought the whole idea is not only impracticable, but impossible. He must have conjured it up on some sunny, auspicious morning when possibility defied reality. Then he breaks out in a sweat, feeling as though he has built a kingdom on quicksand. Perhaps it would have been better to leave the country right away, abandoned his relics, his reliance on the system he wanted to escape. He should have relied more on his ability to improvise, without the assurance of a lot of money behind him. He could have been safe and sound in Manaus by now, building a life there, but instead he's here, a common criminal, trying to escape the country undetected. What an absurd reality he's created!

And the Beumers? Just a needless distraction, an unnecessary detour.

This thought adds to his dissatisfaction. His time spent with them made him a pariah, hunted and persecuted; every day that he spends in Amersfoort makes his situation more tenuous. Even after a week, he gets no further than staring apathetically out of his hotel window, watching traffic in its mundane weekday flow. He orders room service for breakfast, lunch, and dinner, eating more out of duty than pleasure. The only commitment he seems capable of making, or keeping, is to avoid being seen on the street. Ever since seeing his photo printed in the paper on his first morning in the hotel, he has been guided by a neurotic paranoia; he trusts nothing and nobody. In the most dismal moments of his atrophy, he feels connected with the rapist and murderer, as if his own depravity somehow led to Suzanne's death. Then he feels dirty and his self-loathing begins again in force.

It is Christmas time. N. watches from his hotel window the middle-class frenzy of buying useless items from deft advertisers in an attempt to mask their emptiness and boredom. They pull everything into their instant atmosphere, to which he thought he was totally immune. But the worn-out jingle bells thrumming in the stores and on the city streets infects him when he finally leaves to do his own shopping (extra clothes, underwear, toiletries, hiking boots). The imposed Christmas spirit makes him long for home and hearth, a cozy family and an average amount of happiness. He imagines the Beumer house decorated with candles, starched napkins and glasses bubbling with champagne and a delicious meal, the three of them together, celebrating their last Christmas in Holland. He imagines spending the first Christmas night with the mother, the second Christmas night with the daughter; or, perhaps, both nights with both women at the same time, a symbolic and literal embodiment of their everlasting togetherness.

Damn, what a loss it is!

The holiday even unearths a sense of longing for Paula and Anke. The child's birthday was in November. Would she have missed her stepdad? Where would they be these days, what would they being doing? He wonders if they think of him still, or if Paula's grief has quickly passed and she no longer thinks of him. She was a beautiful woman, and if she was ready for a new relationship she would not have to look far for opportunity. She speaks well, dresses elegantly, and isn't unintelligent by any means.

N. mopes at the thought of all he's lost. His thoughts are dark, and his desires all seem wrong. He has never felt so lonely.

And then of course there is *the* question, constantly nagging at him, always in the forefront. Who is the man who called him by his name in the woods? The more he thinks about it, the more convinced he is that it was the man he passed on the walking path, the man with clockwork regularity. The thought haunts him like a phantom, an angry dream.

This way of seeing things doesn't do much to help strengthen his self-confidence or lift his spirits.

Christmas passes and the when the remainder of the holiday spirit is covered by a layer of snow, daily life returns to its disenchanting reality. N., feeling somewhat emboldened, wanders into a bookstore, digs through a discount bin and finds a few books that look like they have reasonable substance, including a Tip Marugg. He spends the days between Christmas and New Year reading. He eats, sleeps, and keeps to himself. On clear afternoons he strolls through the center of Amersfoort. At night, the temperatures drop below freezing and a light snow falls.

Now that he no longer wears a beard to disguise his face, he has gotten in the habit of wearing a hat with a wide brim that partly covers his face, and glasses with tinted lenses. Although there is no one he knows living in this city, he has a deep fear of being recognized by the authorities. Or worse, that someone from his previous life may recognize him in the street, a look of shock as they crow: Heeyy Chris, what are *you* doing here? Ever since he was called out by the stranger in the fog, N. can't shake the unpleasant thought that there might be someone within the circle of his family, acquaintances and colleagues, who is unconvinced by the story of his disappearance. He has begun to wonder if everyone has long been waiting, arms folded in disapproval, for his inevitable return to common sense, take up his place once again in his boring existence.

To make matters worse, his cost of living has suddenly increased dramatically. His meager savings will not last much longer. He is currently spending about a hundred and fifty euros a day on room and board. When he took up residence here, he had over thirty-five hundred euros in cash, adding to his previous reserves by saving his meager salary from Piet de Wilde. If things don't change soon, he will be flat broke by sometime during the third week of January. He needs to find a dealer as soon as possible to liquefy his relics. That's all there is to it.

This looming predicament does nothing to improve his mood.

The turn of the year has been rather quiet. There is still the usual vandalism carried out by the youth and riffraff in the Keistad, but according to the hotel manager, it is clearly less than in previous years. In the first week of the new year, with his reserves diminishing at an alarming rate, he decides to bring about a swift change in lifestyle. He wants to avoid paying for a train ticket to his former hometown in dimes and quarters. He has decided to run the risk of returning there because he wants to work with an art dealer who is known within university circles as being capable, reliable and, perhaps most importantly, discreet.

So he moves out of the hotel in Amersfoort to Hilversum, where he takes up residence in a relatively cheap bed and breakfast in the south part of the city. The guesthouse is ideally located to serve as a base for the operation, the risks of which are incredible; indeed just the thought of its audacity makes N.'s heart pound suddenly. Above all, he wants to get this part of the plan over with as soon as possible. With the relics sold, he will at least know where he stands in a certain respect, and can create concrete plans for the days and years to come. This small step toward activity eases his frantic nerves a bit, and his mind becomes busy with calculating and contemplating.

With the move to Hilversum, N. feels alive again, his sense of purpose suddenly restored. The renewed freshness in his veins feels akin to winter giving way to spring; there is new hope and expectation, strength and vigor. And indeed, yesterday, while walking through a city park, he heard the song of a blackbird. And in another more spacious park, one for the better situated, he will soon take stock, in the next few days, certainly, with a first practical test of his theory so far, as well as the chances of success in the short term of his dangerous, but also challenging, mission. All of a sudden, it's as if he has shed an old, bad skin; damn, it feels just like that.

On his first night in the bed and breakfast, N. drinks a glass of good cognac, which he had purchased at a liquor store on the corner that afternoon.

38.

Hans. When was the last time he had even spoken to his dear brother? It must have been about four years ago when he last visited. He had come with his mother who was already quite ill, in the house N. had bought a few years earlier. Hans is ten years older than N. He studied international law after business school. He began his career as a diplomat, and since then has been a trade attaché for a number of national companies and Dutch-based multinationals. Because of his position, he spends a lot of time abroad. This is not, however, the main reason the two brothers have such rare contact with one another; since the death of their parents, their father five years ago and their mother three years ago, their relationship has in fact become non-existent. N. calls the cause of their division *"animose* envy", a nonsensical adjective that, in his opinion, gives the noun its deeper meaning and application to their situation.

Their relationship has been icy ever since childhood, but when N. was awarded his doctorate cum laude at the age of twenty-seven, such an achievement was too much for the elder brother to ignore. Hans had tried frantically for a similar achievement—how nicely it would have jumpstarted his career—but it had proven too much for him. He resented the fact that *petit frère* had proven some level of superiority, and on such a sensitive point. Since then, the older brother had mostly ignored the younger brother's existence. His position in the international community had given him a certain status, and with his business dealings he had amassed a small fortune; Hans, feeling sufficiently elevated, had effectively distanced himself from N. and the rest of his working class family.

Hans's wealth, N. thought, was plainly evidenced by his real estate holdings. His country home was really more of a castle, set on a lot of over a hectare on the edge of a wooded area in the middle of the Gooise. N., aided by a walking map, covered the distance of about five kilometers to the estate on foot. He had revisited the more sensitive moments from their past during the walk and hesitates now, standing at the gate to his brother's exuberant retreat, half-hidden in the back of the garden from the rare passers-by by bushes, shrubs and tall evergreen pines between which the gravel driveway meanders. The house has two stories and fanciful architecture that lend it a kind of King Ludwig playfulness. It was built in the seventies of the last century and its facade of dazzling white turrets and battlements which give the unmistakable impression that it is not only solid, but imperishable.

N. rings the doorbell, hoping to find the fortress unoccupied. He has no desire to reestablish their blood ties; Hans has always preferred not to spend the holidays in Holland, and N. prays this hasn't changed and that there will be no response rattling of an electric lock, no sound of a voice as an intercom button is pushed. N. listens carefully, ready to turn on his heel and escape notice. But there is no response. He rings again, just to be sure. Again, no crackling of a microphone or rattle of the mechanism. If Hans is away from home for any measurable amount of time, N. knows that Martha, his wife, is with him. The childless couple is inseparable and their marriage might, under different circumstances, serve as an example to the less committed younger brother. He tries the gate, knowing the likelihood of it being unlocked is extremely low. It doesn't budge. He stands before this implacability for a moment, scaling the monstrosity and joyfully deliberating how he might break in. The Janssen's fortress is the second or fourth in a row of five. Behind this row, there is a dirt road through the woods to Lage Vuursche. The path leads past the row of estates to the public road.

N. walks around to the back of his brother's house familiarly, trying not to look suspicious. On this side, too, the fence turns out to be an impenetrable barrier: it is made of steel and very tall, running the distance of the back of the house where it joins with the fence of the neighbors. It towers as grimly as an iron curtain above the evergreen. N. realizes that breaking into the house is a monumental task, maybe even impossible. And that's just his evaluation from the exterior; he is sure that there are additional alarms and safeguards on the interior. But this knowledge somehow does nothing to deter N.'s determination. The challenge excites him. For now, he has one approach that can help him. He can see between the bars of the fence into a window of the spacious garage. Four years ago, when he last saw the couple, they owned a Mercedes S-class and a so-called lady's Porsche for Martha's personal use, a toy she would take on shopping trips to Hilversum or Laren, or to show off in front of her equally exquisite girlfriends in The Hague or Blaricum. From his vantage point, he can see the smooth contours of the German sports car. With this knowledge, he can move forward.

N.'s next target is protected inside the house, where locked safely away (or at least such was the case four years ago) are some precious Cobra and a De Kooning, the darlings of the money-investing *nouveau riche*, with a total value, Hans had "accidentally" mentioned once, of about one and a half million (although still in old guilders).

N. leaves the estate and has lunch in a nearby inn. In the phone book at the reception desk, he looks up the name of the nearest Mercedes dealer—Jagersma garage—as well as the names and phone numbers of the neighbors on either side of Hans's house, one De Wit and one Wameling family. He tries De Wit first. After a few seconds there is a man's voice. N. introduces himself as the administrator from the garage where his neighbor, Mr. Janssen, is a customer, and asks Mr. de Wit if he might know where the

Janssen family is, since he has tried in vain several times in the past few days to get in touch with them by telephone.

"I wouldn't know, sir," is the measured reply.

"But can you..."

"Sir, listen carefully. I don't know the family next to me at all. We don't have any contact with each other, so I can't give you any information. Good afternoon."

Curt and grumpy. N. hangs up the receiver, a little taken aback, and thinks for a moment. Why don't the wealthy fraternize automatically? *As a destitute homeless person*, N. thinks, chuckling, *I suppose I might well ask myself that same question.* He tries the Wameling family.

After at least ten rings N. is about to hang up when someone picks up.

"This is Mrs. Wameling."

"Hello, ma'am. This is De Vries from the Jagersma garage. Mrs. Wameling, may I ask you something?"

"You may."

"Mrs. Wameling, it's like this. I've been trying to get in touch with your neighbors, the Janssen family, for a day or so. Do you happen to know where they are?"

"Abroad, sir."

"*Abroad...?* Well, that's nice! With my money no doubt! You know, ma'am, I've had an outstanding account of two thousand euros here for a year, and we've corresponded and phoned about it a lot. Mr. Janssen was supposed to visit me the day before yesterday to make things right. And now he's gone on vacation."

The lady laughs, a short laugh. "It's not a vacation, sir; the family is traveling on business. I'm telling you this to keep you from trying... By the way, I didn't know they'd changed garages."

"Well, that's nice," N. lays on some extra indignation and ignores the lady's last remark for the sake of convenience. "If Mr. Janssen really is a businessman, he will understand that our garage business cannot run on customers who are so slow to pay their bills! It really is a fine kettle of fish to me. If he's back home in a day or so, I'll tell him..."

"Mr. and Mrs. Janssen won't be back in the Netherlands for another three months," Mrs. Wameling interrupts delicately. She laughs again, no doubt delighted with this free bit of gossip regarding the payment morals of her closest neighbors.

"What did you say? *Three* months?!" N. lets his indignation explode again by making his voice crack.

"Yes sir, they left a few days ago, and hope to be back at the beginning of April. I'm sorry, you'll have to be patient until then I think."

Now the lady chuckles unabashedly and N. knows enough; in fact, he's amazed at how easily he obtained this information. He has everything he might need to know. An excellent overture and the first hurdle to possible success has been cleared. He has three months. He says goodbye to the lady with thanks, due indignation, of course for so much impertinence and so on. He hangs up and leaves the reception desk, rubbing his hands with contentment. The first blow and half the battle.

The coming days, he realizes, will undoubtedly require more fortitude, but N. is encouraged. Such a long absence will allow him to work in peace and quiet. He no longer feels the sense of urgency that might trip him into a mistake or make him overlook essential things; he has the necessary space and time for deliberation and reflection. That evening he eats in an excellent restaurant somewhere in the center of the media village as if the expected proceeds of his plan are already burning a hole in his pocket.

39.

After spending several days in a celebratory mood, the contents of N.'s wallet had become severely diminished. He decides to monetize his icons quickly. On a beautiful sunny, somewhat windy day at the end of January, he takes the train north. From the station, he walks to the city center and then into a nondescript alley.

Weinberg's antiquarian bookshop has been tucked into the back alley since time immemorial. N. hopes that his hat and glasses will make him unrecognizable in the off chance that he may bump into someone from his previous life. After a brief hesitation and with a strong dose of anxiety, he enters the store with the relics in a package tucked into his bag. If the Weinberg man behind the counter—the fourth or the fifth generation of a family with a somewhat tragic history—knows him at all, it would be at most a superficial relationship. He recognizes him from an appraisal he'd done once at the university; he was the expert that had been called in when an archivist had doubted the authenticity of a few medieval books.

The old man is busy with a customer. N. does his best to look inconspicuous as he occupies himself, waiting for the store to empty. After about fifteen minutes, the customer leaves, and N. shows Weinberg his treasures. The way he pulls the package from his bag—with an almost shameful pleasure—he feels a bit like a pederast entering a room of little boys. He tells the man he wishes to sell the icons for nine thousand euros a piece. Weinberg examines each relic carefully, asking N. where they had come from. He tells him the truth, that he had bought them somewhere in Poland ten years ago.

The old man inspects each one carefully, examining their backs, their frames, even uses a magnifying glass, turning them over and over. Then he pulls a book from one of his shelves, probably a catalog, and thumbs through some pages. N. grows increasingly nervous (he suddenly imagines that he'd been fooled in Krakow all those years ago). The man checks a long list of figures, silently, then disappears into the back of the store for about ten minutes. When he finally returns, N. finds out that he does indeed possess a voice after all, and he offers N. four thousand euros a piece for three of the relics, and a thousand for one because he cannot verify its authenticity. In passing, he asks N. how things are going at the university, looking directly at him for the first time. His eyes are large and magnified by thick glasses, and N. thinks that there may be two thousand years or more of Jewish history contained behind those eyes, from his personal experience of the horrors of WWII to the centuries of antique dealership that has been passed through his family for generations. It's as though he can see through people's secrets and stirring souls with a mere glance. N. suddenly feels a quiver pass through his legs, and tries to sound casual when he responds, "Pretty good," implying that the same answer applies for him personally as well. He tells the man that he is selling the icons personally, not for the university, and that his asking price is not negotiable. Weinberg smiles his professionally, perhaps a tad villainous, and offers fifteen thousand for all four. N., convinced that he would be a fool to accept this offer, says he'd be willing to part with the one in question for a thousand if necessary, but that he'd like twenty-five thousand for the other three together. The reality is that he'd like to get out of the store as soon as possible.

Weinberg IV or V examines the pieces under his magnifying glass again and sighs as if he is the one being taken for a ride now. He inspects them from all sides, even smells them, and looks again at his catalog. He walks into the back office again and after a few moments, N. hears him talking on the phone. After about half an hour and a bit more haggling, the antique dealer finally folds, offering the "well ok, because it's you" cliché, and N. leaves the building with seventeen thousand euros, relieved but also dissatisfied with the feeling that he was likely swindled out of ten thousand euros or so. But what is a man to do when he has only about eighty euros left in the purse and less than half a bottle of good cognac?

With mixed feelings, he walks back out of the alley and onto the main road.

Ten minutes later he is at an address on the fourth story of an apartment building where he had once heard second- or third-hand that a person might be able to have themselves "measured" for a passport. He's not entirely sure if there is any legitimacy to the rumor, but in any case, he wants to try. N. rings the doorbell. A rather sleazy-looking Turkish woman answers the door with a whining child on her hip. He asks her if what he has been told is true.

Without answering him, she yells into the apartment behind her something that sounds like "Kürüs!" A Turkish man appears like an apparition, as if he was listening behind the door. He is quite young with surprisingly blue eyes, a square build and a balding head. He eyes N. suspiciously. N. repeats his question. The man looks at him for a moment longer, then looks out of the door and checks the hallway in both directions. Closing the door behind him, the young man leads N. into a narrow corridor.

"Passport photo is two and six thousand," Kürüs says in a tone that does not suggest negotiation. He looks at him directly, rubbing his thumb and index finger together. N. has come prepared; he gives the man his new passport photos, a new name—Dormaal, Jan-Hein—as well as a new date of birth and address which he has written down. The man tells him that he requires a down payment of three thousand euros and in a week, he can pick up his passport.

As promptly as he put seventeen thousand euros into his pocket, he now promptly removes fifteen two hundred euro bills again. He is greatly relieved that there will be no paper trail of the transaction and wonders at why more business cannot be conducted in such a way. He says he'll come back in a week.

Then he does something he will come to regret deeply (and, indeed, in some part of his soul he regretted it immediately) but the temptation is far too great. After leaving the Turkish family's apartment, he walks to the university, believing himself to be reasonably protected by the hat and glasses. He even walks with some sense of disdain towards his old life (*at least I was brave enough to step away*, he thinks). It's lunchtime; the morning lectures are about to end. In the courtyard, surrounded as always by a multitude of students and always teaching and knowing better, Hans Wagenaar, one of N.'s esteemed former colleagues and associate professor of English language and literature, saunters towards the cafeteria. He is lively, shiny, brimming with health and good spirits, working, eating, sleeping and copulating. He has the look of a man who loves his profession and who, for as long as N. has known him, has always given the intimidating impression that someday he'll do something substantial in his field.

Moments later Jan Bierman passes by, always in a rush and giving the impression that he has no time for anything. Jan, a man in his mid-forties, became a professor of general literature by kicking and screaming his way into a tenured position and therefore lacks the respect of his colleagues. But he is nonetheless a popular teacher, literary researcher and text exegete among the student population. N. wonders if he's still flirting with that young student, a pretty timid thing from the high country; she had been about eighteen then, but it was probably two years prior when they had hooked up. The professor had seemed to be happily married with a beautiful wife and two cute adolescent daughters, but (for quid pro quo) taking some pre-candidate as a concubine should be possible. It had surprised N. and perhaps made him a bit jealous that the man could so quickly and easily pluck the most willing girl from a batch of freshmen for private pleasures. Always in her room, of course, and as often as he like; N. found the whole situation perplexing because the man looked more or less like a stuffed scarecrow with a ragged haircut and a protruding belly and his moth-eaten wardrobe from about a hundred years ago.

He sees a few more colleagues walk by and a few students he still knows by sight. He presses on, struggling with an almost paralyzing feeling of alienation. The he is suddenly struck with a wounding realization that the majority of campus has long since forgotten him, like he stepped out of their world and into another. It's as though a mirror has been placed between the two universes that is transparent on one side, his side, and there is nothing more for him on the other side. And even if he did decide to step back across and make himself known, they would push him back, like Jesus had been pushed back by the Grand Inquisitor for his violation of the order of things.

It is with the same almost paralyzing feeling of alienation that he strolls through the city center. He is not foolish enough to return to campus again, like a criminal to the scene of the crime, but he is attracted to the city quarter where he had lived for about five years in rather unhappy family circumstances with a house and mortgage. About fifteen minutes later he is at the shopping mall where the Janssen family had once stocked up on weekly groceries and sundries from Blokker, Zeeman and Bruna (for growing up with wealth, Paula was actually rather pennywise).

It is past one o'clock when she enters his field of vision. N. still couldn't say that he intentionally went that way, but of course he knows that this is when Paula picks Anke up from school every day (today is the free Wednesday afternoon for the child) and then the two of them go shopping together before returning home. He sees no reason why she would have abandoned this habit. And indeed, he cannot claim coincidence or circumstances beyond his control when he spots her. The former Chris Janssen—husband, step-father, teacher—stands at the window of a pharmacy when he sees his former wife (but of course he realizes later they are not "former" or "ex" at all, simply because he disappeared) on the other side of the square heading towards the supermarket, pushing a shopping cart in front of her. Next to her, Anke skips and laughs; the girl is radiant, with one hand on the cart next to her mother's. A man walks beside them, with dark hair and eyes. He is muscular and tall, perhaps even taller than N. He can't deny having thoughts about his wife and stepdaughter from time to time over the past few months, wondered at how they might have coped with losing him. When he thought of them, he always imagined mournful faces, with Paula spontaneously brought to tears. The thought had been quite painful to N. at times, and he could not resist falling into a pit of self-loathing over it all. So the sight of his once faithful partner gives him a shock; whatever the scene playing before him, it certainly is not one of tragedy. They appear to be a lively family of three, cheerful, frisky even. The talk and laughing, kissing each other on the sunny square (Paula kisses the man for no apparent reason, and N. feels a sudden pain; she was never so spontaneous with him).

And suddenly with a shock, he is struck by the impermanence of life, how quickly people adapt to new situations, how easily old stories are erased, wounds are healed. He had always thought—for exactly these reasons—that it was nonsense to grieve, to mourn the loss of loved ones, specifically and most recently his mother. Life and death go on. What he is faced with here is just a taste of his own attitude, and he pushes himself not to dwell on it. Two people who were left behind, processed the loss of husband and stepdad; with the great financial bliss of an excellent life insurance policy and afterwards an excellent survivor's pension, the house mortgage-free, the mother in good health, who could blame Paula? She's provided herself with a good-looking new life companion. N. wonders if he also benefits from the proceeds of N.'s premiums and one-time deposits. What more could a person melted by fire and turned to ashes wish for?

He pushes himself a bit further against the shop window, although they don't move in his direction at all, until they disappear around the corner of the supermarket. He must not be seen here, not now or ever. He has been tossed from their lives, his return to it would only be a disturbance, and abnormality, an abomination to all parties. Here too, Sartre's die is cast, a chapter closed.

Nevertheless, it feels even strange to him. Once again he feels excluded, as though watching from an afterlife. He is disillusioned as he walks through the city center, and by the time he reaches the train station, he has sunk completely into a deep pool of sadness.

"I shouldn't have done this, I never should have done this," he mumbles; it's his own fault.

Back in his Hilversum guesthouse, he counts his money. Including the one-off proceeds from the small plan, he now has 14,063.22 euros at his disposal. A reassuring amount, one might think. But N. is somber, and compares himself for a moment to the day laborers from Steinbeck's epic; when they would get a few dollars, it was but a drop in the ocean of their relentless money worries. A funereal mood weighs on him like lead, and only lifts when he indulges himself again that evening with a copious meal and an animated conversation in the vestibule of the guesthouse over coffee and cognac with another guest, an American violinist. She is approximately his age, homely but very engaging. She is visiting Holland as part of a radio music program and will be flying home tomorrow afternoon. Later, in his room, they drink a couple of whiskies, and she purifies his dejected soul when she gives herself to him with abandon. The next morning in the breakfast room, from an invisible sound system, he hears the song *Delicado* played by Percy Faith's orchestra. The overwhelming staccato rhythm of the full orchestra repeats in his head and brightens the mood of his day significantly.

A week later, having long since returned to good spirits, N. takes the train back to his old stomping grounds, pays the remaining three thousand euros for his passport, and returns to Hilversum post haste, enriched with a new identity as Jan-Hein Dormaal. Incidentally, he thinks as he touches and examines the document, the municipal authorities really ought to improve the security of their civil affairs department.

40.

It takes N. an hour to walk the five kilometers from the guesthouse to his brother's house. He has now done the walk about ten times, approaching from both the front and the back, on different days and at different times of the day, to make sure the house really has been vacated. He's even made the trip in the evening, gazing through the closed gate, watching for light, movement or sound. Two weeks have passed and the house has remained silent and dead.

He decides to trust the information Mrs. Wameling gave him.

But breeching the fence line, let alone the inside of the house, will prove a challenge. The top edges and posts are wrapped in garlands of barbed wire, forming an implacable, impregnable barrier to him. There are two gates—one at the front and one at the rear—and both are equipped with heavy steel locks and hinges. In fact, in the entire row of country estates, the only gate that N. has seen open or close at all is the front gate at the Wamelings' home, to let in or out a silver-gray Jaguar carrying an elderly couple. N. assumes they are the Wamelings. He also sees a young woman who apparently lives in the house; she drives a Jeep to and from the house every day and opens the gate with a remote control. Between the Wamelings' yard and his brother's is a tall stone partition, far too high to scale unsupported. But during one of his reconnaissance outings, N. found that a somewhat unsecure looking wooden door has been cut into the wall further down. Perhaps, N. thinks, the two neighbors are on rather friendly terms; or more like, N. predicts remembering his brother's rather solitary nature, the door was already there when he bought the house.

N. considers his options. He buys a pry bar and a powerful flashlight at a hardware store, wraps these and a few other tools in a jute bag that he discarded in a market in Hilversum, and on a clear afternoon he walks with the bag to his brother's house. It is half past five when he arrives, almost dark and near freezing, and the Wamelings' gate is closed. He knows, however, that the Jeep always comes by six. He waits in the bushes along the road for six o'clock. Then until a quarter past six, half past seven. He is getting cold, and is about to give up when down the road, he sees the Jeep arriving at last.

The gate opens and N. quickly and stealthily follows the Jeep inside before he hears the gate slide mechanically and click into the lock. The shadow of the wall offers him protection from any remaining evening light. Cautiously, he moves towards the door in the wall, located not far from the Wamelings' garage, which protects him from accidental glances from the main home. He tries the latch, and to his great surprise, it opens with a slight creak. He closes it behind him. Then suddenly, sooner than he would have thought possible, he is standing in his brother's garden.

N. is certainly no expert in security but is of course familiar with the concept of a "silent alarm". As an amateur in the field of serious crime he has prepared excessively, and is now almost at the point of hyperventilating. He regains his awareness, forcing himself to calm down. His mind once again begins calculating. He realizes now, of course, that he is like a rat in a trap. The crowbar will not help him jump back over the fence. His only path out is forward. In the darkness N. sneaks along the other side of the dividing wall. When he reaches the side of the garage, he stands up. Nothing moves. He waits. Still, nothing happens. He walks around the garage, stumbles over a paving stone, and reaches the kitchen door at the back of the house. He holds his breath and waits again. Still nothing. During one of his reconnaissance trips he found a window which he suspects provides access to the basement (the house has a partial cellar). He comes upon the window and sees now that it is made of wired glass. A metal handle faintly reflects the flashlight beam behind this glass.

N. hesitates; breaking the window will inevitably make some noise. He is getting cold again. It must be four or five degrees below freezing, at least. His toes are starting to tingle, even in his thick walking shoes. He waits for about half an hour, not knowing what to do. Then an airliner, undoubtedly just departed from Schiphol, growls and shrieks in the clear freezing air overhead. As the noise of accelerating jet engines grows, he thrusts the crowbar through the glass, making a hole big enough for his arm to reach inside and turn the handle. But the battered window is not wide enough for N. to fit through. He quickly digs through the jute bag and pulls out a screwdriver, pliers and several wrenches. With the screwdriver and pliers he manages to unscrew the hinges of the window from the frame. He shines the flashlight into the cellar and waits. There are potatoes and a few other food items, but no movement. The broken glass has shattered into a potato barrel, making his landing area quite tidy. He lowers himself carefully, standing on the potato barrel, then jumping to the basement floor, about a meter and a half below. He places the window frame back in the groove to minimize any suspicious appearances.

He stands dead still for a moment. He's suddenly swept with fear that he's gained access to the house only to be locked inside a cellar vault. What a pyrrhic end, he thinks, as he imagines the headlines: *Owner's missing brother found as burglar in his house.* For a quarter of an hour that feels like an eternity, N. stands petrified. He collects himself, and is just about to walk up the stairs to the first level of the house when he hears voices. At first he thinks it must be walkers on the sandy path or voices from the neighbors; but then he hears a door squeak directly above him, and he is forced to accept that he is no longer or never was alone in the grand house. Heavy footsteps shake the floor above his head, keys jingles, a lock clicks open, and then all at once a door opens and the basement is flooded with light. In three silent steps, N. moves behind a cupboard under the stairs, with just enough space to kneel and bend down. Casting an almost loxodromic double shadow on the basement wall in the bright, contrasting light, a large figure comes down the stairs, breathing heavily. Two powerful farts escape as the man steps down. In spite of the light now filling the cellar, the man shines a flashlight around, including over the cupboard and right over N.'s head, but miraculously not along the battered window.

After ten or fifteen excruciatingly long seconds, the large man works his way up the stairs gasping from the effort, and N. hears a distant male voice. "Probably cats… a rabbit maybe…" "Should have put it higher…" a woman says. The words die away and turn into laughter, then coughing. In the cellar a mild stench of sweat and shit remains.

Much to N.'s distress, the man locked cellar door behind him. He is now painfully aware of how precarious his situation has become. Obviously, the house is being monitored by some security company, apparently through some kind of hotline.

About ten minutes later, he hears car doors slam shut and a diesel engine starts and backs away. After another fifteen minutes of waiting in the cool basement, he walks up the stairs. By the light of his flashlight, he uses the crowbar to pry open the door. It gives way quite easily, and there is little noise or damage. He stands in the kitchen, which he can assume hasn't been used for a few weeks.

At first, he barely dares to move, afraid that he has or is about to set off some kind of silent alarm again. He pulls out a kitchen chair and sits in the dark for about fifteen minutes, reflecting. Then he stands, slides the chair back into its original position (N. realizes he needs to consider everything now) and with a vague memory of the layout of the house, he gropes his way down the hall to one of the living rooms. The door is open. Some light enters through the open curtains from the street, and N. can see a sample of his brother's artistic possessions, worth millions. Carefully, he closes the curtains. When he is sure that no light can escape outside, he switches on his flashlight and scans the paintings on the wall. He is sure they are all hung by wire attached to some ticking alarm system. The painting he has come for, the one by De Kooning, is no longer there, and in its place are two hideous nineteen-fifties nonsense canvases by the man who calls himself Corneille. N. feels that the artist's success and name recognition reflect the sad state of affairs of pictorial taste then, now, and in the future. N. worries that even the slightest vibration here will set off alarm bells all over Hilversum. How, he wonders, could the current situation between art and capitalist tastelessness more saliently be depicted than by this wall in my brother's house?

He finds a mobile phone lying on the kitchen table, and uses it to call the guesthouse. He tells the front desk that he'll be away for the night and probably for the next few days. He puts the phone in his pocket and walks up the wide stairs to the first floor. In a guest room where he once spent the night, he takes out a comforter by feel, spreads it over one of the two single beds and locks the door. He doesn't undress. He simply sits on the bed for a moment and thinks over his situation again until, finally, he lays down and falls into a deep sleep.

41.

Waking up in a house that has been entered unlawfully is an uncomfortable experience. Criminal activities don't come to N. naturally, and the echoing silence of the huge house feels oppressive. The objective of the home is clear at every turn and in every nook and cranny: merely an investment of money. The house is far too large for two people, but N. thinks he can finally understand why his brother's marriage has lasted so long. Each partner has a separate wing, likely sharing a room only when the house staff prepares and serves them a meal.

N. (alias Jan-Hein Dormaal) is well aware of the house staff: a housekeeper, a gardener and, he thinks he remembers, also a private chauffeur. He realizes he'll need to take into account that the housekeeper probably has a key. This suspicion is reinforced by the note on the kitchen table, torn from a notepad, with the letterhead and telephone number "Hafman Securities" and then the following text written in ballpoint: *Mrs. Jager, 02.12 at 19:30 in connection with an alarm. Could not find anything. Probable malfunction. Regards.* Then initials. N. realizes he must not leave any trace that he's been in this house.

He walks back to the guest room, folds the comforter and places it back in the closet. He runs his palms over the mattress to make it look freshly made. It's half past seven, and before it gets light, he opens the curtains at the front again. Then he rummages around the kitchen for something to eat and drink, finds tea bags, tea cookies, crackers and butter and improvises a sparse breakfast. When he is finished, he carefully puts everything away.

After breakfast he wanders about the house investigating, keeping as far from the windows as possible. He discovers an even better hiding place in the basement behind the potato box where there are some empty burlap sacks he can easily crawl under in the event he may need to hide again. At half past nine, N. sighs and says to himself, "the sooner it's done the sooner it's over," and he calls the security service.

"Hafman Securities. This is Inge."

"Hello madam, Mr. Janssen speaking (N. gives his brother's address). I'm calling to inform you that circumstances have made our stay abroad much shorter than initially planned, so I..."

"So we don't need to do our rounds anymore?" interjects Inge. She is clearly a businesswoman and only needs half a word to get the point, for which N. is incredibly grateful; lacking any knowledge about security firms and their agreements and contracts, he didn't have the slightest idea how to continue the conversation.

"Yes exactly, in about a month we think we will leave again. I'll contact you around that time."

"So you want to continue your subscription?"

"Certainly, ma'am, no reason to cancel."

"Okay, thanks. Yes, then I can make a note of that."

"Great. Goodbye, madam."

"Goodbye, Mr. Janssen, have a nice day."

He is somewhat astonished that his idea worked, and he sits and stares out in front of himself for a while. Initiative, determination and audacity; these will have to be the pillars on which he stands for the coming days and weeks. He'll need to act with deliberation and above all, keep things moving.

He begins a tenacious search of the property, which results in the discovery of a bunch of keys with which he can open the front and back door, as well as the inner door to the storage space and the attached garage. The Mercedes isn't locked, but he finally finds what he's looking for in his sister-in-law's Porsche: the remote control that opens the gate to the street (N. tries this out later in the day after seeing the neighbor's silver-gray Jaguar drive away). He also finds the key to the lock on the back gate, and decides to carry it on him so that he may escape the property unseen at the back and disappear across the dirt road into the woods.

This key suddenly gives him a pleasant, secure feeling, as though he now has things somewhat under control.

N. makes coffee and turns on the vent hood to eliminate the smell of it. He keeps an eye on both the driveway and on the back gate to be able to parry any surprises. For the rest of the morning and afternoon, he keeps himself busy reattaching and repairing the cellar window and concealing the damage to the cellar door lock. After that, he pokes around in his brother's study upstairs. There is a large mahogany desk and lining the open shelves along the walls are Elsevier's Encyclopedia and other thick books about travel, foreign countries, atlases, books on law, dictionaries, and a row of old novels containing works by Zola and other French naturalists. In another closed cabinet, there are several binders labeled with all kinds of subjects.

Feeling that he is on the right track, he decides to spend the next night in his brother's home as well. The next day, he busies himself studying all the binders and related items from the closet, which provides him with an increasingly clear picture of not only his brother's financial position but the total of his possessions and debts. The house was purchased eight years ago for the price of three million Dutch guilders and considering the exorbitant rise in the housing market since then, N. estimates that the current value of this property is now worth the same figure but in euros. He notes the name and address of the real estate agent and the notary with whom his brother signed a contract at the time. Then he practices his signature. After a few hours he has mastered it, and he starts humming softly.

By six o'clock it is practically dark. N. starts to feel hungry and craves a hearty meal. After a sharp look around the interior, putting things back in their original position and emptying the garbage bin, he leaves the house through the front door and closes it carefully behind him. The weather has softened, the temperatures have risen above freezing and there is a drizzling rain. In the street, a car passes by swishing through puddles. He opens the gate using the button on the remote control and steps onto the street. Behind him, the gate slides closed and clicks into the lock, and the house is once again hermetically sealed.

N. strolls towards Hilversum, protected from the drizzle by an umbrella he took from the house, satisfied with himself and the situation. He was able to take control of his brother's bastion with relative ease and maintain his presence of mind. And now here he is, his task accomplished and the prospect before him of a hot meal and a bottle of wine at the inn down the road, the lights of which are already appearing in the mist.

42.

But when he reaches the guesthouse, alone in his room, he is struck once again by the old pain of loneliness. After surviving the tension of his mission, which was not entirely without danger, he has no outlet, no one to whom he can convey the harrowing details of his success. He thinks also that the silence in his brother's immense house, the chill, the big rooms, the impersonality and desolation of his brother's barren materialism, make the feeling of loneliness that much more poignant. He longs for another being, warm and lively and engaged, a woman undaunted by his immense sexual desire.

There are beautiful women in Hilversum, to be sure. When he wanders around the center during the day, drinking coffee or eating lunch, they are all around him: beautiful, healthy, well-dressed women, touchable according to physics, but more or less a universe away according to social acceptability. To avoid going completely mad with desire, sometimes he lets his imagination take refuge in the vision and attitude towards women of maltreated medieval monks, or to Lammetrie's anatomy, but even that does not temper his desire. His lust is so enormous that the thought of blood vessels and intestinal systems, muscles, organs and secretions hidden behind such a beautiful and sometimes provocative shell only heightens his desire. Being surrounded by these lovely women, these beautiful constellations, who simply look past him with little more than a fleeting glance makes him wither. After all, he is a stranger with an average good figure, and in this village where media is king, appearance is everything. And with his unvarying wardrobe, his eternal hat and dark glasses, which despite being timeless make him look boring and mediocre.

Here in this glittering city inextricably linked with the entertainment industry, the last thing he's doing is stealing the show.

He realizes it would have been different if he'd been able to brandish his former profession, showcase and engage his social contacts and networks. He would have been able to color his bare guesthouse room with the warmth and scent of a woman at any time, even without relying on an escort service. He is surprised to find that the thought actually bothers him deeply in his heart. His insight, sharpened by experience, is that women's natural propensity to monogamy is, for the most part, only a theoretical construct used to control women within society. N.'s experience has taught him that women are more enabled, by or because of cultural and economic factors, to live their lives according to their own standards and insight in the direction they want to take.

The flipside, of course, is that they are free in who they choose to make them happy. Many women are satisfied with the prospect of an exciting evening, a one-night stand, a beautiful weekend together if necessary, and that's the end of it. Here in the more liberal Gooise region N. is therefore one of the many who does not represent any added value, and therefore, like a humble street dog waiting for a morsel thrown in pity, he has to wait and see whether he might catch a woman's eye.

The thought of this makes his loneliness unbearable.

He longs for a bosom in which he can bury his fears and hesitations, his loneliness and doubts for even just a moment. At times of despair like this afternoon in his empty guesthouse room, the faces of Olga and Sonja rise up strongly in his mind. The pain is so immense that N. picks up the mobile phone, ready to dial their number, if only to hear only their sweet, affectionate voices on the answering machine. Twice he begins to dial the number, etched permanently into his memory, and twice he puts down the phone. That door, he believes, has been closed.

43.

The next day, he contacts the escort agency whose phone number he has kept in his wallet all this time. The woman answers in a terse voice and he identifies himself again as Kees and asks about a Nelleke.

She can recommend several girls sir, but Nelleke is no longer available.

"No Nelleke? But…"

"I don't know any Nelleke, sir."

He was with her just six months ago.

"I'm sorry sir, but girls come, and girls go. Six months is a long time in this business. We have a few new girls. Shall I tell you…"

"No, no need, thank you."

N. hangs up, deeply disappointed. Of course, it's the most normal thing in the world that girls come and go. *Rise and decline*, this business, a cog in the eternal impermanence of life, this raging merry-go-round, this screaming beast of Time. Nelleke, or whatever her real name is, she got out, not out of life (he sincerely hopes), but out of "the life". Perhaps she's earned enough for her further studies or working at such ungodly hours started to bother her, always with another drooling, horny guy. Perhaps she tired of having to live in lies, always having to look at Asmodeus's grinning face. Maybe she became engaged or married, who knows, moving in with some guy, turning her priorities elsewhere. Didn't she hint at something like that back then? And why is he so stuck on Nelleke anyway? There are so many beautiful young women. She was blond, tall and slim, with a beautiful figure, to be sure, but there are plenty of those in Holland.

Half an hour later, feeling still depressed and indecisive, N.'s cellphone buzzes. He answers, assuming it is his landlady because she's the only person with the number.

"This is Nelleke… is this Kees?" Her voice is clear and cheerful, a little expectant, a little provocative.

"Heyyyy… aren't you? I thought…" She has caught him by surprise, and he has to regain his composure. He feels his heart in his throat.

She says she is no longer registered with the escort agency, that she has not officially been in the business since the start of the year, but that she still has an arrangement with an acquaintance of the agency. If someone asks for her specifically, they will call and she decides whether to contact the client. She tells him that she has always remembered him.

When he asks how she knows his number, she tells him that they store it so they can trace people who don't keep appointments. It happens sometimes. If Kees hadn't disconnected so quickly, they would probably have asked for his number directly. She tells him that she'd like to spend a whole weekend with him, and if he could arrange it, she was available next weekend.

He doesn't try to hide his excitement when he tells her will arrange every day, every minute, every second to be with her. With giddy exuberance, he makes reservations for Saturday morning in the restaurant of a motel near Apeldoorn. She also loves walking, she says, so she'll bring a pair of sturdy shoes, a pair of hiking pants and a warm coat. Perhaps they could prowl around the Veluwe together one day, he suggests, and she responds that it would be wonderful! Her voice is still lively, and full of provocation.

"I'll see you next weekend, hopefully the weather will be nice," she says, finally.

"See you next weekend," N. echoes, still a little out of breath. Then the line is lost.

The weekend falls in mid-February. N. rejuvenates from slow seconds to syrupy minutes, and the prospect cheers him up more and more, it begins with powdered sugar and white marzipan. A lot of snow has fallen. N., who, after Amersfoort, sees unreal white forests glide past from the train compartment, has the feeling of being pulled into a fairy tale by electric traction.

In the motel he drinks coffee overlooking the parking lot. He isn't there long before he sees her pull in. She still drives the same car, a metallic-green Citroën Xsara. When she gets out of the car, dressed in a suit over which she drapes a long coat, he catches a glimpse of her long legs, and feels himself sinking into that purple-pink cloud of euphoria described so aptly in romance novels. He is so overcome by the joyful thought of this young woman coming here, just for him, for a whole weekend, that he forgets completely the true purpose of her coming. In the hall, he walks towards her expectantly, his arms wide, but she doesn't recognize him with a clean-shaven face and looks at him strangely. Then she hears his voice and her face widens into a captivating smile which, as the poets once wrote, was so lovely that it might even make gods fall in love with a mortal being. They embrace and kiss, and he leads her to the bar where they have a drink together.

That afternoon, at Nelleke's request, they visit a painting exhibition at the Singer in Laren, and then in the evening they go to the theater in Apeldoorn. That night they explore and feel each other's bodies. On Sunday morning, there is a light frost, but the weather is otherwise sunny and nice. Dressed in walking clothes and wrapped up in discussions about art in general, they trudge through the snow in the woods near Laag-Soeren and over Het Loo. She takes pictures of him, he takes pictures of her, and then there is a picture of both of them together, arm in arm. In the evening after dinner he is struck again by euphoria, and all his principles and plans are pushed aside. He asks her plainly if she would like to become his steady partner. She rejects him, of course, shortly and sweetly; she has no doubt well practiced in the art of sweet rejection. She says she has a steady boyfriend she wants to share her life with (an announcement, incidentally, that she lets slip again later). And when he hears a hint of irritation in her voice for a moment, a brief moment, he realizes he should not press the point.

The night is hectic, and because he knows this is the very last night he'll ever see her, he becomes daring. And then, with his face between her thighs, looking deeply into the entrance to the beating secret of birth and death, he suddenly has the groundless desire to crawl back into the womb. At his request, she spreads herself open with her fingers, and he wants to lie there quietly rolled up like a four- or five-month old fetus, in that warm cocoon of flesh. He wants to be with and in her all those years of her life, then die together with the mother body, to become ash together with Nelleke. Suddenly he understands what real Loneliness means and how unprepared he is for real life in spite of his experience. In his confusion, despite the books of prose and poetry that have been written about it over the centuries, he feels that not one grain has ever been dissected, felt, or understood of the phenomena of affection, love and eroticism. It has all been clutter and deception, cobbled together nonsense.

And though he knows he'll be rejected, he can't help but make another, half-hearted attempt at salvation. And when he is of course rebuffed again, he asks if they can at least meet again for another weekend.

Nelleke sighs, wraps her naked arms around his back, her naked legs around his hips, holding him with her whole body.

"Let's leave it at this, Kees. Now we only have nice memories of each other. Suppose we stayed together. Then habit would creep into the relationship, the automatism, the boredom. It's guaranteed to happen. We'd become indifferent to each other like men and women always become indifferent to each other when they stay together too long, the passion ebbs away. Men and women aren't supposed to be together for the rest of their lives. That's absurd… That's what the circumstances, the culture, the history, the church, told us it should be. We'd start to hate each other… I don't want that; I want to keep it beautiful between us. You'll always be in my memory… I know that, that's my eternal partnership with you. That's why we've been so intimate with each other, even spiritually, especially spiritually… Can you just accept (she shakes his shoulders), that in that respect you've been the only man in my life for a long time, and that is why I wanted to see you again, and that all the men who might come into my life can never change that?"

She falls silent, looking at N. with a penetrating gaze. Then she says, "I didn't just contact you again on Wednesday out of the blue. I wanted to. I was hoping all this time that you'd call me again… I wanted to see you one more time. Last summer, it wasn't finished between us. But it is now. It's complete, and incredibly beautiful. Men and women shouldn't spend too much time together. A few times, and when they do it should be done intensely. Drinking each other in… Let the photos we took of each other keep the memory alive. The rest is worthless. It's decay, humiliation, it's getting old and dilapidated… It's the transience that will always play tricks on us, cutting us down again and again. What's the point of holding each other in our arms when we've become old and ugly, cursing our defeat to each other's shriveled faces, only seeing the shadow of what we once were in each other's eyes…

"Oh Kees, I'm so scared of growing old, so *awfully* scared…" She cries suddenly, her tears flowing freely, but he can't comfort her, can't defend her, even though he puts his body around her protectively. All he can do is look into her face, twisted by sobbing.

That Monday morning, they bid each other farewell at the railway station in Apeldoorn. After their breakfast together, she insisted on paying half of the weekend package. She wanted, she said, to say goodbye to him as a friend, not as the girl he paid for. The last thing he sees of her is her receding figure as she waves to him from the platform; the last thing he feels is a poignant kiss on the center of his mouth. Later that day, in his guesthouse room, he falls into a deep sleep.

44.

Her firm, delicate rejection of him sets N. back on his previous course: execute the Grand Plan as soon as possible (he's already wasted so much time) and leave the region for good with the proceeds he's expecting from his recent criminal enterprise. After saying goodbye to Nelleke, it's as if he has left Europe for good (or Europe has left him). The world is big, happiness is everywhere, and the pull of the great melting pot of Manausgrows ever stronger. At the start of a new week, he nestles again into his brother's house. On his return, he has found that the note from Hafman Securities to Mrs. Jager is no longer on the kitchen table, but the neatly arranged pile of junk mail has grown. There is an upside-down bucket on the kitchen counter, with a not-yet-completely dry chamois hanging over it. Downstairs, dust has been removed from the tables, chairs and cupboards. These signs of someone's recent presence make N. nervous, and he makes a note to proceed with extra caution.

N. doesn't know how frequently the cleaning service comes to the house, but in any case, he must now work without leaving even the slightest trace. He no longer throws used coffee filters and the like into the garbage can but instead, flushes them down the toilet immediately after use. He entombs himself in his brother's office and study where there is a decent view of the Wamelings' outdoor activities to the left. Judging from the neighbor Mr. De Wit's reaction when N. had called him earlier, he doesn't worry much about the right side, and besides that, there is a distance of at least seventy-five meters between the De Wit palace and the Janssen castle populated generously with shrubs and conifers and other evergreens and bushes. The two residences are completely invisible to one another.

For two weeks, he watches the Wamelings' movements from the office (his field of vision covers the front door, side entrance and driveway) in order to distil some pattern in behavior. He can cautiously conclude that the elderly couple are in the habit of going out in their Jaguar on Tuesday and Thursday afternoons at about three o'clock and returning around six. The lady with the Jeep (she could indeed be a daughter still living at home, considering how they interact with each other), she is gone by the time N. arrives in the morning (N. sees her driving a couple of times when he is walking to his lookout post), and comes home around six o'clock. In addition to these regular movements, the Jaguar leaves occasionally at random, but almost without exception it is the woman going out alone (the man seems to be something of a homebody). Otherwise, the family receives few visitors, and if they do, it seems as though they enter through the back of the house where N. cannot see. Last week, however, a landscaping company came, running chainsaws and other noisy equipment in the garden for several days.

The days spent purely in observation of the neighbors were, for the most part, peaceful and undisturbed, aside from the occasional jolting phone call which would send a loud ring echoing through the empty halls. He never does get used to the intensity of it, and after a few days, he switches off the ringer on the telephone. Then one afternoon, his peace is disturbed by something far more tangible, more human in nature. One morning—at exactly 9:50—N. feels a presence enter the house, and he is sure that he is no longer alone. Initially it is a vibration, a slight stirring of the inner atmosphere. This is followed by the sound of a door opening downstairs, and then some rummaging and the squeak of a floorboard. A radio suddenly turns on at high volume. The clock strikes 10:00 and N. can hears, loud and clear, the weather forecast for the week followed by the usual commercial *bêtise*. Then a vacuum cleaner flips on, and he can hear the sound of someone pulling it back and forth across the floor. *Mrs. De Jager,* N. thinks, *has returned to finish her work.*

N. immediately freezes with panic. If she comes upstairs, he is lost—or in this case, found. In preparation for this type of disturbance, N. has already surveyed this floor extensively and found that, aside from his brother's heavy desk, there is nowhere he can adequately hide. There is not a single cabinet or closet on the floor, and the large bed in the bedroom is too low to the ground for N. to squeeze under. There is a small floor above where a retractable ladder accesses the attic above, but both spaces are relatively empty and N. could just as easily be found there. The only route to escape detection, N. has decided, is through the dormer window where he sits to spy on the neighbors, and onto the roof of the side wing. However, the roof is rather steep, and the option is not one that could be played out without significant risk. If he were to slip and fall (a highly realistic possibility) he would almost certainly land in the rock garden below, where all kinds of large, sharp rocks would quickly snap his leg or crush his head. Not a pleasant prospect. All things considered, but it may be his only option if the cleaning lady decides to bring her work upstairs.

He waits, keen to every signal of approach. She spends at least an hour pushing the vacuum cleaner from room to room (*there's one benefit to these country homes*, N. thinks sarcastically, *they can certainly keep a person occupied*). Then the house grows quiet and a few minutes later he smells the aroma of freshly brewed coffee. His mouth waters at the smell; if circumstances were different, he'd be brewing himself a cup right now. Around eleven-thirty, the front door opens, then from outside comes the sound of rugs or mats being beaten against a wall. He grabs his jacket (which he never has too far from reach) and moves to the top of the stairs and looks down onto the landing not far from the front door. He hears a mat being laid down, then cheerful humming, and a woman's back appears through the bars of the banister (blue-grey skirt, beige blouse, gray hair in a bun). Singing softly (but not entirely on key) she grabs another mat and takes it out through the front door. N. jumps at his chance, and floats as noiselessly as a butterfly down the stairs—avoiding every creak—then down the hallway and into the kitchen, tiptoeing silently to the pantry and quickly out the back door. He runs to gate at the back of the garden, then disappears behind the fence, onto the dirt road. Sweat is beading on his forehead, and he imagines the eyes of a dozen or so cleaning ladies on his back, but nevertheless wanders back to his guesthouse in good spirits. He stops for a cup of coffee at the inn then wanders into town for a light lunch.

45.

The doorbell rings and N.'s heart races. Is it the person he was expecting, or someone else? There are countless possibilities that are outside N.'s control, and the movements and motives of a single unexpected person, whether intentional or not, could shatter everything. One risk factor seems to have been eliminated: the Wamelings. Just like previous Tuesday afternoons, they drove away half an hour ago. From his brother's office he has a view of the fence on the street side, somewhat obstructed by a few trees. In front of the gate stands a man in a winter coat next to a Volvo SUV parked next to the fence. He assumes it is the real estate agent he called to the residence. The man rings the buzzer at the gate to his brother's house, and after N. confirms through the intercom that it is indeed the agent, he presses the buzzer that opens the gate.

Two days after his near encounter with Mrs. Jager, N. called a real estate agent, Steensma's Brokerage & Insurance. He explained that he intends to sell his house, telling them he would only be available on Tuesday or Thursday afternoons and would like to have a meeting so that they might make an appraisal of the house and, if the meeting went well, would consider possibly sell it through them.

In an attempt to look the part as the owner of such a property, he borrowed a dark suit (double breasted jacket) from his brother, who is a similar build to him (it's just a bit too wide at the waist), as well as one of his designer shirts, designer neckties and a mauve silk handkerchief. N. feels sufficiently disguised as a gentleman to take up the challenge of obtaining a considerable sum of money.

Feeling confident in his high-end attire, N. greets the agent of Steensma's, a fairly young man, probably around twenty-five N. guesses, with short, stylish hair. The agent is also well-dressed in a suit and tie, clearly prepared to match N.'s assumed status. The young man's conversation proves to be as pretentious as his clothes: limited in breadth and unintelligent, but effective because he is straightforward and to the point. The young man introduces himself as Van Dam, Peter van Dam. For the sake of convenience, N. assumes that Peter does not know his brother, and he has no reason to assume that the man before him is anyone other than the rightful owner of this substantial home, in other words the respectable

Mr. J.J.H. Janssen, attaché and commissioner. If he does know his brother, N. will tell him that he is acting on his instructions. That would complicate his plan as he would have to provide written authorization, but he will at least have time to disappear quietly and continue his plan, although with less financial security.

But Mr. Van Dam, exuding the volatile scent of money and decay so common in showrooms of car dealerships and in advertisements for fast and discreet personal lenders, doesn't seem to suspect anything. He looks upon the interior of the decadent home with a somewhat greedy expression. As he guides him on a tour, N. tells him the history of the house as well as he can from what he's learned from his brother's files.

After a tense hour—N. worried unnecessarily the entire time that Mrs. Jager would visit again or the Wamelings might unexpectedly come home early (neither happens)—the young Mr. Van Dam finished a thorough appraisal of the house and land. N. tells him he's in a bit of a hurry with the sale because he's been unexpectedly called out of the country for work, and he will soon be permanently leaving the country, to the US to be precise. He wants to have everything taken care of before then, and inquires what asking price would allow for a reasonably quick sale.

The junior real estate agent looks at him, looks around again, takes a few measured steps, and says decisively:

"Three million. For that amount it will go within fourteen days. There might be a quarter million more in it, but then you'll have to be patient." He looks at the N. with an endearing smile, and tells Mr. Janssen that if he does not need the money immediately, he thinks his brokerage firm would be able to sell it for three and a quarter within half a year.

"Three million is fine," says N., claiming that he doesn't want to worry too much about the small stuff. It's worth it to him to just be free of the headache; in truth, if the sale does not finalize in the next two weeks, he'll have no small amount of trouble. He tells Mr. Van Dam that he wants to buy something in America as soon as possible, and he already has something in mind that he'd like to put an offer on this week.

Mr. Van Dam nods empathetically. He looks around again, and out the window into the garden.

"Including or plus transfer costs?"

"Including is fine," says N., "and there's something else," he says in a firm voice. "I want half a million in cash… in two hundred euro bills." He winks conspiratorially, and the younger man flashes a corrupt smile. "Of course you can calculate your commission on the full amount," adds N., completely ignorant of how such things are done. "I assume you can put that in a contract for me."

That was no problem. The handover will be done on executing the deed.

The shake hands, and the agent promises to call to arrange a viewing as soon as there is a serious candidate. N. gives him his cellphone number (I'm on the road a lot for business, you understand). Just after four-thirty, Mr. Van Dam walks back down the meandering driveway to his SUV. As soon as the young man believes he is out of sight, he does an exuberant dance before climbing in his car and driving away. N. opts for an extravagant dinner at a first-class restaurant in Hilversum that evening, still dressed in his brother's fine suit. He regrets that he doesn't have a woman for company. It detracts from his fine mood and ambiance somewhat, and he sets his mind to meet a regular life companion again once abroad. He's discovered that he is a sociable person at heart, and always being alone is taking a noticeable toll on his mood.

46.

On Wednesday morning, less than 24 hours after their meeting, the young Mr. Van Dam calls with the announcement that a prospective buyer has been found. "They seem very serious," he adds significantly. They set an appointment for the next afternoon at half past three.

N. has been at the house all morning. He is struggling with the turmoil of the uncertainty and it keeps him awake all night. Early this morning he took a tranquilizer to remain functional and to keep himself from abandoning the whole enterprise. On the one hand there was the fear that something could go wrong in terms of business or organization, and on the other hand is the fear that the deception has long been found out and that he's about to walk into a stoically set trap. He cannot escape the unnerving feeling that he is on the verge of being unmasked. After all, he knows nothing about the contacts his brother may have in the world of local real estate, notaries and the like. What if they're keeping quiet so they can catch this *Fremdkörper* in the act?

Still restless, again dressed in his brother's custom suits, he walks aimlessly through the big house. He checks all the paperwork for the tenth time, cross-checking the official documentation that must be submitted when selling a house. When the phone rings at half past one, the loud ringing once again sends a shock through his system. N. is certain it is in regards to his meeting with the prospective buyer, but nevertheless he barely dares to answer. An unclear conscience and the piercing ringing of a telephone in a strange house; N. is not well-suited to a life of crime. This whole affair, N. thinks, needs to end soon.

When he finally builds up the nerve to answer, the ringing has already stopped. He berates himself for hesitating, and is suddenly overwhelmed that the entire deal may fall through because of that missed call.

About five minutes later, the cellphone beeps again. N. answers eagerly this time, so much so that he thinks it must be audible in his voice. But it is only his landlady asking him if she should expect him for the hot evening meal. Yes, he says, she should, please.

Then the phone beeps again. "Oh, Mr. Janssen, it's Van Dam." He explains that the prospective buyer has been delayed on the way, and asks whether it will be a problem if they move the appointment by a half hour.

That is not a problem, N. tells him. With a sigh of relief he shakes himself out, dabs his forehead and loosens his tie. Any rationalist, he muses, who believes there are no leftovers of superstition attached to his soul, should experience a situation like this just once.

At exactly four o'clock there is a knock on the door. The Wamelings having departed punctually with their Jaguar at three o'clock. At the gate is young Mr. Van Dam's SUV and a silver Mercedes S-Class. N. opens the gate and three men and a woman enter the driveway. He waits for them in the front entrance. Van Dam introduces one of the two men—he's an older man, probably fifty years old, balding and with a well-groomed gray beard—as his boss, Mr. Steensma. He assumes that Mr. Janssen has no objection to Mr. Steensma coming along personally, as is customary in their brokerage for transactions of this size. N. says it makes no difference to him, but the man puts him at some unease with his penetrating glance, probably with some depth of psychological knowledge formed by insight and experience.

The prospective buyer is a small, stout man, probably in his sixties, with sharp, inquisitive eyes. N. is increasingly fearful that he is being fleeced and the lot of them might be taking him for a ride. The man is introduced as Mr. Grootendonk (with a double o). He wears a hat and an expensive dress coat over a grey three-piece suit. He offers N. a clammy fleshy hand before presenting the lady as his wife. She is quite voluminous, wearing a short sable fur overcoat over a woolen trouser suit, the trouser legs ending in neatly laced boots. Without wasting any time, Grootendonk inquires after N.'s profession, asking why he's decided to sell the house. N. answers laboriously, repeating the story he's rehearsed several times. The couple, accompanied by the young Mr. Van Dam, then begins a thorough inspection of the property, looking over every square inch of the house and garden.

Steensma stays behind, asking N. to join him for a moment while the other three finish their tour. Once out of earshot of the others, Steensma tells N. that Mr. Grootendonk has been told the asking price is three and a half million, but that the seller is willing to negotiate. "This guy," Steensma says, gesturing toward the buyer and his wife, "has money like water." He goes on to say that, due to the inexperience of his associate, and (no offense intended) Mr. Janssen's apparent inexperience, he wishes he had come himself that first afternoon. He is afraid his colleague set the price far too low, but there is of course always room for negotiation in order to arrive at higher selling price, which would be, in his opinion, a fair agreement.

"I assume you're okay with making a bit more money," Steensma says, letting out a greedy chuckle. N. nods, trying to look nonchalant; in reality, he just wants the whole business over with. After their brief conversation, N. and Mr. Steensma rejoin the others, and whether they'd all like a cup of coffee. The entire party responds enthusiastically, and N. makes his way back to the kitchen. As he enters the room, his heart leaps into his throat; there, standing at the sink, is Mrs. Jager.

In retrospect, he applauds himself for having the presence of mind to handle this crucial moment with grace. Clearly, she is just as shocked to see him—perhaps more, even—as he is to see her. He immediately introduces himself, and in a calm, even voice, explains to the gray-haired cleaning lady that he is Mr. Janssen's *chargé d'affaires*. He offers his sincere apologies for the fact that she clearly has not been informed of anything; Mr. Janssen had in fact told him to do just that, but with everything on his plate at the moment it must have slipped his mind. He explains that he is here to rent out the house on Mr. Janssen's behalf; the Janssen couple recently decided to settle abroad for more than a year, and he is meeting with a potential renter at this very moment. He's actually quite surprised that Mrs. Janssen hasn't already been in contact with Mrs. Jager.

Mrs. Jager's bewilderment does not appear to have settled at all by this explanation, so N. advises her to contact the Janssens herself if necessary. Mrs. Jager replies that she doesn't have the family's address or telephone number, such information is only known to the closest neighbors. This information is music to his ears, reassuring N. greatly. All she knows, she tells N., is that the Janssens are in America, on the west coast near *Sante Frisco*, and that they wouldn't return until the beginning of May. She asks a few more practical questions to which N. is able to provide immediate answers. He shrugs his shoulders, resigning to his position as the bearer of bad news, and apologizes again. Upstairs, he can hear the potential buyers climbing to the second floor of the house and the groaning of the extension ladder as it is pulled down. He promises Mrs. Jager that he will call her tomorrow or the day after with further more information on the services required of her which, incidentally, the Janssen's would like her to continue, even during the rental period.

She still seems somewhat disconcerted as he ushers her out of the back door. N., with sweat pooling along his hairline, under his armpits, and dripping down his back, returns to the task at hand.

When the company descends once again into the kitchen, unaware of the menace that had just taken place, the coffee is ready. He takes it to the kitchen table, and they all sit companionably.

Three-and-a-half million is too much Grootendonk informs him, dismissing the need for pleasantries. N. give a non-committal nod (this hadn't been his original asking price anyway). The prospective buyer offers three million, and although he's reluctant to play the part of haggler, denies the offer, not wanting to rouse suspicion or seem too eager. There is fifteen minutes of haggling, and while the temperature throughout the house is a constant sixteen degrees (as it has been all those weeks), it feels to N. as though the heat has been turned up drastically at the kitchen table. The negotiations continue, a back-and-forth of innocuous agreements over money that seems trifling to all parties. N. realizes, once he's away from the commotion, that the amount they're debating is more than double that of a professor's salary. Finally, to N.'s great relief, they settle at three million, one hundred and fifty thousand euros. N.'s happiness at the agreed amount is firmly contradicted by the dissatisfaction playing across Steensma and Van Dam.

"I understand that you want half a million in cash?"

N. nods, still in a daze. Mr. Steensma asks him to name a notary, which he does immediately. With a second cup of coffee, the clearly disgruntled Steensma makes a phone call and quickly arranges a meeting for next Tuesday. N. arranges to meet Grootendonk in a restaurant near the notary's office for the transfer of the cash.

The four gentlemen and the lady chat a little while longer before N., wanting them gone well before the Wamelings or the lady with her Jeep return home, makes an excuse to usher them out of the house. He can admit to himself, albeit still reeling, that the situation has gone as smoothly as one could expect. At half past five, humming unconsciously and with a slight skip in his step, he walks to his guesthouse in the south of Hilversum.

At one-thirty that Tuesday afternoon, he meets Mr. Grootendonk in Hilversum in the agreed restaurant. The man is alone. A beige overnight bag holds a small case. In a more private part of the restaurant, he hands the bag to N. and asks him to check the amount. As he does, Grootendonk walks to the bar to order a drink, and N. is left undisturbed to run his trembling fingers over the neatly wrapped packets crisp banknotes. It would appear that the entire sum is there, in two-hundred-euro notes. He's surprised with the confidence he conveys when he suddenly pulls out a packet at random and holds it against the light. Within the wrapper he can clearly count one hundred notes. Then he counts twenty-five packets, and is satisfied that the requested five hundred thousand euros are in front of him.

When Grootendonk returns, N. has already closed the bag and reports that everything seems to be in order, at which the other has him sign a receipt. They drink coffee and make small talk (the man turns out to be the owner and director of a trading house where his son is now taking over the reins so that he and his wife might enjoy their well-earned rest in the Gooi area). At half past two, they take Grootendonk's car to join Mr. Van Dam from Steensma's Brokerage & Insurance, who is already waiting for them at Blokzijl notary. The signatures from all parties are obtained without being disturbed by a police raid, criminal investigator or crime syndicate. The purchase is complete, and after a few formalities, the Grootendonk family is informed that they can move into the house in exactly one month, at which time the keys will also be handed over. Mr. Grootendonk offers to give N. a ride home, but he politely declines, saying he's already ordered a taxi. Every minute with the man feels like an eternity.

As soon as the Grootendonk drives away, N. walks to his guesthouse, takes the overnight bag to his room and puts it under the bed before carefully locking the door again. Then he walks back to his brother's house, hangs the tailor-made suit back in the closet, pulls on his own hiking pants, comfortable sweater, and sturdy walking shoes, and strolls casually through the woods back to Hilversum. Back in his boarding room, he flops onto the bed with a deep sigh; a wave of peace and liberation pass over him, and if he lived to be a hundred years old, that would be just fine with him.

The next morning, he checks out of the guesthouse and travels to Utrecht where he moves into a suite in a hotel downtown. The bedroom has a small safe set discreetly into a wall, and he tucks the overnight bag inside of it. What will happen when Mr. J.J.H. Janssen returns from the States in a little over a month's time? How severe is the damage he's done? Regardless of his distaste for his brother, it is beneath his dignity to laugh at his misfortune. Still, however, he feels neutral, and hopes that he'll soon be able to forget the whole thing once he is abroad. The money has come in, his future is secured—at least for the time being— so his primary goal for most of the last year is now accomplished. The rest, he feels, is secondary and uninteresting.

47.

By mid-April, the weather begins to turn mild. Even in the bustling city center of Utrecht N. hears the spring song of blackbirds in the parks, and through the open window in his hotel suite drift the sweet smells of flowers blooming. Spring is near, and so, too, is his future.

Manaus. He can almost feel the blue-green tropical heat, can almost smell the musty gray dirt. He once spent a month there about three years ago, and the city got under his skin. Part city, part no-man's-land, having its own civilization and legislature and surrounded on all sides by one of Earth's last true jungles. He imagines quietly working on a novel there, perhaps a successful one this time; or maybe a travelogue or road story about traveling through the deep jungle, like a modern Bruce Chatwin; or perhaps a script for a movie set in Brazil; his future there feels full of possibilities.

But first, he wants to invest some of his money in the hospitality industry there. A bar, or two, maybe even a small chain. His plan for the five hundred thousand is to use half for an investment and venture capital, the other half in a bank as a nest egg. Jan Versteegh would have to be his figurehead or manager. He knows Jan from the time they were both members of Vindicat's pub committee. They worked together as bartenders in various nightclubs in the city center to earn a little extra money on top of their modest scholarships. He and Jan learned the hospitality industry from the bottom to the top working together, both in terms of operation and environment. Jan never finished his post-baccalaureate studies; young and idealistic, he said the world was calling (and he did have a fair share of noteworthy adventures before eventually settling in Manaus, working in the hospitality industry). As far as he knows, Jan no longer has any ties to the Netherlands, other than the occasional phone conversation with N., most recently about ten months ago, shortly before the historic explosion. He told N. during that conversation that he had the opportunity to take over a successful nightclub in a Manaus suburb, but he lacked the financial means. He had also remarked during that conversation that although the heat could be somewhat oppressive in Manaus, it made people thirsty for drink. After living in Manaus for some time he absolutely did not want to go back to Europe, where no matter where a person went, they'd only see gray hair and balding heads, and this somehow had to do with today's European youth. But he was a hard worker and good colleague, and N. knew that N. could be trusted through and through. When N. calls, Jan enthusiastically promises to arrange a hotel room for him. Then, after a brief and friendly conversation, N. tells Jan about his supply of cash he would like to put in the hospitality industry there…

"But why do you want…?"

"Black money."

"Aha. How much?"

A mumbled two hundred grand.

"Dollars?"

"Euros."

"Damn Chris, that would go far here in Manaus." Even over a distance of ten thousand kilometers, N. hears the tell-tale click of a tongue.

Jan also advises him that once he reaches Manaus, the money would be safest at the branch of an American bank. Jan offers to help him with whatever he needs if he truly does intend to come to Manaus for good, and wishes him good luck before hanging up. N. remembers that his friend lives with a Brazilian woman ten years his junior, a beautiful woman (N. has seen a picture of her) with whom he had a child. And, N. can't forget, the time Jan told him how many beautiful young women live in Manaus.

That night he walks into the center of town and finds a bar where he drinks a couple of whiskies. He manages to seduce a young, blond lady of the night. The sting of impermanence bites at him. This illusion of closeness, a temporary fix for broken connection. He thinks of Nelleke, and then the Beumer ladies. While the bar floozy flirts with him, he gives something pure and unaffected to Olga and Sonja. N. knows suddenly that he wants—needs, perhaps—to hear their voices one more time, even if only briefly. Perhaps even the recording of Olga's hoarse voice on the voicemail message would be enough.

N. feels incredibly lonely again, accompanied by a sudden indescribable desperation. He realizes again that his success overseas is almost entirely dependent on quickly finding a woman to make his confidante and companion. Everyone needs at least one other creature, woman or man, to avoid going insane: if the recent months have taught him anything it's this. He finishes his drink and dismisses the hooker, then realizes that she may be just as lonely and desperate as he is at the moment. The thought makes him even sadder. Wasn't it Emil Cioran who wrote that if you wanted to know what loneliness is, all one had to do was go to a brothel at five in the morning? Or did he mean worldly fatigue? He can't remember. He pays for his drinks and walks back to the hotel, sinking into a bottomless depression.

Will he walk alone into his new future, or will he manage to find a young life companion at his side? If Tipp Marugg claims that as an older white man, you can always count on the open arms of an Antillean, why shouldn't he find the same fate with an underprivileged native in Manaus? He is, after all, not bad looking, and is certainly not a man without means.

That evening in his suite, he's too depressed to move past self-pity, but these thoughts will eventually bring him to another idea for a nice prelude to his adventure. In the end, there's a sense of hubris in it. After all, doesn't he still have the key to his brother's house? As long as no storm has kicked up there (he'll have to be careful, of course), what is keeping him from impersonating his brother as a wealthy landowner? Barely touched by middle-age, carelessly collecting famous modern art, a couple of cars parked unassuming in a garage, he could play the dynamic bachelor, bon vivant and cosmopolitan, bored with life in this country and on the verge of living elsewhere. Doesn't that type of wealth serve as honey in the trap? He could attract a lot of wasp-waisted flies if he publicized that he had not tired of adventure, but of being a bachelor in his genteel civilian life. He could lure in women far more elegant than anyone he might find in his old routine of calling for an escort girl.

His pedophilic brain is already at work writing the listing in the personal ads in his mind's eye: *<M, 35, good looking, traveling, wealthy. Seeks attractive adventurous girl, age 16-22, willing to settle abroad. Marriage possible. Respond w. photo and no.>* Wouldn't this indeed be the most efficient way to select a beautiful, enterprising young lady?

When he really likes an idea, N. finds a way to bring it about. Driven by a screaming desire and a triad of warm ideas, within a few days he had placed a numbered advertisement in the Tuesday edition of three national magazines, and by that Thursday the first responses were already pouring in to the p/a of the hotel. By Friday there are no less than one hundred seventy-three letters laying on his stylish suite table (over the next week, thirty-five more will trickle in). Some are handwritten, some typed on a typewriter, but most typed on a PC, and with only a few exceptions, each one is packed with enthusiastic photos. The ages of the respondents are between fourteen and twenty-three. Reactions vary in length from ten lines to a whole page (a few young ladies added a second page before they felt their exceptional qualities had been described to their satisfaction). What strikes N. most in these letters is the appallingly poor language skills of today's Dutch youth. After the first few dozen letters, he realizes that most of them are reflections of girls whose dreams and aspirations have been crushed or let go, and the thought once again makes him lose his cheerful, excited attitude. The feeling is brief, however, and N. allows himself once again to rejoice in the affection of strangers.

After much deliberation and still a bit surprised by the number of responses he received (how many more would it have been had he used the internet?) he narrows it down two girls he will invite to his brother's charming home, the first this Friday, the other a week later. That is just possible; five days after that, the Grootendonk couple will take possession of the estate. The first girl he chooses did not send along a photo (but she is quite young) and the surprise tantalizes N. Her letter is handwritten in black ballpoint and her handwriting and grammar are flawless. The girl writes that she is sixteen years old and would like to go abroad; she uses a rigid, somewhat archaic writing style that gives the suggestion that the letter might have been written by someone else (a thought that N. finds even more provocative). The second girl writes that she's eighteen and has included a passport photo, though her letter is not without grammatical errors. She has a beautiful if somewhat plain face, with eyes that are gray and perhaps a bit too small. She is dark blond and says she loves to travel.

The Thursday before the first appointment, N. carefully approaches his brother's house again. When he enters he can see that nothing has changed in the past weeks, not even a sign that Mrs. Jager has returned. In the mailbox at the fence, he finds an envelope from Steensma's Brokerage & Insurance, containing a bill for 53,520.00 euros for mediation and additional fees as well as a request for payment within fourteen days. The envelope does not have postage and must have been put in the box directly by someone from the brokerage. In the time that N. spent at his brother's house, there was never a substantial amount mail, so he assumes that it must be forwarded elsewhere.

He calculates that firm has charged an hourly rate of well over five thousand euros, which seems rather exaggerated, and it is not without some joy that he tears up the bill with a smile and puts the scraps into a waste bin. Later that day, after a few unsuccessful attempts, he manages to contact his former student. She is at first stunned to hear his voice, having almost certainly heard of his demise in an explosion, but after a brief conversation, he finds that she is wildly enthusiastic.

48.

Sixteen-year-old Marianne van Ees from Rotterdam agreed to meet with N. on Friday afternoon at half past three at the inn where he so regularly ate meals on the way to his guesthouse from his brother's house. If everything goes according to plan, his young bride-to-be will arrive by bus at the station right in front of the inn and ask for Mr. Janssen at the front desk. That's the arrangement.

N. is there at a quarter past three, dressed in one of his brother's respectable but sporty outfits. He has a slight headache and is more anxious about the meeting than he expected. But there is a pleasant nervous anticipation; he is in the fortunate position of being able to wait, watch, and judge. He orders a cup of coffee and stares out the window to the road along the restaurant. A bus comes to a stop and two women step off, each holding a small suitcase. The older one wears a short coat, the younger one, still a girl, a short leather jacket. They look like a mother and daughter, both wearing blue jeans; N. muses at how blue jeans are the outfit of choice for both the young and old. After some discussion and gesturing, they walk across the gravel path to the entrance of the inn and disappear into the hall.

N. consults his watch and wonders what time the next bus is scheduled, worrying that his young companion has gotten lost in the labyrinth of Hilversum's public transportation system, and a short moment later he is overwhelmed by anxiety that this whole dating idea is idiotic. What sixteen-year-old girl makes an appointment with a more than twice her age? And just as a gloom sets heavily over him, a waiter comes to him and asks if he is Mr. Janssen. Indeed he is, or at least he has been until almost twelve months ago. He looks around in amazement. How did he miss her arrival? The server tells him there are two ladies in the hall asking for him.

N. stands up, somewhat wary, doubt setting in. The two women from the bus are standing there, looking at him expectantly. He doesn't try to hide his surprise. They—or, more correctly, the mother—introduce themselves as mother and daughter Van Ees from Rotterdam. Registering his obvious surprise and burgeoning disappointment, she suppresses a nervous laugh before continuing that she hopes Mr. Janssen doesn't mind that she has come along. Taking into account her daughter's age, as a mother, she feels it's her duty to find out exactly who they are dealing with. She tries to give her explanation a diplomatic tone but makes it clear that her presence is non-negotiable. Mr. Janssen swallows, nods, and invites both ladies to sit down, ordering coffee and apple pie. He adjusts quickly to this unexpected turn in the situation, but after silently taking stock of the two ladies, the daughter in particular, his disappointment grows.

"There's a lot of forest here," the lady breaks the silence. She speaks with a slight Rotterdam accent. She adds that where they're from, there isn't any forest.

N. agrees, explaining that he has lived here for so long, he barely notices how heavily forested it is. The mother has dark brown hair cut short and gray eyes. She is a little on the chubby side, and so ordinary in appearance that there is something agreeable about it. She looks well cared for, and he estimates that she certainly cannot be older than about forty.

But of course, his eyes are drawn to the girl. She has pale, freckled skin. Her figure, perhaps normal for her age, is skinny and undeveloped, and wonders if she really has reached the minimum age required by his personal standards. She looks as though she's just finished (or perhaps is in the midst of) a recent ruthless growth spurt. Overall, sees enough potential in this teenage girl to think she will grow into a nice young lady in the years to come, especially since she seems to take after the mother in every way, from her physical appearance to the gestures and occasional half-closing of her right eye. She cannot conceal that she feels awkward, maybe even a bit embarrassed, and it comes across as shy modesty. The situation is just as strange and unfamiliar for N., and he tries to put her at ease by asking if she had a good trip.

Suddenly, young Marianne goes off like an alarm clock, telling him that they had worried about the trains being delayed, it being Friday afternoon and all, so they left an hour earlier just to be on the safe side. But it turned out that the trains were running on time, so they had an hour to spare in Hilversum where they've never been before, so they did a little sightseeing and some shopping as well.

"Mommy bought me a very nice watch. It's for my birthday." She brings her wrist to his face so abruptly that N. flinches involuntarily, which draws some color to her cheeks, and she looks to her mother for encouragement.

N. knows already that Marianne doesn't really charm him and likely never will, but he nevertheless examines the watch attentively, even holding her delicate wrist for a moment. He asks if it was for her sixteenth birthday.

The girl looks a little helplessly at her mother, who explains somewhat sheepishly that she is indeed a little younger than indicated in the letter, certainly he won't mind that. It's only a difference of two years. Her birthday was indeed four days ago, she turned fourteen, but girls these days mature so quickly.

Marianne nods vigorously and thinks she can easily pass for a girl of sixteen, perhaps even seventeen. At school they always think she's older than she is.

"And Marianne is also mentally very mature for her age," the mother adds immediately.

N. understands the endorsement. He says that if that is the case, of course he cannot object to her age, although he does think fourteen is quite young. He asks, almost mischievously, "Don't you think I'm way too old for you?" At this, the ladies assure him in unison with the solid conviction that it is not age but love and good rapport that matter.

Yes, Mr. Janssen can't object to that.

N. and the mother drink another cup of coffee. Marianne has a soft drink. Then he tells them that he lives nearby, only a ten-minute walk and that he enjoys the exercise and has come to their meeting on foot. He asks the ladies if they wouldn't mind walking a little bit, and they both agree. The ladies exchange what N. takes as an enterprising glance at one another as he pays the bill and picks up the lady's suitcase.

They arrive at his brother's house after a chatty walk, the conversation carried mostly by the mother, and he presents the house from the road as proof of the wealth he mentioned in the advertisement. Then he guides the Van Ees ladies through the garden gate via the sandy path. He offers them a tour, and they gladly accept, examining the place closely from top to bottom. They pause for a moment to look at Corneille's cut-up forms (the mother asks if the paintings were done by N. himself in his spare time). He shows them their guest room (his brother and sister-in-law's bedroom). Then they walk to the kitchen, the pantry and the garage. N. mentions casually that the Porsche Carrera belonged to his wife, who died two years ago. He invites Marianne to sit behind the wheel, if she wants to (which invitation she eagerly accepts). In one of the living rooms, he offers the ladies a drink. The mother would like a sherry, the daughter a mixed juice. N. pours himself a generous helping of his brother's *Joseph Guy*. During the aperitif, he says a little conspiratorially that he unfortunately can't use the car for a few months—another reason he came to the rendezvous on foot—because, well (he makes the well-known gesture of the wrist, the invisible cup to the lips).

"You know, one too many and a police check, bad luck really. But it was the second time." He nods his head, attempting foolish regret. When he suddenly sees the mother's face light with concern, he tries to reassure her, saying it was in a time when he'd fallen into a bit of a hole after the sudden death of his wife. He admits he's in a bit of an awkward position without a driver's license, especially now that his driver is on sick leave. He does hope to get his driver's license back in just three weeks, and promises that his days of seeking comfort in the bottle are behind him.

The mother's eyes soften at his explanation and they hope, again in unison, that this type of thing doesn't happen to him again.

N. also informs them that his housekeeper and her husband are going to the Canary Islands for a week, so he's called a catering company that will be preparing their dinner soon. Both ladies croon at such a luxury.

At exactly six o'clock, in accordance with N.'s careful instruction, the catering company arrives at the back gate. A young man carries the food to the kitchen quickly and silently. N. pays him while the mother and daughter set to work finding porcelain plates and silver cutler. The ladies compliment the extravagance, and it really is a luxurious meal, paired with a fine white wine in crystal glasses (even Marianne takes a few sips, perhaps her first introduction to alcohol), and N. has heightened the ambiance with the lighting of candlesticks in several candelabras, the motivation behind which is that the light will be less detectable through the curtains.

The mother leads them in a hearty prayer, and N. says his own separate prayer that there may be enough food to go around; he hadn't been planning on three people, after all. Before the mother's lively mood threatens to swallow the entire conversation, N. turns his attention to his young mistress. She tells him that she is Christian-reformed lower general secondary education, and has chosen to concentrate her studies in language arts. She wants to be a receptionist in a large hotel someday, preferably abroad, because her greatest desire is to see a lot of the world. Her eyes sparkle as she tells him her plans for the future, and N. finds himself being drawn to her. Some shift in taste and boundaries, he thinks perhaps because of the influence of alcohol, and he feels a growing erotic attractiveness toward her.

Mrs. Van Ees breaks in then, explaining that she is an administrative assistant at a customs clearing office in the port of Rotterdam. She's had this job since her husband ended up on disability four years ago which, as Mr. Janssen may know, reduced the family's income quite a bit.

When the conversation lulls, N. realizes both ladies are waiting for him to reveal something about himself. Spurred by alcohol and, perhaps, erotic desire, he allows his imagination to take flight. He tells the ladies that he became a widower after his wife was killed in a tragic car accident two years ago. At first he thought, out of respect for his wife whom he had loved dearly, that he would never marry again. He found himself spiraling into a very dark place. But thanks to the spiritual guidance of a pastor, he came to see things differently, and now every time he even thinks of a new woman, he can see Beatrice's smiling down on him from above. Yes, Beatrice, that was the name of his dear sweet wife (N. blots at his eye). He had once considered himself an atheist, feeling that faith was ridiculous, but has now become deeply spiritual. He goes on to explain that he has had dated several women in the past year, all between about twenty-five and thirty-five, and all of them divorced, burdened by children, or products of otherwise broken relationships; in short, women his age were damaged women. He had even briefly become entangled with a married woman with children, and although he quite liked her, she had refused to leave her husband. Such an arrangement, he said, was entirely unacceptable to his own value system (the ladies' faces betray their enthrallment with him). After all of these unpleasant affairs, he decided he was ready to find a companion and began his search in earnest for a younger woman. He admits that he thought the age he specified in his advertisement was perhaps a bit too young, but he'd really like to meet someone without a quote-unquote "past", if they understand his meaning.

They seem to understand perfectly. The mother emits another sigh, the daughter shifts restlessly in her chair, and N., satisfied, pours himself another half-glass of *Joseph Guy*.

After dinner the mother busies herself putting the dishes in the dishwasher, then excuses herself to the guest room, adding that of course he and Marianne will want to get to know each other in private. In an attempt to appear chivalrous, N. explains that it is not necessary because, at least as far as he is concerned, there will still be plenty of opportunity for him and Marianne to, well, really get to know each other. So, the mother stays, and the three of them watch television, the 2040th episode of what the ladies call the "only" word game *If You Know It Don't Say It*. The two are apparently so familiar with the show that the mother digs out a pen and notepad from her purse to take notes, and when Marianne asks N. enthusiastically whether he likes this game, he replies automatically that he does.

The girl sits close beside him on a couch, inching gradually closer until finally they begin to brush each other's hands. After a while, N. slips his hand behind the girl's back and paws at her willingly turned breast; Marianne unhooks her bra. The mother looks on, approving, even encouraging the interaction. After the "only game" is over, N. pours another round of drinks. Then, feeling the growing eroticism in the atmosphere (he has a growing curiosity regarding the mother's desired role in this strange triad) he brings the conversation back to his heartrending past. N. tells them that his young wife (she was only twenty-two) was pregnant when she died, already in her fourth month of pregnancy. He had so much been looking forward to becoming a father, which made the terrible drama even worse. He turns to Marianne, and asks bluntly whether she would be open to having children soon?

"I'd love to," she nods emphatically, for once without first looking at her mother. Then N. suggests: "But of course you're still very young to be a mother now. Besides, you want to become a receptionist and see a lot of foreign countries." At this the mother hastens to say that Marianne has wanted children for a while, and that it might also be wise to start early. Because then, when the children are a bit older, it will be easier for her to find a job. Mrs. Van Ees is of the opinion that women nowadays put far too much emphasis on early careers, and by the time they get around to children—"if they can even still have them," she adds threateningly—that not only is it hard for those children to have such old parents, but such a delay is often associated with complications at birth, increasing the risks of stillbirth and disabled children. There was an in-depth article about this, she explains, in a recent edition of *Libelle*. She makes it clear that her feelings on the subject are rather passionate, and N. makes it clear that he finds no fault in her opinion.

At half past eleven he suggests that it is time for bed. He can imagine it has been a tiring day for the Van Ees mother and daughter, and it has actually been quite emotional for him as well. When the mother and daughter exchange another meaningful glance, he gambles generously that he will make it through this first night without Marianne in his bed... Well, there will be plenty of opportunity for all that in the near future, perhaps over the Easter holidays which are already fast approaching. Then the mother asks, to N.'s surprise, whether Mr. Janssen might at least want to "see" Marianne.

He understands, agreeing vigorously, and fifteen minutes later the child stands shyly in his room in her budding femininity. He gestures wordlessly to her, and sits on the edge of the bed as he watches her undress, slowly, bit by bit, with her face turned away. She is so uncomfortable, which N. finds endearing and pitiable at the same time. He says a few reassuring words when she first takes off her jeans and sweater, then her blouse. She hangs everything neatly over a chair. Her matching bra and panties are both so brand-new that it wouldn't have surprised him to see a Hema price tag hanging from them. Then the girl stands naked in front of him, shivering slightly and expectantly, a sudden flush on her pale cheeks. Then she looks at him, asking whether he likes what he sees. When he says that he does, she asks whether Mr. Janssen wants her to lie down on the bed now or if she should undress him first.

N. feels the pull of a slight temptation, but overcomes it, saying that it is not necessary tonight, he can wait another week. She explains somewhat bashfully that she'll have her period next week, probably the worst on Friday and Saturday. Well, the following week then, he tells her; he has learned to be patient for such things. He kisses her on the cheek, on the neck and the back of the shoulder. There is a faint smell of sweat mixed with the remnants of deodorant. He carefully takes her breasts into his hands, then moves down to her surprisingly moist vagina and asks if she has already been with a boy. She tells him that she is still a virgin. Then he kisses her nipples before helping her gather her clothes and wishes her a good night.

As soon as she leaves the room he is overwhelmed with enormous regret that the child does not pique his desire. After all, doesn't his preference for the *fruit vert* also stem from his aversion to older women who, almost without exception, have been previously mounted by men? He suddenly feels a fierce longing for Sonja Beumer.

A quiet night follows. The next morning, N. wakes early and has a tense breakfast. He keeps his eyes trained on the kitchen door while he listens for possible suspicious noises outside. When the ladies wake, he hears them upstairs using the toilet and shower. They greet N. at the kitchen table like old acquaintances. Marianne, who has actually put on a bit of make-up to make herself look more mature, gives him a warm kiss. He sets out for them aromatic coffee and delicious sandwiches, which he had delivered yesterday by the catering company. He tells the ladies that he has arranged to have them picked up by a taxi at half past ten and taken to the station in Hilversum.

After breakfast, while Marianne is upstairs, mother Van Ees takes N. aside for a moment to tell him that it is her sincere hope that this first introduction to her daughter can be the beginning of a happy and lasting relationship. However, she adds, that she would appeal to the gentleman's sense of responsibility. Of course, she can sympathize with his situation as a widower, having had to live without a steady partner. It's only natural, she continues, that he would like to have a few children. But she does expect that in the event her daughter becomes pregnant, he will of course do what is right and provide for both her and the children. Not that she doubts him, she affirms, but she feels it is her duty as a mother to make this point clear. "And God willing, if a child were conceived in love, perhaps the next weekend or soon after that, then that's just God's will." But if possible, she thinks, it might be wiser that perhaps he could wait until Marianne is out of school. Certainly, he can imagine the trouble a child would have while still under compulsory schooling and already in that position. But of course, if the gentleman would like to be with her daughter sooner in the happy expectation of parenthood, well, she gives her blessing.

The conversation makes N. almost a little impatient and irritable, and he tells her bluntly that he knows his responsibilities and would rather postpone fatherhood a few more years. He's in no hurry at all. But he suddenly feels a sense of urgency for the ladies to leave quickly.

The taxi finally arrives at half past ten (also ordered to arrive at the back entrance). After some passionate exchanges, mother and daughter disappear from sight. Ten minutes later, as N. is about to leave the house, the phone rings. Perhaps it's relief that makes him answer it. It's Mr. Blokzijl from the notary. There is something wrong with the sales contract, he explains, and wonders whether he and Mr. Grootendonk, who is at his office at this moment, might come visit Mr. Janssen in about half an hour.

From the quaking in the man's voice, N. thinks they have likely found out that a lot of things are not okay, probably that nothing is okay. His heart is pounding. He checks his watch and says he will expect both gentlemen in half an hour. The moment he hangs up the phone he rushes up the stairs to his brother's study, taking the giro booklet and transfer cards from the desk, slips them into his pocket, and leaves with the utmost haste. A little over fifteen minutes later, he is at the railway station in Hilversum, where he boards a train to Utrecht.

That same weekend, he sends the Van Ees mother and daughter a polite note saying that after some reflection, he has decided to refrain from further contact. Marianne is simply too young. But he writes further, that he realizes he may have raised their expectations, and in an attempt to alleviate their distress, he would like to transfer an amount of 20,000 euros to Marianne's giro or bank account. He will call in a few days for the number.

A few days later, he uses J.J.H. Janssen's transfer card to transfer the full amount to an account at ABN Bank.

49.

The next morning is a Thursday. From the phone in his suite, he dials the number for Olga's landline. He assumes that, barring any schedule changes, mother and daughter will both be at work and that he will reach the answering machine.

"Hello? This is Sonja Beumer."

This declaration has an unusually violent effect on him, and he hangs up the receiver immediately. Sweat beads on his forehead. "Don't be an idiot!" he mumbles. An hour or so later, after walking a little bit past the hotel and through the surrounding streets, he dials the number again. The line picks up, but no one says anything. N. can hear breathing, but he remains silent. Then:

"Kees, is that you?"

N. remains silent, immediately sweating.

"I know it's you, Kees… why won't you talk to me?"

He clears his throat and summons every ounce of his inner strength to make his voice sound neutral and controlled.

"How did you know it's me?"

"See. I can sense things like that. You called an hour ago, too, didn't you? Where are you?"

"In Utrecht, in a hotel."

"Are you alone?"

"Alone, yes. Are you?"

"Mama is at work. Do you want to talk to her…? She'll be back around two o'clock, and she has a lot to say to you." Sonja's voice relaxes, almost begins to take on an ordinary conversational tone.

"How are you doing?"

"Good. Mama too. But what on earth are you up to? You still have all your stuff here." Then, after a momentary hesitation, "Say Kees… or should I call you Chris?"

N. suddenly feels a biting sting at this. For a moment he feels paralyzed; he no longer understands the situation.

"How the hell did you get Chris?" (His poorly feigned astonishment is useless, he knows).

"Chris… Christiaan Janssen. Mama already knew that when you were still with us. But she never dared to tell you. You shouldn't leave your driver's license lying around." And then: "You weren't a teacher at all, you were at the university."

"How did you get to that, Sonja?" Useless delay, useless surprise, again, he knows. He can't understand why he tries to maintain the pretense.

"Mama has…" She explains that there has been a phone number on a bookmark in one of his books. She had dialed the number, worried about his motives for hiding his identity, and it turned out to be the university. It was the number of the institute where he worked. Because she didn't know what else to do, she had asked for Mr. Van Andel. When they didn't know any Van Andel, she asked for mister Janssen, Christiaan Janssen. They told him that Mr. Janssen—Chris, as he was known casually—had gone missing. The woman on the phone had told Olga in detail about the missing person case. Mrs. Beumer, she said, should assume that Mr. Janssen was no longer alive; he had almost certainly died in the Gunpowder Disaster.

N. assumes that she had spoken to Gerdien Jagersma, receptionist and known chatterbox, and asks, not entirely disinterested, if Olga had told her anything about him still being alive.

"No. We'd suspected for some time that there must have been some urgent reason for you to change your name."

N. heaves a huge sigh of relief.

Then Sonja asks, "Are you really married?"

He affirms.

"And you have a child, a daughter?"

"No, not a natural daughter. She already had her when we got to know each other. The child was two at the time."

"What's her name?"

"Anke."

"Your wife?"

"No, her name is Paula."

"Are you going back to them…? Or are you already back with them?"

"No! Please. It's over, it's over for good."

"Are you really still in Utrecht? Or are you near here? I don't trust you anymore."

"No, I'm in Utrecht. I really am. I don't really think it's a good idea to come back to your area."

"What do you mean?"

"After everything that happened."

"So what? You think we haven't solved all that yet."

"Solved?"

"You know that Kees, don't be stupid."

Kees knows nothing, truly. A deep sigh comes through the ether. "Come on, Kees, don't you read newspapers, don't you ever watch TV?"

No, actually he never watches TV, except for one time last Friday, a stupid game show with a young girl, a child really. He reads newspapers very irregularly. That's what he tells her, omitting the part about the young girl.

Well, if he'd kept up with the news, she tells him, he would have known that Suzanne Heusinkveld's killer—that was her name, Suzanne Heusinkvel—was arrested at the end of December after having confessed during a routine interrogation. They hadn't suspected the boy at all. It had been out of jealousy because Suzanne had broken up with him and had been having an affair for six months with an Egyptian boy named Ismael. He also lives in Q, having been adopted into a family there as a baby, and works as a line cook in a restaurant in Y. He was first boy they suspected of having done it because he and Suzanne sometimes met in the woods behind De Geus. It turned out that her jealous ex-boyfriend had found out about the affair and had been waiting for her there. He told her to break up with him and when she laughed at him, first he hit her then choked her and then ran away. Suzanne was still alive when they found her, but she never regained consciousness and died in the hospital. He hadn't wanted to kill her, Sonja said, just scare her. It had all gotten seriously out of hand. Sonja explains that she had known Suzanne from elementary school even though Suzanne was in a higher grade.

N. heaves a sigh, not of relief, but of powerlessness against the pointless cycle of life and death, and everything.

"You know what's crazy, Kees?"

"No."

"Nobody knows why Suzanne was there in the woods. Ismael said that they hadn't arranged to meet there. He could prove that, because he was at work all afternoon when it happened… That's why they didn't suspect him for long."

N. feels a sudden unbearable pain, as though a serrated knife was being turned somewhere in his head or heart. He is probably the only one in the world who knows why she was there. Her last words to him are suddenly crystal clear in his ears. That poor girl at that bench, her bicycle in hand, the words so provocative. Maybe that was what finally led to her death, this propensity for provocation, perhaps she said to her impending murderer: "So what? Is it any of your business what I'm doing here?" Provocation and self-determination always come with risks in life, especially for heedless girls, even in the supposedly emancipated West. All it takes is a little challenge or provocation for stupid, shortsighted, vain, and selfish men to claim sole control of their bodies. A little independent will and desire and they are blinded by anger, jealousy and wounded pride. N. feels hopeless as he thinks of how many personal and general disasters men's egos have caused throughout history.

A shudder passes through his whole body. For a moment, he feels hopeless, destroyed.

The line is quiet for a few minutes, then in a muffled, shaken voice, he asks: "But why were they after me?" Sonja had said a few things in the meantime, but her words slipped past him, busy as he was bracing himself against a storm of memories. That whole chase suddenly played out in his mind again.

"That was because of Theo," she says. "But mama will tell you that too. She knows more about it than I do… By the way, mama has something else to tell you."

"What's that?"

"Aha… you'll have to ask her yourself."

There is another pause. N. realizes that the mother is pregnant and that the pregnancy has continued. That means she must be in the sixth month by now. He hopes it will be a girl; then, in his heart, he says goodbye to the Beumer ladies for good. His time there has passed. For a moment he doesn't know what to say or how to end the conversation. He stares out the window of his suite into the street, where a constant flow of afternoon traffic passes by, his thoughts on the murdered girl. The world keeps on turning, he thinks, relentless and indifferent, Time never stops to mourn murder or disaster. And then Sonja breaks the silence.

"Will you come back to us? The three of us had such a good time."

N., pulled suddenly back to the present, masters his confusion and offers an emotionless lie. "I think so. I'll call Olga this afternoon."

The rest of the conversation plays out in semi-intelligible, irregular but persistent fragments.

"Kees."

"Yes."

"Kees, I love you so much… even after everything that's happened. Maybe even more."

"Girl," he mumbles, covering the receiver, "for God's sake don't be so sentimental." To end the conversation in a quick but dignified fashion, he lies again.

"Sonja, listen. I'll call Olga sometime this afternoon and then we'll arrange everything. As far as I'm concerned, I'll be there very soon, maybe even next weekend."

Sonja mumbles something unintelligible, and a silence falls again. If he could have, he would have gently disconnected. But then she hangs up and he realizes that, despite the irritation he had felt in the moment, he was nearly ready to propose to this tall, slender girl to go with him to Manaus. Then he chuckles, realizing that her height and her paleness and blondeness would have certainly caused a sensation there.

50.

At eleven o'clock on Sunday morning, a cleaning lady at the hotel became suspicious after finding the door to his suite had been left ajar. She entered to find him on the floor in the bedroom, totally naked, with his skull bashed in and his neck broken, lying in a pool of blood that had long since dried into a dark patch on the carpet. The suite safe had been broken open and was empty. Two months later, there was still no trace of the perpetrator(s), and nothing had been learned about the contents of the safe; the police still have no leads and are no closer to arresting the murderer(s) of Jan-Hein Dormaal, who was without a fixed address. The man has long since been identified as Christiaan Jacob Janssen.

After some unsuccessful phone calls in the course of that week, N. only managed to get in touch with one eighteen-year-old Karin van Emmenes from Castricum. He told her not to come to his address in Lage Vuursche, but instead to his hotel in Utrecht. Karin had provided a passport photo with a plain face, full lips, dark blond hair falling at her shoulders, freckles and something of a turned up nose. N.'s traumatized libido was curious about the rest of her body. The dear girl had written a very charming note explaining that she was still in pre-university education and wanted to someday go into business. For reasons she would tell him later, she wrote, she would prefer an older boyfriend. Of course, if it "clicked" between them, she was also interested in marriage. She wouldn't even mind having one or two children.

They agreed that she would report to the hotel reception that Saturday evening around half past six and that he would pick her up there. At a quarter past six that day, restless with longing for his impending female company, he stared out the window of his suite onto the street in front of the hotel. A dark blue Golf, a somewhat older model, parked on the street. Three young people got out, two guys in jeans and bomber jackets and a girl with a gray jacket over a short black skirt and short leather boots. They talked for a moment, gesturing toward the entrance of the hotel, then the girl crossed the street and out of N.'s view. The two young men watched her, one of them lit a cigarette, then got back in the car and drove down the street. Although he couldn't be sure (a passport photo is too vague to confirm an identity at such a distance) he suspected that it was Karin. A phone call from the receptionist a few minutes later confirmed this suspicion. A Ms. Karin van Emmenes was at the front desk asking for Mr. Janssen. With a slightly accelerated heartbeat, he descended.

He introduced himself in the lobby. "Hans Janssen," he said, offering his hand.

"Karin van Emmenes, nice to meet you."

She was about one meter seventy tall with a soft voice and a very sweet smile framing a row of perfectly white, perfectly straight teeth. She looked at N. with a look, he thought, of slight reproof. Why is a man like this—so well dressed, gentlemanly, and good looking—after young girls? Or perhaps this was simply the work of N.'s conscience reading this in her smoky gray eyes. She asked if she could call him by his first name, and he said that she could, please do. He escorted her to his floor, and while they were in the elevator, confessed to her that he had seen her coming and asked casually who had brought her.

It turned out to be her step-brother and his friend, she said. Still, N. struggled to pinpoint exactly what it was about her that made him uncomfortable. It certainly was not her appearance. Although he couldn't imagine that this beautiful little creature was really eighteen years old; he had the impression that was closer to twenty-three or twenty-four years old.

Once in his suite, she immediately removed her mohair jacket. Her shirt had a plunging neckline, a sight that didn't disappoint, even by N.'s supple standards. It provided a generous view of her young, creamy white breasts, especially when she leaned forward for a moment to sit on the couch. Nothing was left to the imagination. N. felt a fierce stirring in his testicles and had to rub his eyes, as if to be sure that this was a respondent to a personal advertisement and not a call girl. While he was in the kitchenette pouring glasses and distributing some snacks on a platter, she called from the living room to tell him that they'd driven past his house and she didn't understand why he was here in the hotel.

"I actually thought you were home at first. There were a couple of cars parked there, and the gate was open. There were two or three men were walking in the garden."

N. was hit by a nasty shock but recovered quickly. He explained that it was probably the real estate agent with a prospective buyer; he was selling the house in Lage Vuursche. At that moment he realized that he would also needed to disappear from this hotel as quickly as possible, preferably as soon as tomorrow. After all, the transfer from his brother's giro account would lead the trail to the Van Ees family in Rotterdam, and from there to the newspaper advertisement and then inevitably to the front desk of this hotel.

As to why this hotel, he told her quickly that he wanted a change after a long-drawn-out and hard-fought divorce from his wife. The house held too many unpleasant memories for him now. Moreover, it was too big; he was looking for something smaller, something cozier.

"Tell me something about yourself, Karin," he wanted to lead the conversation away from himself.

It wasn't difficult to do. Karin, it turned out, had quite a willing story to tell. The four or five tears shed along the way did not seem entirely sincere to N., and perhaps the accompanying story wasn't either, but it made an impression nonetheless. She said she was from a broken home. Her father left her mother when she was eleven and she had stayed with her mother. When her mother got a new boyfriend, she moved in with him but without Karin; the boyfriend didn't want her in the house. After about a year, her mother and boyfriend left for Australia to build a new life there. She was fourteen then and an uncle of hers was appointed as her guardian. After spending some time in a foster family and then in a home, this uncle, who was unmarried himself, let her live with him. Well, his true intentions soon became apparent. She thought she probably didn't have to tell him what they were. That misery had lasted two years; he threatened to hurt her if she told anyone, and lacking any alternative, she stayed. At the end of last year she had fled her uncle's house and found refuge with a classmate, a slightly older girl who was already living by herself. And that's where she was living now. Karin was in the exam class of the university prep stream, and it surprised her a bit that she'd managed to get this far in spite of all the trouble.

N. found her story less convincing the longer she went on, contradicting herself often. But she had a beautiful body and he didn't want to spoil his final weekend in Holland with trifles. He suggested that they go to the hotel restaurant for dinner, and decided to continue boldly, tell her that he hoped she wouldn't blame him for the fact that sex—healthy and exuberant sex—had taken a rather prominent place in his life. Especially since his divorce. After everything she'd told him, he was worried that she might be shy to…

She interrupted with a mysterious smile and confirmed that it wasn't an issue for her at all. Despite her bad experiences, sex was still very important to her. Before they got that far, though, she just had to go back downstairs as she'd left her bag at the reception.

When she came back, N. was already in the bedroom. He didn't want to lose any time this evening, especially after last week's unsatisfying rendezvous. When she entered the bedroom door, he picked her up, smiling and fully cooperative, and put her on the bed. He undressed her first, and then himself, did some preparatory work and then took her, or rather she took him, because she turned out to be extremely enterprising. She was indeed no longer *virgo intacta* (most likely the work of that nasty uncle) and she clearly did not want for experience. She told him she preferred doggy-style, so that she could feel him deep inside her. If he would work her breasts, she could always cum "like a train". To N.'s sense of aesthetics, this was not his favorite position, as it seemed to him a rather humiliating position for the woman. There was something ridiculous to it, and something disgusting too, the woman on her knees, with her distorted buttocks turned towards the man. But Karin's experienced, backward stretched feminine hand drove the man's burning rod into her longing love cave. She overwhelmed him a bit, to be honest, with her initiative, and almost deafened him with her heavenly sighs, grunts, groans, and high squeals each time she reached her climax, fictitious or otherwise.

N. was completely absorbed in the game, swept up by her anticipation and by the volume of her arousal. He enjoyed every single movement of her hard, taut body, every moment of her surrender. At such moments, he mused, a man should hate that nature forces him to take breaks between his ejaculations.

When he came, he wanted to stretch out, wonderfully exhausted, next to Karin, still vibrating. He wanted to whisper sweet things into her ear, then with his tongue and fingertips, he wanted to start a search over her delightful body, and tomorrow he wanted to stay in his room with her all day, and ask her to go to Manaus with him and… But then in the next room he heard a noise. It was, he thought, the sound of metal grating over metal. He got up from the bed, reached for his clothes…

★ ★ ★ ★

The author

Bernard Lovink was born in 1942 in the Dutch village of Wisch. After graduating high school from the HBS-A school in Doetinchem, Lovink pursued a degree in social sciences at the University in Nijmegen and later went on to work as a policy adviser for several local governments. Long since retired, he now lives a quiet life with his wife in the town of Vries, where he enjoys reading and taking long walks. Perhaps it was on one of these walks that the idea for his first novel came to him: the story of a man whose "freedom" unexpectedly falls into his lap, but who lacks the basic intuition to use it.